Unnatural

KATLYNE MARIE

Published by Katlyne Marie

Distributed by Bublish, Inc.

ISBN: 978-1-64704-146-5 (paperback)
ISBN: 978-1-64704-147-2 (eBook)

Unnatural Series

Unnatural

Chapter 1

0497

"Where am I?" I quizzed myself. Moving my eyes about the barren concrete room, I instantly recalled, "Oh. That's right the same place as always." Straining my eyes to look straight up at the extended ceiling of a hidden away glass-dome, I exhaled through my nose. "Any minute now they will do the same thing as always, and as always I will be powerless to stop them. Well, let's get it over with."

"Go ahead-" I succeeded to hear one of the regular scientists direct to the dome's ceiling controller.

Closing my eyes, I prepared myself for the impending torment up until I overheard one of the other same strenuous voices shout. Shooting my eyes open I listened to the man call back, "No, wait a minute! The Director wants to try that again."

"Why? When the results didn't change the other times."

"Just let me do it, so we both don't get fired."

"Fine, whatever." I heard the controller upsettingly groan.

Hearing the footsteps of the scientist venture into the large dome room, I again closed my eyes for a quick breath. As I waited for the needle to be impaled into one of my many exhausted veins,

I counted the footsteps. What else could I do, but just sit here and let these people do whatever it was they were going to do.

I stopped counting after the seventy-fifth step. Knowing that just like always it was only seventy-five steps from the door to the table where I was strapped down directly under this dimly lit dome. "Alright 0497, I am going to have to inject this drug into one of your many veins that lie within your neck." I heard the adult calmly warn. Using his right hand, he forcefully pushed my head, pushing it over towards the left to expose one of my seemingly still good veins. "Here we go." The man sighed inserting the syringe's long needle into my lax skin. Feeling the liquid get leisurely pushed out of the syringe and into my connected vein, I felt the same usual liquid drug run throughout my system at its usual speed. Counting again the same thirty seconds it took to run through my entire system while the scientist detached the emptied needle and brought my head back up to its same ninety-degree angle with my shoulder. Gazing up at the closed ceiling, I now heard the man annoyingly call, "Don't worry 0497 we will take good care of you."

"Right." I thought, grimacing at the declaration every time I heard someone say it. "It's the same old dreary routine over and over. Just get it over with." Thirty long seconds had come and gone, and now the only thing left was to wait for the ceiling to cradle itself open. Revealing what I knew was hiding behind it.

The loud banging of the collapsible panes echoed throughout the cold, darkly lit room. I was so used to the sound that it no longer phased me, but then again even if it had it was not like I could react anyway. Staring straight ahead I saw the low orange-red light of the moon break through the opening. It's light glimmering down onto the table where I lied. Exhaling another quick small breath, I closed my eyes and prepared for what normally came next.

Excruciating pain shot throughout my entire body all at once forcing it to instinctively react. My back curved upwards, wreathing in agony. On instinctive impulse, I tightly shut my eyes, doing all that I could to bear what was happening. I had gone through it so many

3

times before I had lost count, but there was no way to sojourn this pain. No drugs could stop it, none could even pacify it. Pure tolerance was all I had. I could feel my skull grow, my shoulders split. Trying to keep sane by searching for a happy place, my poor fingers desperately clutched the restraints wrapped around my wrists. All I could do now was just cling to the numbers flashing in my head, those few seconds I had left before the drug would finally stop my contorting and transforming body. "Please hurry up." I anxiously prayed. By the time I had counted seven minutes, the pain in my body finally came to a numbing halt. With a deep exhale and sigh, I opened my eyes to watch the same longstanding enemy of mine once more vanish behind the retracting ceiling. Pleading, "Thank God" in my head.

With a couple of minutes to calm down, I heard the same men who had restrained me to this table who knows how long ago come back into this old, cold, heartless room. As one removed one side of my wrist restraints and another remove the other side, they surprisingly stayed hush. No words were traded between the two men, no expressions were exchanged. It was precisely the same every time, nothing was ever different. Removing the restraint wrapped around my petite neck, I felt a set of hands slip under my neck and legs. Carefully lifted, I watched my world get turned upside down, knowing that my limp neck had slunk back under the man's brute arm.

"Same room?" I heard the man who was holding me ask his co-worker.

"Yeah, same room. Thanks to that Rebel Syndicate, we're having to relocate the Unnaturals into the off-grid rooms. You know that." The other man returned to his co-worker as if he had asked a foolish question while grabbing what I assumed was the Saline Bag attached to the I.V. needle painfully stabbed into the back of my hand. Taking the bag off its small hook to carry it to our next destination.

"It would be much easier if we had them all in their old rooms, instead of these rooms off the grid. I mean better for all of us transporters." The first man said as we started to move.

"It would be but, for now, I wouldn't complain. The Director has made up his mind, and besides be glad it's only five of 'em that are being kept hidden from those Rebels, compared to the hundreds being kept in this laboratory."

"It is easier to keep track of only five Unnaturals." The same man joked, ending the discussion as he carried me back to the same room I was being secretly restrained in.

"Here we are, Room A-1." The less muscular and statured transporter stated carrying the I.V. bag. Putting what I believe was the same PIN into the keypad, he unlocked the foremost door. Behind that remained a bullet-proof plexiglass door that required a key to open. Listening to the jingling of the keys I could tell he is shifting through the metal objects though the sense was overwhelmed by the terrible sensation of the blood rush to my head from being held in this drooping position. "A-1, 0497. Ah, here it is." He quickly stated to the world that it was the key not only labeled to this door but my identification as well. Within a few seconds, we were again on the move. Gently sitting my unresponsive body on the hospital bed that was locked in the epicenter of the room, the employee carefully adjusted my legs and my arms so that I wasn't lying on them potentially putting any deadweight on the deteriorating appendages.

"She's the only one out of the five with no fight left in her." The transporter sighed softly to his companion.

"Yes and no. In that form, she has no will to fight, but you haven't been here long enough to see her in that other form." The other said changing out the near-empty I.V. bag for a new one. "And besides her Number Identification should tell you how long she's been here. Visualize yourself in 497's shoes and you would most likely also lose the will to fight just as she."

"True, 0497 is one of the lower numbers compared to 5789 or 6024. And you are right I may have lost the will." Quickly changing the subject, he asked, "What about this other form? I have heard stories about it but-"

"No one is allowed to talk about it!" The first man ordered, finally taking their leave. "Now let's go. Got to get 0996 ready."

Soon after the men had left, I could hear through the double door system that the 'Alarm' had been triggered. Every week that same alarm had gone off, so much so it was no longer unusual to me. In the dark, computer-screen lit room, I stared up at the blue-green glow on the ceiling form the computers that were injecting sedatives, injecting drugs; and measuring the continuous stats of my blood pressure, blood sugar, and heart rate. "None of it changed. It was all the same. Everything was the same as always." I upsettingly pondered before enthusiastically wondering, "Would I not be here if we had not gone to see that Blood Moon? Mom? Dad?"

Chapter 2
0497

"Hey, honey you want to go see tonight's 'Blood Moon'? I know the picture-perfect place for the three of us to go see it." I remember my dad ecstatically talking. He was a tall, slender man with brown hair, and deep, dark blue eyes.

"Yes! I want to see it!" I cried back, in the same manner, jumping up and down. "I can't wait to see the Blood Moon! Dad, do you think you could see any Constellations or Comets on the same night?" I shouted with high hopes and expectations.

"Who knows-" My mother returned saying something I could not recollect. I wanted to say it could have been my name yet, I no longer remember what it was. "But why don't you go read up on the Blood Moon while I get dinner ready okay, honey?"

"Okay," I cheered running up the cherry wood stairs to my room. Inside my messy childhood room, I went to the bookshelf and began to scan through my collection of Astrology and Horoscope books, finding one of the newer ones my parents had bought for me for my eighth birthday last month. Glancing through it I flicked through my favorite chapters attempting my best to keep my imaginative expectations of the uncommonly usual moon phase and its unfamiliar powers locked deep down. "It says that the Blood Moon can gift Unnaturals strange powers as well as curse others with those same powers," I read aloud. "I wonder if I will see any

7

'Unnaturals' there?" Picturing the possibility of seeing a Vampiric, or Draconic, or even a Lycan also under the same moonlight so they could absorb the power of the red moon filled me with tons of excitement. Although, it also reminded me of the possibility of being attacked by an Unnatural Creature, and that horrified me. Remaining headstrong I shoved the thought of being bitten by a Vampire or being preyed on by a Lycan out of my head because this was a one in an only chance of seeing one until December and that was SO FAR AWAY!

Hearing my mother again call out what I believe my name was I ran downstairs for dinner. Savagely eating the perfect spaghetti my mother had swiftly prepared for dinner that night. I asked to be excused so I could rush back upstairs to my room and get my Telescope ready for the evening's planned event. "Well, why don't you have your dad help you get it ready, while I clean up."

"Okay, mommy." I cheered getting out of the dining room chair and eagerly waited for my dad to hurry up. Dancing eagerly up the stairs, I hurriedly ushered him to speed up. The thrill consuming me.

As we took apart the logic tool that allowed me to see the beautiful stars in the sky every night, I continued to impatiently bounce around, even jumping onto my star covered bed. Jumping up and down while my father took apart the extensions so it could properly fit inside the case. Once it was all put away, we went downstairs and loaded everything up into my mother's small four-door navy blue car. I couldn't remember the brand or model now. Sitting in the backseat, I observed through the sunroof all the stars that started to shine back down at me. No clouds interrupted the sight of the white dots in the sky.

When we finally arrived at the place, I walked beside my mother as my father carried the Telescope case, a basket full of snacks, and a blanket. Arriving on top of this nice hill, my parents hurriedly set the Telescope back up so I would be out of their hair for the time being. Observing the sky, I was able to recall the beautiful color of the night. It was such a gorgeous midnight blue color, further allowing me to identify all the constellations I could. Only able to name the basic ones that everyone was taught when they were little such as the Big Dipper and Little Dipper, the Polaris, Mizar, and Alcor Stars, Merak, and Dubhe stars. I was depressed that I could only see the base stars, yet I do remember how happy I was about seeing the Blood Moon. I did not need the Telescope to see it. The moon that night felt so close that I could have touched it if I tried hard enough. Its red glow raining down onto my happy family, making my mother look even more beautiful than she was normally. Her petite five-foot-seven body with bright hazel eyes and dirty blonde hair shining so gracefully under the bright light. Lying on the wool blanket my parents had brought along with us, I stared up at the red glowing moon. Its many colors were ever so prominent.

The longer I stared up at it, the warmer the light felt to me. The happier I felt being under its Supernatural yet scientific occurrence. "You love its glow don't you-" I remember hearing someone ask, reading the very thought I was thinking at the time. The voice did not sound like the voices of my parents but somehow it felt like I had known it for a long time. "Do you want to feel its power?" I heard the voice continue.

"Power?" I inquired standing back up on my feet. Trying to pinpoint the location of the voice, I spun myself around to trace the source. "What power?"

"This power." I heard the man's deep voice speak. Appearing before my eyes, I saw a thick dark shadow mass with fiery glowing eyes solidify. Before I could react to anything, the shadow grew a skeleton hand that touched the top of my head, its fingers playing through my freshly cut deep brown bangs. "There is no reason to be frightened by me."

Softly agreeing, I continued to stare into his eyes.

"Honey, who are you talking to?" My father asked.

"Probably her friend." My mother whispered to him almost mocking my childhood creativity.

9

"It's alright, my little Reaper." The shadow said, his red eyes expressing pure sympathy and calmness. Removing his hand from the top of my head, I felt my chest strain. And before I knew what was going on my legs gave out from underneath causing me to collapse onto the ground, I remember being in pure agony, unable to speak or cry. My body started to feel weird. My senses started to drastically improve, allowing me the ability to sense people down below the hill, to the ability to smell the gasoline from the passing cars on the street, the ability to hear the smallest of voles burrowed deep in the ground and even the softest sounds of the moths fluttering around the street lights. "It's alright, Little Reaper. Just sleep for now." The Shadow continued to speak his red eyes still captivating my child-like attention span as his hidden skeletal skull came sulking out of the deep hood that covered his head. I didn't want to sleep because of my rising fear, although I also felt unrulily calm. The two emotions fought one another, and before I knew what happened to me, I blacked out.

When I woke back up, my body felt stiff, but I was thankfully, still me. "Oh, thank god, you are okay." My father sighed. "Thank god. I'll go get your mother okay." I subconsciously nodded.

When both of my parents entered the awfully clean and dull room, I softly asked my mother, "Where am I?"

"It's okay, you are at the hospital. Everything will be okay." She abruptly answered while trying to hold back her tears. "The Doctor thinks you might have had a seizure, but they are even wary of that."

"I want to go home." I cried, not wanting to be at a Hospital as my mind tried to simultaneously digest the vague information I was given.

"Not yet -" Dad said, his voice blurring out the last word in the sentence. "The Doctor wants to run a few more tests, however, he thinks that come tomorrow you should be able to go home okay honey."

"Fine," I grumbled, sitting up in the hospital bed. "Could you at least bring me my books or something?"

"Sure, honey." My mother said. "Your dad has work today, but I'll bring them after I drop him off, okay?"

"Okay. Thanks, Mom." I smiled watching them leave. I know it seemed horrible that at eight years old my parents had left me alone, but they both worked equally hard to get me everything I wanted and needed, so I didn't complain.

After they left, I lied back down onto the uncomfortable bed and wondered what had happened. Attempting to recap every single event that night. "Was it something to do with the Shadow? Why did he keep calling me 'Reaper'? I wasn't- I didn't become an Unnatural, did I?" So many questions rang through my head that I could no longer decipher what was truly going on. Pushing the thought of everything that had happened to me being related to some sort of seizure, my overactive imagination was quick to consume me. Though, with that, I was oddly enough able to drift off into a nice slumber while awaiting my Mom's return with a few of my books.

When she came back, I was awake again listening to the Doctor tell me that I could instead go home in a few hours. "Yay." I sprang up.

"Are you sure there isn't anything wrong with her?" I heard my mother ask confused. She looked back at me, our eyes locking for a split second. "Can I talk to you outside, Doctor?"

"Sure." He answered with a curious look overcoming his facial features.

"Honey, read some of your books for now. I will be right back."

"Okay." I nodded uncontrollably picking up the book about the Blood Moon again.

"Doctor, you've got to believe me, when I say I watched my own daughter turn into a large black and tan dog who bared her own teeth at me and my husband." I heard my mother clearly express. With her voice sounding pitched full of fear, I curiously tilted my head to listen to more of their conversation. Wondering deep down in my gut if that was what had truly happened, and not some sort of medical diagnosis. I may have been eight, but I was intelligent for my age and did not like to be fooled.

"Mrs. Swallow, I don't know what you saw, but if you really believe in what you and your husband saw last night, I can bring in a specialist to do more tests on your daughter. But," He paused for a moment, "I don't know if you want to be putting her through such horrendous testing." I heard the Doctor answer back. "For now, be with your daughter, and call your husband to converse with."

"Please just call the Specialist! I don't want my daughter to become one of those things!" I now heard my mother furiously shout in the hallway before storming back inside.

Chapter 3
0497

I remember the specialist coming in and telling my mother that from his experience, I looked completely normal. All the tests that the Doctors had done to me when I had initially arrived had all led back to me having a seizure. The reason could not be truly discovered, but it for sure had nothing to do with me becoming an Unnatural. Even if I had indeed turned into one, it shouldn't matter to her what I was because I was her daughter, he resumed to tell her. I guess it worked because soon after that I had been thankfully discharged by her parental/guardian signature.

It took a few months to get everything back in order, but eventually, it did. I had moved on from what had happened, and so had my parents well at least it appeared that way. They never talked about it in front of me, but I could still hear the fear in their voices thanks to my increased sense of hearing. And before I knew anything, the next Blood Moon phase had come around.

"I want to go see it! Please!" I childishly pleaded to my parents not knowing at the time that my endless pleading to go revisit that same lunar phase was a relinquishing relation.

"No, your father has to work tonight, honey. Besides, I don't feel it's safe enough to be out tonight, those nasty Unnaturals are on the rise." My Mom refuted as my father agreed.

Making my typical pouty mad face I screamed, "It's so unfair!" Stomping up the stairs to my room, I began to look at the stars through my stationary telescope. "Why can't I go see it? Why are you guys being so mean to me?!" I argued to myself, stepping away from the telescope I wandered over to my bed and grabbed my little dog plushie, "Why is everyone treating me so bad?!"

"It's not your fault, Little Reaper." I heard the same male voice speak to me. It had routinely spoken to me since I had returned home, however, it only ever made an appearance in my room for some reason. "They just don't understand. They foolishly believe you are corrupted."

Ignoring the voice, I covered my face in the plushie's back, hugging it tightly. "But I'm not corrupted! I'm not possessed! I'm not an Unnatural!" I cried, draining my tears into the doggy's soft fur.

"You are my little Reaper, you are not an Unnatural, you are not possessed by a spirit. You are just my smart, Little Reaper."

"Reaper?" I thought. "How do you know what I'm thinking?" Looking up away from the soft black and tan fur of my stuffed animal, I had named Rose, I saw the same cloak wearing skeletal creature. His eyes were the exact same calm fiery tone as the last time I had seen them. Again captivated, I unwillingly locked my gaze with his.

Using his skeletal hand, he grabbed my chin and pointed it upward before his fingers cuffed my cheek in his boney palm. Pushing the left side of my face further into his hand, I listened to his voice ring in my ears, "You are my Reaper, and you will be okay. There is nothing to fear, just sleep."

"Sleep?" I thought in my head while my eyes still avidly preyed on his burning inhuman pupils. Unable to regain control over my body I watched my surroundings blur as I fell forward. My body slumping over before falling hard onto the cold cherry wood floor. My head hitting the floor with an abrupt thud.

"In time, you learn to understand and control what I have blessed you with, my Little Reaper. I will see you again in due time." The Shadow spoke into my unconscious mind.

When I woke up, I hastily found myself in another hospital bed with both of my parents sitting beside the bed's railings. "It's okay. We're right here."

"The Skeleton isn't here?" I questioned my mind confused and slightly terrified.

"Skeleton? No there are no skeletons here honey." My dad verified while I tightly hugged him. "It may have been something you saw before your seizure."

"Seizure?"

"Yes, you had another seizure -" Mom answered, her voice sounding distanced.

"Mom?" I questioned as I sat back down on the bed. "Are you okay?"

"Yeah, I'm fine -" She continued again saying that blurred word. "I'll be right back, baby watch her."

When my mother came back, she was accompanied by a different doctor, but he was part of the same field as the last one. I remember the Doctor acted as if I wasn't even there while he introduced the new guy to my parents. "Mr. and Mrs. Swallow, this is Dr. Shane Masters; he is an Unnatural Genealogist. He believes that because due to detail surrounding your daughter's seizures some more tests should be done-"

"Tests?" I asked interrupting the man. "It was just a seizure; I am not an Unnatural!"

"Well, that's what we hope these tests will help us clarify-," Doctor Masters spoke, stroking his bleach blonde silvery hair back over the top of his head. "I would like your parents to bring you to

15

the Hospital on Salem Drive once you are discharged. From there we will be able to start giving her some advanced testing."

"Okay, thank you, doctor." I heard both of my parents return.

Crossing my arms, I puffed my cheeks, again giving my usual pouty face. "Not fair."

"Honey, not everything is fair, but this is for the benefit of your health. If the tests come back positive, then we will be able to treat you for your species and you will be able to go back to living a normal childhood." My mentally drained father ignorantly said.

"But I am not an UNNATURAL!" I shouted standing up on the bed frustrated. "THERE IS NOTHING WRONG WITH ME! It's that Shadow! That Skeleton!" I again cried, falling back down onto my knees as tears began to roll down my cheeks. "I wasn't 'sick' until I saw him!"

"Shadow? Skeleton?" My mother asked confused. Staring back at the Specialist she now inquired, "Is that a possibility?"

"It could be, I won't know until we get the tests started." The Doctor answered. "-, should be discharged tomorrow then after that I ask of you guys to stop by the Hospital.

"Okay, thank you Doctor Masters." My father answered, his voice also sounding distanced just like his wedded lover.

Puffed up with complete frustration, I rolled over onto my side turning away from my parents. While they continued to talk to the Doctors, I angrily blamed what was happening to me on the fiery-eyed, shadowy Skeleton. The night was tough to get through after my tantrums and youngling outbursts, but through some persuading my parents got me to go along with the tests telling me that whatever the results were; they would still love me.

I remember the drive to the Hospital was super quiet, annoyingly quiet. At the time, I didn't understand why they were so sad or emotional when it was ME that was going to be tested on. I attempted to put up a show to get not only my mind off what was going on but theirs also; however, I only ended up getting yelled at. The ride became even more depressing from there. I knew why they were acting so pessimistic, but even though they disliked Unnaturals many of these supernaturally gifted Humans were already living side by side with their non-supernaturally gifted counterparts. I knew that my parents were part of the group of Humans who believed they were superior to Unnaturals. They were part of a group that saw those with supernatural powers as spawns of the Satanic Devil, and I had firsthand experience of that when my own parents blessed my room after my first 'seizure'. Making me deeply ponder if those tests had come back positive... "Would they excise their own child?"

Chapter 4

0497

By the time we had arrived at the Hospital for my testing, the sun was starting to set. Being led into a room by one of the many Nurses stationed on the first level of the Hospital, I was then handed a small kid's hospital gown and told to change into it. My mother helped me change into the gown before she decided to fold my blue and pink star and moon pajamas neatly on the back of the guest chair. "The Doctor will be in shortly." The nurse chimed in her happy-go-lucky tone.

"Thank you." My father said as he bypassed the nurse to enter the room.

"I want to go home," I mumbled to myself.

"I know you do -" Mom said, "But we need to figure out what is wrong with you, see if its anything that can be treated or potentially cured."

"Ugh." I sighed, grabbing one of my books and beginning to re-read its contents. Steadily flipping page after page, I ignored my parents.

Ten minutes past by before Doctor Masters came into the small hospital room. "Sorry it took a bit I had to finish up with a patient."

"Oh, no, it's okay. She's content with her books." I remember my mother making small talk.

"Astrology, huh?" The Doctor asked me with a happy smile as he stepped closer towards the hospital bed.

"Yup." I sighed, looking at him for a quick second while twiddling my toes. "I want to know all the constellations, moons, stars, and galaxies."

"Well, you are an ambitious child. That's a lot of work." He continued now standing on the bed's right side opposing my parents. Taking my hand, he felt my pulse mumbling the ten seconds before his voice filled the small room. "Very good, now I want to check your heart rate." He informed as he pulled out his stethoscope. "Breathe in and out." Doing as he said, I quickly hoped that this was the hardest part. "Okay, your base stats are all good. Now here comes the hard part.

"Hard part?" I asked glancing up from my book.

"Well, I will let you choose. We can do the MRI first, or we can do the Blood Draw, Spinal Tap, and Sensory Tests." Doctor Masters spoke up still with the smile on his face.

"Why so many tests?" I heard my father ask, feeling his hand comfort my back. "Why the Sensory tests? She isn't going blind or deaf."

"Well in the past we have missed some important increases in the five main senses of the Human, and let's just say it was not good results. Besides eighty percent of the Unnatural Species that have been discovered over the last two years have had double sometimes triple the senses of a normal Human."

"Double? Triple?" My mother asked muddled. "Is that even possible?"

"We had a patient that had a sense of smell ten times stronger than a Bloodhound, and another that had such an extensive strain on his touch senses that he was able to walk on the ceiling. No tests are going to be missed, as we don't want a mistake to happen."

"Okay." I sighed. "I just want to get this over with."

"Okay honey, go ahead and choose." My dad spoke up.

"Sensory last. The Blood draws first- and then I don't even know what the other tests are?" I listed to the best of my ability.

"Alright how about we get the Blood and Spinal done then after that we can do the MRI, and Sensory last okay -?"

"Okay," I said starting to feel somewhat less nervous about the tests and their fifty-fifty odds.

"Let me get a Nurse in here to help me with the Blood Draw." The Doctor calmly spoke while he simultaneously took his leave back towards the hallway.

A few minutes later Doctor Masters was back in with a Nurse who I attentively watched her disinfect the area with an anti-bacterial swab and numb the fold of my left arm. Soon after she injected the needle and began the draw. Drawing up four full vials of blood, she wrote Swallow on the tags and then awaited the next set of orders for the next test.

"Let's get you something sweet to eat to get your sugar up then we can get you prepared for your spinal tap." Doctor Masters filled in while answering the many questions my worry-hearted parents had. Watching the Nurse walk out and come back in less than a minute with what I believe to remember were a couple of soft-oatmeal cookies.

A little while after my stomach had settled, I was then told to lie on my side, while my gown was partially opened and an additional disinfection template was placed over the direct location on my body around the middle of my back. I was extremely uncomfortable for the time being, at least until the next part came.

"Okay -, here comes the worst part. Ready?" He foreshadowed as he reached for the draining needle.

"Yeah," I said through gritted teeth.

"Hold her one of you, this can be very painful for some children." I heard him explain as he started to inject the needle into my back. Instinctively I cried out in pain trying to move but my father firmly held me down in place. Grabbing the rails of the bed I again cried out. "We are almost done, a few more seconds." It was just as he said the pain seized as if all my nerves had gone numb. "Okay, all done." He said while I felt him tie the gown back up. "Let her rest for now while I go send these upstairs to the lab."

Taking a long exhale, I let go of the rails and curled up into the fetal position. All my fear twisting itself into knots deep down inside my stomach. "It's alright we are done for now honey." My Dad said covering me up with the bed's blanket. "You did very well."

More time wasted away before the Doctor finally came back to take me upstairs for the MRI part. It was a simple test where I lied on a cold hard bed that slid in and out of an extremely noisy tube. Lying on my sore back hurt a bit, but I made it through easily. Leaving the only one left; the Sensory Tests.

"Are you ready for your last few tests?" The Nurse asked as she wheelchaired me to the next room where these Sensory Tests were supposed to be done.

"Very." I tiredly agreed. "I want to go home and sleep in my bed as soon as possible."

"I bet you do. So, do I." the Nurse chuckled as she wheeled me into the exceedingly small room with a tinted glass window and lots of speakers and vents. "Alright, I'll be sitting right outside, okay."

"Okay," I said trying to remain calm.

"Alright -, we will start the smell test." I heard the Doctor speak through a broadcasting speaker to the adjoining room. "One of those dishes in front of you has food underneath it, can you pick out which one from where you sit?"

Without even trying I said the third one to left. "Smells like sloppy joes," I answered excitedly before the next question could escape the man's mouth and transfer through the speaker.

"Okay, good. You are correct. Now Nurse Jackie will turn you around, and we will switch the dishes again. We have two more trials to go."

"Cool I like this-" I said stopping when more people came in, I could automatically smell that there were three people inside, followed by the scent of the sloppy joes, a hint of celery, and the distinctive aroma of coffee. Unsure if this were part of the test or not, I quickly answered what I could smell.

It took several seconds before the Doctor's voice rang through the speaker, making me believe I had inaccurately answered or something along those lines. "Very good, you were right. We were going to exchange out the sloppy joes, with celery and another dish with some grounded coffee beans and there were indeed three people in the room at the time. I am overly impressed."

"Cool," I said smiling at the Nurse who smiled back at me. It felt like one big game to me, though I knew there was something off the more I further in we went. Of course, now I knew that I should've kept my mouth shut.

Chapter 5

0497

"Alright, there is no point for the last trial. I do not think we need to do Taste as both Taste and Smell are similar. I want to test your Sight next, okay."

"Okay," I said as the female Nurse turned me back around to face the tinted glass.

"Ready?" He asked with the same smile on his face.

"Ready." I returned still enthused yet kept an added sense of caution.

"Good. You've had your eyes checked before, haven't you?" Doctor Master's jested before moving on to explain the next phase. "This test is just like that except, I want to see how fast your eyes can send messages to your brain, so the minute I tell you to read the card read it from left to right and down."

"Okay," I said inspecting a man who came out dressed the same as the nurse in light blue scrubs and tape a piece of paper on the tinted glass window. Once he left, I awaited the command.

"Read the first row, please."

"E-R-T-9-P-Q-V-O-L" I quickly answered back as the letters were still big and bold.

"Alright, how about the fourth row, if you wouldn't mind."

23

"I-M-V-B-X-D-3-8-5-J-G-F" I read in a three-second interval. It took a little longer as the letters were quite small, and I was about ten feet away from the window.

"Alright, that is good. Really good. You have really good eyesight." I remember the Doctor praised. "We got Touch and Hearing left."

"Okay." I audibly yawned. My exhaustion overriding my other emotions. "Let's get this over with."

"For Touch, I want Jackie to slip a blindfold over your eyes and for you to just rely on your hands and feet for this test." I nodded again as the Nurse walked up behind me and slipped a small black blindfold over the top of my head, covering my eyes. Taking another long exhale, I could hear footsteps move around the small room, a couple of sets, meaning at least two people had entered. Waiting for the objects to be placed in my hands or under my feet, I respired another breath.

The first object was placed about an inch under the skin of my hand. I could hear whatever it was breath irregularly alerting me to the answer seconds sooner than the questions could be asked. To ensure my accuracy I allowed the pores of my hands to glide over the top of the critter. It's soft fur and unusual flinching instantly backed up my theory. Taking a hard swallow I faced my rising fear and softly mumbled. "A rabbit."

"Correct." The Doctor's voice assured sounding speechless.

Listening to the two people who had entered the room at the beginning of the test exhale a long sigh, I cautiously asked, "Are you guys okay?"

"John, Doug. Come back." I remember the Doctor order the two lackeys. "Okay -, you can remove your blindfold."

"Okay," I answered back using my hands to take off the blindfold. Taking a few seconds to adjust to the low light in the room, I could hear the three mumble to themselves through the wall of tinted glass. "Are we done? Do we need to do the Hearing Test?"

I remember again that there was a long pause making me doubt if I should have asked those questions. By the time the men had spoken up, Nurse Jackie had gone to check in on them. "Oh sorry. Yeah, I don't think we need to do the last test. All of your senses seem to be in a good range and quite possibly a bit advanced for your age."

"But that's good, right?" I asked slightly concerned.

"Yeah, it's good news. Now, Nurse Jackie will take you back to your room-" the Doctor ordered.

"Then I can go home?"

"I would like to have you stay for overnight observation -," the Doctor now ordered me. His voice sounding spooked.

"Oh okay," I said back as the nurse wheeled me out. Something deep in my gut told me to not argue against this, that it was only going to be a night, and one night wouldn't hurt.

Arriving back to the room, I was greeted by my parents who had also received the same news about me having to stay for the night, for 'quote on quote' observation. As I laid in my assigned bed, I was hastily consumed by slumber. Not caring that my parents had left for the night without extending their love.

When morning came, my mother had come to visit me, telling me my father had to work again even though he did not want to. Again, I did not care; I understood he had a job, I understood that it was also this job that the money had come from for all my books and Telescope equipment. So, I was alright with what I had.

"You ready for these results, honey," I remember my Mother asking me. Her voice sounding as if she too had just woken up. I wearily nodded back, while I ate some of my generously gifted breakfast of pancakes and lightly scrambled eggs. "Is it good?"

25

"It isn't your food, but it's good." I returned after swallowing a mouth full of pancakes.

"Glad to know your mother's cooking is appreciated." She joked.

"Well, how is breakfast going?" Doctor Masters inquired as he walked in with a clipboard in hand.

"Good." I smiled while putting a mouthful of the fluffy scrambled eggs into my mouth.

"Alright I am going to go talk to your mother outside for a quick minute, but we will be right back." I heard the man tell me through my chewing. Nodding I agreed, knowing it was about my test results. I too was curious, but I knew that they would tell me in time.

Several minutes had passed by before Doctor Masters came back in. My mother, however, did not follow. "Where did my Mom go?" I asked him, slightly panicked with a bit of confusion.

"She had to go to the bathroom." Masters speedily lied before changing the subject one me, "Now, I am sure you are curious about your test results -. Aren't you?"

"Yeah," I said pushing my plate away to give him my full attention. I heard him take a deep sigh while his heart rate hastily increased. "Are you okay? Your heart is beating really fast."

"I'm okay, just unsure of how to tell you." He said walking over to the side of the bed so he could sit on the edge. "You are the youngest patient I have ever had to test here, only eight years old and your test results-" Doctor Masters paused again.

Before he could answer, my stomach churned telling me the feared answer. My gut warning me of the real reason my mother was not here by my side. "They came back positive, didn't they?"

"Well. Yes, they did. -, you are an Unnatural." He replied looking very softly into my eyes. "What Species you are IS hard to say, but that tends to be the case with certain species this early in the diagnosis. You see, each species has certain characteristics about them that help us diagnosis a breed and a treatment."

"And I didn't have any?"

"Not any clear characteristics that we know of."

"I see. So, what will happen to me now?"

"Well, for now, I and a few other of my trusted associates will be observing you to see if we can clarify any possible characteristics besides your very strong senses and odd spinal ability to change your bone structure."

"Huh?" I questioned the vast vocabulary going directly over my head, making the man lightly chuckle.

"For now, both your mother and father, as well as a few of my co-workers would like for you to stay here for a little while. Your parents could bring some of your belongings, but until we can figure out what kind of Unnatural you are, it would be best for you to stay here at the Hospital."

"Oh." I sadly answered him, "Okay."

"I know it's hard to accept, but you may be the very first of your species, so in a way, it's like identifying a brand-new comet or star."

I halfheartedly nodded my head, quietly adapting to the results of those tests as best as my developing eight-year-old mind could. I had to get it through my head that I was an Unnatural now and not a human anymore, although in my head that Shadow's statement had told me-

"You are my Little Reaper. You are not an Unnatural, you are not possessed by a spirit. You are just my smart, little Reaper."

Thinking aloud to myself in the quietly abandoned room, "Am I really an Unnatural? Is being your Reaper the same thing?" I couldn't figure anything out. Every thought was just another irritating question.

27

Chapter 6

0497

Before I had known what had happened December had flown past and we were already at Easter in early April. I was still holed up in the same hospital but in a different room. I had been moved onto the second floor, room A-1, where I was also given the patient number 0497, and unfortunately saw hardly much of my parents. The last time I had seen them was on Valentine's day back in February. But they had kept up on sending me plenty of Astrology and Literature books, so I could potentially keep up on my advanced reading and science skills, making it okay, I guess. I had yet to develop any signs or characteristics that would aid the Doctors and Researchers in discovering what kind of Unnatural I had become. They thought it was due to not being of age, or because I was only a newly risen Unnatural. Terms I did not understand at the time.

I remember that when Easter finally came around, I had heard a familiar voice walk off the elevator, followed by another. The voices of my parents. I was so excited that I charged out of my room and ran towards them. Eagerly jumping up at my dad so he could pick me up. I tried my best to hold back my tears but failed to do so. It was too hard.

"I missed you guys so much." I cried to both of my parents.

"We missed you too honey, but how did you know we were coming. We didn't want the Nurses to tell you-" my Dad asked me confused yet happy to also see me.

"I heard you step off the elevator and talk to Mom," I answered not afraid of my increased senses anymore.

"I'm sorry we couldn't come to see you sooner, but we both had work and well-" my Mom paused. Looking at her I saw her eyes looked extremely saddened and dark. "Could we go talk about this outside?" I looked at her as she asked the Secretary behind the Administrative Desk.

"Oh mam, you can take her down to the Courtyard, but other than that Doctor Masters, and Director Julious don't want her off Hospital Grounds." The secretary snottily answered.

"Okay, let's go to the Courtyard." My dad said to me.

"Okay." I smiled as he put me down on the cold tiled floor so I could walk beside them holding my father's hand along the way.

When we reached the Courtyard, I watched as Dad led me astray from Mom and towards a bench by the center stone fountain. As we waited for her, we counted the number of coins, and ducks that were in the pond. I remember how happy I was for my parents to be visiting me in the Hospital Institution.

When my mother came back, she was accompanied by Doctor Masters, a few Nurses, and some of the Transporters. "Doctor Masters did you see my parents came to visit me." I smiled at him. The man flashed a small smile back at me, acknowledging me in the same way he usually did.

"I see that." Masters responded before looking back over to my mother, "Are you sure about this, Mrs. Swallow?" Skimming his sights over to my father he too asked. "Mr. Swallow?"

"Yeah, we've had a long time to think about it, and I just can't get past it-"

"Get past what, Mom?" I confusedly asked her. Looking at my father I sought clarification, "Dad, what is she talking about?"

Dad simply returned, "I'm sorry honey, I really am."

"What?"

"I'm so sorry, kid." I heard Doctor Masters speak as he walked up towards me, his tall height shadowing over me. Bending down on his knees, he got down onto my level. "But they will not be able to ever see you again-"

"WHAT?!" I cried looking back at my Dad, then turning around to face my Mom. "What is he saying?" I could sense the sorrow in their voices, I could hear their fast heartbeats and their quick swallows. My stomach churned again, and I again asked panicked, "What is he saying!?"

"Honey, it's exactly as it sounds your Mother and I will not be able to come here to see you again. We will not be your Mom and Dad, but we will always love you no matter what. We will always love you like the people that gave birth to you and raised you."

My eyes bulged out in supreme shock and I felt my heart sink deep down into my upside-down stomach. The tears rushing down my cheeks as I wailed out my sorrow. "No! IT'S NOT FAIR!" I angrily shouted at them. "WHY ARE YOU BEING SO SELFISH!"

"It is hard on us too." I heard my mother speak her voice shaking. "We don't want to do this -, we really don't want to."

"Then why did you sign that!?" I angrily debated. "Why did you give up!?"

"It was difficult on them it, really was, -" the Doctor spoke up again saying that same blurred word as always. "But please understand that they are thinking of the best future for you."

"Is it because I became an Unnatural!? Is that why?" I cried out confused. "It's not like I had a choice!"

"Honey, please-" I heard my Mom try to speak up.

"I think it is time for you to leave now-" Doctor Masters gestured, the tone of his voice becoming profoundly serious, "Before you put her into any further Shock-"

"Little Reaper, I think it's time you show them what you have been hiding from them. From them all." I heard the same male voice speak, his voice sounding so calm, so influencing.

"Shadow," I mumbled aloud. "It was you that made me this way!" I shouted at the Skeleton who lurked from behind my father wearing the same black cloak."

"Get the sedative ready." I heard Doctor Masters order one of the Nurses.

Glaring back at them, I again heard the Shadow's voice whisper this time directly into my ear. The cold air that escaped from his mouth as he spoke moving my hair away from my ears, his long skeleton fingers wrapping under my chin, "It was that man who told your parents to sign away their parental rights, Reaper." The deep raspy voice call as he locked my sight on Doctor Masters. "Now why don't you use that of which I gifted you with and show them exactly what my Little Reaper is."

"He's right." I obediently mumbled. Fully understanding what was going on. "It's your fault I will never be able to see my parents again after today, right Doctor Masters?" I coldly interrogated still looking in the direction of the Hospital Employee with bright blonde hair.

"Who's right? Who are you talking to?"

"The Skeleton," I answered back. "He told me that it was your fault," I growled running straight for the Doctor who quickly stood back up on his feet in fear of me. Skidding to a stop I smiled, "His voice keeps whispering in my ear." I remember telling them. Dropping onto my hands and feet I began to feel my shoulders turn, and my spine reform, I could feel it grow, I could feel my skull extend. Right there in broad daylight, at one o'clock in the afternoon on

31

Easter, I had successfully transformed of my own free will, awakening this apparent canid form with superior senses.

Feeling the long boney fingers remove the gown's ties, on me, I heard him coldly define, "Be free my little Reaper." before he had returned to the dark shadows. As the gown fell to the cobblestone ground, I charged forward, running directly for the Doctor hearing my mother shriek in fear. Her piercing cry making me halt. Regaining conscious, I then locked focus on her. Responding in this canine way, I folded my folded ears back and tucked my tail underneath my stomach, I hesitated on what I was supposed to do now. I did not know what was wrong but everything in my body had stopped.

"Go now." I heard the Doctor order the Transporters and the Nurses. "We got the characteristics we were looking for." Locking my gaze on Doctor Masters, I growled at him exposing my long newly formed teeth. Dodging both Transporters' attempts to grab at me, I side-winded before targeting the Nurse knowing that she had the sedative. Although, I had forgotten about the other Nurses, the two males who were also out on the Courtyard. Both of whom had snuck up from behind me. Getting tackled down onto the ground, I forcibly coughed up saliva.

"Don't hurt her!" My father shouted at the two male nurses confused and terrified.

"Mr., Mrs. Swallow I suggest you go now. Before it gets any worse and you guys do end up getting hurt. You must recall your daughter is no longer human, this is what she is, a type of Unnatural! Although she is eight years old, in that form she could easily out-muscle two grown men. So again, I warn you guys to go back inside and wait, or leave."

"Fine, we will wait." My Father upsettingly growled back to the Doctor in charge.

Feeling all four of the grown men push all their weight into my body, I snapped out a longing cry as a needle was thrust into my neck. Feeling the same cold liquid pour throughout my entire system, I relaxed and tried to regain my steady calmness. "Try to think of a happy place. Think of a happy place." I pleaded as my body went limp. Making it impossible to even raise my head. However, as much as I pleaded for any happy places, any happy memories, I had none. They were gone. All of them were gone.

"Take her back to her room. Restrain her, and we'll be in later to evaluate her." I remember faintly hearing Doctor Masters speak, while I was picked up by one of the Transporters to be obediently carried back to my current room, A-1.

Inside the room, I watched the two transporters tie my back legs together and restrain my neck down onto the bed. Scarcely conscious I waited for them to eventually leave the room before I finally fell into the exhaustion of the drugs that had been injected into my veins.

Chapter 7
0497

Upon waking back up, I quickly found out I was still in the same altered mutation with four-legs and long fangs. I couldn't see, and the rest of my senses seem like they were in a fog. Exhausted and weakened from the recent events, I decided that there was no reason to fight back at this current point in time. A short burst of time passed by before I finally felt someone's presence rub down my fur-covered back.

"You're awake. That's good." I heard Doctor Masters's voice announce as he removed his long-fingered hand away from my fur. "The Director required your senses blurred for now until we can finish the analysis. However thanks to those reckless actions of yours we were finally able to figure out some of your characteristics and identify you with a form of Hellhoundism. The Breed is difficult to identify, unfortunately, but hopefully, with some saliva analysis, blood work, and some tests we will be able to truly figure out what you are." A long pause ensued before the man continued to explain, "I know you are confused, scared, and very frustrated, but with other forms of Hellhoundism, the Unnatural can still talk. So, if you want to spread some dialog, vent, or interrogate you can while in you are in that form."

I growled at him, refusing to speak any physical words translatable in the Human English Language. There was nothing that

I desired for this foul man to overhear, having my heart broken was enough for now.

"Alright, give me the cold shoulder. Once that blindfold is taken off your massive skull..." The Doctor spoke, tapping my furred head with his long finger. "All you will see from here on out are these four walls and the circular wall of the dome. Any socialization you desire will only be through the Researchers, Doctors, Transporters, and Nurses. Your name is no longer your name, everyone from here on out will call you by a number, you are a number, just like the other full-time patients. Your new name will be Number 0497. You will no longer be called by anything else." I remember the Doctor coldly directed.

"Fine by me, not like I matter to anyone in this sorry world." I thought to myself. Once again, feeling no purpose to tell the man how I felt, or what I wondered.

"A Nurse will come by to draw a few more vials, then later I will come back to collect a saliva sample. You try to harm me or any of the employees here, and your life can become exceedingly difficult." Doctor Masters said. His voice fading away just as the hospital room's door slammed shut.

A while later, the Nurse came by to draw my blood. Recognizing the voice as the same Nurse who did it the first time, I relaxed my tension, though I still refused to talk. I felt betrayed by everyone. The Nurse drew whatever CCs of blood she needed, bandaged my arm, and left. Only to return with the Doctor shortly after, or so I believed. Still, with the blindfold on, I could only recognize them by my slowly regaining sense of smell. The skulking scent of drugs and medications made me scowl in disgust.

"Alright, 0497, I will be opening your jaws while Nurse Jackie will swab your inner cheek, and collect a loose saliva sample. Fight back, and you will face some severe consequences." He now harshly growled. Hidden from behind the blacked-out cloth wrapped around my eyes, I ignorantly rolled them.

Feeling his long fingers grab my muzzle before prying my lower jaw away from the roof of my mouth. I instinctively fought back to keep the tough grip from ripping my lower jowl off. Although, it proved useless with the leather shackle wrapped around my neck. "Hold her still, Shane." I heard Nurse Jackie demand the Doctor as she put a cotton swab into my mouth to line the inner cheek wall. "Part one is done."

Moving my tongue around I tried to use my front legs, I tried to push his hands off my muzzle, nevertheless, his gloved hands remained tightly gripped. Continuing to fight back as much as possible even though the more I moved my tongue around the more I had made saliva, allowing them to quickly receive their sample. Allowing my sore jaws to regain control, I heard the two pairs of feet quietly step away, leaving me alone in the dark lit room with the blindfold still covering my eyes.

A few hard days later, I was finally able to return to my little eight-year-old humanoid form. Using my free hands, I grabbed the cloth and began to rely on the intact touch sense to help me unwrap my neck restraint. Thankfully, it much easier with the size difference of my two diverse forms at that current point of time in my young life. With all but my legs free, I began to remove it also with ease. Free, I jumped off the bed and ran into the bathroom located in the short corridor of the room a few feet away from the bed. Once inside, I scavenged around the closet for another gown, or something in the least to cover up my half-naked build, knowing that my parents had taken my pajamas and nearly all of my other belongings home with them when they signed away their parental rights. Finding a child-sized hospital gown, I hurriedly tied the strings on the back and pulled it over my body.

As I pulled the gown down, I saw the Hospital Band tied around my right wrist. There was something blacked out on it. The only thing that was not covered by the black marker was my patient number 0497. All I could see was this new name of mine, I could no longer see my birth name. I knew what it was, yet the more I thought about it, the more I wondered was it really my name now since my parents signed away their rights. "Did I even have the right to my last name anymore?" I inquired to myself. Quitting the pondering once the door panel system ringed its jingle, alerting to me the door unlocking. Knowing that someone was either coming in to give me more drugs, or it was the time for my scheduled feeding, or worse if it was the Doctors and Researchers again.

Using my sense of smell, I identified one of the scents as one of the men who had entered the room. Recognizing that indistinguishable scent I scanned over the bathroom for a place to hide. With no place to hide in the tiny bathroom, I swallowed my breath before weakly stumbling out of the room, preparing a hundred different excuses in my head for why I had escaped my restraints and hid inside the tiny bathroom. As I passed through the threshold of the rooms' doorway, I then identified the sights of Doctor Masters and his Researching Associate, Doctor Galloway with their scents. Their fowl scowls ironically allowing me to somewhat relax.

"I see you were able to freely change back into your human form again. Impressive for a child." I heard Doctor Galloway return. "And you also were able to release the restraints."

"Yeah, how were you able to do that?" Doctor Masters smiled at me through very gritted teeth.

"They were simple knots and buckles. I learned to tie my own shoelaces when I was four years old, and those were harder than the restraints." I sparked, simultaneously flashing a mocking smile at Masters.

"Why you damn brat?!" He cursed aloud as he walked towards me. Slightly intimidated, I backed down, until his associate warned him that harming me physically was not only going to force the Director to terminate his contract but to also decline his medical license. "Just stay in your bed 0497, and everything will be better for all of us. I don't want to have to restrain you in that form." Masters now sighed while rubbing the back of his neck. Trying to keep himself from attacking me.

"Right?" I thought to myself as I walked back to the hospital bed. Climbing back onto the uncomfortably thin mattress, I debated asking them why my name had been blacked out, however, the further I pursued the thought the more it seemed as if the timing was wrong.

"We have come closer to identifying what species you are, 0497, however, the only thing we still don't know is the connection between you and the Blood Moon. Both of your 'seizures', or per your mother, your Transformations happened on nights of Blood Moons. While the other time you transformed, you were talking to a 'Shadowed Skeleton'."

"You are inquiring an eight-year-old to figure what her connection with a Lunar Phase is?" I heard Doctor Masters snap at his co-worker making me feel incompetent. "But then again, she described the Skeleton Shadow as the one being behind her becoming an Unnatural. Right, 0497?"

I looked away from the two Institute employees, but in the end, nodded my head. "So, what tests are you going to put me through this time?" I groaned upset.

"There is a Blood Moon coming up in a few days-"

"It's tomorrow." I moaned astounding the men. "At least that's what the stars have told me."

"Stars?" Probed the Researcher.

"Astrology. It was her hobby before coming here." Doctor Masters now answered ahead of me, again ignoring my presence. "Anyways we will need to see how you react under the light of the Blood Moon. So, tomorrow night, we-"

"It supposed to be the strongest after Midnight, as is most nights where the moon can be seen." I returned interrupting the blonde-haired, white coat wearing man again.

"So, it's tonight?" Asked the Researcher.

I nodded, feeling uncomfortable about saying what was on my mind at the moment. "Anyways." Doctor Masters spoke, "We will be back to get you so you can be Transported over to the Dome. Alright, 0497?" Looking away from the man, I again nodded my head. "Good, we will see you later."

"Whatever." I thought in my head.

Watching the guys leave the room, and hearing the keypad lock the door again, I flopped down on the bed, rolling onto my side, I stared out the second-story window. Watching the fading sunlight, painfully earning to feel its succumbing warm rays again.

Chapter 8

0497

As the sky turned dark, and the sun could no longer be physically seen along the horizon, I rolled onto my back anxiously counting the seconds before the Transporters arrived. Finally hearing the door open, I slithered off the bed, greeting the men at the end of the small narrow hallway from the door to the bed.

"Let's go, Number 0497." One of the men said using such a deep tone that it left no room for playing out an argument. One of the Transporters took the lead while the other fell behind to make sure I didn't attempt a break for it. Following the front Transporter, I walked the extensive distance to this Dome Room, which once more at this current stage in time I knew nothing about. Of course, now knowing that every Blood Moon Cycle or Full Moon Cycle, they stuck me out there. And sequentially, it was offered the same results, creating a boring traditional routine.

Reaching the Dome's main room, I looked up to see the abstract glass ceiling with all the gorgeous white dots I knew were stars gleaming back down at me. Dragged out to the center of the room, I watched as they attached a leather shackle to one of my ankles for safety protocol. I was completely content to keep staring at the beautiful stars, I refused to care about what they were doing to me. Hearing the men leave the room, then hearing the doors themselves lock, I paid no mind to the repetition of sounds. Ten minutes later, I saw the distanced moon start to express its scientific lunar phase, its red-orange, scorching glow filled the room with extreme ease. Allowing me to bask my childish body in its warm light.

Before I could count the full five minutes, I felt my body once more start its alteration. Preparing for the Shadow to make himself known, I dropped down to my knees, my hands touching the cold tiled floor. Feeling my spine reform and my shoulder blades rotate, I screeched out in pain. In seconds, the transformation had completed itself, and my exhausted self-collapsed onto the tile. My limp body falling on top of my newly mutated brown paws.

Staring up at the blackened sky that boldly shined back down onto me, I smiled while the folding ceiling caved over the red beam of the moon and the white glow of the small stars. With the furious emotions flooding back to, I knew it was these people who made me do this without any form of compensation; I forced my exhausted self-back up onto all four of my legs. My toes spreading as far as they could go to grip the tile floor, I quickly realized that unlike other Unnaturals with Hellhoundism, it all originated so naturally to me. It all felt as if I had done this before.

"My, my, so, there is a connection between the two. There is something in the glow of the Blood Moon that made you what you are." I heard Doctor Masters mock as he walked into the Dome room accompanied by two Transporters. Uncovering my teeth, I bared them at him, I still decided to blame him for my parents signing away their rights. "Oh, what's wrong 0497. Still mad?"

Lowering my head as he sauntered closer to where I remained restrained with the leather bracelet, I began to try to slip my ankle out of the bracelet. However, it was so firmly wrapped around my foot that it was pointless. Grumbling, I quickly noticed that the same bracelet had a leather lead about a few feet long, giving me much more of an area to cover than I had expected. Lingering in front of the leather strap, I tried to hide its true length from the Doctor who had stopped about four feet out of my range. I had to coax him to walk closer, I just wanted to make him pay. It was the only thing I could think of at the time. I wanted someone to pay for what happened in this last year of my life, I just wanted someone to pay. Sinking my head even further, I dropped myself close to the ground, and tucked my tail, while practically sitting on the lead. Feeling saliva drool down my teeth and onto my lower jaw, I snapped them together, clacking the long teeth together. I subconsciously challenged him. The man falling for the temptation started to venture step by step closer to where I stood. Now standing a foot from where I remained positioned, he was finally within my perimeter. After being here for so long and seeing more of this man's semi-true colors I charged at him. Knowing that it would bring him in faster.

"Oh, you damn brat!" I remember him snapping at me. Furiously trudging closer to where I now played the submissive dog role. Dropping down onto my legs, with my tail again falling under my stomach and my floppy ears folded flat against my skull. As he stepped even closer, I delayed my intended actions until he nearly stood over the top of me. Baring my teeth again, I curled my lips higher and shot up at him. My long legs reaching his shoulders while my fangs attached to his neck. Clamping down tightly onto his skin, I felt his hands grasp at my scruff in an anguishing panic. Although my fear attempted to petrify me, I remained determinedly put. I could hear him cough, feel his heart beat at an increased rate, hear the blood ooze out of his wounds. "Get this damn thing off of me!" Doctor Masters ordered the Transporters. "Get her jaws open!"

I remember feeling one pair of hands slip into my mouth and commence an attempt to separate my jowls from their boss's flesh. However, what made me finally let go of the Doctor was something being thrust into the back of my neck. I believe it was a syringe needle full of yet another sedative. On instinct, I clung tighter for an additional thirty seconds until the exhaustion from the sedative and transformation had finally bit at my ankles enough times. Releasing my jaws, I fell back onto the floor, no longer capable of moving. Watching through my obscuring vision the Transporters quickly escorted the deranged man out of the Dome Room so he could receive medical attention, I quietly told myself, "In the least, he was at a Hospital, whether or not it was the right one, who knows."

When I came to, I was once again back in my human form and this time restrained to my bed at four posts. My wrists and ankles all were restrained to the bed. I could scarcely make out what was up and what was down, so I remained as still as possible for the meantime. Knowing even at eight years of age that this was most likely due to some kind of drug that was similar to the sensory distortion I was given during my previous change.

"Oh, you're up now." I heard someone express to me, or at least try to. "We had to give you a Sensory Distortion Sedative after that little fallout you and Doctor Masters had a couple of days ago, it was quite a bit of CCs for your age, and body, so you must be feeling the lasting effects of the drug still." Staring at the Nurse that was talking to me, I tried my best to focus on her, but my head was working at an extremely fast pace, so I zoned out whatever she medically had to do to my body. Finding out after I had calmed down some more that she had attached an I.V. to my hand. Unable to stay conscious, I heard her continue to say to me, "By safety protocol, you are to be arranged to be transported to the Laboratory where the rest of the riskier Unnaturals are kept at. And because of that, I had to give you a calming Sedative Drop, next to a Saline bag. I do apologize."

Looking away from her, I looked straight ahead, which again happened to be the ceiling. Remaining conscious was extremely difficult and unfortunately, I fell to the drug's hold once more.

When I had woken up, I was in a similar room to the hospital room I had stayed in previously. Still powerless to move, or use my senses accurately, I paid excessive attention to the Scientists and Researchers, who now moved in and out of my new room. It was hard to keep track of everything they had tried to tell me. The only thing I recalled was when a Researcher had told me that I was

43

considered a new breed of Hellhound, called the 'Infernus Cannis Umbras' or Hellhound of Shadows. Although, to everyone else, I had all the behaviors and appearances of a normal dog breed known to Dog breeders as the Beauceron. It satisfied me to finally know what species I was, but I believe that the Researchers failed to recall that I was still a child; although as everyone grows, they gain newer abilities with whatever species of Unnatural they were. I was a new breed and had other powers that not even they knew how to properly deal with. As I grew and gained more control over my transformation I too gained these unclassified species abilities, however, I felt no need to use those gifted abilities in front of the Researchers; and as much as I am aware even now I haven't used them in front of these scientists. As more time past by, I had also lost the will of ever getting out of this cruel place. Through all the same tests occurring every Lunar phase, the same drugs every day, the same mental torture of no longer belonging to anyone but the Hospital's Institution, I had lost every ounce of willpower to contest against being a guinea pig. To me it was hopeless, and before I knew what happened, day after day, I eventually ended up where I am today.

Facing the same weekly Rebel Syndicate raids, the same tests under the unusual repetitive Blood Moon, the same Sedatives, the same Sensory Distortions, the same Pheromone Blockers, the same tasteless food, the same I.V.s. I knew it was my fault that I was here. I knew I was here because I decided to go see the Blood Moon in August, here because of the Shadowed Skeleton man who gave me this curse called Hellhoundism, here because my parents wanted the best for me, here because Doctor Masters and Director Julious wanted me to be kept as a lab rat for the sake of advancing Modern Science. There were countless reasons I was here, and yet I could hardly recollect where here was, what my original name was, what my parents' names were, what the purpose behind these supernatural powers was.

Staring up at that same blue-green ceiling, I listened to the Alarm continue to ring seeing its red-light pass through the little square window near the upper part of the door. It was nothing unusual, but for some reason, my heart skipped, and my stomach churned. As I heard the computers record the quick rise and fall of my heart and blood pressure, I questioned what was causing the tension on my lifeless body. What was going to happen today? Would it be something different for once? A change in the same old routine?

Chapter 9
Jakob

"Remember, we are here for those in the Off-grids." I heard Mhykal instruct our composed group on the outside of the Institution's Grounds. Observing the brilliant red glow of tonight's Blood Moon, I overheard my fellow Unnatural Rebel Associate continue. "Yalu, I want you to take a small group of our friends here and take the upper floors so we can get the Guards and Researchers to believe we are after those Unnaturals. Jakob, you and I will take an alternative small party to the lower floors we had recently discovered in our last few Raids."

"Gotcha." I sighed, glancing over to Mhykal from out the corner of my eyes.

"The rest of you guys make a perimeter and keep an eye on the Escape Routes. Help any Unnaturals you see. If you do not see any guarded humans, let them go. We are not hunting; we have a job to do here tonight." The normally comical man surprisingly ordered in a stern tone. His voice giving off that type of volume where it left no room for any intolerant questions about our protocol. Grabbing his dark trench coat, he looked back at me again, "Let's go the second Yalu triggers the Alarms."

"Alright." I complied.

"Oh, and here's a small list that one of our fellow spies had made copies of."

"You mean one of the unconsciously willing men I had fooled into making copies of?" I joked back, looking fully into his amber gaze accompanied by short black hair, matching feint facial hair, a solidly built face, and a routinely made bod.

"Yeah, your abilities have come in handy with these raids here recently." Mhykal returned smiling back at me.

"I don't know how handy." I continued to tease, taking the folder of stacked papers. Opening it up, I saw there were few papers inside of the file. "It's a small stack. But then again, I asked only for their Numbers, Species, Abilities, and Room Locations." Skimming through the papers, I saw only five numbers and not necessarily in order either. "Five of them? Huh?"

"Yeah." He sighed answering my cold questions just as the Alarms in the building started to go off. "Well looks like we got to start heading in."

"Give it a few seconds, you know with our speed, that it will only take a few seconds to reach the lower levels of the Institution," I said still browsing through the paperwork. "There is a set of twin Draconics, numbers 2501 and 2502. One with full transformation, and the other with elemental control."

"Rooms?"

"A-3, and A-4. On what looks like a basement level."

"Underground? Hmm. Alright, keep going and fast." Mhykal said as he impatiently stood up.

"Room A-2, has an Unnatural Shaman, with Necromancy. Number 0996."

"So, there is still someone with the older Numbers. Man." My fellow comrade continued to interject.

47

Ignoring him I resumed to inform, "Then there's room A-5, the Unnatural is not specified, but the ability is Telekinesis and Teleportation. At least that is what it says, I have no idea what that really identifies him with."

"Probably still human? What is his number?"

"Umm says, 3457."

"Okay, that's four analyzed. Got about another minute before those slow humans reach the upper levels, so hurry up with who is in the last room. Which I would assume is A-1, right?"

"Yeah, in A-1, there is an Unnatural with Hellhoundism, with its known Ability redacted. They truly don't want it known whatever it is." I smirked. "Could be in our favor if we get that one for sure."

"Could very well be. Now, what about the file number?"

Closing the folder, I placed it on the table next to some of our other remaining comrades who would keep in touch through our Bluetooth ear receivers, "Number, 0497." I answered.

"Oh, that's even older than the Shaman."

"Yeah, it is. That has to be what around twenty years?" I shrugged while ordering the men to discard the folder and all of its papers properly so we cannot be tracked. "Hope whoever it is, they are still sane because that long inside that place could make it problematic on all of us in the future."

"True, nonetheless our job is to get them all out. And we better get a move on, or else Yalu's Trickery will be seen right through." Mhykal groaned. "And I will get my ass kicked."

"We both would." I joked, walking alongside him. "Ready, I guess."

"Good, let's go." He ordered with that sneering smile of his. "Move out." Although he had led one or two raids here and there, everyone unquestioningly followed his orders and followed behind us as we ran at a partial of our full speed to get inside the Institution.

Once inside, we practically flew down the halls, the stairs, and towards the Laboratory. The irritating alarm sounding like a high-pitched buzz in our ears.

Upon reaching the Underground Laboratory, we commenced our descent towards the lower levels where we believed the 'Off-Grid' Unnaturals were being contained.

Corridor after corridor, we finally reached A-3 and A-4. Thankfully, they were side by side.

"The Draconic twins," I answered a tad out of breath.

"You really should run more, Jakob."

"Shut-up, Mhykal." I growled back.

"There's a Keypad for each room. Shit, we didn't think of that."

"They got to keep us out, and them in, don't they? It's fine, though." I exhaled, straightening myself up to a consistent vertical position. Placing my hand on the Keypad, I fixated on where the strongest thermal readings were, knowing that with a diminutive use of my own Psychic Sensory Ability, I could figure out each code. Figuring out what keys were most pressed, I hurriedly punched in the first code, then went onto the second Keypad.

"Jakob, there is a double-door system." I heard one the lower Unnaturals who had trailed us identify.

"Shit," I growled. "Mhykal, can you pick these damn locks?"

"I can try." He said walking up to the plexiglass door. "I'll need my back watched, though." The dark-haired Vampiric Unnatural ordered, cutting into his lip with his sharp fangs.

"I know before you were changed, you were a well-known thief who excelled at Picking Locks. This should be a breeze." I praised my friend.

Laughing back at me, he returned, "Yeah, yeah." Then there was a pause, "Alright door one, opened, let me see the next one." Stepping back a bit, I walked back over to A-4. From which I began

49

to talk to the Draconic, letting him know who we were, what we were doing here, and if he wanted to assist us on our mission.

"Free my brother first, and then we will decide after we get out of here." The male Unnatural with a Dragon faced skull, and some bluish scales spread across areas of his skin spoke. Ripping out his I.V. needle, he walked out of the small room and into the Corridor. His height was a bit menacing even to my six-foot-two height. If I had to estimate he stood around seven feet tall, at least in his current form.

"Alright, door two opened." I heard Mhykal announce. Stepping back, he let the two brothers happily reunite, then returned, "Alright onto the next room. You guys wouldn't happen to know where it is?"

The Draconics shook their heads no at the same time. The younger one in A-3 spoke, "We don't their exact location, but if you head down that corridor there is a screaming Human, and that way there is another man, who sounds like he is constantly praying or something."

"Amplified hearing. It's even stronger than mine." I teased the stone scaled brutes. The twins just cockily smirked back at me.

"Alright, well let's get the screaming human, I believe with a bit of extra help from Jakob, we can get him to ease out. We don't have a lot of time here anyhow. Yalu should be able to keep them distracted for another eight or nine minutes." Mhykal spoke up, as we now ran alongside the Draconics at about half of our original speed.

Reaching the door, I unlocked the Keypad, while my old thieving friend picked the lock on the second door. Once inside the room, I used my Hypnotic Ability. Speaking into his mind, I succeeded in getting him to use his Teleportation ability and get the twins as well as a few more of our beat men back to our stationed Headquarters on the outskirts of the Hospital's property. Taking a quick sigh, I looked back at our leading supervisor, "We still got the Shaman and the Hellhound left."

"Let's get the Shaman first, the twins said he was down this corridor, then we can ask the Shaman for his help in the search for Number 0497." Mhykal breathed.

Running back at our typical supernatural speed, we were able to reach A-2 in less than two minutes. Bringing our deadline down to six minutes. "Alright, while I unlock this, please check in on Yalu, see if she can attempt to hold back those guys a tad longer," I asked Mhykal, who I knew had the easiest time with the female Vixen.

"I will try." He swiftly answered. Then while he used his skills, he chatted with his girlfriend for a few seconds before returning. "She says she can at least grant us an extra three minutes and that's all before she has exhausted all of her Illusionary."

"Okay, that should be enough time if the Shaman can tell us where A-1 is," I answered as the second door unlocked. "Hello, 0996."

Chapter 10
Jakob

"I prefer Crowe," the male Shaman rejoiced. "The Spirits told me that you were coming today. It is a blessing that I was able to stay mentally intact till today."

"Yeah, you're one of the older numbers, right?"

"Yes, except for, 0870, and 0497," Crowe replied in his crackling elderly voice. His long white hair falling over his shoulders as he slowly wandered past the double-doored threshold.

"We freed 0870, five years ago, I believe he is a Club Owner now." Mhykal happily kidded. "A good man, very business savvy."

"Okay, Crowe, would you know where-" I asked remembering that we had a small-time crunch to work with here, but not trying to be rude.

"Where 0497 is? Unfortunately, I do not know young Immortal. The Spirits have told me about a large lingering Shadow that hangs around the spit firing female. They warn of that being and his control over her." Crowe answered.

"Spit-firing female? A lingering Shadow?" I sighed. My mind swiftly wondered why the paperwork had nearly all of 497's info redacted? What did this controlling Shadow have to do with her?

Why were the Spirits this Shaman conversed with seemed so afraid of it?"

"I do recollect that when I was brought down here, A-1 is down that way." The sun-dried skinned Shaman stated pointing down an endless corridor. "It's the closest room to the Glass Dome." Crowe continued thankfully giving us much-desired information.

"Alright the rest of you guys, take Crowe and return to the perimeter base." Mhykal again ordered. "497, shouldn't be too hard to handle." He now charismatically spoke.

"Right, for someone who has been here as long as she has, I do not believe she will leave this place so easily." I returned. "And I doubt YOUR skills with women will be very useful in this endeavor." Raising my brow to mockingly question his updated enthusiasm.

"True-." My friend now sighed pathetically, getting very depressed. Acting as if he had been shot with a horrid arrow of truth.

"Besides, isn't Yalu your girlfriend. I don't think she would like to see you flirting with another woman. Even if your Vixen has a deep history with crossing back and forth between both women and men, I doubt it will work out in your favor, Mhykal."

"True-." He again continued acting more dejected.

"Let's get a move on, thank you, Crowe, for your help," I said respecting the elderly man.

"It was my pleasure," Crowe answered from the back of one of our larger Vampirics who decided to carry the light man back to the base.

"Alright, let's go get 497 and get out of here." I returned to Mhykal who had thankfully regained his adult composure. "You are a Hopeless Romantic."

"Shut-up, Jakob. This is coming from the same man who has only laid with what, three women in the last couple of centuries." He snickered as we ran at our top speeds towards the location of where A-1 was supposedly at.

53

"Well, they were women of their time; I didn't have the energy for the hundreds of women that you had slept with between whatever your relationship status was with Yalu back then."

"It's very complicated." My brunette haired and amber-eyed friend playfully sighed. "We turn down this corridor?" He eventually asked.

"Yeah, I think so." I agreed with my fellow Vampiric. Eventually, after some more running, we came to a room called the Dome. "I think we went too far."

"What is this room anyway?"

"It was on the blueprints, but I don't know it's full purpose. For all we know, it's there for aesthetic appeasement to entice banks to loan them money, and besides the doors are locked." I answered to what seemed to be a usually distracted Mhykal.

"True. We could see what's inside?"

"No, we can't. We have a time crunch, or did you forget Yalu is giving us the necessary time to get all five of the 'Off-Grid' Unnaturals out of this Hell."

"Guess I did." He tried to joke with me, giving me one of his typically fake smiles. "Alright, let's go look for this room-. Oh, wait, here is a descriptive sign. It says that A-1 is further down the same corridor."

"So, we didn't go past it?"

"Seems that way. Let's hurry up now, so we can get back home."

"Tired already?" I teased.

"Shut-up, Jakob."

Running further down the corridor we finally found the room marked A-1. Reaching forward to unlock the Keypad like I had done several times already, I noticed out of the corner of my right eye that there was a clipboard hanging off one of those wall-folder boxes. "Hey, Mhykal did you see any clipboards?"

"None that I can remember. Why is there one-?"

Grabbing the board, I initially scanned through the papers. "These are medical orders that's for sure. It looks like it is signed for 0497, and by a Director Julious, and a Doctor Masters." Flipping through the papers, I slowed my speed-reading to skim some of the orders written by these two. "There are almost twenty different medications they have her on, and damn those are some high dosages." Further flipping through the pages, I continued to mumble, "Then here's a list of food-drug orders. Another thirty or so different kinds of proteins, carbs, sugars, antibodies."

"What does that mean?" Mhykal asked sounding astonished about the number of treatments these cruel people had forced this long-standing patient of theirs to go through.

"I don't know, but I do have a majority of them memorized for now so we can give the lists to Viktor."

"Good idea, now crack that keypad so I can unlock the door."

"Hold this," I said handing him the clipboard. Looking at the keypad, I again put my hand up towards the keys. Reading the past collections of thermal readings, I found the leftover fingerprints. Pushing past the fact that some of these thermal readings seemed surprisingly fresh, I hurriedly punched in the keys. Managing by luck to open this door because of the vast amount of identities on those keys. "That was a difficult PIN." I sighed. Getting the clipboard back, I further studied all the medications they were giving this 0497 to once more run through the list while Mhykal worked on the plexiglass door's lock.

"Alright. Got it."

"Good, now let's go see where she is hiding," I answered noticing from where we stood that there was no sign of anybody at all in the room. Opening the second door, we cautiously ventured inside the darkly lit room. Our vision was not impaired thanks to our Species Abilities; however, it wasn't pure darkness either, the lights bouncing off the machines measuring her stats were providing enough luminescence for us to make out the layout of the room.

"Found her." I heard Mhykal call while standing beside the locked bed.

"You did? She's just lying there?"

"Yeah, I guess so, she looks conscious, but I don't know how to read this. Even her Aura seems odd."

"Probably because of all the drugs they are pushing into her body. Sensory Distortions. Sedatives. Pain Killers. Blockers. Uppers. Downers. All of those can produce odd scents with one's Aura, you should know that." I reminded him as I walked around to the opposing side of my friend.

"Hey?" He asked waving his hand in front of her face. "You there?"

"She isn't dead, or else the machines would be expressing a flatline," I denied, sensing the depressing mood of the room. Gently putting my hand around her chin, I moved her head sideways, seeing a small bandage pressed on one side of her neck. "Injection sight-."

"Yeah, they are all over her, what of it?"

Driving my hands under her neck and legs, I began to gently lift her off the hospital bed. Hastily snarling, "We need to get back now, got less than thirty seconds until Yalu's Illusions fade. Grab that I.V. bag and make sure you also grab a few of those drugs they have close by."

"Okay," Mhykal said. Quickly unhooking the I.V. bag, he gently placed in on her, allowing me to carry it. "She looks completely lifeless. I don't even see a single ounce of 'spit-firing', either."

Growling at the profuse urgency of our time crunch, I ignored his blabbering and continued to carry the extremely light woman, noticing some familiar characteristics. "For the extensive amount of documented time this woman has been here, she seemed much less like how the Shaman had previously explained to us, and more lifeless." Also, noticing the age, I wondered, "She seems really young for the amount of time she has been here, and from all of my past raid experience the Syndicate has only seen a handful of children at the most." Coming back to reality a second later I questioned, "Did you get those drugs I asked you too?"

"Yeah. Ready to go now?"

"As much as I will be, for now."

"Yalu, this is Mhykal, we got them all, move out." My long-time comrade barked through his earpiece. Receiving a quick nod from him, we then prepared to now escape from this underground hell.

"So, this was your true plan?" I heard someone growl to us.

Chapter 11
Jakob

"Stealing all of the High-Risk Unnaturals." The man wearing a white lab coat, and dark blue scrubs said while turning on the light to the room. His bright blonde white hair almost glowing under the soft fluorescent light in the room.

"Stealing? That goes a little far. We are freeing them, not stealing them. If anything, you guys are the ones that stole. Thieving away their rights as people." Mhykal smirked. I could hear in his voice how hard was trying to hold back his raging anger.

Reading his name tag on his lab coat, I then challenged, "So you are the Doctor who signed off on all those drugs and medications you are giving this poor woman?" while still holding 0497 in my arms.

"Poor woman?" Doctor Masters laughed. "It was that damn brat who gave me this scar!" The man then growled his attitude changing as he angrily pointed in the direction of the barely breathing woman. Exhaling a longing sigh, the man retreated his hand before again seizing a mocking smile, "As much as I would just love for you take that bitch, I cannot allow it. Her abilities have been helping the Government in ways you cursed Rebels can't even bother to understand."

Glancing down at the neglected woman, then back over at the man with a long scar off to the right side of his neck spreading from the middle of his cheek to under his stern jaw and onto the upper part of his neck. The more my eyes investigated the scar the more I noticed little details. The scar while resembling deep lacerations caused by either this woman's claws or fangs also appeared to have healing boils at each end. These details made me debate if it was an attack or an odd burn. Turning my attention back at Mhykal, I assured, "We can get passed him no problem. And we should hurry, she won't make it much longer under their care-"

"Ha, good luck with saving that one! 0497 has been the same lifeless vessel for over ten years!" The man interrupted with a sinister smirk. "And good luck with getting out of here... "

"See you later-" Mhykal sneered as we both rushed past him our Vampiric speeds slipping right on by the man.

"Hold on a minute, Mhykal!" I called back, stopping about ten feet past the door.

"What?! We need to get out of here! Now!" He urgently reminded coming to a heel beside me.

"Hold her." I returned handing the woman over.

"Jakob, what are you going to do?!" Mhykal furiously questioned with fierce confusion, taking '0497' in his arms, while unfortunately dropping the vials of medications we stole. The sound glass of breaking on the tile floor instantly hushed my tone as I explained the change of heart. "Jakob, we don't have time for that!"

"Just shut-up!" I shouted back, "I have made up my mind." My dark trench coat flowing upward as I walked back towards the psychotic Institution Employee.

"Now what are you going to do? Kick my ass?" The Doctor chuckled still holding an unusually rabid smile while he pressed the secondary emergency alarm to call more guards down to our location. The noise hardly phased me as I had indeed made up my mind, maintaining the same gait I watched this Doctor Masters fish for some object hidden away in his lab coat's outer pocket. My ears overhearing the man curse under his breath, "Filthy Unnaturals!"

Responding with a curse of my own, I shot back "Disgusting humans!" just as I decided to use my hyper-speed. Coming within range of him in under few milliseconds I hastily formed a tight fist and punched the man in the lower gut, momentarily knocking all the air out of his lungs. As he collapsed down to the tiled ground, I picked him back up by the throat, lifting him back up off his feet and slammed him against the corridor wall, leaving only the tips of his covered toes to grip the floor. "You're weak, disgusting, abusive." I continued to curse however, this time audible enough for the Doctor to perceive while I held him in place along the concrete plastered wall with the strength of one hand.

"Jakob!" I heard Mhykal shout. "We need to go! NOW!"

"IN A MINUTE MHYKAL!" I roared back at him, my eyes remaining fixated on this cruel man who was trying to refrain from losing any more air from his lungs. Snarling to him, I interrogated, "You think that I did not see them, did you?"

"Seen what?" The Doctor now coughed holding onto that same smile.

Shoving him into the wall again, I overheard my friend again call "Jakob!" The pitch in his tone only making the tension climb higher.

"GO MHYKAL!" I bellowed back as my own slightly increased hearing could hear the woman moan in agony. "She needs to see Viktor now!" I ordered. "Don't worry about me, I will catch up with you in a few minutes."

"Don't go get yourself killed." I heard Mhykal upsettingly tell me before he vanished taking the same path we had used to infiltrate.

"You guys all are fucking bastards!" I hissed to the fraudulent Doctor. Stepping closer to where I held the man so I could stare face to face with him. Our eyes quickly locking on another. Tightening my grip on his neck, I began to asphyxiate him, believing that this was still a much quicker death then he deserved, and yet one a man of his traits was owed. Feeling his hands try to grab at my arm, before feeling the man's attempt to also kick at me. "Those scars. You console people like her, tell them that they can be treated, but all people like you do is put them on countless drugs. So many drugs that it keeps her from ever fighting against you and your men as you take advantage, treating them no different than lab rats. Using their unique abilities and genetic mutations to further your science. Its people like you that truly piss the HELL out of me." I harshly exclaimed with my own version of a crooked smile. "How about we see how you do against someone who isn't on those drugs? Against someone with fifteen times the strength of a Draconic!" Holding him away from the wall for a brief second, I released my grip on his thin neck, the sensation of his blood swiftly moving through the numerous veins in his neck was no longer traveling through the nerves in my fingers. As the man attempted to stand on his feet and rile his fists, I lifted my foot off the ground and proceeded to bring my boot in for a nasty kick across that smug face of his. It's hard sole crashing into his cheekbone forcing the Doctor to be meet the concrete wall once more. Quickly recovering, he attempted to weakly swing a fist at me. Dodging the incoming attack with ease, I reached for his wrist and tightly grasped the flesh. Putting my back into it, I swung him around before throwing him into another wall. Walking over to his slumped-over frame, I once more picked him up by the throat. Slowly lifting him back up off the ground, I yet again tightened my hand's grip on his jugular. Just before he passed out, I lessened the harsh grip and proceeded to drag him back over to 0497's assigned room A-1. Tossing the Doctor's barely conscious body into the room, I sneered, "Enjoy your stay in there." Swinging the plexiglass door shut followed by the metal door, I hastily punched my fist into the keypad. Breaking the keys, forcing it to malfunction, and lock him in the small bland room. Taking a quick breather, I ended our one-sided conversation with, "As much as you deserve it, you aren't worth the effort to kill, you annoying prick."

61

Leaving the conversation with that statement, I took another sigh. Shocked that I had not killed the creep. Running back through the same corridor where only a few minutes earlier my ally had taken the last of the rescued Unnaturals through. Quickly reuniting with the rest of my reconnaissance group, I saw that everyone was thankfully accounted for. All the members of Raid, and all the patients we were supposed to free from the Off-Grids, all of them had safely returned to our temporary base. "Glad you weren't killed or captured, Jakob." I heard Mhykal sigh in relief.

"How are they?" I asked jumping into the back of the transport van that had both 0996, and 0497 in it. More of my worry attached to the young woman, then the elderly Shaman.

"Well, the twins decided that if we needed them to ring them up, and well the Human, he surprisingly relaxed once we told him what was going on. I think he's naturally skittish." Mhykal broke down while also stepping up into the van, closing the doors behind him. "He already helped us minimize the group of collected vehicles so we could sneak out under the radar of the police."

"That's good. His ability could come in handy if he decides to stay." I sighed my sights continue to focus on the woman who was gratefully sleeping.

"By the time I had gotten her here, she was in obviously a lot of pain, so Viktor gave her a Relaxant, and a small sedative dose, just to ease her over. He believes she has gone through some sort of Shock Paralysis that is why she could not move of her free will. Viktor also suspects she had been through a lot of mental abuse."

"Was she able to say anything?"

"No, she barely could manage to respond to the sedative let alone say a physical word, unfortunately."

"I see." I exhaled.

"Did you kill the Doctor?"

"No, but I did kick his ass," I smirked. "I should have killed him, but it was as if someone kept telling me not to. It felt as if it wasn't even worth my energy."

Leaning my back against the wall of the van, I heard the Shaman named Crowe speak up. "It was the Shadow that told you not to kill him."

"Huh?" Both Mhykal and I questioned in chorus.

"The Spirits tell me that the Shadow has made himself visible to the Doctor and is speaking with that man."

"Okay, I am confused," I interjected, "How did the Shadow tell me not to kill him? It was just a feeling. I didn't see a being like that anywhere, nor did I feel his presence."

"He can hide from even the Dead," Crowe mumbled to us before he started to murmur something over 0497's sleeping body.

"A prayer." I thought to myself. "I guess it couldn't hurt her any further."

"Her blood is tainted, and her soul is stuck in the Shadowy Depths, yet her heart is still as innocent as a child." The Shaman said ending his prayer a few minutes later. "She is trying everything to keep her sanity in tack. Poor thing."

"Yeah." Both of us agreed.

"Hey Jakob, you said you did memorize what was on that clipboard?" Mhykal asked attempting to alter the subject.

"Yeah, I got the drugs and additives in the least memorized," I answered.

"I see. Well, hopefully, Viktor can help us get her-"

"We're here." I heard the driver clearly state over the roar of the truck's engine.

Chapter 12
Jakob/ 0497

"Put her on one of the beds." Viktor ordered me as I followed him into the room we had put aside as a 'medical ward'. Gently placing her down onto the twin bed with its metal head and footboards, I again heard my comrade's voice speak up, "You can hang the I.V. bag from the small hook against the wall."

"Okay," I said. Grabbing the bag, I stretched it to place the hook through its perforated hole. "I'll go ask Yalu or Nancy for some clothes that hopefully will fit her."

"Ask them to dress her, I know you are not like Mhykal, but if both of our suspicions are right, any trust she has in men is gone. Even if we too are Unnaturals." Viktor continued to express as he stood over his usual desk. Looking most likely over the names and dosages of the drugs I had written down for him.

"Yeah, I think you're right-" I paused when I saw her eyes open. Exposing the lifeless, pale, ice blue tones in the iris. "Hey, Viktor-" I now called. "She's waking up."

"The Sedative must have worn off." He calmly returned. "Just tell her-well you know."

"Where was I?" I thought to myself. "I remember being carried out of the Room, and from what I recollect the outside world before I was once more sedated. But-"

"Hey-." I heard someone softly say. "I know you are most likely wondering where you are, but I promise you it's okay. You are in our current hideout." The male further explained. Out of the corner of my blurred sight, I faintly made out the man's physical traits. It was the same man who had taken me out of the room, only to exchange hands with his friend so he could beat up Doctor Masters. From what I could make out he had a slender build with a slight muscular stand. A slender European face. Short dark dirty-blonde hair that seemed stylishly messy accompanied by these dominant ember green-hazel eyes. All of it added up to what I recalled. "I'll be back. I'm going to go see if there's anything else you can wear besides that short hospital gown."

"It had been so long since I had worn anything else." I thought to myself, still unable to speak. "You can sure try; not like I can fight back anyways." Watching him take his leave, I tried to absorb my new surroundings, but before I could even attempt it, I saw someone else come into my line of sight, the only other person I had around for conversation the Shadowed Skeleton. "What do you want now?" I coldly mumbled to myself.

"Little Reaper." He said stepping up to the side of the bed. "My little Reaper has made it back to the Outside World."

"Hardly feels that way."

"It may not seem like it now," The Skeleton said, his fiery red eyes still captivating me the same way they did when I was eight. Leaning forward he used his long skeleton fingers to rub my dyed hair off to the side of my face. "But it is still the outside, my sweet, Little Reaper."

"Sure, it is. So far, this seems like the same old, same old world."

"Now it may be, but in time it will be different. In time, my Little Reaper it will be fun again, for both you and me."

65

"Is that a promise?"

"It all depends on you, Reaper." The male voice said in my ear before he disappeared again into the shadows.

"Right." I groaned in my thoughts.

"I don't know why you are asking me; I think my clothes might be a bit big on her." Yalu sneered. "Hell, do you even know what her breast size is?" The Caucasian skinned, black-haired, yellow-eyed Vixen casually asked in her usually soft raspy feminine voice.

"Umm-"

"Jakob isn't that kind of man, to go fondling women's breasts-" Mhykal smiled in my direction before he cut the sentence to change the subject. "How is she doing anyway?"

"She woke up before I came down to ask you about what clothes you had free off-hand," I said sitting on the dark red Victorian accented sofa across of them. "She still hasn't spoken or done any purposeful movements yet."

"In the years we have been doing this since creating the Syndicate, we have had our cases of Amnesia, Addictions, Paralysis, and many other medical problems, but I think it is the first time I have seen anyone in as bad of a state as 0497."

"She's nothing but skin and bones right now." Yalu interrupted as she began to walk towards her bedroom. "But, I will still look. Who knows I may have something? Meanwhile, you should also ask Nancy, or Alexsandria, or any of the other women who live here."

"But only you and Nancy seem more like her age and possible size." I continued. "I think Alexsandria is still too young to be close to her size."

"Whatever Jakob." Yalu continued disappearing into her room.

"Tell her that I went to ask Nancy-"

"Nancy isn't here, she went out to the club tonight. She should be back in a few hours." Mhykal coldly reminded. "Besides though is it best for 497, to be changing clothes? I mean if you think about how long she has been there, she may not know how to wear a bra, let alone a shirt or pants."

"True, but still, she needs something different than that hospital gown." I returned, again wondering if she really was a child when she was brought in.

"Besides stop worrying about her so much. We just got her out of there and now we have to wait for Viktor to-"

"How can you not be worried about her? You are a Hopeless Romantic, aren't you?" I growled standing back up. "We are most likely the first people she has seen treat her kindly in who knows how long and building that bridge of trust takes someone showing that they care about her."

"Jakob, we do care for her, but if you show too much care, she may not know how to handle that. She may become nothing more than a lost puppy stuck by your side all the time." Mhykal calmly stated. "Besides what makes believe you have to be there with her? I have only seen you like this twice since you and I became friends two hundred years ago."

"Don't ask," I growled as Yalu came back with what seemed like some clothes.

"I managed to find a sports bra, a t-shirt, and a pair of sweatpants. As it tends to be cold during the night here, not like you Blood Suckers will know the differences." Yalu said handing me the clothes.

Giving them back to her, I returned, "Viktor said it will be better if you changed her." Before I walked off. Knowing I needed time to cool my head before I went back into the medical ward.

"Jakob-" I heard Mhykal call in his usual teasing manner.

"FUCK-OFF MHYKAL!" I yelled back at him, ending our conversation with my middle finger raised into the air, waving the digit back at them.

Chapter 13

0497

"Heya-" I heard a woman express coming into the room with what I recollect was the other man who had come to save me last night. "God, she looks worse than before. Or is it just me?"

"Hey, I am right here, and I can hear you quite well-" I thought flustered with the woman.

"She can hear you know-" I heard the dark-haired man who was still sitting off in the corner of the room. Who if I remembered correctly went by the name Viktor.

"Oh-" the woman said. "My bad. But for all, it says you really do look bad."

"Yeah, I know, crazy woman." I continued to mutter in my head.

"My name is Yalu, and my friend with me who I am sure you have already become acquainted with, his name is Mhykal." The woman who allegedly called herself Yalu introduced. "Jakob, wanted me to help you get out of that short gown. Okay."

"Then, where is he?" I wondered, knowing she must have been talking about the European looking man. "With the number of times I have had my gowns changed while there was a female always present, there was still a male-"

"Jakob is a bit too respectful around those of the opposing sex, so he didn't want to be here."

"You're lying." I quietly groaned.

"So, I brought Mhykal to help me out. Don't worry he won't hurt you." Yalu continued to tell, giving her friend a dark glare with that golden gaze of hers. "Alright, let's get you sitting up, so we can untie those ribbons."

Feeling what I believe were Mhykal's hands just by their size and callused skin reach under my neck and back, I felt my body be slowly lifted up into the desired sitting position. From where I felt female hands begin to untie the ribbons. One by one, they were all freed.

"Umm, Mhykal do you see this?" I heard Yalu ask, knowing that one of my hidden secrets had been exposed.

"Yeah, that is one large scar, and its shape is peculiar." Mhykal returned.

"Of course, it's peculiar looking." I mimicked. "A cross-shaped scar that stretches from the top of my back to the top of my tailbone and from one end of my ribcage to the other end. Believe me, it's weird."

"Hey Viktor, could you come document this for me?" The same man now asked the other male-"

"Yalu, hold her gown up-" Viktor said as he casually stepped up beside the bed. I could not turn my head to see what was going on, but if they document just like the other guys did, then it was all accomplished through a camera. "Everything has been documented. I'll email it to my computer and put it on file to show Braedon when he comes back from wherever he has wandered off to."

"Okay, thank you, Viktor." I heard Yalu speak. "Alright, I am now going to get the sports bra on you."

"Bra?" I thought to myself confused. "Oh, that's right I had grown breasts a while back. But what made me need one?"

Sliding the sleeves of the gown off my arms, she then had Mhykal hold my arms up over my head. I felt weird being handled like a children's doll, but I guess it could not be helped. Feeling the cotton-fabric material be pulled down my arms, I watched the grey-trimmed, black bra get pulled past my head, and stretched down over my breasts. It felt a bit tight and restraining, but in a way, it also felt better than the leather restraints I had been put in countless times. The only annoying part, for now, were the straps that dug into shoulders.

"At least we are similar sizes, I think you're about half a cup smaller than I, but for now it should work." I heard Yalu speak. Trying to lighten the mood. "Next I have is a man's tank top, which will go on the same way."

"Yeah, I know how a shirt goes on, I just can't put it on myself." I mocked.

The white shirt was pulled quickly down over my arms, head, and breasts appropriately fitting my body type despite being a little bit big. Though, it was a lot snugger than the same old hospital gown. "Okay, here comes the pants."

"Again, I know how it goes."

"You can lie her back on the bed, I can do this part myself." I overheard Yalu hushedly order Mhykal.

"Okay, I will just be outside." He returned venturing away from the side of the bed and out of the room.

"Okay." Yalu sighed, leaving the gown over my private area, and beginning to slip what looked like gray sweatpants over my legs. Cuffing them up until my bare feet poked out through each leg hole before she began to pull them up around my bare butt. "Alright, all dressed. Later once you put on some more weight, I will help you get some fitting underwear."

"Great." I sighed with an imaginative roll of my eyes. "Though I do appreciate the clothes." I knew I couldn't verbalize my true feelings however I still desired to at least think it. Even if it was still in my head, this was the first time in a long while that I had used a positive word.

"I will be back later to check in on you." She reminded just before she wandered out of my line of sight. Her cocky voice seeming calmer and more laid back when Mhykal wasn't around. Odd behavior.

Looking up at the marble crested ceiling, I began to attempt to make out the symbols and art carved into the ceiling, successfully managing to make out people, deer, dogs, a lion, the moon. Unfortunately, it didn't take long for me to make out all the characters in the marble. Everything returned to being the same old boring stuff. "GO FIGURE!" I grumbled. Closing my eyes for a quick second, I now thought, "How long did I have till this would be over? Was I dreaming all of this? Were the new location and the new outfit all just a dream? Did I make up these people who had not only rescued me from the Laboratory and all those Researchers, Doctors, and Scientists? Were they made up by some new drug that had been injected into my mind? Was this another test? Was all this made up to extend my leftover sanity?"

I couldn't figure it out, and with the doubt creeping in, I began to panic. Hearing the heart monitor, I had been hooked back up to begin to loudly beep made my fearing anxiety only worsen. In seconds, I saw the man called Viktor enter my peripheral vision. Clutching my wrist with his thumb, index, and middle finger the Unnatural began to read my heartbeat. Ten seconds quickly went by before he let go. My heart rate was still steadily increasing as my panic worsened. The rate was so high the necessary organ to live strained for a break. I knew with the pain coming back that I was one step short of transforming. I had to calm down. I HAD TO CALM DOWN! But I couldn't! No matter what I tried, I could not relax.

"I'll get you a relaxant, hold on." I barely saw come from Viktor's mouth. Enquiring what I had perceived only made it worse. Feeling my eyes water, I began to feel tears roll down the side of my face.

When Viktor came back with a syringe in hand, I flashed back: Seeing Doctor Masters with the same syringe in his hand and a crooked smile on his face. Panicking even worse in my head, I called out for anyone to hear me.

With the needle pressing in my upper arm, I could only ask in my head, "Someone please help me!" Shouting it to myself.

"It should take effect in a few seconds. That should help calm you down-" I heard Viktor's blurred voice speak through Doctor Masters's lips.

"PLEASE! Someone!" I again cried to myself.

"Be calm, my little Reaper." I heard the Shadow's voice echo in my ears.

"Please-" I thought my mind beginning to stall on the words, hesitating on what it was supposed to say next.

"There is nothing to fear, Reaper." He again assured. I could feel his long skeletal fingers rub away the escaped tears on each side of my face despite not having the ability to see him. "Remember you are in the Outside World. If it were one of your dreams, I too would not be here."

Chapter 14

Jakob

"What's wrong?" I asked Viktor as I stormed through the medical ward's door followed by Mhykal.

Viktor was sitting beside her bed, checking the monitors we had her hooked up to, checking the machines that kept an eye on her overall stats as she still couldn't physically let us know what was wrong before going back and checking 0497's pulse.

"What's wrong, Viktor?" I again requested walking up to the bed to see the woman asleep in fresh garments. Her head slanted off towards one side.

"I believe she had a panic attack." Viktor answered, now looking back up at Mhykal and I. "But, I'm not sure."

"A panic attack?" Mhykal asked. "Sure, it wasn't a heart attack or something like that?"

"Well if it was one, there would've been a much faster rise in her heart rate, but the monitor read a quick rise and fall, then another rise and a slow fall." Our fellow Vampiric ally answered. We were thankful he had served countless centuries as a Doctor and a Scientist because if not things would have been a lot more complicated for us. We wouldn't have a single idea on how to treat this poor woman.

"Well, what about withdrawal from all those drugs she was on?" I now questioned.

"No, surprising she has had none today. Even if there was one, I doubt it was the source of her attack." He speculated. Pausing for a moment to return to his desk, I overheard the Vampiric continue to theorize. "I have been able to remove eighty-percent of the medications she was on from the list you gave me. I would assume it was her extraordinary healing powers that extinguished the drugs from her system, however not having much experience with her species I can only hypothesize a possibility."

"Okay." Mhykal shrugged. Trying to diminish the tense mood in his usual comical way. "But she is okay?"

"For now, yes. I did have to give her a Relaxant to get her to calm down though."

Stepping closer to the side of the bed, I saw that her cheeks had dry streaks off to the side of her eyes. "She was crying?" I wondered.

"A little, but her eyes still didn't move, blink, or anything."

"So still no reaction?" My friend asked.

"Not exactly. I believe that I saw her fingers spasm as I gave her the drug. Whether it was from the muscle contraction or if it was purposeful movements, I cannot tell you." Viktor continued to debrief. "She will be out for a little while, but it will be best if she sees someone beside her when she comes to."

"Okay, I'll stay here." I reacted after a swift pause. Locking eyes with Mhykal as I remembered our little dispute that had arose a few hours ago.

Sighing, my century-old friend gave up on the challenge and rubbed his hand over the back of his head while saying, "Do whatever you want, Jakob. Just remember what I warned you about."

"I'll keep it in mind," I growled.

"I'm sure you will," Mhykal answered before he made his exit as Viktor returned to his desk.

Coming back to the bedside, he grabbed the little tube flowing Saline into her system took it out of the I.V. bag and replaced it with one of ours that we had in storage. "It hasn't been even a full twenty-four hours since we had done that Raid, and she is already proving to be trouble. Yet, I am still confident that she will prove to be worth all the preparation, and arduous work you guys went through to retrieve her and the other Unnaturals." He peacefully encouraged.

"I hope so. She was supposedly being used to further some sort of Government project, or at least that was that creep Doctor said."

"You mean the one you beat up?" Viktor cheesily grinned before he returned to his desk. "If she starts improving we just might be able to figure out what part of her Species they were using for the project, and either prevent it or-"

"I don't want her to be used like that. Not again. Our goal is to stop that cruel abuse those bastards are forcing Unnaturals to go through over the centuries." I hastily countered restating our organization's cause.

"True, but stopping the abuse is hard when Humans still abuse one another over the simplest of things. And over the years, we have figured out how to obscure our truths allowing us to blend into the 'Human' lifestyle quite well." Viktor calmly spoke while flipping through some sort of paperwork. "You should know Jakob; you are one of the oldest Vampirics we have here besides Braedon and me. And all of us have seen plenty of changes in the two different societies."

"Yeah with the more well-known species, the Draconics, the Lycans, and us Vampirics having figured out how to adapt to 'their' society while those less known species such as Hellhounds, or those with supernatural abilities like the Shaman and the Humans with psychic powers have yet to adapt."

"In other words, Jakob, you are saying that to stop the 'abuse' means having to teach those like 0497 how to adapt to that society with their new abilities. It's easier said than done when at one point in time those people such as 0497 were once human and to do what you wish is a lot more difficult than shutting down the Hospitals and Laboratories all over the World."

"Yes and no. It's easier than changing the laws that are in place calling Unnaturals secondary citizens and allowing places like those we are shutting down to also get away with the treatment, however, I also believe that with the right help from those same species it will become easier in time."

"So, says the immortal one. I don't think that those other species you are describing are immortal. Draconics can live from anywhere between six hundred years to a thousand years. While Lycans live the usual human lifespan, depending on what the exact definition of their curse is. Last I knew Humans don't live past one hundred years unless they have good health, and Hellhounds well from I have read live odd lives varying on their species and family history before the genetic mutation." Viktor continued casually explained.

"Guess you are right. Our goals seem nearly impossible, but it's those small possibilities of it being accomplished that has kept my hopes up all these years. I suspect that there was something with what they were doing to her that made me want to fight so hard for it." I serenely stated looking down at the sleeping woman who we barely knew anything about besides her species, and the Patient Number 0497 she had been given again who knows how long ago.

The hours went by before the woman had finally woke back up. Her pale eyes staring into the nothingness ahead of her. Just like Viktor had said, I made my presence clear. "Hey. It's okay now." I started slowly. Leaning closer to the side of the bed, I noticed that her left hand's fingers began to convulse. It was small but noticeable. Gently grabbing her hand, I waited for the next little twitch. Before I knew it, her fingers had wrapped slightly around my hand. It was all I needed to know that this Unnatural was on the verge of regaining some of her mobility. While it would still take some time before she would be able to fully function again, this was a good start. "It's alright," I assured her before calling Viktor over to investigate if this truly what I had hoped I had seen.

"She is starting to have some purposeful movements indeed." I heard him tell the both of us.

"That's very good," I said now using both of my hands to hold hers. "It's a great sign."

Chapter 15

Jakob

Three months had passed since the Raid on Salem Drive's Hospital Institution for Unnaturals, and 0497 was on a steady road to regaining all proper and purposeful movements. She had yet to talk to anyone, but she could use both of her arms and sit up. The Hellhound had also started to regain some of her leg strength as of last week. While she had shown this almost instant comeback, we also had miraculously managed to almost fully wean her off the complete list of medications. She still needed a little help from the painkillers to get through the muscle contractions, which was a small-side effect from the dystrophy, but nonetheless, she was recovering. And she wasn't the only one doing well.

Our Syndicate had officially closed three national Institutions in America. Of course, there were many more to whom desired our attention as well. All in all, our large force of several rebelling groups had managed to shut down fourteen here in the States, and another thirty-seven internationally. While Yalu and I had switched shifts with 0497, we would also help Mhykal and Braedon make Raid plans on other Institutions. Everything was coming along well, but as the law of physics says when something good happens there's usually something bad that was going to follow up, what it was yet to be decided. Although we all had the feeling, that gut feeling it was going to be bad soon.

All of us were on edge about our next Raid in Ohio and something was telling me to not go with my friend and his on-again-off-again girlfriend.

"I'm telling you; you are too attached to her." Mhykal jested with me his arm swathed around his girlfriend's lower back.

"Sure I am," I growled playfully rolling my eyes. "What about you two? Attached to the hip again?"

"Hey-" Mhykal now barked back at me with still a smile stretching from ear to ear, like usual.

"She may not talk still, but we all have gotten close to her, and if you feel that something is off about the Raid, then don't go." Yalu voiced to me. "However, we could still use your great mental abilities, besides Viktor is going to stay here to supervise 497 in case something does happen. If he does see something, he will be contacting Braedon first thing, okay?"

"I know he is staying here-" I returned glancing back at 0497, who was leaning against Viktor's arm for support as she watched the setting sun. "I just can't help but shake this feeling." I murmured to myself. Shrugging off the odd sensation I was feeling, I continued. "I guess I'll go. If anything bad happens, I can get back here by foot in about fifteen minutes anyway."

"Yeah running at full speed all the way here," Mhykal said, mocking our Species Abilities.

"Alright, well, we got to get going now," Yalu said checking the time on her newer dark purple smartphone. "If we're late to the checkpoint, Braedon will rip into all three of us, and I don't feel like getting my head ripped off."

"He's more bark than bite." Mhykal teased.

"I don't know how you guys get away with it so often."

"Somehow, we manage, right, Jakob?"

"Yeah." I sighed following them down the stairs onto the first floor to walk into the garage and pull out in our black tinted window Escalade.

A few hours into our raid, I heard through the Bluetooth earpiece that Braedon, our group's leader had gotten a phone call of some sort. My stomach dropped, but I kept my mind clear of all doubt, putting trust in our medically trained Viktor.

"This section is clear," I reported into my earpiece. "Moving onto section B-4 and C-7."

"Roger that. Meet up with Mhykal at checkpoint B-2 before moving onto the next section." One of our tech lackeys explained.

"Alright." Darting through the corridors I hastily caught up with my friend. Both of us wearing our usual black trench coats. "Hey, Mhykal."

"Hey Jakob, from here we work together and free the Unnaturals. I guess they're all simple electronic swipe locks." Mhykal filled me in as we began to walk towards the next two sectors.

"That shouldn't be difficult. Compared to our Raids on Salem Drive, these just seem like child play."

"True, even I could unlock those doors." I heard him laugh.

Quickly we opened all the doors in each sector, freeing in total seventy semi-healthy patients. While many seemed like Humans with powers either gifted or cursed upon them, few were specifically diagnosed as species of Unnaturals. Leading them all back out, we collected them onto a 'Stolen' public bus, from there I used my hypnotism to order the driver to take the humans up to a 'Human/Unnatural' safe house. From there, our leader Braedon and a few other leaders in charge of the large safe house would help teach the humans how they could fit back into whatever their lifestyle they once had as well as how to keep their abnormal abilities in check. Sitting in the passenger seat of the Escalade, I anxiously waited for us to complete this 'Raid'. Glancing up at the brilliant Blood Moon with its infamous glow, I exhaled a longing breath.

"Ready to go?" Mhykal probed as he stepped into the Driver's seat of the vehicle, his girlfriend following into the back seat.

"Yeah." I sighed. "I'm ready for bed."

"So am I." the Caucasian Vixen yawned. "Thank god it's finally over."

"It is exhausting work, but it has to be done, unfortunately. If there was no one to rebel against the harmful treatment of our fellow Unnaturals, all of us would either be hunted down with deeper discrimination or captured and put through those 'treatments' of Humanity. Then most of the ones we had freed would most likely be living their last days in the same room, or the same cell, undergoing the same painful torture day in and day out." Mhykal heavily sighed while he drove the vehicle out of the hidden shadows and into the paved asphalt road secluded by the thick forest.

"Or Unnaturals who represent breaks in science and technology would end up in similar situations as 0497 did." I reminded.

"True. Out of all the Raids, I can remember she was the first one I had physically seen in that rough of shape." Yalu returned. "Can't imagine myself if my life had been as rough as hers."

"I don't think any of us could."

Arriving back at the Manor, we all noticed that something was wrong. All the lights were off inside the place. Stating the obvious, I ordered Mhykal to stop the vehicle.

"Jakob, hold on. Let me park it first. You don't know what is inside, or if there is indeed anything wrong in the first place." My friend pleaded.

"I am not waiting around," I growled back. Jumping out of the vehicle I stormed towards the large front doors and went inside. My first instinct was to check in on the woman who had been steadily regaining most of her mobility, but I decided to handle protocol first. The first thing I had to do was check the many rooms and common areas in the Manor. Using the Bluetooth earpiece, I contacted both Mhykal and Yalu. "I'm checking the rooms of our weaker parties before I head up to check on Viktor and 497. Could you guys check on our other dorms and make sure everyone is accounted for?"

"Yeah, Yalu, will take the east side of the property, and I will check the south side. Be careful Jakob, and try to keep a positive head on your shoulders."

"That made no sense Mhykal, but anyways I am almost done checking the rooms here in the Manor," I said rushing room by room to hurry up and get into the Medical Ward. Once the protocol was finished, I flew back down to the second story towards the Ward. Approaching the room where the Syndicate treated the Unnaturals were set out to be medically treated without being abused, I noticed Viktor leaning against the wall adjacent to the door. Hurriedly running up to his side I frantically inquired, "Are you okay? What about her?"

"I knocked my head on the bed railing, but I am okay," Viktor assured, holding a cloth up to the back of his head. Dabbing it to dry the blood from his gushing head wound while it healed. "But 0497, she transformed."

"Transformed how? As in, to her Hellhound form?" I questioned confused before rapidly ordering into my earpiece, "Mhykal, Yalu, hurry up and get back to the Ward, Viktor could use some help cleaning up."

"Okay, we are on our way." Yalu and Mhykal spoke in unison.

Seconds later, they arrived up to the landing. "Viktor, are you okay?" Yalu said as she began to help him clean his head wound.

"It's already healed over." He panted.

83

"Apparently, she transformed and tackled Viktor causing him to bash the back of his head against the bed's footboard," I answered gazing up at the two interspecies lovers.

"She transformed? It's only been three months-"

"It's got something most likely to do with the phase of the Moon, similar to the way the full moon effects newly turned Lycans," Yalu said upset.

"That would make sense, except she's not newly turned," Mhykal ecstatically said. "That woman has been a Hellhound for almost two decades per those papers."

"I need to go in," I said placing my hand on the old Victorian doorknob. "I need to see this for myself."

"Jakob, take Mahkyl with you." Viktor returned. "The way she was acting it was as if there was someone else in the room; as if there was someone else in there telling her what to do, and although I couldn't see anything, I wouldn't trust that behavior."

"Okay." The three of us spoke at the same time, digesting the analyzed information our friend had just told us.

"The only way I could keep an eye out for her fast movements was the tagged collar she wore, her claws clicking against the wood floor, and the silent arguing with the hidden identity." Viktor continued to describe his mind trying to solve what happened to him.

"What about the power, why did it go out?"

"Oh, I don't know; it went out right after she completed her transformation."

"Okay. Well, let's get in there. I'm curious to see what a Hellhound looks like." Mhykal sneered trying to again bless the mood in his typical fashion.

"Be careful, both of you," Yalu ordered us.

Chapter 16
Jakob/0497

Entering the Medical Ward, I began to scan around the moonlit room for the supposedly transformed woman while my friend quietly closed the door behind us. Hearing him walk on the wood floors, I heard the quick clack sounds against the paneling. Confident the noise was coming from behind me, I swiftly spun around, however my advanced night vision could not decipher where the mutated canine was hiding.

"Stay on guard," I whispered to Mhykal.

"Okay." My friend responded, pausing when the sound of the metal tag rang out. "There's the tag-"

"Mhykal?" I called out his name just as he was cut off. A loud thud soon followed deep in the darkness. Spinning around to face where I believed my friend was, I finally caught a glimpse of what I assumed to be was 0497. Standing on top of his chest, with its long jowls' inches away from his face was the transformed woman, her masculine hand-sized paws standing on his chest. "Mhykal-" I urgently called out, running towards the madness.

"No, stay back!" I heard him swiftly order through soft gasps. Observing the large dog flash her long snow-white canines, I tried to remain calm and listen to my friend. Moving his hand gradually into the air, Mhykal began to reach for the left side of her morphed head. The black dog swiftly shied away, snapping her massively powerful jaws at his approaching hand before refocusing on his face. Her fangs even closer to ripping into flesh. "It's okay. 497, we aren't going to hurt you." Mhykal encouraged, his hand finally touching the side of her elongated thin face clarifying that this black dog was indeed 0497. Attempting to take in her appearance, I instantly realized how much she did resemble the Hellhounds told in books, a giant black dog with an intimidating figure. Enveloped with her unique figure, I noticed 0497 fade her snarl. Hiding the long teeth back under her lips before pushing her head into his hand and gently treading off my ally.

"0497-" I softly spoke, looking directly into her eyes. The pupil's color no longer that vivid blue but a fiery red-orange. Even in the dark, they glowed like the lasting embers of a smoldering blaze. Captivated by them, I fell onto the floor and crossed my legs as I watched the harsh red color retreat to that cold icy blue. The canine strolled closer towards me shortly after. Almost within my arm's reach 0497 swiftly recoiled, returning to the darkness. The sound of her lips curling again filled the silent night. Confused, I stood myself back up, only to notice that her attention was not directed towards me. It felt as if she was staring at something else. The exact behavior Viktor had warned us to be on guard for. Quickly thinking back to what the Shaman's Spirits had told us was hanging around her, I began to wonder if this behavior and the possibly unseen entity was what he was referring to were related.

"Jakob," I heard Mhykal soundlessly call.

"She's not focused on me." I returned aloud. "I think she is communicating with that Shado-" I hesitated when the both of us clearly watched her canine body drop on to the cold wood floor in such a sudden pattern that it instantly concerned us. Worried for the Unnatural's health we rushed to her side. Hunched beside her the both of us began to patiently analyze 0497 attempting to fight to stand back up on her own feet. The brilliant smoky red coming back into her eyes shadowed by a painful snarl. "Hey-" I gestured to the mutated animal. Leisurely sitting myself down in front of her, I again called. "497-?"

"Why?" I thought to myself, hearing my body scream out in violent agony. "What's happening to me? Shadow-!" I growled, looking up passed Jakob to see the Skeleton Shadow standing over him.

"Little Reaper. You have extended your time in-"

"Tell me what's happening!" I snapped, trying to force my legs to work while my head slumped back on the floor. "I know you can read my thoughts!"

Hearing the Shadow blow out a heavy sigh conceding my outburst, the being sadistically exclaim. "My Little Reaper has challenged me." Speaking now in an unusually quiet, dark voice. "You have extended your muscles, too long in that paralyzed state with those defying drugs to retain your human form. This is your first complete transformation in eight years." Floating through the European Vampiric, he grabbed harshly at my jaws, lifting my head off the ground, exposing my vital neck. "Now, my stupid Little Reaper challenge me again, and I will make you not only lose your sanity, but I will make you watch as I use your body to kill those people who saved you." The Shadow coldly whispered into my now cropped canine ears. Releasing his hold of my jaws, he threw it onto the ground. Staring at his red eyes, he aggressively interrogated, "Do you understand me, Reaper?"

Trying to get back up, I looked away from his harsh glare before softly murmuring. "I understand."

"Good." He smiled fading back into the dark shadows.

"I understand." I heard a female voice whisper. The tone quiet, and soft. Looking shockingly down at the only woman in the room, I saw her miserably shaken expression.

"Did she just talk?" I overheard Mhykal question also stunned from his position behind the canine.

"I think so-" I wondered aloud while I reached my hand out to touch the top of her fur. The black dog with light brown markings like a Doberman, or a Rottweiler quickly jumped back. Distancing herself from me. Forcing herself to stand up on her shaky legs, 0497 limped herself passed me.

"Okay. Did I miss something?" Mhykal asked confused.

"I don't know." I returned as we both watched the female canine drag herself back over to the same bed she had been sleeping in for the last three months. Looking up at the bed, she lifted onto her back legs and placed her front legs on the mattress before relying on all the strength in her transformed arms to finally creep on to the bed. Successfully crawling onto the cot, she lied herself down with her head lying in her paws, at least that was what I saw under the poor lighting offered by the Blood Moon. "I have no idea what is going on with her." I sighed.

"That makes two of us." Mhykal snarkily shot back just as the lights flickered back on. "Hey, look the power's back."

"Yeah, it looks like it was because of her transformation." I hypothesized. "She isn't a regular Hellhound that's for sure."

"That's for sure." My friend repeated as he walked towards the door. "Are you coming, Jakob? We should all go get some rest, it has been an awfully long day."

"Yeah," I agreed taking one last glance at 0497 before following my friend out of the room. Stopping by Yalu and Viktor first to exchange what information I had obtained. "She has calmed down now; I don't think she meant for you to get hurt Viktor. She did a similar tackle to Mhykal but didn't physically harm him, and I do believe that she is being haunted by that Shadow the Shaman said his Spirits warned us about."

"Yeah I know she did not do it purposely. But I think for now we should all call it a night and leave her alone in there." Viktor said with all of us agreeing to the notion of sleep. Splitting up, Yalu and Mhykal went off to her room together, while Viktor went off to his, and I too wandered in to my assigned bedroom.

Entering my semi-large room, I flung my trench coat onto the small sofa at the end of my queen-sized Mahogany Victorian Canopy and sauntered into my private bathroom, deciding at the last minute to take a hot shower. As the water warmed up, I began to undress. Throwing off my athletic t-shirt, and my dark jeans, I stopped to look at myself in the vanity mirror. Seeing I needed to shave before my stubble got any more prominent, I quickly grabbed the men's razor and shaving cream to begin. As I swiped away the stubble, I noticed that my golden eyes were not showing in the mirror. A frequent occurrence that came as a consequence to our handy adaptation of appearing more human, such as our ability to create reflections, and while it was quite a handy adaptation that allowed us to fit into the human lifestyle it didn't hide every secret. Our eyes still exposed our hidden truths, though we could easily remove any suspicious Humans with the stir of contacts. A trick that wasn't just used by Vampirics. Now if one preferred the all-natural look, they could up their feeding to maintain their previous traits, and if I recalled the last time I had fed on Blood was almost three months ago; the night before the Raid. Taking a deep sigh, I decided I would feed in the morning before I went to check on 0497. Finishing up with my shaving I rapidly took off my gray boxers and stepped into the shower. Stepping under the hot water face first, I permitted the water to hit my face. Spraying onto my chest and draining down the rest of my lean body. I may not have the ripped eight pack like Mhykal, but I had some strong lean muscles, declaring my body as 'fit'. Rubbing my hands through my greasy dark blonde hair, I flashed through the entire day, the entire process of our Raids, and then the event of whatever had just happened.

Reaching for the hair shampoo I kept on the small shelf in the frosted glass shower, I extracted a handful of soap and began to wash off all of the dirt, blood, and built-up grease from my pores. Dispersing the soap throughout my hair, down to my scalp. As it sat under the water, I repeated the same process this time with some body wash and a scrunchie, spreading the soap over my semi-cleaned chest, stomach, arms, and steadily working my way down. A few seconds later I rinsed everything out of my hair whilst the showerhead spewed more hot water onto my figure.

Finished with my shower, I stepped out grabbing the towel to swiftly dry myself off, running it through my hair at the end. To which after I wrapped the towel around my waist and walked out into my room so I could grab some new boxers in the least. Putting on some black fabric boxers, I pitched the towel into the hamper, then flopped onto my queen-sized bed. Not considering the thought of slipping under the red comforter I passed out right there. Ending my day with a clear and clean head.

Chapter 17
Jakob

"Hey, Jakob-" I heard a familiar voice speak from behind me. "Finally feeding, aren't you?" Mykal expressed as he took a seat across from where I sat at the kitchen's island counter.

"I needed to," I answered placing the human blood-filled whiskey glass on the dark grey marble counter. "It has been three months since the last time."

"That's a record for someone that usually drinks like what once or twice a month." He joked seizing the Blood bag to drain its last few droplets, and plasma.

"Shut-up," I growled. "Do you know how hard it was for me to hold back and not feed on that lunatic back at our last Raid." Sipping more of the thick consistency, I quickly huffed a large exhale. "So, have you visited 0497, yet?"

"Yeah Yalu and I went to visit her after our shower-" Mhykal teased.

"I don't want to hear about your sex life, Mhykal." I groaned finishing off the glass.

"Well. Fine, I won't tell you about it." The Vampiric now laughed at me. Rolling my eyes, I hinted at him to continue with what he had originally planned to tell me. "Anyways we went to see her, and she was still in that canine form sleeping. According to Viktor, she was asleep even when he had strolled into the Ward earlier."

"Whatever happened last night, must have required a lot of energy."

"Who knows, but before I left to go see if you were awake, 497, had woken up. Yalu decided to stay with her while I left." Mhykal expressed as he stood up from the kitchen's bar stool.

"Well, hopefully, Yalu doesn't rub off on 497, too much." I jested as I began to collect the several Blood bags I had gone through. "I don't know how I could deal with two of them."

"Yeah, I think having one version of my girlfriend is all I need and even that it is a handful sometimes." The man continued to joke as he leaned against the wall watching me clean up the mess that I had made. Grabbing the whiskey glass, I walked over to the sink and began to rinse out the stacked blood cells and left-over plasma. "Besides, I don't think 0497 has anywhere near the same attitude as Yalu."

"True, but we still don't know anything about her besides what kind of Unnatural she is, what she looks like in her Hellhound form, and what her Patient Number I.D. was," I said over the running water. "I mean the Unnaturals we had rescued over the last three months a majority of them knew what their names were, even that old man, Crowe recognized his name."

"If you call that a name."

"Yeah." I sneered leaving the glass to dry itself off. "But you get where I am going with this. We don't even know what 497's real name is-"

"She just started to talk last night, Jakob. Besides, you don't even know if she remembers it. She could have been a child when she was brought in, for all we know." Mhykal reminded me as we began our journey through the seventy-room mansion towards the Medical Ward on the second floor.

"Again, you could be right, but I just don't want to think about her parents leaving her like that. I mean to be tortured like how she was is hard enough to reminisce." I continued slipping on my short-tailed leather jacket over my usual white t-shirt. "It is definitely a subject I wouldn't even try to bring up unless she does first."

"You are still so attached to her. Maybe you are the lost puppy-"

"Right, asshole," I smirked.

"Has she opened up to you?"

"What about you? I don't see her warming up to you?"

"No. She hasn't." Mhykal shrugged getting all depressed again. Slumping his shoulders and losing his composition. "Usually I can get them to open up-"

"Well she doesn't fit into that circle, and I don't think you should be talking like that in front of Yalu. She might kick your ass." I interrupted, our eyes glancing over at one another for a quick second. "I am sure she will open up to us in time."

Reaching the ward, we both entered the room at the same time. I paused to see that there was nobody in the room at all. Walking over to Viktor's desk for any clues I could hear Mhykal ask aloud, "Where did they go?"

"There's a note here," I called back, clutching the folded piece of paper up from the stack of Unnatural Medical books.

"Well, what does it say." Mhykal sparked running up behind me.

Rapidly reading it in my head, I then reported it aloud, to my moronic dope of a friend. "Says Yalu took 0497 out to the garden, and that she dragged me along in case of any possible medical occurrences. Although that would most likely not happen. -Viktor."

"Why would Yalu take her outside?"

"I don't know why. Isn't that a bit dangerous for 497 to be outside so soon?"

"Well maybe it is also a step in the right direction, did you ever think of that?"

Nodding my head off, I agreed. "I didn't think of it, but after so long without seeing the outside world, I just don't how it could be encouraging."

"Well, we won't know unless we go see how she is reacting in person."

"Alright let's go see them." I shrugged putting the note back down on the desk. Following my friend, we casually strode out of the Ward, closing the door behind us. Descending the grand staircase, turning around the banister to pace towards the back of the house, I wondered how the Hellhound was acting. Was she acting scared and timid? Or, was she acting more like how Mhykal, and I thought she truly was?"

Finding one of the five glass doors that connected to the back part of the Manor, we stepped outside into the sun-blasting world. Its blinding light uncontrollably warms our immortal bodies at an extreme rate. We did not combust, or turn to dust, or explode, or glow, or anything like those other myths. Although it was still an adjustment, keeping hydrated, fed, and close to shaded locations to cool off aided us in not having some sort of heat-related diagnosis.

"Hey Jakob, Mhykal-" I heard Viktor call to us. "Over here."

"Hey, Viktor," I called hiking up to where he was sitting under the covered gazebo positioned beside the property's large pond. Using the little patio table to work on his usual workload.

"God, why is it so bright?" Mhykal complained.

"It's called sunlight, it comes from the sun, and it is always bright." I scoffed back. Focusing back on the subject at hand I asked Viktor, "Where is Yalu, and 0497?"

"Over there." He pointed off to his side not even looking up from his electronic device. Following the index finger, my eyes led my sights to the location Viktor had indicated. The two were stationed over by the stables we had on our grounds. "Yalu thought 497 getting some actual fresh air, and some feminine time would help her heal faster."

"She doesn't want us to be involved?"

"No, not really. She just asked me to come along and see if I could observe any unusual behaviors that she could not pick up from up close."

"And, did you see anything?" Mhykal piped in.

"No, nothing like what had happened last night. She was ready to get out, but it took her a few minutes to physically come outside. Then it took a few more minutes before she was comfortable enough to adventure further beyond the patio, but then after 0497 had touched the grass for the first time I believe I saw a smile seize her face finally." Viktor smiled.

Chapter 18

0497

Glancing up at brilliant, blinding light of the warm sun that blared back down on my black and tan fur coat, I couldn't help but feel another positive feeling. I felt happiness, and contentment with where I now stood. Dropping onto my stomach, I rolled over onto my back allowing more of my fur to soak up the glorious sun. Looking over to Yalu who had put her long black hair into a ponytail, while wearing the same dark pants, and form-fitted leather halter top, I saw that she was upside down.

"You really are enjoying this, aren't you?" I heard her raspy feminine voice quiz.

Rolling back over and bringing myself up to a sitting position, I hesitated. I wasn't sure how to answer the question. I knew that I could talk once again, but I didn't know how I would sound; if I could even manage to say the right words. I had not talked in so long, that everything I said in my head didn't sound right to me.

"It's alright if you don't want to tell me." I heard her spark with a light shrug of her shoulders.

Without thinking, I lunged forward, tackling her down onto the soft grass that tickled my paw pads. Jumping off, I privately giggled to myself.

"Why you." She growled at me with a sly smile on her face. The Caucasian woman's hands reaching for the tagged collar buckled around my neck. Easily dodging her, I darted a few feet away. This all felt instinctual to me. Trotting closer to Yalu, I paid close attention to her movements, preparing to again retain a distance. I was gratefully able to fully use all my muscles in this form and without much pain, yet as we played around, I swiftly realized that I unfortunately did not have all of my energy back. Flopping back down onto the grass again under the blinding rays of sunlight, I smiled to the Unnatural woman who sat beside me. "You sure are feeling better though."

With a flicker of my standing ears, an answer finally came to my head. "Yeah. I am."

"Hey, an answer to my questions finally." Yalu grinned. Looking away from her, I proceeded to hear her request more answers. "Why haven't you switched back to your human form?"

Hearing the inquisitiveness in her voice, thanks to my regained heightened ability of hearing, I tried my best to contemplate an answer. Harshly playing many responses over in my head, I eventually answered. "I like this form better. I feel more in control of myself."

"That's an unusual answer. Lycans with similar abilities prefer their human form to their wolf form. But then again you are not a Lycan. Hellhound." Glancing over at her, I nodded my head, choosing to not vocalize my thoughts. "Although I still don't see how you were in control last night."

"I wasn't trying to hurt anyone," I said looking down at the ground, folding my cropped ears flat against my head. "I really wasn't."

"I know you weren't, so, do they. Everyone knows that you weren't trying to hurt us, but it happens. Everyone loses control occasionally. I'm sure though that the more you work with your instincts and mind, you will be in complete control one day."

Looking at her, I stared into her golden yellow humanizing-fox eyes, questioning whether I could trust what she was saying. After all this time with this 'power', I have never been in complete control over my actions on Blood Moons. However, I wasn't in the outside world either, so it left me open to the possibilities. Eventually answering her; "One day, huh?"

"Yeah."

"Could you help me?" I asked her using simpler terms compared to what I had put together.

Staring into her gaze, I saw there was a look of shock and confusion, making me regret inquiring for help. Looking back at the grass I apologized for my behavior. "Don't apologize." I heard Yalu return her voice sounding unusually stern this time. Deepening my feeling of insecurity. "I'm just not the right person to be asking for help when it comes to control, but nonetheless, I will still aid you where I can." Returning my gaze to the free Unnatural, I observed her facial expression beginning to relax. "Besides, as members of this Syndicate, it is our job to help any Unnatural who is willing to accept our help. Although, when we rescued you, you weren't able to deny our help."

"I would have accepted it if I could. I needed to get out of there, I truly did."

"It would have ended up killing you-"

"If it was supposed to have, it would have happened long ago." I boldly expressed steadily feeling more and more comfortable talking to her as time went on.

"You make it sound like if it weren't for something that happened-" Yalu said looking straight at me with a confused expression.

" I don't know how to explain it without getting myself in trouble."

"Trouble? What are you talking about? No one here is going to punish you for telling your story." The woman now urged. Sensing her blood pressure rise, alerting me to a wave of rising anger, I hesitated.

"I can't tell you." I snarled, my lips curling as I slammed my eyelids shut, grimacing in absolute fear. "Believe me-" I paused before softly continuing, "I wish I could tell you. I really want to, but I can't."

"Okay, I won't push it then." She sighed. Sensing her hand press gently against my left cheek, I pushed into the soft skin of her small palm. "We won't push you to tell us. You can tell us, whenever you are ready, we will be here."

Nodding my head, I eventually broke away from her hand. Looking over at the gazebo where I had smelled the three male scents, I flattened my ears, wondering deep down if I could trust them the same way I did Yalu. I mean I didn't feel like I could completely trust her either, but my instincts were warning me to be cautious around the males. "Looks like they're here too."

"Yup, they have been there for a little while. I had Viktor leave a note before we left, because both Jakob and Mhykal, especially Jakob, are worried about you." Yalu expressed.

"Are they really?" I asked, partially believing her statement. Looking back at her I further probed, "They're not just saying that to back up how they truly feel-?"

"No, I can assure you they are genuinely concerned about you. Especially Jakob. He has this abnormal soft spot for women. He gives them high regard even though not all women can neither understand nor see it. And Mhykal, well he is nothing but a big flirt, and Hopeless Romantic, with a deep heart for women as well." Still, on the fence, I just slightly hummed in agreement. "You know it was Jakob who beat up that Doctor. The one who put you on all those medications."

"Yes, I know it was him. I saw him punch Doctor Masters in the stomach."

"Well, aren't you going to thank him?" Yalu cockily asked me.

"In time," I acknowledged, before deciding to revert to a little bit more of our chase game. I was tired of chatting.

"We only got a few more hours until the sun sets." She breathed, "We should get you back inside." Upset that she was not willing to play with me anymore, I closely followed in behind as we went to meet up with the male Unnaturals. Noticing along the way to the gazebo the massive number of other people staying here at the Manor. The numbers of 'freed' Unnaturals sanctioned here made it difficult to stay confident in everyone, made it difficult to bury the doubt that none of them were going to bring me harm. Putting those thoughts in the back of my head, for now, I focused on staying close to these four, putting what trust I had built up with Yalu on the table with at least these guys.

Chapter 19

0497

A week later I finally managed to transform back to my human form and had begun to feel more and more comfortable in my new surroundings, but I still did not feel one hundred percent safe. I felt I could put more of my trust in Yalu as our acquaintanceship embarked on its trail to hopefully a good friendship. The men, on the other hand, I didn't know what to think or feel. We had started some type of relationship, though I couldn't figure out what to classify it as or if I could even trust what I was feeling. Recollecting what my Vixen friend had told me, I continued to try to keep an open mind and heart.

"Hey, 497." I heard Yalu loudly call. Startling me out of my wandering thoughts. "Come on. I got a new outfit I want you to try on. I think it will fit you perfectly." She said, dragging me out of my cot.

"Okay." I reluctantly agreed. As I began to put on more weight, the outfits started to routinely change. And adjusting to wearing clothes for the second time in my life at first was hard, but as the months rolled by and the clothes started to fit more, things began to feel normal. Following her down the stairs, I was dragged past Jakob and Mhykal. The two were just sitting in the formal living area, grinning from ear to ear while I was dragged towards what I believe was Yalu's room.

"Here we are." She said pulling me in.

"Where?" I thought to myself as I absorbed these fresh surroundings. It was something completely different than my previous accommodations.

No longer able to take the silence, my newly acquainted friend announced. "This is your room."

Spinning around, I stared back at her deeply confused. "My room?"

"Yup. It is right across the hall from mine, and everyone thinks that you in the least deserve it. We believe that after living in that Hell for so long, you deserve something to call your own." She cheerfully returned, further entering the large room.

"I don't-" I said still in shock, trying to not doubt their honest intentions.

"It's alright to be in shock. Most people feel the same way. I know I felt the same when I had first received my room." Following her up the small platform, I watched as she dropped onto the dark-wooded Victorian Four-Post bed with a deep blue comforter. "Now, it isn't anything extravagant, but its a lot better than that hospital room you had, right?" Still stalled for words, I wandered over to the matching dark blue fabric sofa arranged at the end of the bed. "You even have a bathroom. Grant it, a lot of these rooms have the same layout, but not many can say they have their very own bathroom."

"Thank you." I finally mustered the energy to say aloud.

"You don't need to thank us," Yalu said in her raspy voice. Making it clear that if I had disagreed with her, she wouldn't let me go that easily. "This is what we do. This is our job." After a quick pause, I then observed the Vixen get up and walk over to an Armoire dresser off to the far side of the room by the bathroom. "I went ahead and got you a few outfits to start out with, after all, you are my size. Now, I only bought whites, greys, and blacks, with a few light-colored jeans, hope that's okay?"

"It's fine." I quietly acknowledged. Trying to digest all of this information, I decided it was time I at least return some of their kindness. "Yalu-" I paused.

"What is it?" She returned looking back at me with a softer yet still stern look on her face.

"In the least, let me tell you my story," I offered. "I won't be able to tell you all of it, but at least...at least let me do this."

"Sure, but you can do it after you shower and change." Yalu sneered collecting some fresh garments from the Armoire. "Hold these while I go start your shower." Taking the clothes, I froze. "I will be right outside if you need me." She continued understanding that from what she had seen, I hadn't been able to complete the most basic of 'human' actions in years. Watching her set and prepare the water temperature, I paid remarkably close attention to the process attempting to learn how to start one of these. "Alright, it should all be set."

Afraid to verbalize my gratitude at this current point in time, I simply nodded my head. Once she left the bathroom, closing the door behind her, I began to undress. Thankfully I hadn't forgotten how to do that. The only thing I still had some difficulties with was the bra, but with Yalu's great teaching skills I was well on my way to mastering that contraption. Sliding the clear glass door open, I slipped into the shower, the nice warm water instantly hitting my face before careening down my petite hourglass figure. Turning around I saw the soap sitting on a small shelf in the back corner of the shower. Again, recalling the differences between the hair wash and body shampoo, I began to properly use the complimentary soaps to clean off all the dirt that had collected on my body. Once I had effectively rinsed the shampoo out of my long hair and off my body, I slipped out of the shower. Closing the door behind me, I grabbed the folded, white towel and began to dry off my soaking wet body. Unsure how to properly dry my hair, I decided to go ahead and put on the newly received clothes. Slipping the undergarments on first, I reached for the pair of jeans to put them on next. The

103

faded, light blue jeans conformed to my petite figure, becoming tighter at the ankles. I didn't know what they were called, but through the fogged-up mirror I could easily make out how much they showed off my lower half. Grabbing the black shirt, I pulled it over my arms and head before lastly pulling it down over my breasts. Straightening the low V-neck collar so it would sit along my small cleavage, I decided I looked decent enough to venture back into the world beyond this tiny bathroom.

"Oh wow, I was right they do look good on you-" I heard Yalu happily chirp.

"Really?" I inquired deeply mystified. "Weren't these just clothes?" I asked inside my deranging mind. "What made them so special, that they 'looked good' on me?"

"The skinny jeans might take some time to adjust to, but..."

"Really? They feel no tighter than the countless leather restraints that were used to restrain me."

"Okay?" She bewilderedly returned. The facial expression on her face speaking in clarity that I had spoken some undesired vocabulary. Changing the subject Yalu quickly resumed, "Before you go into any more detail, let me trim back your hair, and then while I'm brushing it, you can tell me all about you're past, okay."

I nodded my head and wandered over to sit on the bed beside her. From there, Yalu tied off my long hair with a ponytail in the middle of my back and began to snip through the thick dyed black hair with magically appearing scissors. Once she had snipped through the last strand of hair, Yalu showed me just how much she had cut off. "Was it really that long?" I questioned looking at the length of hair. Estimating it to be at least eight maybe nine inches long.

"Did you ever have it cut?"

"Not that I can recall."

"Well let me go grab a towel and a hairbrush then you can start telling your story."

By the time the slightly older Vixen had finished drying and brushing my hair, I had told her how at eight years old I had gone to see my first Blood Moon. The same moon that caused me to change and how eventually through many tests I had ended up at the Laboratory. However, I did leave out some parts I felt they didn't need to know, both for their sakes and mine.

"Wow, only eight years old?" Yalu inquired, thankfully waiting till the end of my story before asking.

Looking away from her, I nodded my head, trying to hide the true amount of trauma I had gone through. Although I think she had gotten the gist of it all.

"That Shadow you talked about? Is it the same one the guys thought you were talking to last week?" She now asked her attention fixating on the one thing I didn't want to.

"He was the only one I could talk to during my state of paralysis, the only one who kept me sane-." I paused. Glaring deep into her eyes, I tried to remain as calm as possible. Swallowing, I breathed a deep sigh before coldly ending "That's all I'm going to say on that."

"Okay." She returned putting her hands up in that way to say 'Woah, I get it'. "Well, what about your Species's Ability? Jakob told us that it had been blacked out, along with many other things."

"They call it Iron Blood, and Blood Scythes," I responded. "I can't say why they were crossed out, but I do remember the abilities' characteristics."

"So, this was a newer ability? Like your Species's Breed was?"

"I guess." I shrugged. "Blood Scythes was something relating to the blood coming out of my pores to create a weapon of a controlled substance. And the Iron Blood was a term they came up with to describe my advanced ability to clot my blood and heal my

105

wounds. The Researchers described them going hand in hand, however, they also said that if my blood had encountered other physical entities it could potentially be used as a different type of weapon. I can't remember the specifics."

"You don't even know how to properly control it, or even how to at least awaken them?"

"Not really."

"It's okay, I'm sure when the time comes you will figure it out. Just like how you will learn to control your transformations." Yalu smirked.

"Thank you for putting all of your faith in me." I cried while doing everything I could to not tear up.

"Your trust in me is what has allowed my faith to be put in you," Yalu said using her hand to push my long-parted hair off behind my left ear. "You are a very strong person for telling me all that you have had to endure."

"Please don't tell them about my abilities. I'm not yet comfortable enough to tell them." I pleaded to Yalu as she got up to leave the room I was supposed to call my own.

"Alright, I won't tell them about your abilities, 497. But like I said before when it comes to those idiots, you have nothing to fear." She returned with that same smile that always made me feel at ease.

Chapter 20

Jakob

When Yalu finally came out 0497's room, both Mhykal and I noticed a distinctive look on the Vixen's face. "Babe, what's wrong?" Mhykal fearfully questioned as she sat beside us in the living room.

"Her past is just purely horrifying." Yalu quietly whispered.

"It is?"

"She was only eight years old when she became an Unnatural."

"Then she was human?" I asked, getting one of my many wondering questions answered.

"Yeah, regular doctors told her parents it was a seizure. But after her second transformation, her parents urged to see a specialist."

"That creep of a Doctor, right? The one who accused us of stealing?" Mhykal snarled.

"Most likely." I agreed with a deep growl.

"They did all the usual tests plus the Sensory Tests."

"Which of course, came out positive."

Yalu nodded, pushing her fallen strands of black hair behind her ear. "After that, her parents left her at the Institution and only visited her once in three months."

"Now that's just cruel," Mhykal growled, his body hunched over with his elbows on his knees and his hands blocking most of his facial expressions. Both Yalu and I could tell that our comical Mhykal was becoming extremely frustrated.

"That's not the worst of it, is it?" I asked his girlfriend, encouraging her to proceed.

"No. On Easter, both of her parents relinquished their parental rights to their daughter. That Doctor was the very person who told her. Of course, at her age, she didn't understand why, but she knew enough to blame it on her powers."

"She lost control didn't she-, with help from her emotions."

Yalu nodded.

"And it was after that when she went into that paralysis?" Mhykal asked.

"No, she says she didn't lose full control over her body until she was older, but she did stop talking shortly after. She did, however, mention after a few incidents she had gone into some sort of paralysis."

"The scars on his face-" I paused remembering the Doctor shout at us that it was 0497 who had given him those scars.

"They looked more like lacerations burned into his skin," Mhykal said, also vividly recalling the grotesque scars.

"When you got closer, you could see the boils." I described in deep detail before prying Yalu for more information. "Was that all she told you?"

"Yeah, all the stuff she was comfortable with telling me at least-" the Vixen acknowledged, momentarily pausing to fix her sleek ponytail.

Doubting the Vixen was telling me the entire truth, I held off prying any further, knowing far better than to question the extent of her proclamations. She would kick my ass if I even attempted to

108

interrogate her, so I let it go. "Did you in the least get her name-" I now asked without thinking. "Like her actual birth name?"

"No. She told me that she couldn't recall what it was. Even when she had dreams of her traumatic past when people said what she believed her name was, it sounded blurred or faded." Yalu returned. "When I tried to further investigate, she would say that as far she could remember her name was 0497."

"We have to change that-" I declared. "It's a memory of that same past."

"You can't just go and do something like that. She's already having problems trusting you guys." Yalu aggressively blurted out, warning me that I was about to cross the line. "Sorry, but if you are going to try to give her an actual name, first try to build a better relationship with her."

Both of us Vampirics looked up at Yalu who had stood up to debate her well-made point. "Okay, we will try to further develop a relationship with her, babe," Mhykal spoke, trying to end the conversation and stay on his girlfriend's good side.

"Good. And don't rush it either." Yalu snarled storming away from the sofas. "I'll be out for a little while to help Braedon with our next scheduled raid, I suggest while I'm gone you guys try to build her trust and break down this wall she keeps putting up around you two." Then before she had made a complete exit her soft voice coldly ordered us, "And whatever you do, do not ask her about the lurking Shadow. She is more afraid of him than she is of you two blundering idiots."

After Yalu left, both Mhykal and I decided to follow through with our promises. Making our way to 497's recently assigned room, I held my breath as I knocked on the thick bedroom door. Though, before my hand could finish the first knock, my ears heard the Hellhound's voice speak up from the other side, "What do you guys want?"

"That's-" Mhykal whispered, astonished by her species advanced hearing.

"Can we come in? Yalu told us about some of your past." I politely called from my side of the threshold.

"Sure-" she began. I could hear the terror on her voice as she pursued attempting to remain open-minded and friendly with us.

"It's okay we won't hurt you. And if Mhykal tries anything you can tell Yalu and I'm sure she will kick his ass for you." I spoke, still maintaining my composure.

"Really Jakob?" Mhykal whispered with this surprisingly funny expression of betrayal written all over his face.

"You can come in-" I heard 497, softly announce her feminine voice sounding so sweet and calm, making me completely disregard the fact that she was supposedly a dangerous Hellhound.

"Okay," I said as I twisted the brass doorknob to open the door. Seeing the woman wearing one of the new outfits her recently acquainted friend had bought for her, I was taken aback. "You seem to be enjoying your room..."

"Wow-" I heard Mhykal loudly interrupt. His mind just as overtaken by her simple get up as I was. Backhanding the back of his numb brain skull I ordered him to immediately apologize.

"No, it's okay." I instantly heard her dismiss flashing the two of us a soft smirk. "He is so full of energy that it is quite optimistic."

"See, Jakob, I'm optimistic." Mhykal chirped, his hands flexed on his hips, and his chest puffed out. Already over me beating him in the back of the head. "Unlike you-"

"Not true. I like Jakob's quiet nature and sweet temperament." The woman now said with this soft look in her pale blue eyes that made them seem full of life.

"Awe, there went my chances-" I heard Mhykal depressingly mutter aloud as he slumped over.

"So, why are you so afraid of us?" I now asked, attempting to keep my distance so I didn't intimidate her.

"I don't how to say it-" she returned. Sensing her temperament change, I calmly waited for the Hellhound to finish her statement. "It will take time."

"That we understand. But it still doesn't mean that you have to fear us-"

"If I truly thought of you guys in that way-" She paused for a little bit. I could see her eyes were fiercely trying to debate what her next words should be. "Then that night, I would have attacked Mhykal."

"Huh?" Mhykal and I questioned together. Of course, my friend's first image of that was getting a scar like the one that Doctor had.

"So, you don't fear us?" I persisted.

"No, I just don't know how to trust you guys. As I said, it will take me more time." She presumed to say as she stood up from the bed.

"Well Yalu, wants us to make peace. Try to build a 'relationship' with you." Mhykal spoke up after he had finally regained his composure. "And while she may not hurt you, she could still hurt us, and personally I would like to stay on her good side."

"I am willing to try to figure out this relationship thing myself." 497 said strutting closer towards our personal space with a surprisingly feminine gait.

"Are you okay if we call you our friend?"

"Sure." I heard her sigh, once more flashing a faint smile. "I could use some more friends."

"You sure have come a long way from that woman we rescued three months ago." I complimented returning her smile with one of my own. While 0497 had closed the gap between us, I could tell she

111

still was very stand-offish. Her eyes watching every one of our movements preparing to dart back if she saw anything her rational mind thought would be dangerous.

"I still need to thank you for that day." 0497 said, her eyes looking up into mine. Watching her deeply exhale before she spoke again, "I am deeply grateful for what you have done for me. For everything."

Chapter 21

0497

Almost a full year had passed since the Raid which had fatefully saved my life, and things were going seemingly well. I had regained all of my mobility, as well as gained some close friendships with three of the people who saved me that night. I was no longer feeling like an Outcast. I hadn't seen the Shadow in months. I had gained a substantial amount of control over my transformations to the point where I could switch in and out of the forms on command with little to no pain. My Species' Abilities were still a hit and a miss, but I clung to Yalu's words about eventually learning how to fully use and control them. Thankfully there were no Blood Moons in the past nine months, giving the appropriate time to accomplish all that I had, however, I still feared what would happen when one finally showed.

"Hey, 497." I heard Jakob call to me from the other side of my bedroom door.

"Come in." I returned, staring out my first floor, floor-to-ceiling window.

"What are you doing?" The several century-old Vampiric asked closing the door behind him.

"Watching the stars." I softly replied. "I used to do this all the time before I would do important things in my life."

"A hobby?"

113

"Yeah, when I was locked up the only time I was ever able to see their bright white glow was when I was restrained to a cold slated table in the Dome Room," I answered. "But before that, I had read hundreds of books about everything there was to know about the opera of the night. I knew the names of countless stars and constellations, each lunar phase, several neighboring galaxies, but-" I paused hearing Jakob walk closer towards where I stood. "Now, I can barely even read when the next Blood Moon is."

"If you want, I could get you some Astrology books?" He asked, finally standing beside me after slowly creeping under my cautious barrier.

"No, don't worry about it, Jakob." I returned. "That was just a childhood dream I had before-"

"Before you became an Unnatural, right?"

"Yeah. Now they just stand as a symbol of my newly gained freedom." I smiled, deeply gazing into his unusual eye color.

"Well, you couldn't have picked a better symbol." Jakob agreed, now turning to directly face me. "I was thinking that I would ask you before I left for tonight's Raid, would you like for Yalu, Myhkal, and I to help train you so maybe one day you could join us in-"

"Jakob, just stop," I said. Staring directly into his eyes, I continued, "I am content with where I stand for now and if I was to go with you guys on one of your Raids to free the Unnaturals..." I paused. "There's a chance that any one of those Hospital Institutions could report me back to the one I was held in and try to either take me out or recapture me."

"I'm sorry, I forgot about that." He said very sympathetically. "But if you still want to learn to protect yourself, we can help teach you."

"Thanks, and who knows I might take you up on your training offer later, but currently I am alright where I stand. I know I will need to learn to fight in this form-" I hinted towards my human form, "just in case that day ever comes, and I can no longer change."

"Yeah. It could come in handy for sure." Jakob said with his calming grin. "I had to learn to fight without using my Psychic Abilities myself. Just don't forget that against Humans, you have about the strength of five men in your human form alone. In your canine form, I'd say its more like seven or eight men."

"And what about you, I think I remember you saying something about the strength of fifteen Draconics one day way back," I smirked, playfully swinging my shoulders slightly back and forth.

"Yeah, it's something like that." He laughed, stepping closer towards me. Now standing in my space.

"Um, Jakob-" I softly spoke. "You are in my-"

"Oh-" the Vampiric quietly returned in a shocked tone. Stepping back a little he then apologized, "Sorry."

"No, it's alright." I returned. "I sort of let you get that close anyway." I happily teased, flinging my grown out bangs off to the right side of my face behind my ear. "Besides, you got a lot closer than I ever let Mhykal get."

"Oh yeah? I guess he can't help it, that Hopeless Romantic."

"Guess not." I chuckled, walking away from the window towards my comfy bed.

"Hey, though-" I heard Jakob now ask. The tone in his voice sounding serious yet sincere, making me unsure how to appropriately react.

"Yeah." I hastily called, turning away from the bed to face the European Vampire. "What is it, Jakob?"

"What would you think if we could come up with another name for you? Something to call you by besides Number 0497." Jakob endlessly requested.

"Sure, however, I am not yet ready to forget my past."

"Are you sure?"

"Yes. You can give me a new name, something that I can use besides a number, something that is all my own. I just don't want to forget what I have been dragged through. I want it to remind me of what other Unnaturals like me are still going through, to remind me of that until this is hopefully all over."

"I will talk it over with Yalu, and Mhykal, and we will come up with a name for you to call all your own." I overheard him say. His tone now less serious, sounding more relaxed. "I guess I will let you get some sleep." Jakob ended treading around the bed, and back over to the thick door.

"Okay-" I said. "Goodnight, Jakob."

"Night, 497." The caring man told walking out of my room, gently shutting the door behind him.

Chapter 22
0497/Jakob

When the morning finally came by, I decided the best way to embark today was with a nice hot shower. Strolling over to the Armoire that sat by the bathroom, I picked out today's outfit; ironically, it was that same outfit I had first received. Placing the clothing items on the bathroom counter next to the sink, I began to prep the water temperature for the shower. Hearing the water exit the showerhead crashing onto the floor with its usual pressure, I began undressing. Taking off the sweatpants, and my undergarments, I finally stepped into the shower, the steaming hot water feeling so refreshing against my still waking skin. Rubbing the flowery scented body-soap that Yalu had loaned me, all over my skin I wondered what today would bring me. There was a typical pattern, but it was never the exact same every day.

"What fights would Mhykal and Jakob get into? What kind of meal would Yalu cook? What was today's breakfast? What was planned?" I wondered. "Well, no matter what it was, it couldn't be worse than my previous routine."

After I had finished rinsing the soap off my skin and out of my hair, I turned off the water and began to dry myself off. As I dried my mid-back length hair off with the white towel using a trick I had learned from Yalu, I stopped to look in the body-length mirror. It's steamed covered reflecting glass, fuzzing the refined lines of my body, however that was not the only thing I saw in the mirror.

"You're back," I growled as I finished drying myself off.

"My little Reaper." The eerie voice spoke to me, his tall shadow standing behind me.

"What do you want?" I interrogated, reaching for the woman's underwear. Not afraid of this guy seeing my naked body when had he not only seen me in the nude before but could also invade my thoughts.

"My little Reaper, I want you to keep an eye out on someone for me." He said his fingers playing through my long wet, dark, black hair. "You are now strong enough to start doing some 'work' for me, Reaper." He continued those same fiery red eyes staring directly at me through the steamed-up mirror.

"What is it?" I unconsciously asked. Knowing deep down what would very well happen if I had tried to go against these 'work' assignments.

As I began to pull up my light-blue skinny jeans I heard that cold, dark voice speak "There will be a night where your 'friends' will not be here at the Manor and someone that does not belong will arrive."

"Someone will try to break in-" I questioned, pausing as my mind began trying to inquire about the possibility of that occurring. Hysterically thinking, "How is that even possible? I was told there are Alarms that can sense Auras-."

"This one is an ally of the Syndicate, granting the ability to sneak past." The Shadow verified, reading right through my anxious thoughts. "I want you to keep an eye out on that Man if he proves to be what-"

"You want me to live up to that Name?" I audibly asked, interrupting the being. Not even knowing how the words skated right on by my thought process. Getting a bad feeling in my gut, I began to wonder what had just happened.

"If he ends up doing what I believe he will do, I am sure my smart, little Reaper will figure out what to do." He finished with a harsh warning moments before the embers dissipated.

"What the hell does he expect me to do? Kill the man?" I snarled while I swiftly put on my black, V-neck short-sleeved shirt. Exhaling a heavy sigh, I slid open the bathroom door and tried to drive the thought of 'my assignment' into the back of my head. Strolling towards the formal living room, I stopped when I saw Jakob and Mhykal were already waiting for me.

"Hey, 497." The brunette-haired Mhykal greeted.

"Hey, Mhykal, Jakob," I replied with yet another heavy sigh.

"Is there something wrong?" I asked the Hellhound who descended the two-step staircase towards the two parallel sofas in the common area.

"Huh?" She spoke, snapping herself out of the stationary thought process. Stepping up towards us, she eventually answered my question with her semi-childish facial expression, "No. There's nothing wrong."

"Something's wrong, we can see it." Mhykal specified. "If you don't want to tell us it's okay, but if Yalu catches on, she might pester you about it."

"I had a conversation with the Shadow, but I can't tell you the details." 0497 responded, her eyes swiftly avoiding eye contact.

"I thought we had seen the last of him nine months ago?" I questioned concerned about her change in behavior. Around six months ago, all of us were finally able to crack open her personality; her sweet, sincere but childishly mature demeanor was what

119

everyone liked about her. Yet now it seemed like her wall was reconstructing itself. The feeling of a much more serious, dark, and mature mindset was beginning to poke through.

"No, he comes and goes." The Hellhound answered her tone distanced. "I don't want to talk about it: so, can we go get some breakfast and forget about this?"

"Sure." We both said in unison, confused about this newer version we were seeing. Watching her walk towards the kitchen, I overheard Mhykal gabble to me, "Oh yeah Yalu is for sure going to interrogate her. She likes 497's more playful self."

"Yalu does?" I queried as we followed in behind the young woman. "I would think your girlfriend would rather enjoy this somber side."

"So would I, but I don't know. That woman can be very confusing and complicated." He teased, rubbing the back of his head with that typical smile and a small chuckle.

"What was that Mhykal?" Yalu's raspy voice interrogated. "What about me is confusing and complicated? I thought you liked those things about me?"

Hearing 0497 lightly laugh lifted the mood while Mhykal tried to console his girlfriend that it was just a tease. "Come on Yalu, I didn't mean it." He expressed following the Caucasian Vixen around the kitchen as she tried to finish cooking whatever it was she was throwing together. Grabbing myself a couple of Blood bags I began to prepare myself the habitual drink. "Hey Jakob, can you make me one?" The fellow Vampiric casually asked.

"Make yourself one. You are standing in a kitchen you know-" I joked back as I finished draining the blood out of the clear bag.

"Yeah, it is a kitchen where food goes and not your guy's feed bags," Yalu growled back at us, holding a dangerous piece of cutlery like she was prepared to use it. Again 0497 laughed.

"Well, we got to eat too; it is not our fault that we have to have some blood from time to time." Mhykal barked. "Besides this is the only room where we can store it, so-"

"So, what! I don't care." The Vixen playfully snapped back before kissing her Vampiric boyfriend. Their relationship was too complicated for me to understand. "Oh, 497, here is your food." Yalu now said as she spun around to hand the young twenty-four-year-old woman a plate full of a well-rounded breakfast. The plate contained some cooked bacon, a couple of sausage links, and a couple of scrambled eggs. Lots of proteins and carbohydrates, but it was nothing unusual for her: Hellhounds were like Lycans and other Carnivorous Shapeshifting Unnaturals. "Sorry, we didn't have anything else."

"No, it's all good. Thank you." I heard the woman speak up with an eager smile.

"No problem," Yalu said, accurately throwing the large kitchen knife into the sink and swiftly grabbing her own plate full of high protein fried eggs. "You two can just feed on that." She now growled as I handed Mhykal his marked Blood bags before sitting down across from the women at the island.

"Whatever." Mhykal sneered.

Sipping on the whiskey glass, I witnessed everyone settle down and eat their meals. The quietness of the morning filling the moderately-sized kitchen. "So-" I eventually questioned after a few minutes. "What are today's plans?"

"Well most of the Unnaturals here are preparing to get relocated to other Safe Houses in our Neighboring states, so we can have some room for the expected newcomers after tomorrow night's Raid," Yalu responded. "Braedon wants us all to be there by noon Thursday, so we can go over each group's assignments."

"Okay. It's a Lycan Institute, though right?" I asked recalling our Syndicate Leaders' plans. "Why don't we just leave it up to them?"

"Who?" 0497 chimed in.

"While we both save as many other species of Unnaturals as we can, there are many kinds of Syndicates, but the biggest ones are the main three," I answered the Hellhound's inquiry. "Those three have higher collections of individual species. For example, here, there is a mass number of Vampirics. Well, the Lycans have a high number of those-"

"Flea-bag, drooling, mongrels," Mhykal spoke up, sticking his tongue out in teasing disgust. Backhanding his skull again, he returned, "Sorry I didn't mean to offend you 497."

"No, I'm not a Lycan or a werewolf." She returned still with the same grin, ripping into the bacon with her brilliant white teeth. "It offends me a bit because I do like my canine form more than this form, however, I know you weren't directing it at me, so I am not offended." She returned after swallowing her mouthful of food. Her tone and vocabulary sounding more adult than prior.

"Anyways-" I said trying to return the focus to the subject at hand.

"I understand it now. The three most common species are Vampirics, Lycans, and Draconics." 0497 answered. "Even when I was human, I had been taught that."

"You guys are quite popular." Yalu joked.

"I guess so." I sneered back, content with the tease. Finishing the rest of my drink. "So anyway, why didn't they take it?"

"Rumors are that Calem has failed in numerous raids, and requested our help," Yalu exclaimed.

"That is not like him, it must have been really bad," I said getting up to assist in the cleaning process.

"Yeah he's usually very stuck up and tries to steal our Raids-" Mhykal interrupted. "So how bad did Calem screw up?"

"Reportedly, ten of his best Lycans and Unnaturals have been apprehended by three different Institutes."

"Ten?" I asked. "What kind of drugs were they using to capture those guys."

"Most likely high doses of Sedatives, and Pheromone Blockers." I perceived 0497 voice. "Those were the same drugs they gave me during the Blood Moon phases to keep me from transforming. I assume that the Lycans tend to do their raids on Full Moon phases for the power increase, and probably weren't expecting the Doctors to figure out that they could use those medications to catch them." She continued to explain, appalling all of us with her high-level prognosis. However, as I had recalled what 497 had said about her hobby with Astrology, I was confident she had a higher level of scientific and thesis understanding.

"How did you come up with that?" Mhykal naively asked her.

Getting smacked on top of his cranium by his own partner Yalu, she returned, "She has always been that intelligent. I figured that out when I had taken her out to the Garden." Picking up the plates I saw the Vixen glance down at 0497, before continuing, "You should have also figured that out, Mhykal."

"Huh? I knew." He argued now standing up to help her clean up. Returning to their traditionally peculiar relationship dialog.

"Sure, you did." I groaned. "So, besides the Unnaturals being moved around, what else do we have?"

"Nothing really. It's another day to relax." Yalu happily returned. "Though 497 and I were planning on going hiking today."

"Mind if we tag along?" Mhykal asked.

"Sure." 0497 smiled. "Why not."

Chapter 23

0497

After our hike, we all returned home to be met by Viktor and Braedon, the leader of the Rebel Syndicate: Vampiric Syndicate that is. He was the eldest Vampire in the group, yet he seemed no older than Jakob or me for that matter. Guess immortality had its perks. Taking in his features once more, I noticed his short-long, amber-brown hair pulled back into what Yalu called a small man-bun. That same golden amber gaze that the other three Vampirics had. Braedon's frame was just as fit as Mhykal's was and he dressed much differently than either one of the boys. It felt more mature, almost business-like. A dark, blue-black suit with a royal, red tie, and shoes. It seemed he carried himself with an arrogant amount of pride, or at least this time around he did. Although I do recall once seeing the man dressed like Mhykal and Jakob did on their 'Raid' nights.

"Hey 0497, I see you are enjoying your life here." He introduced fluently speaking with a heavy, old New York accent. Standing in my human form, I acknowledged him with a slight nod. My instincts feeling no reason to fear, distrust, or dislike him. "That's good. Now, if you don't mind would you please allow me to talk in private with these three? I would like to discuss our plans for Thursday?"

"Sure." I sighed. Waving a temporary goodbye, I strode past our Leader to saunter back towards my room eavesdropping in their conversation along the way:

"She seems to be adjusting well." Braedon chirped.

"Yeah, she is. I was hoping for her to tag along with us on Thursday, if possible." Yalu asked in her distinctive tone. "But, I don't think 497 is confident enough in the world outside this place."

"In time, I am sure 0497 will either leave here and go on with her own life, or she will remain here to help us with our Cause. Now, how about our plans for-."

"For helping out Calem and the Lycans." I heard Mhykal loudly refute, making me softly chuckle as I further distanced myself from the location where they were commencing their secretive meeting.

Deciding to ignore the rest of the discussion, I continued to tread in the direction of my room. Once inside I opened the think blue curtains draping over the Victorian floor-to-ceiling window and altered my appearance again, mutating back to the form I was more content in for reasons I could not explain. Lying down in front of the window, under the bright sunlight, I rested my head in my paws to wait for the day to seize itself. Easily becoming overwhelmed with the thought of a nap, I drifted off.

When I awoke, the sun had set behind the horizon, leaving only the lively stars to shine back down at me. Responding to their call, I smiled for a quick second. "Another clear night-" I tried to say. Hesitating the minute my heart started to rapidly beat. The organ demanding more air to fill my lungs, so it did not have to strain as heavily to maintain a steady flow of oxygenated blood. "No, it's-it's n-not one of those nights. It-it can't b-be." I coughed, quickly realizing that it was one of those irregular Blood Moons. Fighting to regain my footing, I sorrowfully wept, "Why?"

Already being in the designated form for the lunar phase, I insecurely evaluated my choices. I wasn't sure how to accurately confront this situation. Hoping to calm myself, I looked back over to the stars. Viewing their still white glow in the corner of my eye, I questioned what was going on.

Baring my teeth in pure pain, I collapsed back onto the wood floor, my long nails digging into the wood, scratching its polished surface. Screaming out in anguishing whimpers and crackling snarls the longer the pain lasted and the longer my heart hungrily stressed; I called out for someone to help, for anyone to help me. This was the first time I had been in the form before the rise of the moon, and yet I had been in more physical pain than ever before. My head was spinning. My senses were blurring and ringing. My nose burned and bled. My gums started to swell while my teeth curved outward in absolute agony. I couldn't figure out what to do.

Hours dwindled by before I finally felt everything start to calm down, granting me faint control over my own body once more. Lying on my side with the bottom of my paws facing the window I continued to pant and heave for air. My senses had yet to return, the bleeding in my nose and mouth had thankfully apprehended. Lying there in a puddle of blood, I cursed the moon who seemed to always be present, knocking me down several pegs.

Before I lost consciousness again, I felt a hand briefly touch my short-medium length fur. Expecting it to be the bony skeleton fingers of that cruel Shadow being, I was surprised to make out the soft skin rubbing through my black fur. "Hey, hey." I faintly overheard someone's voice call out from the outskirts of peripheral vision.

"Finally, someone is here-" I prayed in my mind.

"Hey, 497 why are you bleeding?" I heard the same voice question. Trying to differ the familiar voices I knew in my head, I attempted to figure out who it was speaking to me. The more the voice panicked over my befallen body, the more I singled it out as a male's voice, however, I could not decide whether it was Mhykal or Jakob. "Hey, come on talk to me-"

"Jakob?" I guessed, concluding it to be the more relaxed Vampiric of the two.

"There you are-" Jakob sighed with much relief. "Sorry I barged in, but when you hadn't come out of your room in a little while, someone had to go check in on you. Especially when today was-"

"The Blood Moon." I whimpered. Doing all I could to retain control over my breaking emotions.

"Is all this a reaction?"

Without the nerve to continue talking, I began to nod, but my spinning head swiftly put that to an end. Remaining silent, I glared back up into what I believed was his humanized amber-green Vampiric gaze.

"It's alright." Jakob assured me, "I'll go get some towels to get both you and this mess cleaned up.

"No-" I yelped. "Please don't. Just-just stay here."

"Ok-okay." The Vampiric whispered. Gently lifting my head, he slowly laid it down in his lap. Coaxing his fingers up and down my stomach, Jakob assured: "Okay, I will stay."

Chapter 24
Jakob

Once the moon had disappeared and the sun took its shift in the sky, I decided it was time to get up. My dark denim jeans were soaked through with dry blood. Slowly picking up 0497's canine head, I tenderly placed it down on the blood-liquored floor so I could fetch some towels and embark on the rigorous task of cleaning up. Observing the soundly sleeping canine I noticed along her back where that weird cross-shaped scar was hidden under her thick coat, the canine had somehow spawned spikes out of her back. Before I could further investigate the mutation, my eyes followed the bone-colored spikes return to a dark blood-red material before reforming inside her spine. Certain whatever it was had something to do with the passing Lunar Phase, I pushed the horrifying image to the back of the deep abyss in my endless thoughts. Heading into the restroom, I grabbed a couple of towels that weren't white and returned to the adjoining bedroom. Laying one of the towels down on a clean spot of the floor, I put the rest of the folded cloths on the sofa and strode over to where 0497 lie sleeping. Gently slithering my hands under her large canine form, I proceeded with slowly lifting her up off the floor. Attempting my best to not harm the Unnatural, I listened to the poor beast howl out a loud painful shriek.

"Sorry." I hastily apologized, carrying her over to the freshly lain towel I positioned her blood-covered head on the towel. Looking at the thick leather collar wrapped around her neck, I saw that the Number Identification tag had some dried blood all over it. Still aimlessly wondering what made that item so important to her that she could not part with it, I wondered aloud, "What memory is it that has made you so attached? It couldn't honestly be for all the others that have yet to be rescued." Grabbing the other two towels, I went back to the large semi-dry blood puddle that the wood floors were eagerly absorbing. Throwing one of the fabrics down over it, I began to tirelessly scrub away. Not even five minutes into cleaning away the dried blood, someone knocked on the door, a hard, double knock. Recognizing the knock as Mhykal's I responded, "Come in-"

"Whoa, Jakob I didn't think you would've slept-" was the first astonishing remark that flew out of my friends' mouth as he swung open the door. Striding inside, Mhykal was quick to interrogate. "What the hell happened?"

"Last night's Blood Moon that's what." I huffed still scrubbing with both hands tightly clenching the towel. "She didn't answer any of my knocks, so I walked in to find her lying in a puddle of blood. She didn't recognize it was me until moments later. Then when I wanted to get it cleaned up, she-" I paused as I draped the second towel over the spot to take a quick break. "She asked me to stay, so I did."

"So that's why your pants are soaked in blood?" Mhykal interjected, standing hunched over the canine, his hand softly stroking the Beauceron's fur. "For her to seek out your aid like that, it must have really had her panicked."

"I don't know but, even I could tell she was in a surplus of pain."

"Looks like she still is."

"Alright I am going to go change, can you get Yalu, and possibly see about some light painkillers from Viktor. 497 may need them even though she may very likely refuse treatment." I alleged, venturing towards the opened door.

129

"Yeah." My dark-haired friend sighed, standing back up to follow. "You know we're supposed to leave at noon, right?"

"Yeah, I know that's why the faster we can get her cleaned up and cared for, the faster we can go complete that damn job." I snarled. "However as of right now, those furry Lycans can kiss my ass-"

Using my species' enhanced speed, I hurriedly ran upstairs to my room so I could switch into some clean clothes. Changing one of pair of jeans out for another, I then exchanged my bloody fit-shirt for a dark-grey t-shirt, before lastly throwing both dirty items into the hamper and rushing back downstairs. Returning to 0497's room as fast as possible.

By the time I returned, Viktor and Yalu were already inside the Hellhound's assigned bedroom. "How is she?" I impatiently demanded Viktor, who was slowly inserting an I.V. into her transformed canine leg.

"She has lost potentially a little less than half a liter of blood, making her anemic. I gave her a painkiller to help ease some of her pain. A low dosage for now. If she needs more, we can administer more." Viktor patiently remarked using only a few of his fancy scientific vocabulary terms so he would not lose us in the translation.

Glancing over at Yalu, who had flipped 0497 over to wash away the dry blood from the Hellhound's face, I overlooked that all around the canine's sleek coat the blood had dried. Caking itself deep into her fur. It made me feel terrible that I had not gone to get help sooner. Hell, Yalu was right across the hall. Looking away from 497 for a second, I could see the Vixen's dark glare locked in my direction, something I knew was coming. Feeling sick, I sat there on the small sofa at the end of her bed, surveying everyone who had assembled around the sleeping Hellhound.

"We got half an hour to get over to the checkpoint," Mhykal spoke up through the deafening quiet.

"She should be okay for now." Viktor sighed. "Jakob, come pick her up and put her on the bed. I can tie the I.V. bag to the post for now. It should have an eight-hour hold, that should be long enough for us to finish our Raid tonight."

"Okay," I said. Gently picking up 0497, I carried her over to the bed, lightly placing her large frame down on the left side of the full-sized mattress. Analyzing Viktor tie the bag on the post, I then watched everyone surround the piece of furniture. "I finally thought of a name for her." I quietly murmured.

"You did huh?" Yalu snipped, her frustration clearly directed at me. "What did you come up with?"

I paused. "It came to me last night when I saw her eyes change color. Cinder. Cinder Salam."

"Cinder?" Mhykal exclaimed confused.

"Like the dancing flame," Viktor responded.

"When her eyes turn red, it felt like I was watching the fiery-red pirouetting embers of a roaring fire," I said trying to describe the same thing I saw last night when she begged for me to stay. "So, I thought of Cinder. It's unique just like her."

"It is a great name, but why the last name?" Yalu still growled, her arms folded under her breasts, expressing her level of disgust over the surname. "You do know Salem was the street name-"

"Yes, I DO know that." I swiftly bit back. "I chose that not because she is not willing to forget what happened to her, but because she, just like all the other Unnaturals are being hunted down like the Witches were during the Salem Witch trials. And besides, it isn't spelled the same."

"Oh, then how are you going to spell it, Jakob?" the Vixen fiercely debated.

"S-A-L-A-M, Salam." I spelled.

"You do know that Salam is spelled with an 'E' not an 'A'." Viktor interrupted.

"Yes, I do know that but, no matter how you look at it, it is still the same, just has a different spelling." I continued. "Her name is her own, that is why I mixed up the vowel, giving her the other spelling of it." Putting my hand on her head. Caressing it along her skull and spoke directly to the unconscious creature, "Your name is Cinder Salam. And it is all yours, nobody can take that away from you."

"Okay, great name, but we do have somewhere else to be as of right now." Mhykal urged breaking the hesitating uncertainty of the room.

"Alright, let's go." I sighed, upsettingly removing my hand from the dog's soft black hair.

"Well look who decided to show up?" Braedon angrily mocked the four of us. "So, what in the world made you guys five minutes late?!"

"An incident with 0497," Yalu answered, her amber-colored fox eyes angrily slanted at our Syndicate's Leader.

"So, why didn't you bring her?"

"It wasn't that kind of an incident." I sighed, also locking my gaze with the leader as if he were asking a moronic question.

"Alright, whatever the reason you can explain it to me later. We got business to do." Braedon persisted, taking a long sigh. "Calem, these are among my best men. Jakob, Mhykal, Yalu, and Viktor."

"Ah, yes. It is a pleasure to finally place faces to your names." The Lycan leader remarked, making an Old English bow. Speaking in the same Old English accent, he continued, "Jakob and Mhykal, you two were the ones who led that raid in New York last year, right?"

"Yeah, but it was Yalu that did most of the work," I replied. "If it weren't for her Illusionary, then we wouldn't have been able to get those 'Off-grids' out."

"I see. So, it was the Vixen then." The older middle-aged Timber Lycan said, locking the traditional golden wolf gaze on the Vixen.

"Alright, back to the subject at hand here." Braedon began, breaking apart the intense staredown and pointing to a recovered map of the targeted Raid. "Six of Calem's men are locked in these off-sanctioned rooms. We both believe that they are on heavy-duty Pheromone blockers."

"That's funny, Cinder thought the same thing," Mhykal whispered into my ear.

"Mhykal, care to elaborate?"

"No, I'm good." He instantly answered, standing at attention.

"Good. Viktor believes that if you add these Uppers to them, then we should be able to get them back to their true forms and hopefully be of some aide to get out the rest of the Unnaturals that are being held inside." Braedon planned.

"Okay, so how do you plan for us to get down there?" I asked. "I'm sure that these doors and entryways are more than likely protected with heavily armed guards. So-"

"Well, that's where some of our men become useful," Calem spoke up, his hand running through his small greyed beard. "If we can get the help of your Trickster: Yalu was it, then we can most likely sneak my men in and wash them out by intimidation."

"That will require a lot of energy. I can at most hide two or three away for that amount of distance." I overheard Yalu's voice argue. Her sassy attitude pouncing back to the surface.

"I will only be sending in six of my best men, if you can keep four of them of them hidden then, we should still have them by surprise."

133

"Scratch that-" I interrupted. "The Doctors and Scientists are two times more likely prepared for a rescue attempt to be made by one of the Lycans. If Yalu can remain in her Fox Sprite form, and hide both Mhykal and me, it will be much easier than trying to hide four brute seven and eight-foot-tall Werewolves. They will not expect to see Vampirics helping out Lycans, even if it is just the two of us."

"That could work-" Braedon acknowledged.

"Besides from the little scuffles your men and the two of us have had, you should know quite well we can handle ourselves against some pesky humans with no problems at all." Mhykal sneered, smiling his same old goofy smirk for a hasty sec. "And as Jakob said, it would be much easier on Yalu's energy level. If she extends all her energy, then her Illusions won't work properly. That should be common sense, even for a Lycan." The Vampiric said his tone becoming serious as the subject focused on his partner.

"Mhykal!" Braedon snapped.

"Sorry." He moaned with a heavy roll of the eyes.

"It's no problem. Years of scuffles and some brute violence between our two groups is sure to arise some of this teasing." Calem sighed, shaking his head. "I just want my men back."

"We will get them back, Calem." Braedon returned, placing his hand on the Lycan's tall shoulder.

Chapter 25
Jakob/Cinder

Thanks to Yalu's Illusions, she managed to camouflage the two of us into the backdrop of the changing background while she remained in her two-tailed black fox form sitting on one of the Werewolves' broad shoulders. Easily sneaking into the basement level from one of the fire-escapes, the group swiftly reached the doors that separated the targeted 'Cells' from the exterior hospital rooms. It was here that we were finally stopped by a horde of, of course heavily armed guards. Six were armed with semi-automatics, and another seven seemed armed with both firearms and what I believed were Pheromone Blockers, that again just as Cinder had suspected these employees were using against the Wolf-shifters.

"We thought you guys were going to come here-" one of the guards barked to the collection of Lycans who're still in their human form.

"Of course, we aren't going to leave behind any of our Pack Members." Lucious, the Lycan whom Yalu was sitting on, smiled as he triggered his transformation.

"Mhykal, take the three semis off to your left," I whispered.

"Okay."

And while the Lycan's continued to alter their forms one after the other, we quickly darted in. "Yalu remove the Trick once we are

135

within three feet of the semis," I ordered the Vixen. "We need to hit them before they fire off their fifth bullet."

"Right." Mhykal happily barked. Racing towards the men using our heightened mobility to our advantage, we quickly closed the three-foot perimeter. Seeing Yalu yellow eyes glow a luminescent green in the reflection of the glass doors, she faded the Illusion just as the fifth bullet was fired out of the automatic. Timing our punches perfectly, we each punched the initial enemy square in the face. Crushing their skulls on impact. Before the other guards could grasp the unfolding situation, we took out the next set of men. Only two guards left, and they hesitated at the sight of two 'human-looking' men with abnormal strength teamed up with six pissed-off Lycans who were now charging in to make their own kill. Not hesitating another second, we took out those last two with our matching right hooks. Each fist contacting the mirror side of their jaws. Once we finished eliminating the guards holding the heaviest firepower having only a total of ten bullets fired off in less than fifteen seconds, I looked over at Mhykal. Making a small acknowledgment before we removed ourselves and headed back behind the frontline full of combat-ready Lycans.

Resetting the time, this time the werewolves charged in and took out six of the seven remaining guys. Some ripped the men's throats out, while others slashed at chests breaking through their bullet-proof vests with ease. Following every detail of the plan, we left one man alive and conscious, allowing Yalu to mentally freeze him as he became surrounded by empowered Lycans just in case she lost all her energy. Ascending into the circle, I pulled my hand up towards his face and closed my eyes to focus on my strengthened Psychic powers. "You will tell me where the rooms of our friends' comrades are being held in," I demanded. My voice the only one singing out in the eerie quietness.

"All six are being held side-by-side." The hypnotized man obediently returned.

"Now, I want to know how many men are in the next corridor."

"There are twelve men in total behind the other door."

"Good," Clenching my hand into a fist, I altered my powers into erasing his mind. Knocking him unconscious. Once I reopened my eyes, I almost collapsed onto the bloody white tiled floor.

"Jakob," Mhykal called appreciatively catching me.

"I'm okay. I just used up a little more energy erasing his mind." I spoke, slowly retaining my balance. "Let's go and get your comrades out," I remarked, directing my conversation at the Lycans while standing up. Wandering over to the door and punching in the code that I had stolen from the guard's memory, I easily opened the door leading to the next corridor. Once the passage had exposed itself, I proceeded to tell each Lycan the code I had memorized for each cell. "Make it quick, so we can get out of here and save some of the other Unnaturals on the upper levels."

When I had come to, I saw at the end of my muzzle was the dark blue comforter and firm white pillows, telling me I had been moved from the floor to the bed. Forcing my exhausted body up, I saw through the window that the sun was again setting along the forest's horizon. Looking around I noticed a small tube had been jabbed into my front limb, following the I.V. up, I found the drip which was full of some sort of numbing painkillers.

"Might as well chain me to the bed." I kidded, seeing the I.V. bag tied to one of the Victorian bed's posts. Sitting up on the bed, I wondered what had happened to me before I had lost consciousness.

"Your name is Cinder Salam." A voice suddenly said out of nowhere.

"Okay-" I audibly stammered, trying to recognize the voice. Thankfully, it was not the Shadow's. Thinking hard about where I knew the voice from, I again heard it call out from the darkness:

137

"Your name is Cinder Salam. And it is all yours."

"Whose voice was that?" I wondered. "Oh, it's yours." Upon realizing whose it was I exhaled a heavy sigh. "You did it. You came up with a name, one that I could call my own." Feeling my lips curl back into a large grin, I made one more look out at the setting sun. Judging that by the time of the day, everyone was long gone, out on that Raid with the Lycans. Leaving me and a handful of other Unnaturals here ALONE at the Manor. "Great." I groaned aloud. Reversing the forms, I stood up and began to untie the simple knot keeping the I.V. bag attached to the post. Carrying the bag with me into the bathroom. Taking off my clothes, I irritatingly forced the bag through the small women's shirt sleeve before entering the glass-walled shower. Hooking the bag up to the hook where the scrunchies were hung, I finally started the water so I could finish cleaning off the forgotten blood. Under the hot water, I began to pull out the long I.V. needle. As soon as it was out, I expected to see at least some blood get washed down my arm, but the deep prick healed over instantly. Nothing unusual to me. Allowing the needle to fall, I finished washing myself off.

Once I was done, I took the I.V. bag and strolled out of the bathroom with only a towel wrapped around my petite frame. Sitting the bag on the Armoire, I began to search through the drawers for any clean clothes I had left. Grabbing some undergarments first, I hastily put them on before continuing my search for an outfit. Ending up with a beige tank top, and some dull grey but comfy form-fitted women's sweatpants, I finished getting dressed. As I closed the drawers on the Armoire, I stopped when I remembered what the Shadow had previously warned me.

"An ally who seeks harm was sneaking into the Manor when no one was around, and it was my 'assignment' to live up to my name." I repeated standing before the Armoire with my hands firmly placed on top, "Right, Shadow?"

Shutting my eyes, I focused on the many physical scents that had remained behind. Canceling out the ones I had already associated with being connected to the Syndicate, I began to sort out what scents did not belong. What scents were not routinely shifting through these halls? Focusing on several scents, I stopped when I heard a shout echo through the halls.

Shooting my eyes open, I attentively focused on using my hearing to try and locate if it was the sound of terror, or like Yalu and Mhykal, a sound of pure ecstasy. Putting that thought out of my head, I waited for it to rise again, even though my gut was forewarning me otherwise.

Listening to my gut, I ran towards the door of my bedroom. Swinging it open, I ran out into the adjoining hallway only to now hear a male scream out in pain. His voice echoing through the corridor so clearly. I could feel my heartbeat race, but for some reason, it wasn't fear that was telling me what to do. It felt more like anxious excitement, I felt excited and eager to investigate the screams. Running down the hallway, I began to feel the uncertainty cling to my physique all the same. It was the same sensation I had questioned when I had blindly asked the Shadow about eradicating the target whoever it may be. I felt like I was being controlled or hurled towards the sounds of chaos.

Upon locating the sound of the second scream, I found myself before the collection of glass doors attaching the back of the house to the small patio and Garden below. Scanning through the glass and into the darkness, I saw a pair of shadows moving around in the distance. "Were they my targets?" I questioned. "No. He told me it was someone. A single target not two." Straining my sight to focus on the silhouettes in the darkness, I saw that the height belonging to one of the unusual scents was double the height of the other. The smaller shadow was trying to pull back, to fight. Seeing that was all I needed to know something was off. Placing my hand on the arched handle I opened the glass French Door and quietly snuck passed the threshold. My bare feet embraced the exchange from the polished wood to paved cobblestone bricks as I steadily prowled closer to the shadows.

Chapter 26
Cinder/Jakob

Hearing the woman savagely yelp into the darkness for anyone to help her made my heart drop deep down into my stomach. I knew I had to get over what fear I had, what trauma I had already previously endured, and help that woman whom by her scent alone I could tell was a species of Unnatural like Yalu, a Vixen. Feeling my heart skip a beat as my mind positioned my close friend there instead of this other woman, I felt something switch in my head. The fear had vanished. Running as fast as I could to reach this person, I relied on the male's scent to pursue them, learning along the way that it had a mutual mix of Human and canine scents. I didn't know what to make of it and personally, I could care less. All I knew was that I needed to chase after them.

Dropping onto all fours, I morphed into my alternative form. Drastically increasing my speed by another twenty miles per hour, I encouraged myself to hurry. With each complete gait I made, I began to feel something take over my body. The hairs of my colic arching along my back and between my shoulders. My cropped and pierced ears retaining their stand-tall position. I could feel my tail uncurl while its tip instinctively curled up in attention. The feeling of doubt disappeared the more my body enticed the 'thrill of the hunt.' Ten feet away now, I began to calculate the best angle to accomplish eradicating this threat, impatiently licking my curled lips.

Watching the man who looked approximately seven feet tall, toss around this short screaming woman whose characteristics made her a few years younger than I, I forced myself to hurry. Making a right, I angled my tail for a sharp turn and swiftly ducked behind one of the tall brushes I had previously scouted. Secluding my presence, I compelled myself to wait until the perfect opening arose. Each movement they made further triggered my natural hunting instinct. "Taking him from the back seemed cowardly, yet the best angle." I hastily speculated to myself. "Yet if he goes to swing her around, or if he stands over her, he will also leave his chest and neck wide open."

"Someone please help me!" The young girl screamed out, her voice blaring into my sensitive hearing. "Please-"

It was just then that the man did exactly what I feared he was going to do. Swinging her around thanks to his unusual height and supernaturally gifted strength, except instead of landing on top of her, he threw her. Tossing her like some broken toy. The young woman's body hitting one of the thick trees with such a brutal force, I knew that it more than likely had broken her spine, or at least fractured some bones along that same vicinity. Keeping concealed under the brush, I counted each footstep he took closing the distance between the injured woman who moaned in pain and this brute man. Just as this violent being took the tenth step, I finally darted out from under the brush. Ordering myself, "Give him a three-second count to figure out who had interrupted his fun, then strike. He shouldn't have enough time to react to me running towards him." I wasn't sure where my reckless planning was coming from, and honestly, I didn't care.

Dashing right in front of this dangerous man, I stood over the crying woman and began to count down my three-second interval.

"Three." I thought as I bared my fangs, lowering my head.

"Who the hell are you?!" He growled, baring his fangs at me as I continued to count down.

141

"One-" I smirked, charging forward.

Just as I had expected to happen; the moment I ran forward to close in the fifteen-foot gap between us, the man took a step backward. Running at about twenty miles per hour, I rapidly closed in most of the gap in less than two seconds. Arching my body to jump up at the man once the gap was less than three feet away. Using more of the poised strength in my back legs, I kicked off the ground and swung upward so my jaws could reach the middle of his neck. Springing open my jaws, I curled my long fangs and finally latched them onto his neck. The taste of his blood quickly spraying out of his wound and into my mouth. Spreading all over my tongue. I felt disgusted but thrilled at the same time. The man now attempted to scream out in pain, but I did not allow that. As much as it was pleasing to hear him scream out the same fear he had put this young woman through, I felt I had to keep this as covert as possible. With my ninety-eight-pound canine weight and fast speed, I was surprisingly only able to make this tall man stagger back. Surprisingly still conscious, he now tried to reach for my neck, but again I was not going to let that happen so easily. Using more of my collected energy, I began to shake my body the same way any other dog did when they had dying prey in their mouth. A couple of shakes later, he finally collapsed onto the hard fall-frozen ground. Landing on top of him, I kept a tight hold on this thick neck, feeling the arteries and veins in his neck spasm. Draining all the blood they had out of his lacerations. Shaking my body again, I growled at him, trying to tell him how I felt about his actions. The longer I held his struggling body there allowing him to bleed out, I eventually saw the Shadow phase-out of the moonlit night's shadows.

"Reap, little Reaper." I heard him praise. I wanted to let go, to disobey what this being was encouraging me to do, however it felt too thrilling to pull away now. My mind was fixated on the idea of making this man pay for this. "You want him to pay, don't you, my Little Reaper?"

Letting go of the dying man's neck, I grinned back at the Shadow, staring directly into his warm fiery red eyes seeing my own red eyes reflecting back. Exposing my blood-covered fangs, I licked my lips and snapped my jaws together in agreement.

"Then activate your most known Ability." The Shadow voiced to me, his cold tone matching the endless depths of the black massed cloak he was wearing. Recapping what abilities, I knew of, I first thought of the only powers I had discovered, the Blood Scythes. Yet, I heard him continue, "The one that Hellhounds are known for, my Reaper. The power over Fire."

Feeling my heart skip in more excitement, I gazed back down at this dual-scented man. My lips curling so far back that it now showed all the teeth I had in my mouth. Chomping down again at the man's neck, I began to feel my body begin to exert all its collected heat. Focusing directly at burning this man, I placed one of my paws on his right arm and the other ahead of where my mouth was on the ground. Beginning to excitedly feel his body heat increase.

"That's right, Reaper." The Shadow laughed, his fingers rubbing down the top of my spine. Feeling the Shadow's cold presence standing beside me, I felt his faded voice whisper into my cropped ear with a terrifyingly cold laugh, "Reap."

Just as I felt the Shadow disappear, I also felt the heat of the fire dance around his near lifeless corpse. Letting go when out of the corner of my eyes I saw the burning embers of a fire sizzle on his face. Stepping away from his body, I shook my body to free all the collected blood on my face and neck. With my excitement fading, I finally turned my attention towards the hurt Vixen, who was miraculously still conscious. Trotting up to her, I pushed my muzzle against her face to ensure she was indeed awake. Hearing her mumble out in pain as her green eyes stared up at me standing over her, I took a long sigh of relief.

"I think your back may be broken," I said to her quietly. Receiving the look 'of you think', I wandered behind her and lied

143

down beside the woman. "There is no one else at the Manor that can help you and I don't have the strength to carry you. I'm sorry." I breathed watching the man who I had killed still burn, the smell of his flesh overwhelming my nostrils.

"No, don't be-" she coughed. "You saved me." Shivering from the cold, from all the physical pain she was in, I began to sense her core body temperature start to plummet.

"I will stay here with you until someone of use comes home." I said while focusing on using this 'Fire' Species Ability to help keep her warm without harming her. Using my own body as the spawn of the heat, I maintained a temperature warm enough to keep her body heat centered and her blood flow properly circulating, while also low enough to not make her combust up like the man that had attacked her. "I will stay right here." I again assured her.

"Thank-thank you." She cried.

Rounding up the last of Unnaturals on the upper levels, I rapidly recounted the heads of everyone. Once I was sure we had all the leftovers that the second entry group had missed, Mhykal, Yalu, and I began to lead all the freed patients outside of the Institution.

As we neared the same basement level entry, I stopped, our group sensing that something was off. "There is a group of men collected maybe three hundred yards out."

"Well, that's the only way out of this place." Lucious snarled back in his dark burly-haired human form. "Guess we will have to breakthrough. Smells like there are maybe twenty or so people. Should be no problem."

"Easy for you to say. Can you smell how many firearms they have on them as well." Mhykal sneered with another irritating smirk, "Or how about what kind of drugs they have?"

"You idiot!" Yalu snapped, attacking Mhykal's left ear with her small yet sharp fox fangs. Of course, still in her small black fox form.

"Ow-" Mhykal now cried, trying to get his Vixen girlfriend to back off.

"Stop fooling around-" I now demanded of my comrades. "Lucious is right, we need to break through, even with my own powers I can't tell all that they are carrying on them until we are within hundred yards. By then, they would be able to see most of our group."

"So, I was still right." Mhykal continued to snark as Yalu soared over to my shoulders.

"What's your plan Vampire?" Lucious growled at me, while the rest of the group were obviously bothered about the possibility of what was going to happen to them.

"You said roughly twenty people?" I asked him.

"Yeah. Leaning towards twenty-five."

"Okay, we got a total of twelve Lycans, two Vampirics, and one Vixen. A total of fifteen Unnaturals that know how to fight." I sighed, looking up at the curved tunnel ceiling of the basement corridor. "With both Mhykal and I's speed, we are capable to take out a few people in three seconds but to eliminate that many people we need to create a wave or a blockade. And your strongest people don't have their full strength back even with the Uppers administered. So, your guys' healing will not be able to work fast enough to withstand any form of heavy gunfire from their Semis, if they even have any. It's a rather difficult bind we are in now because they know that we have gotten out the six strongest of the Lycans, as well as all the overlooked Unnaturals."

"Jakob, I have collected enough energy now that I can recreate an Illusion. I may not be able to suppress the mass amount of people we have, but I can falsify the human's sense. Flip them." Yalu said as she sat on my right shoulder. "But you guys will have to rush them."

145

"Okay, that will work, just don't overexert yourself," I ordered the petite Vixen.

"Roger." She barked, hopping off my shoulder and taking off ahead of us to start the illusion. "Give me about a thirty-second head start."

"Roger that." I grinned back. Turning to direct my next set of orders to the collected party of about forty Unnaturals, including the twelve Lycans and the three of us from the Vampiric Syndicate. "Alright, the Illusion Yalu will most likely use is changing your directional senses. Left is right, and up is down. While they are disorientated, Mhykal and I will be able to eliminate most of them, the rest of you just need to sneak past them."

"Let us help-" I heard one of Calem's tops call as he hung over his friend's shoulder.

"No. Our job was to help you and your men get out. Besides, we have the most experience when working with Yalu's Trickery Ability." I returned.

"I may act like an ass; however, Jakob and I are telling you guys to place your trust in us. This is our job." Mhykal assured, standing next to me.

"Alright." Lucious sighed. Looking at his fellow Werewolves for their acknowledgment he eventually continued, "We will put our trust in you guys. Just this once." Cockily smiling back at us while he continued to hold up his superior ranked ally.

Returning the smile, I continued, "Good. Alright, Yalu's thirty seconds are up. So, you guys ready?" No words were uttered back, just a pure nod of agreement. Leading the pack of Unnaturals we disembarked on our last hurdle in this complex rescue assignment.

Chapter 27
Jakob

Quickly reaching within two hundred yards, Mhykal and I activated our heightened speed. Rushing straight for the group of disoriented guards. Skimming through all their carry-on items, I noticed sixty percent were carrying some sort of firepower. The guns all ranged from small handguns to semis, to full auto. Increasing our speed to at least eighty percent, we ran for each side's center. Punching one man in the face, then elbowing another in the throat right at their trachea. Not paying much attention to Mhykal, I focused on taking out my designated section of guards I had picked. With Yalu's Illusion and our speed, in less than fifteen seconds we had taken out the group of twenty-four men. Lucious's sense of smell wasn't too far off regarding the number. As both of us collected our breath, we watched the Unnaturals scream in joy at regaining their freedom upon reaching the last door blocking us from the outside world.

Watching Mhykal tread over to Yalu who was back in her braided black-haired, Caucasian skinned human form also trying to collect her breath, I smiled. Hearing them do their own celebratory kiss, I allowed them to do their thing and began my journey towards the exit.

Stepping back into the brisk fall night-time air, I looked up at the sky that was full of dark clouds. The stars obscured behind the puffy wall of who knows what kind of chemicals and molecules. "Wonder if Cinder is up, now?" I thought to myself, calling 0497 by her new name. Hoping that she had heard me call her that and had approved it.

While we rounded up at the assigned checkpoint, I could not help but overhear Braedon arguing with Calem about the usual stuff:

"We get the Unnaturals this time that was our deal." He barked to the English Werewolf.

"Most of them are just like us." Calem snapped back, his voice low.

"Fine, you can have the Lycan-like Unnaturals and we get the rest." Braedon heaved with a heavy sigh, eventually giving in to the Lycan Syndicate Leader after a long brutal stare down. "A lot of the Unnaturals your members had forgotten about were other species besides Lycans, and Canine Shapeshifters, right Jakob?"

"Oh, please don't get me involved." I exhaled, sitting in the back of the Escalade vehicle we had driven up herein, "I frankly don't care how many Unnaturals we get, they're finally free out of that Hellhole, and as long as they can get the protection of either Sanction, I don't care how many we get."

"It's about the Number we can set free," Mhykal spoke up, sitting next to me. His temper back to the normal don't care, happy self. "I mean, I'm all for outranking you drooling mongrels and those fire-breathing lizards, but it isn't about that here. We are rebels serving to free and protect the Unnaturals who're being forced to live in confinement as test subjects, and lab rats."

"How about we just let the Unnaturals decide? No matter, who they pick we will continue to give them sanction." Lucious said, stepping into the conversation. "Give them a few minutes to decide then we can round them up and go our separate ways."

"Seems like your men are more willing to co-operate than you are?" I heard Braedon arrogantly snicker. "So Calem what about it?"

"I guess." He growled back to our Syndicate Leader. Leaving our checkpoint table, he went and told the gathered Unnaturals their choices, giving them a few minutes to elaborate whose sanctuary they were accepting.

"This is the first time I had seen entire families here, though," I spoke aloud to the remaining members of the Lycan Syndicate.

"Not for us." Lucious continued. "This is our fourth time seeing families collected. Seems like the Government is starting to agree with those guys and trying to eliminate our Kind altogether."

"Sensitive but much more torturous." Mhykal agreed. "It doesn't surprise me though, to them, they see a benefit in making our kind extinct, yet in my opinion, this still does not come anywhere near the New York Raid."

"Yeah, everyone heard about that Raid. Taking 'Off-grids'. That must have been a long time coming."

"Five years of it." I chuckled. "Five long years in between other Raids of course, but yeah. That institute had some of the oldest numbers we have ever seen."

"Like 0497?" Lucious returned.

"You heard about her?"

"She was a Hellhound. The first one to be seen in several decades, and from what we gathered, she is supposedly a newer breed. As I said, everyone has heard about it, well at least the rallied Syndicates."

"Wow, what else do you know about her?" Mhykal interrogated, preparing for a fight.

"Not much else. You guys seem to be keeping a tight leash on that one. But then again, it's probably your best bet to."

"What do you mean?" I interrupted, also feeling the urge to start kicking this guy's ass.

"From the research, we had gathered about 0497, she has several Species Abilities, and they can end up being bad for you guys if it ever gets out." The Werewolf continued, smirking his fang tooth smile.

"If I were you, I would stop trying to talk about her like she is some weapon or almighty being," Yalu warned, standing behind the werewolf with a profoundly serious glare on her face. The same glare that made both Mhykal and I cringe. Lucious turned around to stare down at the petite Vixen. "Cinder is not any of that. And if you ever try to talk about her like that, or even try to talk to her, I will rip that thick ass numb brain-skull off your large extended neck. Got it!" She continued to growl; the ground started to mold around her the angrier she got.

"Lucious back off." Calem's top man, Joseph, spoke up, coming up behind Yalu. "We're leaving, we got what we needed. Fighting those Vampirics will only get you seriously hurt."

"Fine." The Lycan submitted, walking away from us with his Superior.

Hearing Yalu still snarl I tried to hold in a small amount of laughter. Growing serious when I heard Mhykal voice, "He almost made it seem like we took her from them."

"Yeah, he did. But there is no proof-" I returned, stopping our small conversation as Braedon came back with Viktor and told us to head back to the Manor. "You're going to set up the Unnaturals back at the Manor?"

"Yeah. I'll be helping get them settled in." He moaned. "Glad that is all over with and we can get back to our own business."

"Really? Any longer and I would have had to beat that mongrel's head in." Mhykal barked his laid back-temper soaking in Yalu's anger.

"Well it's over with now, so go home. Get some rest." Braedon ordered before sulking away.

Properly getting into the vehicle, the four of us took off ahead of our Syndicate Leader on our journey back home. With Mhykal, and Yalu in the front while Viktor and I sat in the back we rushed home, all of us hoping that Cinder was okay, and in the same place, we left her.

Chapter 28
Jakob

The Manor appeared to be alright upon first glance. The lights were still on in many of the rooms, including the common areas. Bringing the vehicle around the long half circle driveway, closer to the Manor, Mhykal carefully parked beside the garage before removing the key from the ignition.

Exiting the black Escalade SUV, a faint gust of wind blew through us, the stench of something burning traveled along the breeze. It had either recently been extinguished or just had burned itself out a little while ago. With the wind changing directions, it was difficult to track the exact location, so we assumed it was nothing more than impudent adolescents.

Walking through the foyer, everyone took a massive sigh of relief. Going our separate ways, Viktor went back up to the Ward, while Yalu went back to her room to take a hot shower, Mhykal and I decided to go into the formal living room for some downtime. Reaching the living area, we hesitated when we saw a familiar sign, blood on the wood floor. Nearing the source of the drag marks, we saw one of our guys knocked unconscious. A nasty gash sat along the top of his forehead. Certain that the Unnatural had just knocked his noggin on the dark mahogany coffee table, we decided to wake him.

"Charlie, hey Charlie," Mhykal called, smacking his face. "Wake up, Charlie."

Eventually, the freshly turned Vampiric stirred. His initial reaction to scream out, "Valeryie!"

"Valeryie?" Both Mhykal and I questioned.

"As in Yalu's little sister?" I now inquired.

"Yalu?" Mhykal called panicked, knowing that her room was just down the corridor. Running off towards her room, I heard him barge inside.

Whirling my attention back to Charlie I asked, "What happened to Valeryie?"

"Logan showed up." He cried. "He took her by the hair and started to drag her around, calling out for someone else by the name of Cynthia Swallow. Calling out for that person to meet up with him, or else-"

"Cynthia?" I probed. "We don't have any Cynthia's here." I continued. "Why was Logan here looking for someone named Cynthia?" I knew that Logan was a hybrid Lycan, and part of Calem's Betas until a falling out occurred, but none of that told us why he would have shown up here, nor why he thought we had someone named Cynthia here.

"He took Valeryie outside, saying that she would suffice until Cynthia arrived." I listened to Charlie recount, "That was after he..."

"He hurt you?" I interjected, "Alright. Can you walk up?"

"Yeah, I think so. Are you going to go look for Valeryie?" the young teenager Vampiric now insisted as he weakly got back up to his feet.

"Yeah, I am," I assured Charlie. "Just get up to the Ward. Get that gash looked at." Waiting for the Vampiric to enter inside the Medical Ward, I hoped deeply that Logan didn't kill Valeryie; however, also knowing some of this Lycan's past, her demise was a possibility. Glancing over at the Grandfather clock beside the archway leading towards the back doors, I saw the time was shortly after four-thirty in the morning. The Raid took us six hours, and another hour to round up all the Unnaturals, then another hour and a half to get back here by Vehicle. Hastily running towards the nearest backdoor to the Garden, following the direction that Charlie had pointed off into, I saw that the glass door had been left ajar. There was no blood on the door, reassuring me that so far that Logan had yet to hurt Valeryie. Walking out, I hunted down a trail of Auras left behind. Tracking the Hybrid's and Vixen's Auras up towards the woods, I continued to hope for the best outcome while expecting the worst.

When I located the source of the trails, I saw some charred skeletal remains, and almost fifteen, maybe twenty feet away was Valeryie lying on her side mumbling in pain and behind her was a familiar figure lying her head on the Vixen's shoulder watching me. The brilliant cold blue eyes inspecting to see if I was foe or friend.

"Cinder-" I softly called, trying to familiarize her with her recently given name as I cautiously approached.

"She needs to see Viktor-" I heard the Beauceron Hellhound tenderly state, thankfully recognizing me. "I think she has a broken back and a few broken ribs."

"Okay," I said, rushing up Valeryie's side. The young juvenile was still dressed in her loungewear and despite how thin the fabric was, she was still quite warm.

"I did my best to keep her warm until you guys got back."

Grasping Valeryie very gently up in my arms, trying to not make her wounds any more serious, I heard the poor girl still screamed out in horrendous agony. Her frail arms clinging tightly to me. The grip was so strong that it started to make my arm go numb.

"Valeryie, it's okay," I assured, trying to still her petrified nerves and save my arm. Once she released that tingling grip, I started to descent back to the Manor, walking as fast as I could manage.

Pausing for a moment and call back to the person who had saved Yalu's little sister, I questioned, "Cinder you aren't hurt, you can walk, right?"

It took a few seconds for the Unnatural to recognize that I was talking to her. "Yeah I can walk, I'm not hurt, just tired." She eventually responded.

"Okay, come on then," I said turning back around to journey back towards the house. The metal tag attached to that collar wrapped around her neck ringing in the silence of the night, notifying me that the Hellhound was bounding up to my side. Sticking close to my side, the hairs still raised on her colic as we swiftly re-entered the Victorian Manor. "I will ask you what happened after we get Valeryie medically cleared."

Cinder whined in agreement. Not saying a single word, making me wonder if she dreaded the consequences of answering a few questions. Pushing away from the thoughts of comforting her, I focused on getting Yalu's little sister up to the Ward. Reaching the living room, I saw Mhykal and Yalu were already waiting for me. Yalu was completely distraught about her sister's condition, pushing herself into Mhykal's arms for comfort.

"She's okay. If it weren't Cinder, I don't think she would still be alive. I need to get her up to see Viktor first, so can he commence her treatment." I said, strolling past them and ascending the stairs. Still hearing Cinder follow me up each step in her canine form.

Once inside I called Viktor, telling him what previously called 0497 believed happened to Valeryie's back. As the medically gifted Vampire examined the younger Vixen, he clearly stated his prognosis, "There is a small spinal fracture, and-" he paused, lightly passing his hands over one side of her chest to the other, "And what I believe are three bruised ribs on each side. She got really lucky if it's Logan we're talking about here."

"Yeah." I sighed with much relief.

"Logan?" Cinder questioned, changing into her disliked human form.

Glancing back at the Hellhound, I noticed there was some dried blood on her tank top, but I knew just by how she was acting that she wasn't hurt, or even afraid for that manner. This was the other side of her that Mhykal and I saw yesterday morning, that cold dark side.

"But she will be okay?" Cinder probed, the worrying nature returning to the surface.

"Valeryie will be okay. Just watch Viktor." I answered. Both of us watched the Vampire begin to move his hands around her body, his eyes focusing on the spinal fracture that was in the middle of her back. A light golden-green glow illuminating from the palm of his hand. "Viktor has the psychic ability to undo anything that has been done to any form of physical matter. In a way, he can heal physical energies, but mental energies are a whole different matter."

"I understand." Cinder spoke, her eyes avidly watching his hands move around the girl's ribs now.

"Viktor doesn't rely on the ability due to the amount of energy it takes to accomplish such a feat. Plus, the longer the wound exists the longer it takes, although there is a maximum amount of time allowed before the ability won't work at all. Hence why the scar on your back couldn't be healed." I continued to educate, staring down at Cinder I saw her holding her arm, while simultaneously biting her lower lip. I could tell she was blaming herself for what had happened. "Come on we should let Yalu and Mhykal in for now," I said, ushering her out of the room to let in Valeryie's older sister and her sister's boyfriend.

Passing the threshold of the Ward, I followed Cinder back to her bedroom where she began to scroll through the dresser for another clean shirt. Changing her shirt right in front of me, without any fear, or committed acknowledgment of privacy, I wondered just who exactly was I seeing. The two sides were becoming confusing to separate.

"Thank you for the name. It's nice. Something to call my own." Cinder said out of the blue, obviously attempting to distract herself from the chaos.

"Well it makes sense considering everything you had been through, but I know you are trying to change the subject. What are you so afraid to tell me?" I interrogated, quickly catching on to her diminutive reasoning.

Plopping herself on the couch, she took a long sigh. Curling herself into an upright fetal position with her head resting on her knees. "I should've moved in faster. I waited too long to stop it." I heard her mumble.

"It was still your involvement that saved her," I assured, starting to put together that the charred skeleton was something she had done.

"Was it really?" I heard her mutter, leaving the fetal position. Confused I waited for Cinder to continue, "I killed that man. I can still taste his blood in my mouth-"

"Cinder?" I questioned seeing the expression of pure disgust and fear in those blue eyes of hers. Thinking to myself, I wondered, "Was she afraid of herself? Or was she afraid of what had happened in the past?"

"I recall waiting for the right opening and charging in right for his neck. I can remember vigorously shaking the life out of that man, and-" Cinder again paused. The terror in her voice sounding both pure and true. "I can still taste his blood in my mouth. I can still smell his burning body- I can still smell it. I can still smell it-"

"Cinder, it's alright." I comforted, putting my hand on her back, gently rubbing it up and down along her spine.

157

Swiftly she stood up and faced me, tears streaming down her face, "No it's not alright Jakob! I killed a man! I killed another Unnatural!"

"Cinder, it happens. We have all been there. All of us have killed a person in our-"

"No, you don't get it!" She snapped at me, "I was told to do it! I was told to kill that man! I was-" Cinder went dead silent, her body behavior changed. Her hands relaxed, her fingers twiddled, her blue eyes began to look even colder than before. When she finally spoke up, her voice quietly mumbled, "I enjoyed it. I enjoyed every moment of it-"

"That was an annotation that I was not expecting." I surprisingly wondered to myself concerned for the mental wellbeing of my friend. "Who told her to do it?" I proceeded to think. Swallowing I now probed, "Who told you to do it? Who told you that you had to kill Logan?"

Looking very coldly into my eyes, I heard Cinder reply with a whisper, "He did. The Shadow told me to-" Stopping mid-sentence consecutively, the black-haired haired woman paused for a moment. I could see her stalling on the words, her mouth slightly gaped open. Waiting for her to speak again, I finally heard Cinder voice this time in a softer tone, "I wasn't supposed to tell you that."

Chapter 29
Cinder

"Why were you not supposed to tell me that?" Jakob asked me with an overly concerned look on his face, rushing up off from the sofa.

"Go ahead, tell him, little Reaper." The Shadow laughed at me. "Tell the Vampire about your job." He now said, leaning over my shoulder. "Tell him Reaper."

"Cinder?" Jakob asked again, his tone worried over my elongated silence.

Looking back at him, I took a deep breath before deciding to answer. "No one has ever believed me when I have said it before."

"Just try me." I heard the Vampiric smirk, "Remember I am several centuries old, I have heard, and I have seen many odd things in that time."

Taking another breath, I proceeded to hear the Shadow still pressuring me to tell Jakob, "The Shadow. The Skeleton Shadow. He is the one that gave me this power. He was the one that turned me into an Unnatural. Into his-" Feeling the skeleton finger press against my lips I hushed up. My mouth clenched.

"That is between you and me, Little Reaper." The cold voice hissed.

"Okay-" I thought to the Shadow. I had learned at a young age to not speak with, nor about in the public eye. Regaining control of my mouth again, I resumed, "He told me, that morning of the Blood Moon, that this guy was coming to the Manor when all you were not going to be here. He told me that I needed to eradicate that man."

Jakob seemed in a state of confusion as if he were trying to digest what I had told him, trying to agree with what I had said. Feeling unnerved that this man was also beginning to doubt my sanity, I fought back my fears to investigate.

"You don't believe me, do you?" I pondered aloud.

"No, I do, Cinder. I believe you one hundred percent." Jakob finally said before sitting back down, "It's just a lot to digest, but it is still far from what I've heard before."

Feeling completely overwhelmed, I felt the tears begin to again stroll down my face. The words I desired to hear my whole life, that feeling someone had finally understood me, that someone had finally not seen me as crazy, I could no longer contain my heartaches.

"So, you were told to kill a man that was going to sneak into the Manor? A man that would be able to sneak past the Aura-Tracers?" He now pursued.

"Yeah-. At first, I didn't know what to think of what I had been told, then before I could question the intentions or even disagree, I ended up senselessly agreeing to the 'Assignment."

"That explains why you were acting off that day." He spoke, finally catching on.

"Yeah' I sighed looking away from his yellow glare.

"Well, it was that assignment that saved Valeryie." The European Vampiric continued to speak, "Yes, you may have killed Logan. Yes, that may have been your 'Assignment' given to you by that Shadow, but remember this; it was 'you' who saved Yalu's little sister." His tall physique once again standing within my personal space.

160

"Thank you," I whispered, stepping closer towards the man that seemed to finally understand what was occurring in my entire life. "Thank you, for believing me, Jakob." I cried, wrapping my hands around his lean muscular frame. Lying my head against his chest. Feeling his hands shawl around my body, bringing me close. Holding me dear. Feeling the presence of the Shadow vanish away, I felt more tears uncontrollably flow from my tear ducts. The false sense of security and serenity leaving with the entity.

"It's all over. Everything is over now. We are all okay, thanks to you, Cinder." Jakob said, resting his head on mine. His presence helping me feel secure the longer I stayed in his strong yet lean arms.

After a couple of minutes, I backed myself up to wipe away my tears. Soothing my still fringed nerves, I ran my hands through my hair, grouping it up, I took the fabric rubber band off my wrist and began to wrap my hair up into a ponytail. Taking another exhale, I whispered, "We should go check on Yalu's sister to see if she is alright."

"Yeah, our support could be used." Jakob agreed. "You sure you're alright?"

Looking up at him, I calmly smirked, "I'm exhausted, but I am okay."

"You should get some rest then-"

"No, I need to check on Yalu and Valeryie-" I returned, strolling towards the door. Hearing the tall Vampiric follow, I released another exhale while waiting on him out in the hallway.

Wandering out of the hallway towards the stairs and the Medical Ward, I tried to push aside that thrilling feeling I had felt prior to the incident. However, the more I tried to push it out the more I was remembering my face making that dreadful smile. My exposed fangs feeling the cold breeze brush against them. The blood and saliva drooling down my teeth. The pure 'fun' I was having observing the light leave that man's eyes while he bled out. Stopping

161

at the Medical Ward's door, I hesitated and tried to put away all those memories. Push them deep down. Shaking my head, I backed away from the door. My butt running straight into the banister.

"Cinder," Jakob called. Calling me again by the new name. "Are you okay? You really should get some rest."

"No. It will go away in a minute." I cried back, tightly holding onto his upper arms. "It will go away," I assured, simultaneously pleading to my head for the memories to stop. I did not want to see them again, to feel them again.

"Cinder, maybe Viktor can give you something to relax you-" I heard Jakob plead with me. He was worried about me. I could plainly see the nervous facial expression seizing his face.

"No. NO DRUGS!" I argued. "I don't want to go back on those horrible things!" Crashing onto the floor with my back leaning against the banister rods, I completely shut down while simultaneously bringing myself into the fetal position.

"Ok. Okay. Cinder-" Jakob sighed to me. "Okay. No drugs." Sitting down in front of me, he continued, "Look at me. Cinder. Look at me."

Dragging my head up, I stared into the Vampiric's amber yellow eyes, I watched them fade and return to a human blue-green. "Your eyes-" I said completely captivated by their unique human color. With pure silence filling the common area, I started to feel my conscious slip. The memories went hush, hiding deep down in the dark abyss of my mind. No longer feeling terrified by the meaning behind what the 'thrill' I had endured when I killed that man. Feeling my conscious slip more, I continued to focus on Jakob's eyes. Everything around started to distort the longer I stared into those humanizing colors.

"It's okay, Cinder." I heard Jakob's voice call. The deep relaxing masculine European tone in his voice soothing my heavily beating heart. "Everything will be okay." The Vampire continued to tell me his voice deeply penetrating my mind.

"Jakob-what, what a-are you-" Was all I could gather before my head fell forward, and I fell into a world full of abundant darkness.

Chapter 30
Jakob/Cinder

"She's unconscious." I thankfully breathed. "Sorry, Cinder, but I had to." Rotating her body around, so I could pick her up I again asked for forgiveness. Once I had positioned her comatose body in my arms, I swung around and began to transport her back to her room. Stopping when I saw the Medical Ward's door open.

"Hey, Jakob. Is she okay?" Mhykal inquired, seeing the limp Hellhound. "Are you okay?" My Vampiric friend questioned.

"I had to use my powers to knock her out, unfortunately." I returned, trying to retain the steadiness in my legs.

"Here let me take her." Mhykal offered, taking Cinder's sleeping human form. "You go sit down."

"Yeah." I moaned. "Thank you." Following him back down the stairs, I parked myself on the sofa while my long-time friend carried our newly acquainted friend back to her bedroom. Sitting on the regal Victorian sofa, I rested my head in my hands using my thumbs to hold the bottom of my chin with my elbows positioned on my knees. Bent over the edge of the sofa, I looked down at the dark royal red French Rug and began to aimlessly wonder what I had seen. With my ability, I had entered Cinder's memory to discover which one was arousing her panic. As soon as I found it, I reviewed the memory, mentally placing myself there to see its events. After the memory had played through, I ended up relinquishing it to the darkest part of her memories. I typically did this activity on Humans, so I wasn't sure how long the memory would stay dormant in an Unnatural's mind, especially one who is haunted by a controlling Shadow, but I had to do something to stop her panic.

"So, what did you do?" Mhykal requested exiting out of the hallway and arriving to sit on the couch across from me.

"First, how is Valeryie?" I asked, looking back at him. Staring into his own mimicked fearful gaze.

"Valeryie is doing a lot better thanks to Viktor's Time Abilities." The Vampiric sighed, rubbing the back of his head. "Yalu is still worried, but she is extremely grateful that Cinder was there to stop it from becoming worse."

"Yeah, she may have indeed saved Valeryie from Logan's brutal strength, however at the cost of some of her sanity." I exhaled.

"So, you buried the memory?" Mhykal sustained. "Does that even work the same way?"

"I don't know. But I had to do something to stop her from freaking out, especially when she did not want any form of medications and relaxants." I deeply exhaled. "Besides, I didn't entomb the entire memory, just the portion that was giving her the most distress."

"Distress? What the hell was it, that had her so spooked?"

"Her enjoyment-" I answered back coldly.

"Enjoyment? Cinder enjoyed killing Logan?" Mhykal sparked, completely in shock. The same countenance I had when she told me.

Flashing myself to the memory, I recalled seeing her amused grin in the bleak shadows of the night. But it wasn't the darkness, there was something she had fixated on that was ten times darker than even the gloomiest part of that cloudy night. Knowing it only to be a shadow with the same red eyes I had named Cinder for, I watched the Hellhound smile even harder. Her lips curled so far back it showed her brilliant white long fangs. The blood just drooling down her canines onto her lower lip and crashing into the ground underneath her muzzle. Her colic was sticking straight up, her tail was curled up to the point it nearly sat along her back. Cinder's cropped ears pitched as far up as they could go. I could hear the Shadow talk to her, and laugh into the darkness, his voice extremely cold. It was clear why she feared ever talking about this creature. As she smiled, she quickly went back to holding down Logan. The poor hybrid could barely maintain the strength to fight against the Hellhound any longer. From there, I observed his body combust. His skin charring and bursting under the orange glow of the bright flames. Once Cinder had seen the flames, she backed off the corpse leaving it to burn itself out. It was there that I stopped the reel, making that small part of her memory dormant.

"Jakob?" I heard Mhykal call, his voice snapping me back to reality. "Was it that dark that even you were stalled by it?"

"Yeah. It was very dark. Definitely like she was under some sort of stimulus." I returned, looking directly into his eyes. "She seemed fine all the way up until she clutched the doorknob. I guess the motion it must've triggered the memory."

"Ouch. Cinder has already been through enough, now to fear her own capabilities-"

"The powers are not the problem. She seems to have a healthier control over them the longer she is well, her. But it's that shadow being she talks about who she fears more than anything." I returned. "I understand why. He comes across as a strict, dark, and controlling being. Something that definitely has the potential of making Cinder crazy."

"Oh wow. So, you did see him?" Mhykal queried, taken aback by my dark gaze.

"Yeah."

"The enjoyment, you were talking about do you think it was by whatever this Shadow-"

"Possible. It is hard to explain." I interrupted, feeling interrogated by my friend.

"I can see that." He sighed back.

"We will just have to keep an eye out for any more new behaviors that I am sure will arise as time goes on." I continued, slowly standing up, "I am going to go check on Valeryie and Yalu."

When I woke up from passing out along the banister, I began to sit up only to see Jakob, sitting on the sofa with his back turned towards me. Getting out of my bed, I strolled around the far side of the mattress to see why the Vampire had been sitting on my couch for who knows how long.

"Oh, you're up?" He staggered, completely flabbergasted about my apparent revival. "How do you feel?"

"Got a slight headache, but other than that I'm alright. How are Valeryie and Yalu?" I returned, walking over to the Armoire for a change in clothes. I too questioned, "Why do you seem so surprised that I am up?"

"Well because you have been in a coma for three straight days." Jakob returned to me. "After a full twenty-four hours, we all switched out with one another to make sure you were still just sleeping. And it just so happens that you wake up during my shift." The Vampiric explained. "Yalu is doing much better now since Valeryie has gone back to her old self. Of course, she's still a little traumatized, but she isn't hurt, so I guess that's a plus."

"That's good." I breathed with much relief whilst I closed the dresser drawer. "Alright, I am going to step into a shower."

"Okay. I'll wait here." He said with that same old, sweet smile. "After that, Yalu should have breakfast ready."

167

"Okay," I replied as I headed into the restroom to prepare myself a shower. Once the sliding door was shut, I rested against it, beginning to sense my stomach churn. My gut instinct was telling me there was something off, something was missing from my recollection. Taking a deep breath, I felt the sensation wash away, permitting me to again attempt to take a nice hot shower.

Chapter 31
Jakob

In the coming weeks, that day seemed more and more like a distant memory. Everyone knew of it, but we all had also forgotten about it. Well, most of it. I still could not get Cinder's memory out of my head. That look she had in her eyes, that smile she had snarled on her face, I almost wanted to say it traumatized me. However, as the third or fourth week came by, I had also outgrown most of that fear: it was becoming more and more of a miracle how she was able to endure that amount of insanity.

Walking down to the Garden, I saw that Yalu and Cinder were back to sparring, another thing that had arisen from that incident. Cinder's childishly scared aura was developing into a more laid-back, mature, and dare I say a dark aura. While learning how to defend herself, some of Cinder's unusual abilities had also surfaced. They were unique and because of the level of curiosity the other Syndicates had in our Hellhound we decided to keep the tricks on the down-low, only allowing the five of us to know: The five of us being Mhykal, Yalu, Viktor, Braedon, and me.

One of those abilities consisted of the control over her blood, giving her advanced healing and some sort of weapon use. The healing properties were much faster than our Vampiric healing and were even faster than Viktor's Time Control. Viktor also told us that according to his research, a single cell was about twice as light as a

169

Human's Blood Cell, however, it was also twice as dense as a single Draconic's Blood Cell. This made Cinder completely capable of using a single Blood Cell as a weapon. A clot could very likely create a worse outcome.

While the second ability was her Specie Ability, one legend says all Hellhounds have control over; Fire. Which according to Yalu and Mhykal, who had both spared with her previously, Cinder had gained almost absolute control over. A single punch could potentially fire a twenty-yard range fireball, however, for now, it consisted of way too much energy to attempt. She had also learned to create combustion. With little to no focus now required to activate it, Cinder can combust whatever she desired into an orange-yellow element of destruction. The longer she focused, the greater the range was, and the greater the temperature was. How Cinder managed to use that same 'Fire' technique to keep Valeryie from freezing to death in the fall temperatures of that scary night, none of us could even begin to describe.

Sitting beside Mhykal, we both continued to observe this sparring match between the two women. However, I noted that there was something unfamiliar about today's training lesson. "She isn't in stance."

"No." Mhykal smiled. "Yalu is trying to teach her how to correctly fight without creating a stance to give away what she was going to do." He explained. "Or something like that."

"I guess it makes sense. Especially if she gets cornered or something like that." I returned, noticing how easily Cinder had picked up the tactic.

"Oh, watch this." Mhykal grinned. "Cinder has gotten really good with this sequence."

Deeply investigating her movements, I noticed the Hellhound start to run towards the Vixen. Remarkably spawning these arched scythes out of her wrists. The blades extending along her forearm, leaving less than an inch gap between her skin and the back end of the scythe's blade. Scanning my eyes over to Yalu, I watched her unsheathe her own small dagger and begin to defend against the countless strikes made by her sparring partner. If neither one of us had increased ocular senses, we would have inconceivably missed several blows. The two women were moving at remarkably fast speed.

"How long can she keep them out for?" I asked after thirty long seconds, with neither side showing any physical signs of exhaustion.

"Oh, I don't know she can keep both up for the entire sparring time without showing any form of exhaustion," Mykal answered back. "Hard to believe in these last four weeks, how much she's improved."

"Yeah, she has gotten quite good at fighting in her human form, but she is still using her abilities." I sighed, noticing that the Hellhound was almost entirely relying on her Specie's powers.

"Oh, you think so?" Mhykal questioned me. "In the beginning, Yalu told her only to use her fists and kicks, which she quickly mastered in a week flat. So, they decided to move on to her Species Ability, and she quickly mastered that. And so finally, we are on her Breed Ability. Which is working as you see." Taking a quick pause so he could lean forward along small bench stationed in the shade under the second-story deck, my friend resumed. "I know Cinder has a high I.Q. and is like super smart here, but for her to be so gifted in combat as well; it's like she has always been that good."

"Who knows." I returned, seeing precisely what he meant. It was surprising that Cinder was able to pick up any combat skills at all, let alone master them so effortlessly. "It could have been from something else too-" I thought privately to myself. "There is no way someone locked up inside a hospital room, stuck in such a deep level of paralysis for as long as she had been, would have been able to pick these skills up so quickly. Maybe if we had started the same day she had finally regained her mobility, but Cinder would still be nowhere near what she is now. It could potentially be instinctual, just like how she had picked up her Canine transformation."

171

"We could really use someone like her in the Raids, though I don't think she feels comfortable enough." I heard another voice speak over the noises of combat.

"Sneaking up on people, now are we, Braedon?" I joked, flashing him a sneering smile.

"No, I saw those two from up in the study, and thought I could use some fresh air, so I wandered down here to watch them spar in person." The leader of our Syndicate leered. "0497, or Cinder was it, has become quite the fighter, and it appears her Species Abilities are also accurately coming along."

"Then again, she does have a great teacher." I happily returned, complementing Yalu from a distance.

"Yeah, Yalu is a great instructor when it comes to her combat and weapon skills. Besides those two are pretty close." Mhykal grinned, standing up from the bench, still observing the two women spar, their speed not once faltering even after fifteen straight minutes.

"Those two sure do seem close." Braedon smiled. "Surprised Yalu hasn't dumped you for her yet." The Leader now teased Mhykal, reminding us all about his odd relationship with the bisexual Vixen.

"I don't think Cinder is interested in getting into an intimate relationship with Yalu anyways," I assured Mhykal. Watching now as the women took off their tank tops to fight in their sports bras, their bodies most likely starting to wane and sweat heavily from the extended workout.

"Glad to see they are having fun nonetheless," Braedon said after a few quiet moments. "Jakob, Mhykal, could I speak to you two in private?" He then altered the subject.

"What about?" I dragged.

"It will be easier if you see it for yourself." He continued, stepping through the glass door to reenter the Manor. "Meet me in the Study."

172

"Okay." Both Mhykal and I said in unison, confused.

Walking up into the Study, both of us saw Braedon standing over his desk, impatiently waiting on our arrival. "About time." Our Leader growled.

"Well, what was it you wanted to show us?" I snarled back. "Something about Cinder, or something else."

"Why don't you see for yourself?"

Stepping in front of the computer screen, I began to read through everything the computer's monitor screen reflected. "What are these?" I asked, looking back at the Vampire.

"Those are emails sent to me, by both Calem and Saylene, as well as a few other major International Syndicates."

"I can see that, why are they all emailing you?" I continued to question, believing, or rather expecting it to be something relating to Cinder. "Are they wanting her?"

"No, well not really." I heard Braedon answer, "However, I have received threats talking about what could happen if we don't comply with their demands."

"So, what. Whatever it is, we can handle it." Mhykal confidently jabbed.

"I appreciate your confidence in the matter, but that is not the real reason why I asked you guys to come in here," Braedon said as he sat down in the same regal Victorian fabricated chair. "We have another Raid to assign and this time it's a Government Based Institute."

"I thought all of the Institutes were Government-"

"I should have explained it better, this is Federal Government Based Institute. This is one of the Newer Institutes, where the highest-risked Unnaturals are being held at. Some species have not been seen since the early seventeenth century. Others are so old that they can be linked back to the B.C. era. And some of them are

173

similar cases like Cinder's. Old species, but a whole newly undiscovered Breed."

"So, what are you saying?" Mhykal questioned, his eyes dancing around trying their best to understand the value of this information.

"I believe that he is implying this would most likely be a base those bastards would have sent Cinder to if we had not rescued her." I restated using simplified vocabulary.

"I believe that would have been a strong possibility." Braedon heavily sighed. "However, to change the subject, I am attempting to collaborate this Raid with the other two Leaders."

"What?!" I growled. Stepping away from the computer to lean against the desk's front edge. "We may get along with the Draconics, but they can be finicky on certain days, and the Lycans well you know where both Mhykal and I stand."

"Look, I can understand where you are coming from, but did you forget our dream, Jakob? Our goal?"

"No." I stammered, looking away. "I just don't see why we have to collaborate with either one of them."

"For the sake of those Unnaturals that also deserve their rights at freedom," Braedon said, stopping when the double doors to the large study abruptly swung open.

"I think you guys should do it." Cinder said as she and Yalu walked inside. Viktor following in behind closed the thick doors. "Braedon is right." She proceeded, wiping her forehead free of sweat.

"Why thank you for the vote of confidence." Braedon smiled.

"Jakob, you told me once before that the goal of all the Rebelling Syndicates was to create an equal ground for Unnaturals. To stop the abuse that Humans cause to us. To free others from that same abuse." Cinder reminded as she casually strolled closer towards us. "I know I have no right to put my opinion on the table, but the three Main Species have gotten along this long for a reason.

That reason is the safety of their kin. I know you guys all have your differences and I believe that not only you two are debating valuable points. However, saving those people should be your top priority over whether or not you can get along with Draconics and Lycans."

"Cinder's right," Yalu spoke up, too inviting her own opinion to the debate, although the Vixen did have a vote on the table. "Whether it's a Government Based Institute or not, Humans are still torturing are fellow kin. I never understood why you guys all fought anyways, nor do I care. Unnaturals are Unnaturals and those that currently do not have a voice need a helping hand! SO, stop being a selfish couple of asses and just fucking collaborate already! Braedon wouldn't have asked your opinions if he didn't already know what was at stake." The Vixen now growled, her cold glare sending chills down both of our spines.

"Fine." I moaned. "Do whatever you were going to do."

"I will send out the invitation later today and whether or not we get both to collaborate, our first meeting will be in two weeks." Braedon too vouched with a heavy breath. "Now you are all dismissed. Except for you Cinder, I would like a word with you."

"Okay." The Hellhound spoke, still trying to catch her breath.

Chapter 32
Cinder

Once everyone had left, Braedon asked me to sit down so we could have a civil conversation. Still drenched in sweat and trying to keep a clear head, I listened to what he had to tell.

"How much of that conversation did you hear?" I heard him enquire.

"Not a lot just something about Emails, then well the argument between you and Jakob." I returned curiously.

"Okay." Braedon thankfully sighed back. His demeanor making me feel somewhat on edge now. The hairs on the back of my neck standing up. "I know you still don't feel comfortable going on these Raids, but I would like to seek your insight on some things."

"Triggered." I thought to myself. "You want me to again open up my past?" My stomach churned, my heart skipped, but somehow, I was able to keep the worried thoughts down. Eventually speaking up, I asked, "Okay, what do you want to know?"

"If we do this, this Raid, I want to know what's the possibility of us losing some of our men?" The Vampiric Syndicate Leader questioned me, staring directly into my eyes.

"By use of heavy drugs, it's most likely a high possibility," I swiftly responded. "By use of violence, it is also another high possibility. I am sure that most of the bullets will be laced with varying weaknesses for different species as protocol requires for any escapees. However-" I paused knowing that something was still off. "That isn't the reason why you wanted to talk to me, is it?"

"You catch on quick." Braedon lightly smiled, the surprise in his voice not getting past my advanced hearing. "No, it isn't why I wanted to talk to you originally. But your input on that question does seem like useful insight. The original reason I wanted to talk to you in private was about your recent outings in the middle of the night."

Feeling the presence of that cold-hearted Shadow, I anxiously returned, "What about them? There's nothing stated here about a curfew anyways." With the skeleton's hands pressing down into my bare shoulders, I froze.

"Tell him that you wanted to head out. Do not tell him what you were actually doing. Let his doubts consume him, Little Reaper." The Shadow ordered me, his cold voice ringing deep down into my left eardrum.

"While that may be true that there are no curfews posted, you have left the Manor's property on your own several times in the last three weeks." The Leader said obviously telling me that he had gone through some of the hidden surveillance cameras I had found in between my 'hunts.' "Here we prefer that someone who is still as high-risk as you, to be escorted around."

"So, what are you going to do? Make me a prisoner here as well?!" I snapped at him, angrily standing up from the chair.

"Cinder, calm down," Braedon ordered.

"No! I am tired of being kept here!" I continued to snap. Exhaling a quick breath. "I just wanted to explore some of the same human stuff I used to be able to do as a kid. And I know that the nightlife is about forty percent safer than me going out in pure daylight with being an Unnatural and all."

"Yes, it is safer for Unnaturals at night, and while I do understand where you are coming from, I would prefer for someone to go out with you when you decide you want to head out, especially with you being such a highly-sought after Unnatural by not only the Government but also the other big-name Syndicates. It's for your safety." Braedon tried to calmly lecture.

"Sure, doesn't seem like it." I thought to myself, knowing if I kept challenging the Leader of the Syndicate, it could potentially lead to much worse consequences than having to a guard follow me around the city.

"This could make it difficult on your work, Reaper." The Shadow now snarled at me, his hands tightly clenching my shoulders.

"I know that." My thoughts growled back, agreeing with the skeletal Shadow about my assignments suddenly becoming more difficult. In the last three weeks, I had gone out to complete several 'assignments'. As much as I still didn't like 'Reaping' and as much as I had started to lose some of my sanity when I got lost in the 'thrill', I had learned to manage the crazy events. Even learning how to manage the lunatic memories of my insanity, thanks to that same entity who had sent me out on those missions. "In two weeks, they have their first meeting, I am sure I could do some work then." I privately disclosed, now knowing that this was how I had to unfairly repay that Shadow for keeping me sane all those years and keeping my friends still alive.

"Two weeks would calculate a lot of heavy work, Little Reaper." The Shadow continued to growl at me.

"I know that." I refuted. "But that is most likely the best time to slip out from under this guy's radar." I could sense my Aura changing, as well as my very own personality the longer I was under Braedon's intense interrogation, but I knew I had to keep calm here.

"Cinder?" Braedon called, noticing I was slightly distracted. "So, you agree to have someone chauffeur you around when you now venture off the property?"

"Yeah." I sighed. Keeping my rising frustration hidden down by the skin of teeth, I maturely dismissed myself. Storming out of the study, I cursed the Vampiric Leader for practically tying me down to this place. I could not just tactlessly blab to him what I was doing because if he truly knew the reason, the man would have never let me out of the Manor, to begin with. "Why did he have to make it so difficult-" I sighed, coming down the stairs connected to the foyer and walking back to my room, hoping I would be able to avoid Yalu and the others. Not in the mood for their many questions.

And sure, enough they tried to stop me from going directly to my room. "Cinder, hey, are you okay?" I heard Jakob probe.

"I'm fine." I sighed, not halting, not even flashing a blink of my eye in their direction. "I just want to get back to my room and take a nice hot shower."

"Okay," Yalu said, her usual cruel glare thankfully telling Jakob to relax. "Hey, Cinder, tomorrow do you want to go out shopping with me? I know you haven't left the Manor in the year you have been here, but I think it will be good for you." She continued, of course not knowing about my previous outings.

"Sure." I continued to painfully sigh the longer our conversation lasted. Receiving enough hesitation, I finally ducked away into my bedroom. Once the door closed behind me, I collapsed against its wood panels. My mind finally emotionally breaking as it returned to my semi-usual childish self. "Why is it so hard?" I complained.

"You will figure it out eventually, Reaper." The Shadow continued to speak, his hand rubbing his cold boney palm along my cheek, in the traditional way he comforted me. Pushing my head further into his palm. "I will let you rest for now. In two weeks, I will give you your assignments, my Reaper." His cold voice spoke before he vanished like normal. The skeletal presence of his lingering hand, the last thing to dissipate into the vanishing black mass.

"Yeah, yeah." I sighed out. Forcing myself up I grabbed myself a pair of clean clothes and tiredly walked into the bathroom. Still

179

thinking to myself, "Why was it so difficult? So unfair? So-" I stopped, collapsing down on the shower's tiled floor. Letting the warm water sliding down my bare skin. "Why am I always a prisoner?" My thoughts deeply pondered.

When the next morning came, I could feel the bright warm sun rising up above the tree line, casting its glorious rays through my north-facing window. As I got myself up out of the bed, I began to skim through the Armoire. Picking out what clothes I believed were 'tasteful' to go out for today's events that Yalu had planned, I began to undress. Stopping mid-way through taking off my bra and before removing my sweatpants to stare at my mirror's reflection, reminiscing that the long cross-shaped scar had started to burn late last night. The pain was bearable, but barely. As I examined the old scar, I saw how red and inflamed it had gotten. Thankfully, the skin had yet to blister, though it was still quite sore. Not wanting any drugs, I did my best to hunker through the pain, to push it out of my mind. Returning to dressing myself, I put on my old, worn at the knees, light blue skinny jeans, a white semi-see through, low V-neck, mid-sleeve shirt on over a beige camisole. After which, I put on my fur-lined collared, burnt leather jacket, and topped off the outfit with some three-inch wedged, light beige sneaker booties. Content with what I chose, I looked back at myself in the bathroom mirror. Pulling a brush through my hair, I tossed the recently trimmed back middle-length deep black hair over onto my left shoulder.

Confident with my tasteful choices, I ventured out of my bedroom and began to stroll towards the Garden for my usual morning stroll. A usual routine I had done to clean my head from my still haunting nightmares. Upon reaching the usual hangout area for the Unnaturals, I saw Yalu and Valeryie were sitting together twiddling away on their smartphones, something I did not see a purpose for. The two siblings really did look like one another, the only difference was when they were in their Fox Spirit forms, and that was Yalu was straight black while Valeryie had white little socks on her paws. Other than that it was only their age and scents that separated them.

"Oh hey, Cinder." Valeryie chirped, noticing me observing them from a distance. Our close friendship forming from that same night I had been assigned my first assignment. "Wow, don't you look pretty today."

"Thanks, Valeryie. It's because of your sister that I have this taste in clothing." I teased back to the nineteen-year-old Vixen who still seemed to dress like a fifteen-year-old. Wearing dark blue skinny jeans, black Converse tennis shoes, and what I believe was some band's tank top named something I could not make out from the way her white hoodie was zipped up. While her older sister was wearing the usual attire, a typical black jacket, black spaghetti-strapped tank top, and dark boot-cut jeans.

"Going for your usual stroll in the woods, are you?" Yalu asked, finally looking up from her own recently bought green-and black flowered outline smartphone case.

"Yeah." I sighed.

"Mind if I tag along?" Valeryie chirped. Her very friendly demeanor was completely different from her snarky sister's temperament.

"Sure." I agreed.

"Come on Yalu, you should come with us."

"Alright. Hold on." Yalu said her fingers moving around the phone's screen at supernatural speed.

181

Chapter 33
Cinder

Walking along the trails, the three of us decided to turn forms. Shifting into our Canine Forms, the two Vixens morphed into their black-furred Fox Spirit Forms while I mutated into my familiarized Beauceron Hellhound form. Traveling around the trails, we all ran around each other. Playing in the fallen leaf piles, and small shallow creeks that we flew by.

"Is it me, or has your canine form gotten larger?" Yalu questioned once we had begun to settle down. Taking a small break beside a fallen tree presiding over a short but sheer cliffside, the elder Vixen continued as she sat on top of the coniferous log, "I mean it's not too significant, but I don't think that the actual breed of dog you are supposed to represent is supposed to get that big."

"Oh?" I questioned confused. I had noticed that I had grown a few inches taller in the last couple of months, but I didn't think it was that noticeable. I hadn't noticed any weight gain since returning to a recommended healthy weight in my human form, however, I knew it could be tough noticing a direct change upon yourself.

"It isn't bad. It's just based on my 'Human' experience, you are about as tall as young Kangal or Great Dane, or some breed like that, not a Beauceron."

"I don't know dog breeds all that well." I returned, sitting on the leaf-covered floor.

"Well anyway, I thought I'd ask." Yalu sneered her sly smile, exposing her tiny fangs.

"Ready." Valeryie chirped up, finding her second wind. Her boisterous energy level returning. "You guys mind if we walk in our human form now."

"Still haven't mastered your energy control, have you?" Yalu now interrogated her younger sister. Reminding me that although Vixens could change into their unique species form of little Fox Spirits, they had to maintain a collected amount of energy to stay in that altered form, which also required a great amount of control.

"No." Valeryie barked at her sister, transforming back into her human form. "It's SO hard."

"I bet it is." I returned, trying to settle what felt like was a rising sibling feud. "I know my form doesn't involve much energy to transform, nor stay in, but I do have difficulties maintaining control over the rest of my abilities, as they desire an excessive amount of energy to utilize."

"How did you learn to control your powers, Cinder?" The younger Vixen enthusiastically probed.

Changing into my human form, I answered, "Through time and patience. It doesn't come as easy as everyone thinks it does. But I'm sure with enough devoted time and a great amount of determined patience, you will figure out your own way to control your powers."

Seeing Yalu flash me a small grin while she too morphed back into her human form, I listened to the elder sister graciously say, "Thank you, Cinder."

"Well, it is true. It takes time and patience, to learn anything. Nothing comes overnight." I half-heartedly lied while we proceeded to hike along the trail. I knew not everything came as quick to everyone as it did me, regardless it still encouraged my reasoning.

"True, well except maybe for those who're born Unnaturals." Yalu now teased me as we proceeded to walk along the trail.

Agreeing with her, I now inquired, "Vixens are created on the same day of their birth, right?"

"Yeah." The elder Vixen heavily exhaled. "Our parents gave birth to us and raised us till I was fifteen and my sister was seven. Then to save us from being caught by the Hunters, we were dropped off at this very Manor, from there I met Jakob and Viktor. I knew what was going on, but when I tried to explain it to my little sister it took a long time for her to understand the truth."

"I'm sorry," I said not knowing about this part of Yalu's past. However, I knew what her younger sister must have thought, what she felt. I had gone through something similar, except her parents didn't drop her off at a Hospital Institute.

"Well, we're better off here anyway." Yalu embraced as we reached the end of the trails, finally returning to the Garden. "My parents' home was raided and they were killed about three months giving us up." Feeling worse, I again apologized to the Vixen. "Don't apologize. It wasn't your fault for what happened. It's those damn humans."

"That's why you decided to join the Syndicate?" I asked.

"Yeah, in a nutshell, that's why I joined the Syndicate."

"So how did you meet your boyfriend, Mhykal?" I now eagerly gossiped.

"Oh. Um." Yalu blushed, her face turning a slight shade of red. "I was going out with his current girlfriend when we met, and well that relationship turned into a hell pit pretty fast. After that, we both broke it off with her and ended up dating each other off and on over the next few years. Currently, we have been together for two years without a breakup."

"Just summed it up." I laughed as we returned to the large Manor.

"I guess I did. It's a complicated history."

"I can see its complexity."

"Alright, just let me get my credit card and we can leave." Yalu ended, separating from me and Valeryie in the formal living room.

"So, I take it you and Yalu are going shopping?" The younger sister asked.

"Yeah, she wants to get some new Winter clothes or something like that," I answered back. "Plus, her Raid attire is becoming worn."

"Ah, so you guys are going downtown then. That's a fun place to be at night when all the Clubs and Lounges are open up." Valeryie cheered as she started to dance on the Victorian sofa.

"I'm sure they are." I cheered watching her best imitation of a night club dance, pretending I hadn't been inside one yet when, unfortunately, I had on one of my assignments.

"Ready, Cinder?" Yalu asked, coming back out of her room and descending into the common area.

"Yeah. Maybe a bit nervous about finally seeing the outside world, but I am ready." I responded to the older Vixen, trying to maintain that naïve front. Following Yalu, the two of us made our way towards the front door and the four-door garage in the front of the property.

"I got permission to take Mhykal's sports car." I surprisingly heard Yalu tease with an ecstatic grin written all over her face.

"Or more like took his keys when he wasn't looking." I chuckled back with a similar smirk.

"Yeah. I have him wrapped around my finger fairly good, don't I?" the Vixen chuckled with her pinkie finger raised.

"Sure, seems like it," I said, slipping into the passenger side of the red sports car.

185

After Yalu had started the car up, she roared its engine before putting the vehicle in reverse. Driving in reverse, she exited out of the opened garage door and pulled out along the half oval driveway before shifting gears. Closing the garage door, she sped off down the driveway, allowing us to make our way off the secluded property and towards the city I had only partially been able to explore.

"So, did you ever go shopping when you were still human?" Yalu asked after ten minutes of absolute silence. Her amber eyes locked with an exciting concentration on accurately driving.

"If I did, I don't remember all the details. The only thing I can remember was the etiquette my parents had taught me about being out in public." I responded, watching the background speed by. "I, however, do remember riding in the car a lot-"

"I'm sorry if this is triggering a bad memory." the Vixen apologized to me as we turned onto a suburban street.

"No." I smiled. "I mean the ride I remember up to that place well, I wasn't thrilled about what was going to happen, but I wasn't frightened either."

"That's good. We got about another five minutes till we are in City Limits. Once we are within the City, I am going to put in some contacts to hide my Unnatural eyes. If I were you don't change or use any of your abilities." The Vixen now warned me. "Remember we look Human, and to stay under the radar of being discovered we need to act and look like humans as much as possible."

Chapter 34
Cinder

"Alright, here we are," Yalu said after parking the red sports car in one of the scarcely remaining parking spots. Before we got out, she gripped my arm forcing me to react and look directly into her now cold human green eyes. "Remember what I had told you."

"Yeah, I got it," I replied. "Make the Humans believe I am Human. No transforming, no powers."

"Good." She breathed. "Alright let's go."

Stepping out of the car, I on instinct smelled the 'fresh' city air. Keeping stride with the Vixen, I shadowed her into the back entrance of the city's mall. Once inside, we stepped straight into the food court, the smell of varying meats, pasta, bread, spices driving my hunger levels. I was so hungry, that I could feel my canine sense of smell jolting into overdrive the longer I fixated on the kiosks. Maintaining pace with the fellow long-legged Human-formed Vixen, I asked her aloud, "There are a lot of people staring."

"Yeah, it happens all the time." Yalu sparked, flashing this popular girl's smile. "The guys think we're much hotter than their current girlfriends, and the girls either find us attractive or are just plain old jealous of us." The Vixen explained over the sound of many conversating people. The young twenty-five-year-old striding with so much swing as if she was the average female model. My body of course naturally syncing with hers.

"Okay, it's an odd feeling."

"Yeah. It is odd at first, but before you know it you will grow numb to it." Yalu continued, pushing away a few guys who tried to ask her for her number.

"I wonder how Mhykal acts when he sees that?" I teased.

"There's a reason I do not bring him out with me into the Public eye."

"I bet."

"Ah, here we go. The first store." Yalu cheered, dragging me inside the small store full of dark almost gothic clothing. "If there is anything you want just let me know okay?"

"Okay." I stammered, my eyes scanning all around the store. Seeing the dark trench coats, the leather jackets, the leather boots, dark jeans, and black shirts, I nearly drowned. Walking around the store, I weaved in and out of the display shelves and customers, leaving my hands in my jacket's pockets along the way.

After about ten minutes of walking around the store, I found Yalu checking out at the cash register, "Did you find anything?" She enthusiastically inquired. Observing the Cashier fold up the long-tailed trench coat, I nodded against her question. "Aw, that's a shame."

"Have a good day." The female cashier said, her voice sounding harsh and scripted.

"Thank you." Yalu snarled back, grabbing the plastic bag before eagerly strolling out of the store, me following right behind. "Look, if you see anything just ask."

"I heard you the first time." I returned. "So far, there's been nothing I have seen that-"

"That has called out to you?"

"Yeah."

"It's okay, it's only your first time back out in the viewing Public eye," Yalu said, while I shrugged. Nodding off that I felt nervous about being in front of so many humans, while simultaneously continuing to act as if it was my first time. "It's another thing you will get used to. Hey, at least you have a name now, calling you by that other one, would've just given you away." The Vixen teased, playfully elbowing me. Dodging her elbow, I nudged her back, keeping up the humanized teasing that two friends did. After a few minutes of walking around the enclosed mall, we came across the next store Yalu wanted to go in, this time for the upcoming Winter months. "This place has some expensive clothing attire, however, the clothes last and are pretty fashionable."

"Okay." I sighed, wandering around the store, following behind the Vixen who was effortlessly navigating through the display cases. Stopping when she came across the jacket section. Eyeing up the wall of three hanging sections I saw on the second row in the middle was a nice light beige soft faux leather women's jacket. The collar was longer in the front and decorated with a white and grey fur lining. The cuffed sleeves mirroring the fur pattern of the collar.

"Oh, you like that one?" Yalu grinned at me, observing my reactions.

"Yeah, I like it," I replied.

Watching Yalu flag down a sales associate, she then requested the young woman to get down the jacket. Handing the jacket in my size down to me, the associate then walked away. "It's six hundred dollars, but that's okay."

"Are you sure?" I worriedly queried.

"Yeah, all of us Unnaturals that are highly ranked in the Syndicate have a joint account that is stacked full of countless wealth collected over the centuries from the elder Vampirics." Yalu told, "So, six hundred dollars is chump change. Now let's see, I like this one." The Vixen smiled, grabbing the black jacket with a black-fur line

189

hood attached to it that was hanging a shelf down. "And in comparison, yours is much cheaper than this one."

"By how much?" I inquisitively pursued.

"Another five hundred dollars."

"So, it is eleven hundred dollars?!" I shockingly shouted, completely astonished by the price.

"Yup. With all that decided. There are a few long sleeves, and sweatpants I would like to look at." Yalu announced, walking over to the other side of the separated wall.

Not much caught my attention liked the jacket had, that was until we had gotten to the sweatpants section. Grasping a couple of ones that had caught my eye, I examined if I indeed liked what I had picked up. Thirty minutes later we finally exited out of the store, stepping past the threshold. I had left with three sweatpants, two black, one grey pair with black French cross pattern stamped onto the left's leg at the thigh height, and that Winter jacket. While my close Vixen friend came out with five pairs of sweatpants, four form-fitted long sleeves, and the black Winter jacket she had decided to buy. All in all, everything cost close to two thousand dollars.

"See as I said, it's expensive, but worth it," Yalu smirked while carrying her own bag of clothes. "Now there is one more store I want to stop by before we can leave."

"Okay." I returned while carrying the plastic bag from the store, called 'Winter Holiday,' which according to Yalu, was a Seasonal Store. Pondering what other stores she had in mind, I felt tempted to ask, yet before I could get out a word, we had already arrived at the store's entrance. "A pet store?"

The Vixen simply flashed a grin in my direction before speaking in code, "We all believe that your dog can use a new collar."

"Oh, I don't know." I stammered, backing up from the entrance. "I just can't." Trying to retain the code.

"Why not?" Yalu asked me.

"There's a lot of memory attached to it." I paused, slightly breaking character. "It was the last gift I ever received from my-my parents."

"Oh, I didn't know." The Vixen returned empathetically.

"I know they never bought it themselves as it was one of the collars the hospital provided, but it was covered with their scent. So, to me at nine years old it was-"

"It was still a gift from them, even if it was placed there by other people's actions."

"Well, we should still get one because that one is years old and looks like it's about to snap at any minute." Yalu tried to convince. "And if you still want a good memory of it, all of your friends can rub their scent on the new one."

"You would guys would do that?" I asked, trying to hold back from crying in public. Persuaded, I nodded my head in agreement following the Vixen into the 'Pet store' called 'Cozy Palace Pet Store.' However, as soon as we entered the venue, I felt the hairs on the back of my neck rise, alerting me to something not being right. Something was going to happen and soon.

Chapter 35
Cinder

Inside the store, I saw plenty of human customers playing with the young puppies and kittens. Children adopting little vanity pets like hamsters, or mice, or birds. It reminded me of way back when I tried to convince my parents into getting me a pet as a little girl. However, now I had deeper sympathy for the poor animals resting in cages waiting on someone good to adopt them and take care of them; it reminded me of the same feeling of waiting on someone to rescue me, to get me out of that Hospital.

"Hey Cinder," Yalu called, redirecting my full attention back to her.

"Sorry." I exhaled soundlessly.

"Just think positive." Yalu continued to express, holding my hands in her own, comforting me. "Alright, let's find where those large dog collars are."

"I believe they are on that back wall." I continued pointing at the section named Collars and Harnesses. Following the Vixen up to the wall, I wondered did I really need a collar. I mean the only reason I had one on in the first place was that the people at the Institute wanted to keep me under their control. Yet, I recollected why I kept it on, to begin with, I wanted to keep that memory until the last

Institute was shut down. Telling myself that the collar would stay, I would wear one for that same purpose.

"Hey here's one that's nice," Yalu said, grabbing up a navy-blue nylon loop choker collar. "The color will match her eyes." She persisted returning to the covert wordplay. "And it feels much softer than that leather." Nodding my head, I was unsure how to appropriately respond, when the only thing I had ever known, the only thing I had ever felt was the harsh leather wrapped around my neck. "So, would you like this one, Cinder?"

"Sure." I gave in. The color indeed went along with my blue eye color and the feel of the nylon felt different. Much better than the leather I was currently wearing.

"Okay, and how about a harness?"

"A harness? Why would I need both?" I asked, again sort of breaking character as people strolled around us.

"Well, just something different. Most harnesses are supposed to stop pulling; however, it has been known to also keep the chest muscles of canines, fit." Yalu answered.

"No. I do not think I will need a harness." I again returned. "Let's just get the collar and get out of here." Feeling the raised hairs on the back of my neck again, this time much stronger I began to worry.

"Yeah, I am getting the same feeling," Yalu whispered low enough so that only my supernatural hearing could catch the audio. "Alright, guess that will be it." She said putting the extra-large dog collar for canines between ninety pounds and up, on the counter. "Just pretend he isn't there, for right now." The Vixen continued to mutter while interacting with the Cashier.

"Have a nice day." The bright sales associated offered, handing the collar in a small plastic bag that Yalu stuffed inside her trench coat's plastic bag.

"Thank you." Yalu returned to the woman in the same preppy mannerism. Exiting out the store I overheard the Caucasian woman order, "Now keep track. If he figures out what we are, then he won't have a problem pointing us out to the entire mall."

"Okay," I whispered back. Using my hearing and my nose I began to concentrate on the man's footsteps and scent. He wasn't that hard to separate from the entire population of humans stuffed inside this mall, at least up until my senses caught onto four other similar-sounding and smelling men. Their footsteps the same distance apart. Their scents still reeking of blood and drugs.

"We got about five minutes until we are back in the food court. Keep a slow pace, remember act human."

Nodding my head, I began to feel my heart rate rise the longer I kept focusing on their unusual characteristics. "Two of them are closing in, about eight feet behind us," I whispered to Yalu while sustaining the same counterfeit grin, lightly elbowing her in that same playful manner and keeping my head straight.

"Okay. Just stay focused." Yalu expertly ordered as we entered the open-concept food court. Walking through the dining area, we continued to stroll towards the back entrance into the mall. Seeing that the sun was still up high in the sky made me more nervous about our slip away. If we were in the pitch blackness of the night, we could easily accomplish breaking away, but as always life was throwing the curveball.

Reaching the outdoor parking lot, we sustained a calm pace towards the red sports car. Pretending that we had not felt the presence of Hunters on our trails. As Yalu grabbed for Mhykal's car keys to unlock the vehicle, I noticed her hand was slightly shaking. I hadn't sensed any other signs of panic emanating from her up until now. And seeing it was enough to make my own anxiety ten times worse. Once the car was unlocked, we slowly slid inside, continuing to keep up the front. Closing the passenger side door, I stretched around and began to pack the bags in the backseat of the car, which had more room than the trunk did, unfortunately. Coming back around, I saw that Yalu was doing the same, dropping the plastic bags of clothes and accessories on top of my own. Whirling back

194

around, the Vixen then proceeded with putting the key into the car's ignition. Revving the car up, she put the vehicle's gear stick into reverse. Pressing her foot slightly on the gas, I prepared to feel my body shift as we moved backward, however my body shifted forward. The car jerked to an unruly stop.

"Shit!" Yalu growled, hastily moving the vehicle's gear stick back into park.

"What?" I questioned, trying to keep my racing heartbeat under control.

"I can't back up." She snarled.

Looking in the rearview mirror, I saw that someone was standing right in the direct path of the vehicle. Fixing my sights on the man, I absorbed all his visible characteristics, noting that under his bulked-up light Fall Jacket, there was a vest strapped across his chest. I did not need another glance to know who this guy was. "So just run him over." I returned, feeling my usual dark side overrun my currently panicked personality.

"I can't!" Yalu shouted. "I wouldn't mind to but if I had in the least harmed him, I would have a Felony on my record and for us Unnaturals that is automatically a death sentence." She inaudibly mumbled. "If we get caught, all I have to do is press a button on my phone and the GPS tracker will go off alerting Mhykal and all the others ranked high in the Syndicate to our location. Okay? So, do not panic. Stay calm." Yalu voiced, attempting her best to remain also tranquil for not only my sake but for hers as well. "Just stay calm." The Vixen repeated, this time directing the statement at herself.

Leaning back in the leather seat, I attempted to release a slow breath 'til I overheard a knock on the car door window. Jumping three feet up in the air, completely spooked, I glanced over onto my side, then back over to the driver's side of the car. Perceiving that all the men who had pursued us inside the mall had surrounded the sportscar. "Great." I thought. "Now what?"

195

"Turn off the vehicle!" One of the men ordered Yalu. His voice sounding incredibly low, and of high authority. Cautiously observing his behaviors, the same man voiced a second order for us to exit the car.

"Just get out of the car." Yalu quietly whispered to me as she turned off the vehicle. Leaving the keys in the ignition, she pretended to put them in her pocket, yet it was the same pocket her cellular phone was located. Slyly pressing the GPS phone tracker, Yalu began to unbuckle her seatbelt and proceed with finally stepping out of the sports car. Deciding to follow her procedure, I ensued the same routine. From there, I watched Yalu effortlessly go along with the human's commands. I knew I had to also follow ensue, however unlike the 'Rebelling' Vixen, I had slain plenty of people and I was not afraid of a 'Death Sentence', I would rather get 'Euthanized' than go through all that torment in another Institution.

Chapter 36
Jakob/Cinder

"JAKOB!" Mhykal shouted from up on the second story, his body intently leaning over the banister, "Get your ass into the Study!"

"Why?" I confusingly wondered while I lounged in another section of the Manor that sat right underneath the study's hidden staircase. Not getting an answer, I slowly stood up and began to climb up the stairs. Once on the second floor and inside the study, I saw Mhykal was anxiously pacing back and forth. Not a good sign grounded on past experiences. "What's up?"

Braedon who was standing over his computer, swiftly answered my question; his voice sounding standoffish, but much more tranquil than the other Vampiric who was running his hands through his black hair. "Yalu's GPS tracker on her cell phone went off."

Hearing those words made my breathing temporarily seize. Snapping back to reality, I hurriedly stated, "Did she accidentally press it?"

"It is a possibility, however with Cinder also being chaperoned by her, I don't want to chance it," Braedon responded. "We have to keep in mind that there is a high likelihood the Government hired Hunters to track down the Hellhound. After all, she is the highest-risk Unnatural we've had in the Manor since the early days."

I identified all the possibilities that could arise from this spree they went on, but this was her first time out in the public eye. How could they have tracked her down that quickly? Knowing how Cinder was maturing, and how Yalu was in general, I wasn't sure how the event was currently going, however just like Mhykal, I knew we had to hurry, so we could intervene.

"We need to go help them-." I finally spoke up after thinking through all the variables and probabilities.

"No!" Braedon sternly ordered, making both Mhykal and I stop from storming through the Study's double doors.

"WHY NOT!?" Mhykal angrily shouted. His emotions further developed than mine due to the level of intimacy with one of the women in our missing party. "THEY NEED OUR HELP!"

"No. Mhykal calm down. If the reasons that Yalu had indeed hit the Panic Button were Hunters, then it will be our best intention to avidly watch the tracker until we can allude to where they are taking them-"

"That may be a promising idea, however, what happens if they search her. They just may confiscate and deactivate the phone." I theorized, opening up a wider amount of probabilities.

"Another gamble that we might have to take. But the tracker is attached to the inside of the SD memory chip. So even if they take apart the phone, and take the SD chip out of it, the tracker will still work. If they confiscate the phone, they will two to one bring it along them to check it for signs of 'Rebelling." Our Leader endlessly explained, as he avidly surveyed the blinking dot on his computer's monitor. "So, for now, it is our best bet to stay calm, watch where they are taking Yalu and Cinder, and plan a rescue once we know exactly where they are being taken to."

"GOD DAMN IT!" Mhykal shouted, grabbing one of the Victorian chairs and throwing it fiercely against the nearest bookshelf.

Although I was just as frustrated, I sat in the yet to be thrown chair and began to hope that we could trust our Leader. Trust in his words that everything was going to be okay.

"Don't fight them!" Yalu shouted to me while she was already being dragged around with both of her arms handcuffed behind her. I knew she could easily disable the Hunters with no problem at all, so why didn't she. Using my nose, I managed to manipulate a distance between myself and the four men surrounding me, I sniffed out a heavy metal encased in the objects wrapped around her wrists. It was most likely one of the weaknesses that Vixens had, so it stopped any of her Species Abilities from being useful.

"Keep to your human form. Keep to your human form." I thought to myself. "Don't use your abilities, right now." Swinging a punch at the first man that stepped forward, I felt my fist make a solid connection with the underside of his nose, the cartilage instantly breaking on impact. His body dropped surprised by the strength behind my small petite frame, his nose angrily bleeding. Not hesitating I backflipped, then subsequently kicked the next round man. The same strength now crushing a few of his teeth out of my opponent's mouth. Blood following.

"Just tase her!" I heard the guy holding Yalu order his colleagues. "Tase the damn bitch!"

Hearing a quick electric volt startup, I attempted to pinpoint where it was coming from. Of course, the sound was coming from directly behind me. With little time to appropriately strategize how to eliminate the target with missing teeth, I barely managed to dodge the electric prongs racing towards me. Switching targets, I looked for fresh meat, noticing that this man had a small handgun hidden under his jacket. Not afraid of the firearm, I continued to dart headfirst into the confrontation. Retaining the lament fighter's stance, I prepared to punch this man with one of my left hooks, however, something stopped me. My body froze, and I wreathed in pain. My back started to burn uncontrollably. The pain alone dropped me to my knees.

Doing everything to hold in the pain, I heard Yalu continue to scream at me, this time the tone full of a tremendous amount of fear. As it rang through my ears, flowing down into my eardrum, I tried to force myself up. Though it was a futile effort. Bending over my knees, I savagely bit my tongue to keep from screaming.

"Cuff her now!" The alleged lead man commanded his cronies. "But be vigilant!"

I could feel someone heavy stand on my burning back, crushing it. Knocking all the air out of my lungs. "Get-get off me!" I snapped as I tried to summon up my lost breath. With the weight crashing further on top of my back, I gagged for more air, bringing saliva and froth up with each cough. Feeling one of my arm's get aggressively pulled behind my back, I began to feel nausea spill over my stomach. The sickness of being forced to submit made my doubts succumb to the surface. Sensing cold metal handcuffs get wrapped around one of my wrists, I felt my other arm proceed to get jerked around. Feeling like it was going to tear out of my shoulder's socket, I tried to enter round two. Quickly a hand grabbed onto the back of my neck before my head came crashing down into the parking lot asphalt. Cracking open a gash along the side of my forehead. The wound only lasted a few seconds before it stitched itself up, leaving only the blood seepage behind. The same blood I could use as a weapon, yet I fought myself from using it in order to protect Yalu. Using what remained of my conscious strength, I refrained from activating the weapon that had become second nature to me while my other wrist felt the cold metal of the handcuffs rip around its soft skin. I knew that most of my fighting capability had departed the second my hands were restrained, however, it did not mean I was out either. When two of the men picked me up off from the floor, I instantly prepared my lower half for combat. I knew I still had my kicks, which according to Mhykal those muscles were both faster and stronger than my fists were. Relying on them for now, I pushed aside the excruciating back pain and began to take advantage of having these two men ground my arms.

"No! DON'T FIGHT THEM CINDER!" I heard Yalu angrily order. The fear in her voice even heftier than when she last called.

"You should listen to your friend Unnatural!" One of the Hunters spoke. The same one who was holding one of my cuffed arms, before clutching my neck. Throwing my body into the tail of the red sportscar to hold me steady. Beginning to feel someone's hands check my back, my front pant pockets, and lastly my coat's pockets, I glanced back up at Yalu. Seeing for the first time the petrifying terror shining brightly in her eyes, I relaxed my will to fight and put my faith in her cellphone's tracker, which now resided in the confiscated hands of these harsh Hunters. Keeping fingers crossed that our friends and allies would rescue us. Relaxing my restrained body, I now screamed out in anguishing pain from my burning scar. The pain drastically increasing each passing second, only made me wonder where that cursed Shadow was when I needed him.

"Of course, you don't ever show up anymore." I thought to myself, "Unless it is to give me assignments, right?"

"Just get them loaded up in the truck." Another man sternly barked as a heavy truck drove slowly up to where we stood. Feeling my frame coldly get half-pushed half-dragged towards the 'Prisoner' Transporter, I shadowed the men who were pushing the Vixen into the same truck. Observing Yalu stroll of her own accord into the truck, I was thrown inside behind her.

"I told you to just do as they said." Yalu scolded me once we were alone in the makeshift transporting cage. The brunette-haired Vixen was full of fear in addition to rage. I was content being scolded, it felt more sound seeing her furious anger, then it did to see her pungent fear. Leaning over so my chest touched my knees, I did what I could to catch my breath. Silently alerting the Unnatural to my agony. "Cinder, are you okay?"

"My back burns. It burns-" I panted, tears streaming down my face. "It burns-burns really bad." I painfully mumbled. Intensely fixating on the words so I could cling to my sanity. "I'm going to have to chan-"

"No, Cinder." Yalu continued to whisper, her voice strictly commanding. "Just think of us, all of your friends, and the happy memories you have made. Think of a happy place."

Nodding my head, I attempted my best to think of a happy place while every blood cell rushed to my head. Think of the positive memories I had made in these last twelve months. But just like in the past nothing came up, I couldn't think of anything. "I knew I had pleasant times here, so why couldn't I remember any of them? Why couldn't I imagine them?!" I fearfully thought, allowing the fear I kept hidden deep down to make its swift venture to the surface. Screaming out in pain, I tried to grab anything with my free fingers, but the only available item was a small chain used to tie the handcuffs to these rods that were running along the interior metal wall of the Prisoner Transport. Tightly clutching the material, I continued to scream out in agony as my back savagely burned.

"Just remember that my GPS tracker is still running." I heard Yalu whisper to me, reminding me that for now, we had to place our faith in our friends in the Vampiric Syndicate.

Chapter 37
Cinder

When the vehicle finally came to a halt after what felt like forty-five minutes of endless driving, I lifted my woozy head from its resting position over my knees. The blood swiftly rushing back down to the rest of my body, making me see spots.

Adverting my gaze over to Yalu, I perceived her say, "We stopped."

"Seems so." I panted. "A short distance from the mall. Maybe half hour, forty-five minutes."

"So that knocks out a handful of Institutes, but-" the black-haired Vixen paused. The horrified look on her face growing worse, "The airport. There's a small airport on the other side of the city and it's within that time range."

"Airport?" I questioned aloud, my heart dropping down into my stomach as I smelled the stench of fear running through Yalu.

"That opens a vast array of places they could be taking us-" Yalu announced, pausing the minute we both heard the heavy doors to the transport vehicle start to unlock. Keeping her gaze locked on me, the woman now ordered with her intact contacts hiding her amber-colored pupils, "Now this time do not fight them, Cinder."

"I don't think I have enough energy right now." I wheezed, my scorching back pain finally slimming down to tolerable levels. Though with how sore the entire muscle had become, I knew I could not further risk harming myself. As much as I wanted to add a few more human lives to the list of 'Reaped' souls, the risk was too great.

"Don't fight." Yalu quietly reminded just as the double doors swung open, exposing more Hunters. Adjusting to the harsh light of the high sun that shone brightly into the dimly lit vehicle, I quickly counted a total of fifteen men, and from what I had also glanced over, several of them were armed. Some of them were armed by drugs over weapons. I could smell the familiar scent of sedatives, the odor of pheromone blockers, the irritating stench of potent medications. Those same scents of those drugs they once had injected into my veins every day for sixteen years. The fear level striking ten times higher now as I flashed back to the same day of the thirteenth moon, that dreaded night I got this same scar:

"Sorry 497, but its that time again." I heard Nurse Jackie tell my sixteen-year-old self. I at that time had just started my paralysis. The doctors just put it down as losing the will to fight, which I had, but I see now that it was a form of shock caused by my trauma, per Viktor's explanation. The large hands of the Transporter gliding under my hospital gown and softly lifting my limp physique.

"Take her to the same place?" The man questioned his average male tone sounding sympathetic about my condition and my usual torture.

"Yeah, I will be in shortly to help you get things set up."

"Okay." He responded while carrying me out of the initial room I was contained in, up until the regular weekly raids had started four years later.

Once they had lain me on the cold floor, I had the same leather ankle restraint wrapped around my leg this time with a much shorter lead. With the inability to move, I impatiently waited for my same old enemy to show itself. The ceiling began to retract, exposing the glass-domed ceiling and the red-glowing Blood Moon on the other side. It's warm powerful light beaming down on my limp body. In seconds, I felt my heart cry out, the muscle straining to keep beating so it properly maintain the necessary blood flow. Knowing that my uncontrollable transformation came shortly after, I blanketed my thoughts and counted the time away. Five seconds slowly past by before I regained mobility in my body and painfully sat myself up. My vertebrae twisting itself while my head rested ahead of my knees now folded underneath my malnourished sixteen-year-old body. My back wreathing in pain followed in behind with the rest of my exhausted frame. I could feel my muscles start to contort themselves, also preparing for the change that had yet to happen. As I screamed in pain, I could hear the several stationed employees rush inside the room.

Before they could close the seventy-five-foot distance from the door to where I remained chained, the pain rapidly spread like a wildfire all over the entirety of my spine before it had miraculously disappeared. The numb tingling muscle, however, endured. Little did I know it was here, that my back was forever branded by that unusual scar. Effortlessly alternating forms into the one that had seven years ago seriously disfigured Doctor Masters, I caught the voice of the familiar calming red-eyed Skeleton Shadow say.

"Now, my Little Reaper take your new powers and reap." He smiled, placing his long skeletal-fingered hand on top of my square-Rottweiler formed head. The eyes captivating my full attention.

Feeling a similar smile spread across my face, I curled my lips up exposing the long dire-like fangs that hid underneath. Instinct consumed rational thought, putting me into a mindless rage. Although my body somehow knew exactly what to do. I remember it was on that night for the first and only time at my stay in the Institution, my Blood Abilities activating. A small scythe swiftly grew out of my back leg, easily slicing through the ankle restraint, freeing me. Once free to roam in the dome, I turned to face all the people who had swarmed their way inside the dome. Surveying the humans' shocked faces, I spread my smile higher and fed my movements off their fear. My legs started to propel me forward and before I knew it, I had clung my jaws onto the first victim. The disgusting taste of blood swarming the inside of my mouth. Once the man collapsed onto the cold floor, I charged for my next victim, leaving the first one to slowly bleed to death as his co-workers split up. Running into three separate directions. Picking out the slowest, I blindly attacked the next employee.

Jumping onto the human's back, I attacked the thin shoulder and prepared for the light person to also collapse onto the tile floors. With this human easily falling, I let go of the shoulder, noticing that it was a scrub wearing nurse, the one who had been 'treating' me all these years, Nurse Jackie. My mind from that point on mentally broke. Staring down at her lifeless body, I tried to nudge her head, unwilling to accept that I had just slaughtered the last caring person I had in my sad life. Eventually accepting the consequences of feral actions, I stepped away from her bleeding carcass, my drained body collapsing a few feet away. The senseless paralysis returning.

"Such a strong Little Reaper, you did well for your first time." I heard the Shadow speak up, his hand patting the top of my skull. The bones rubbing through my short black head hairs untraditionally calmed me. Remarkably I retained my tranquility. "For you doing a respectable job, I will allow you to keep your sanity, Reaper." The dark voice continued to mutter, his fingers cutting away a portion of folded ears. The sheer pain reminding me of my awareness before I collapsed into the blackness of my unconscious. "Your back may hurt for now, however in times to come I want you to understand my Little Reaper, that this marks you to me. It will always mark you to me because you are my powerful Little Reaper." I recalled the fading voice utter into my thoughts, haunting my memories.

"Cinder!" Yalu shouted at me, snapping me back to the events that were currently unfolding. With my full awareness returning, I noticed I was being carried onto some sort of aircraft. A small live cargo plane, I believe. Scanning around for the Caucasian Vixen's who continued to shout my name, I tried to hunt down the location of her apprehensive voice.

"Yalu!" I yelled back, noticing that she was still restrained in the truck, chained, and handcuffed to the bar of the Prisoner Transport Vehicle. Right away, I figured out that she wasn't going to be transported alongside me. That they were going to separate the two of us. In my head, I remembered those words from the Shadow, I was marked to him with that scar etched into the skin. Quickly figuring out that I would not be able to fight the Hunters, I made up my mind on the next plan I could think of. Silently crying, I pleaded, "Shadow, please I beg of you, protect her, protect my friends from harm." With no response, I decided to up my plead, "I will be your Reaper. I won't fight you anymore. So, please, please do me this favor. I beg of you-"

"Fine then, my arrogant Little Reaper." The haunting Shadow finally answered. Seeing his entire cloak wearing body as I was thrown into a flat seat. Landing on my hands, I felt the same restraints begin to tighten around my wrists, ripping into the skin. "I will protect the Unnaturals you have grown attached to until you and I are reunited once more."

Staring up at the white roof of the plane, I returned to the Shadow, "Thank you. Thank you, Shadow." Feeling the sharp prick of a needle jam deep into the vein in my outer thigh, poking through the slim material of my skinny jeans, I felt the heavy dose of sleeping sedatives drain into my bloodstream.

"Alright, we're ready to take off." I heard the man growl as he sat beside my drug-induced tiring body. Hearing the engine of the plane roar, I barely managed to feel the air vehicle lift off the ground before my exhaustion became too much to bear, and I finally fell into the depths of slumber.

Chapter 38
Cinder

With the drugs wearing off, I opened my dreary eyes to see I was again being pathetically carried somewhere new. Through the dimly lit lights, I scarcely made out the tall ceilings of what appeared to be a long corridor. My returning scents alerted me to the sheer sounds of screaming creatures, other Unnaturals. I could clearly make out the painful howls of Canid Species, and shrewd growls of Draconics, the hisses of large cats. Curses being said in multiple different languages that I could surprisingly understand, although I had no memory of ever learning these dialects. I could tell it was a new place, full of both Unnatural and Human scents that I had yet to clarify, and it fearfully bit at my will to challenge these employees.

Fighting both rising fear and panic, I began to struggle. "I needed to continue to fight back." I told myself, "I do not belong here!" Feeling the handcuffs still wrapped around my wrists, binding my arms behind my back, I hurriedly revised my next plan of action. I knew I couldn't escape, however, it didn't mean I couldn't do other things, so in the meantime, I would refuse to submit.

"Sir, she is fighting us-" I overheard the unfamiliar human carrying me shout to his superior.

Before I could attempt to see who this man was, my petite physique was tossed around, and I was upright once more, standing on my feet. With two men holding down my arms and one of those two, holding one of his large hands against the back of my neck, I began to operate a way to combat these brutes. "I wouldn't try to fight this." The higher ranked employee spoke up, his tall slender white coat wearing frame now facing me. Frustratingly glaring up into his dark-brown pupils, I observed his movements as he strolled closer, trying my hardest to stay infuriatingly calm. Stopping within range of my long slender legs, I pretended to continue to heed his ranting over the same old crap, while I tried to silently shifted my sore legs around and alert him to my newly revised plan.

Taking advantage of the men tightly gripping my arms, I kicked off the floor tossing both of my legs up into the air. Using my increased speed training, I crossed my ankles behind the man's neck before dragging him closer to my restrained body. My knees pushing back into my small, lush breast muscles. Precisely executing my plan, I leaned forward and head-butt the brunette-haired man. Our foreheads making brutal contact. Noting he was still conscious, I again head-butted the man, this time simultaneously releasing my wrapped legs. While this man in Doctor-like attire staggered backward, I lifted my left leg. Kicking the underside of his square jaw with the top of my bootie. Lifting it higher, I again brought my leg back down, hitting him over the top of his head with the heeled wedge of my shoe this time. From there I surveyed my work, although the observation was short-lived when I was tackled into the nearest wall and plastered flat against its cold concrete wall by one man as his partner checked on their superior. Everything was still going according to the plan. Using my regaining strength, I pushed my hundred-pound physique off the wall. Getting slammed into the wall again, I felt a forearm drive horrendously into the back of my neck. Forcing my actions to temporarily seize. Still unwilling to give in, I yet again pushed off the wall. This time succeeding. Granted enough room for my legs to touch the partition, I crawled up its concrete material continuing to fight. Yet, surprisingly the employee seemed prepared and equipped for my attempt to break free. Swinging around, he body-slammed me into the same concrete tiled floor, busting up my chin with the blow. Knocking all the air out of my lungs, as he pressed his large knee into my upper back.

Coughing out a painful yelp, I overheard the doctor-like man shout to his men, "Don't beat up on her! Her Blood is a weapon-!"

Smiling I when I quickly reminisced that no one was around to tell me how to use my skills now, I licked the blood from my split lip and finally activated my Blood powers. Creating the blade-like spikes out of my boney spine, I felt the weight release and knew that the quick draw had indeed struck its intended target. Now free from that heavy brute, I clashed with my body to stand back up on my feet again. Taking a breather as I stood there looking down at the Doctor, I melted down the handcuffs now knowing that I did not have the same metal weakness of that putrid Silver like the other Canid Unnaturals had. With the melted silver falling right off my bruised wrists, I finally freed my hands from those unbearable restraints.

Rubbing the soft skin, I continued to listen to the Doctor curse at his men as he slowly stumbled on to the soles of his feet. Through the instant swelling of his gums, I eavesdropped on his angered rambling "You guys are absolutely pathetic! You cannot even contain a simple Hellhound! We have other Species of Unnaturals here that are much more dangerous and psychotic than this bitch!"

"Watch your mouth, you foul human!" I growled back running towards the man and his two other goonies. Quickly dropping down onto my hands and knees, I illuminated myself in my orange flames to swiftly transform from one form to the other. "I don't have anyone here holding me back anymore!" I recklessly thought inside my apparently deranged mind seconds before I erupted out of the flames in my Beauceron canine form. Charging directly for the remaining humans, I directed my attention to the Doctor. Before the man's lackey could step in front of him, I had already jumped onto the man, my paws bracing his shoulders as I threw the rest of my weight into his small stern frame. Once again, forcing the man onto the hard ground.

Stopping myself from ripping my fangs into this man, I altered forms, returning to my bloody human form with the ripped jacket. Spawning a scythe blade out of the top of my right wrist, I morphed the blood so its formation would concave along the flow of my hand. Still maintaining the iconic crescent moon shape of the scythe, I increased the density of the clotting cells and further strengthened the weapon. Hearing both of his men shuffle around to once more attempt to break me away I hastily pointed the needle-like point directly at his right eye. Fully prepared to drive the Blood Scythe right through that dark brown iris.

Forcing our eyes to lock, I readjusted my bodies' position over the top of his. My left hand stationed on the concrete beside his square-chinned face, my long deep-black hair falling over my shoulders and lying across his face and chin. Coldly commanding the Doctor, "Tell your co-workers to step down, or you will end up losing much more than this eye."

"Stand down!" He immediately shouted to his co-workers, afraid for his sight and life.

"Now then, I want to be escorted out of here." I again demanded, keeping my blade positioned directly on his eye while rearranging my hair with my free hand.

"I'm sorry I can't do that." The man blurted out, the tone of his voice darkening.

Pushing the blade's tip into the pupil, I observed the blood rapidly break apart. The cells unmolding and splashing down onto the man's tan skin. Before I could try to remold the blood cells, I observed my body uncontrollably fall forward. Landing directly on top this man's body, my upper half draping over the top of his face. "What is going on?" I stuttered confused. I knew it was not my powers that had failed me, even though it looked that way.

Feeling my lifeless arms both get harshly clutched by the still conscious lackey, I was then swiftly lifted off of this unexpectedly prepared man. Intently observing the man begin to stand himself

211

up, I frustratingly listened to him calmly remind. "You must have not heard me before when I said we have seen plenty of dangerous Unnaturals come through these walls."

"Wh-what did you do-do to me?" I panted, feeling all my breath in my lungs constrict.

"You were so focused on trying to get out of here that I was surprised you didn't feel the syringe I had in my hand, jam into your leg that saddled my stomach." He sighed, using an annoyingly sarcastic tone.

"A sed-sedative?" I weakly asked, my mind racing to figure out what drug had been pushed into my system for the second time today.

"You are very intelligent indeed." The man said now having a hold of my chin to keep me fixated on him. "However, you are still off on what it is exactly." He paused, expecting me to talk back to him. "Yes, it was a sedative, but I had it also laced with a Pheromone Blocker and some cleansed salt. All of your abilities and powers are on a temporary pause, as well as most of your muscular function." The doctor laughed, letting go of my limp head. "Go ahead and put her in her room. I will be in shortly after I get myself cleaned up." Getting picked up so I could be properly carried, I tiredly watched the man walk out of the line of sight as this man embarked on his current task of transferring me to some 'designated' room. "Oh, and get someone to help Bryan, here before he bleeds out."

Chapter 39

Jakob

"Yeah, we found Mhykal's car," I informed Braedon, speaking through my black smartphone. "The car was locked, and the keys were left inside. Mhykal picked the lock easily and swiftly barged in to find any clues."

"And?" Braedon requested, the sympathy barely there in his voice, making me feel that other things were going on which the Leader was keeping confidential.

"Well, we didn't find anything worthwhile besides the clothes that Yalu said she was going to get, although a few seemed more like Cinder's style." I rambled on about. "No real clues about where they had gone off to."

"Okay, well considering you both ran there, take Mhykal's car and stake out the next location that Yalu's cell phone GPS tracker had pinpointed to," Braedon reported back to me. "I will send you an image of its location."

"Okay." I anxiously sighed, furiously hanging up.

"Well?" Mhykal growled, his rampant pacing not helping the situation at hand.

"We take your car and stake out the next location, which..." I paused as my phone vibrated from inside my back pants' pocket. "I got the marker." I quickly answered, walking over to the passenger's side of the red sports car.

"Look, I am just as in a hurry to get Yalu and Cinder back home safely as you are, but why the haste?" Mhykal snarled as he stepped into the car's driver seat.

"Yalu's tracker stopped at the exact same location we spent five years investigating blueprints and schedules to free those five 'Off-grids'." I heavily sighed, remembering that crazy-ass Doctor we had, unfortunately, ran into.

"I am not going to stake out at that place!" I heard Mhykal snap as he drove the car right out of the parking lot and towards the Institute on the other side of the city, on Salam Drive. Flying at speeds almost thirty miles faster than the twenty-five-speed limit, I could sense his fear and anger just overflowing out of Yalu's boyfriend. I had not seen this type of animated emotion coming out of him in almost five decades. "Besides why stake it out when you and I know all the halls, rooms, and routines of that place."

"True, I do remember all of that, and with our speed and abilities we should not have a problem taking control of that place again to free Yalu and Cinder, however Mhykal I need you to try to calm down. If you cannot control yourself, then sneaking in will be much harder." I pleaded with my old friend.

After speeding straight through a red traffic light, I finally saw the words reach his slow brain. Slowing the vehicle down to about fifteen miles over the speed limit, he agreed. "I guess so."

"We will continue with a small stakeout just in case there are any newer changes to the staff or structure of the Hospital in the year since." I continued, feeling surprised that the building had not been shut down after our Raid. I knew we had gotten all the 'Patients' that were being kept there out that same night, but then I guess when the population of Unnaturals is about a fourth of the human population in the world, it made it easy to obtain more patients. And with the vast human population the state of New York,

I guess it wasn't that miraculous that somehow Salam Drive's Hospital Institute had managed to stay open. But as much as saving the Unnaturals was our goal, our primary achievement was to save Yalu and Cinder today. The others could hopefully hold out for a bit longer.

"Okay, Jakob," Mhykal said before speeding up the mileage in his fancy sports car to again rev through two more traffic lights. "I, however, want to get there as fast as possible. The longer we wait on Braedon, the more I am imagining the pain and torture those 'Doctors' and 'Researchers' are doing to those two."

"I hear you Mhykal but getting us possibly injured or KILLED on the way won't allow us to rescue them any faster!" I shouted at him.

Surviving the rush hour traffic, we finally reached the Institute. Pulling into the same shared parking lot with the ironic Human therapist building, we sat in the car and anxiously counted down the next ten minutes to look for any possible shift changes so we could grab someone and get some much-needed information. It had only been two hours since Yalu's GPS tracker in her SD Memory Chip had been triggered, but in that small period these people could have already gotten our two women friends assigned to a room, I.D.d and possibly even started testing on them. The endless possibilities were fearfully struggling.

With no one coming out in those ten minutes I could sense Mhykal's rising frustration about having to stake out. "Mhykal just wait, someone will come out-"

"NO! I AM FUCKING DONE WITH THE SITTING AROUND!" He screamed, getting out the vehicle, slamming his car door shut with such a heavy force that if the door were, for instance, a chair it would have been shattered.

Forced to follow him, I quickly got out of the car and began to jog beside him. Our Vampiric speed easily able to outrun the Guards and the rest of the Hospital's employees on duty, we quickly stormed the administration desk. Not seeing anything on either Cinder or Yalu on the first floor, I painfully nodded my head no.

"Alright let's go to the second floor." Mhykal continued as we again took off at our super-speed, taking out the guards who tried to stop us, maintaining the image of nothing more than a blur in the cameras' lenses.

Reaching the second floor, I had Mhykal occupy the employed Humans while I again searched the list of rooms. "No sign of them on this level either." I irately hissed, my frustration level rising higher. "Where are they?"

"What about the third or the fourth floor?" Mhykal probed after kicking one of the arms guards' square in the face. Fracturing his skull and throwing him against one of the weaker walls.

"I doubt that they would be on the higher levels." I sighed, recalling that Cinder was considered a High-risk. "We need to check the lower levels. I believe that they would have brought them down to the basement levels."

"What about 'Off-grids'?" Mhykal eagerly questioned.

"I think that they would take Cinder there, but Yalu will most likely be put in one of the Laboratory rooms as she and her sister are the only Vixens in the States." I returned, clarifying my theories and suspicions. They were not as pin-point accurate as Viktor's or Cinder's prognosis, but thankfully Mhykal's simple vocabulary understood the speculations.

"Okay, let's get down there before these guys regain their conscious."

"Umm, Mhykal I don't think some of them will be regaining their consciousness any time soon." I returned, pointing out the fact that five of them had their skulls completely bashed in, the likelihood of fractures extremely high.

"Sorry, I guess that I lost control during the commotion." The Vampiric apologized.

216

"Don't worry about it." I smirked, "After hunting down not only our species but also hunting down our close friends, I believe a little payback doesn't hurt. Now let's go before any of their co-workers find us."

Chapter 40
Jakob

Reaching the only underground level of the institute, we pursued each room reading the attached clipboards that had documented all forms of data on each patient. Despite the urgency to hurry up and locate Yalu whom we believed was on this exact level, the two of us decided against splitting up due to the surprising amount of armed guards we kept running into. Of course, though between the speed needed and the effort used to dispose of the guards, we were steadily running out of steam.

"Where are you Yalu?" Mhykal growled aloud, his head swinging side by side to quickly skim over the names still on the papers. "Damn it!"

"Mhykal calm down, we will find her-"I paused as out of the corner of my left eye I saw her name flash by on one of the clipboards. "Wait, here she is." I hesitated, flying to a halt several feet passed the room. Walking up to the arm, I quickly used my gifted abilities and unlocked the door to her assigned room on my first try. Thanking myself that in only an hour since our arrival, we had successfully located her without running into much misfortune.

"Yalu?" Mhykal whispered, speedily walking to her beside the bed.

"Mhykal?!" Yalu loudly called, her voice sounding flabbergasted.

"Are you okay, baby?" The Vampiric interrogated, his hands gently holding her head up. Using his left hand, he parted her long black side-swept bangs over to the side of her petite feminine face. "They didn't hurt you, did they?"

"No. A couple of sedatives and a 'pheromone blocker' I think." The Vixen returned, rubbing her template. Trying to remember what the Doctors had exactly injected into her system.

"Those ASSHOLES!" The other black-haired Unnatural growled, his furious temper poking through.

"It's okay, they probably didn't give you a high dosage according to these papers." I hastily interrupted, glancing through her chart. "Yeah, it's an average mild dose of Pheromone Blockers and Weak sedatives." I continued to read, stopping when my sense of hearing alerted to the sound of hastily approaching guards. Dropping the clipboard, I now urged our departure. "Now we need to get Cinder and get out of here as soon as possible. So, where is she?"

Yalu hesitated. Her yellow eyes looking down at the tiled floor.

"Yalu?" Mhykal asked. The tone in his voice overwhelmed with absolute concern for his girlfriend.

"She isn't here." We both heard her hysterically cry.

"What?" I inquired, deeply bewildered. Hearing the footsteps near our location, I swiftly approached the subject from another angle. "Well, we'll have to figure out where she is later. We won't be of any use to her if we all get caught."

"True." Yalu sighed, wiping away her tears. It was only the second time I had ever seen her cry, so I knew that this alone had terrified the poor woman.

"Can you walk?" Mhykal worriedly questioned.

"Not really. The feeling in my legs has yet to fully return." Yalu answered her boyfriend. I could feel her heartache as she spoke. Yalu the strong dignified, snotty woman with a bad attitude was now feeling defeated. She had been split up from one of her only female friends other than her younger sister, Valeryie.

Mhykal picked up the Vixen, knightly carrying her in his arms before he followed in behind me. Leading the group, I quickly took on the oncoming squadron of guards to clear up space. Telling the Vampiric that he should rush ahead and I would follow. Using my fast speed, I outran the firing bullets from their advanced weaponry. Ducking under a round of three fired bullets all aimed at my head, I tripped one man, then grabbed his skull as he fell and swung his still-living body into the line of fire. Dodging behind the same guy, I locked sights on one of the three guards off to my left and dropped onto my hands before spinning around, roundhouse kicking all three of them back to back with the back of my black short-tongued construction boots. While they motionlessly fell to the hard ground, I quickly configured that based upon the simple laws of physics, I had done enough to get the ball rolling. Enough people in the way of one another that with four of the guards falling either into the line of fire or the line of movement, I decided to run after Mhykal and Yalu, who had taken a hidden passage we had discovered while deciphering the blueprints last year. The passage led straight out to the opposing parking lot and back out into the open world.

As I caught up with them, I entered the brightly sunlit open asphalt parking lot. The rays echoing off the dimmed windows of the those 'Doctor' salary cars, and Guard salary SUVs. Adjusting my sights, I saw Mhykal still carrying a semi-drugged Yalu who was leaning her head against his chest, her arms lightly wrapped around his neck. Thankfully, the Vixen was still wearing the same outfit she had picked out this morning, well except her Fall/Winter jacket, which we assumed was in inventory.

Catching my breath, I heard the usual jokester tone of my couple century old friend: "Man, you really do need to work out more, Jakob."

"Shut-up Mhykal." I teased back before fixating on our next task. "We need to hurry up and get back to the car, so we can get back to the Manor and regroup. We cannot allow Cinder to be in Human or Government care for long."

"Yeah." Mhykal and Yalu simultaneously agreed. Running back to the car, I quickly got in and began to move around the plastic bags full of clothes so that there would be room for Yalu to slide in. It would have been much easier if she could have transformed into her tiny Fox Spirit form, but the three of us knew those creeps had drugged her with Pheromone Blockers to keep a majority of her Species Abilities under their control.

"Okay, there's room right behind your seat," I said as I walked around the front of the car to help move the driver's seat so the Vampiric could slide his Vixen into the backseat. Hastily strolling back over to the passenger side of the vehicle, I finally parked my exhausted ass in the seat. Watching Mhykal gently lie his girlfriend down in the backseat, half crawling over the folded driver's seat, he proceeded to comfortably position her in the backseat. When the Vampire tried to help seat belt the Vixen, she finally snapped at him, ordering him to hurry up and get all of us out of here.

"I can seatbelt myself. I wasn't able to walk; I still have use of my hands." Her raspy voice hissed.

"Okay. Okay." Mhykal smiled back; adjusting the seat so he could finally get inside the vehicle. Swinging the sportscar's door shut, he turned the keys in the ignition. Revving the sports car engine, he swiftly pulled the red vehicle out of the adjoined parking lot.

While we lawfully drove back towards the large Victorian Manor, I had been gifted with by a good human friend I made back in the early eighteenth century; I finally fired up the courage to interrogate Yalu about the recently succumbed events. Before I could ask the first question relating to the incident, I saw out of the corner of my eye that the Vixen was cradling something in her hands. "What is that, Yalu?"

The Vixen softly answered, "Before we were shadowed by the Hunters, I had managed to persuade Cinder into getting herself a new collar."

"How the hell did you manage to get her to go along with that?" Mhykal questioned, this time stopping for a red traffic light.

"I told her that the tag could stay attached to the keyring, based on the same reason she told you she would keep wearing that raggedy old collar. However, it was not the only reason she clung so heavily to it." Yalu sighed, strongly clutching the nylon.

"Okay, then why else?" I asked, feeling lied to.

"She said although it had been administered by the Institute, a nurse working at the Hospital had her parents rub their scents on the leather."

"Okay? So again, how did you manage to persuade her?"

"I told her that we would rub our scents on it." Yalu smiled, handing the blue-collar up to me. Investigating the unusual nylon slip collar, I noted that there was a small choker chain looped through the keyring. It was unique and I could easily imagine it on Cinder when she was in that black and tan, bright blue-eyed Beauceron form. "It took a bit of persuasion, but she agreed to it eventually."

"She probably gave in, so she didn't have to continue to hear you pressuring her." Mhykal sneered back to his girlfriend.

"Anyways, I want to know what you recall seeing when you guys were split up," I said, changing the subject advertently quick. "And I would like if you could tell me before we make it back home."

"Why?" Mhykal and Yalu quizzed me at the same time.

"I have a feeling that Braedon is keeping something hidden from us," I answered, putting my index finger and middle finger up to my forehead, trying to think of what it may be.

Chapter 41
Jakob/Cinder

"You saw her get put on a plane?" I shockingly questioned Yalu after she had told us the last thing she recalled. "An actual plane?"

"Yeah, I did," Yalu answered, her voice still full of defeat. "Cinder did try to fight them on it, but she-"

When the Vixen stopped mid-sentence, I knew there was something else up that had happened at the Airport, something that Yalu did not want us to know. Looking back at her, I gently probed, "What happened?"

"Jakob, don't push her too far." Mhykal barked, sympathizing with his girlfriend's emotions.

"Mhykal it is okay," Yalu spoke, her voice returning. "There was something that had stopped Cinder from fighting completely, something to do with her back. I believe it had something to do with that scar. She said it was burning. I don't know what the scar had to do with her pain, but nonetheless, the amount of pain she was in, incapacitated her. Of course, she never listened to anything I told her-" Yalu heavily moaned, her usual tone returning with that last sentence.

"She fits in with all of us." I smiled, returning to facing the front of the car.

"Yeah, she sure does." Mhykal chuckled as he pulled up into the driveway of the Sanctioned Manor. "So, Jakob I have to ask; why don't you trust Braedon?"

As the vehicle drove into its usual spot in the Garage, I returned, "It's not that I do not trust him, I, however, think that he is hiding something from us. I think that he is hiding something about Cinder, from us."

"Why would he do that?" Yalu growled.

"I don't know why he would." I returned, slithering out of the low-lying vehicle. Helping Yalu, I asked which bags had Cinder's clothes in it, so I could go put them in her bedroom. Wondering as I grabbed the Hellhounds clothes, "Where did they take her? The fact they had used a small cargo plane to Transport her this time around only widened the number of other Institutes she was possibly being held inpatient at. Although, it probably wasn't anything less than six thousand miles or so, and with only seven institutes left open in the eastern half of the Continent, we are left questioning where?"

"Don't worry Jakob, we will find her." Mhykal barked at me, giving me his usual jokester grin. "We will save Cinder." He repeated, his Vampiric gaze stern and serious.

"My, my, that is a large scar on your back." I had overheard the Doctor I had only recently attempted to kill voice. Sensing his male fingers run over my sore, bare back, I reacted, however, I quickly found out how futile that was. Unable to get away thanks to his brutes cuffing my hands above my head and connecting the cuffs to a long hanging chain, I was left contorting this way and that. Even my feet too had been restrained, stuck in spread-eagle anklets, the soles bore down on the cold concrete floor. "There is no reason for you to flinch." This sarcastic and sadistic cruel man returned, sliding his fingers down my back. Deeply driving the digits into the etched skin along my cross-scar. "I have seen the documentation on your old files your old Doctors so generously faxed me. Though I only had a few hours to skim over the charts, I have to admit that the picture of this long scar in your file does no justice to its massive size."

"Shut-up." I weakly growled at him, again trying to fight the chains I had restrained around my wrists and ankles. My entire body having been stripped down naked, just for this 'examination'.

"Still trying to fight me?" The man sneered, pushing his fingers deeper into the middle of my vertebrae. Bellowing in pain, I bit my lower lip to keep from screaming. After twenty seconds of deeply prodding along my spine, he removed his long digits from the scarred skin, allowing me time to catch my breath. I could hear his footsteps move around this 'designated' room I had been carried into. His irritating voice, rambling on and on about what he had found in my transferred file. "Now before I get you settled into your new home; I'm supposed to tell you what to expect from here."

"Expect?" I thought to myself.

"This is not one of those Unnatural Patient Hospitals or whatever it is that those Rebels call it. A Hospital Institution, right? This is not one of those. To you guys, it probably is the same thing no matter what way you look at it." The Doctor rambled on, slightly getting off-topic once more. "This is a Government based and Government-funded Laboratory. You guys are nothing but prisoners here without a say about how we do things."

"Nothing unusual." I soundlessly thought. There was no need to tell this man what I was wondering and currently, everything would be kept in my slightly insane delusional mind.

"Judging by your silence, I believe that you understand all that I am telling you." Deliberately pausing for a few seconds so I could 'obediently' reply to his hypothesis. Not being dragged into that again, I kept myself quiet while this man rampantly muttered. "Anyways, you will return to your Unnatural/Patient I.D. Number of

0497, and you WILL allow us to do what we are being paid to do." I rolled my eyes, continuing to listen to his footsteps get closer and closer to where I was helplessly restrained. "Before we can get started on our research, I need to first get you sedated."

Upset I snapped at him, my tired soft feminine voice growling, "No more drugs!" I knew what to expect back from this man, and although I refused to care, I had to at least make that statement clear. I honestly didn't want to go back on all those medications.

"I know that you were on a lot of medications-" the doctor said as he injected the usual sedative filled syringe needle into my bare thigh, "that you were on, but here you will only be going on sedatives, pheromone-blockers, and a flash of cleansed sodium here and there. Pain killers aren't given to anyone unless the Unnatural is in so much pain that it stops us from our intended research." Feeling the liquid drain into my leg, I welcomed the few seconds of silence. Once the entire dosage had emptied into my vein, the Doctor removed the needle. "That is all we will most likely ever be giving you during your stay here."

"Whatever." I rolled my eyes, ignorantly refusing to believe what he had just told me.

Focusing on the man's footsteps as they moved around, I heard him speak, his voice directed at his underlings, "It should take about three minutes before the dosage will take over 0497's body. In about a minute, she should lose complete muscular control, so after that I want you to remove her restraints and carry her over to the table so I can get the Upper into her."

"Upper?" I thought, beginning to feel my entire body start to go limp, I felt my head lose its stability, drooping down over my shoulders.

"Speaking of which it's already starting to take effect."

Hearing several sets of footsteps, I equipped my mind for what was coming up next. With the hanging chain increasing in its available length, I felt my body start to loosen up. Unable to catch myself, my body began the process of falling towards the concrete floor. Awaiting to be reunited with the cold hard floor, I was surprised to feel myself get caught by one of the fresh-meat. The man hastily rearranged my nude figure, removing the restraints so my wrists and ankles could regain their freedom prior to carrying me over to the medical table I had seen in the middle of the room when I was brought inside this darkly lit room.

Gently placed onto the freezing cold metal table, I watched this unusual Doctor or was it more like a scientist, I could not decipher between the two. His small, slender, lengthy physique with brunette hair and dark green eyes now stood over me. Exposing another syringe in front of my eyes, this time he flicked the dripping needle before continuing his endless rambling. "This is a Pheromone Upper." Poking the needle into my limp arm the man began to slowly inject this newer medication into my bloodstream while finishing his explanation. "This drug forces your body to start emitting the level of Pheromones needed for any Transforming Unnatural Species to morph into their breed's natural forms." Removing the syringe, he continued, "Unlike the Hospitals who try to research ways to repress your Unnatural abilities for the intended use of allowing the Unnaturals to potentially return to a human life, which only a hundred cases have ever been successful in accomplishing; we try to research ways that species, such as the breed you are, can potentially be useful for both Military and Scientific Advancements."

While the sensation of my body began its explained process to morph into my Hellhound Canine form, I continued to keep my eyes on this 'Researching' Doctor, still unsure of the exact title he held. However, my ability to stare this man down was suddenly cut short as I uncontrollably started to change. My skull altering its formation from human to the Beauceron Canine skull shape. My hands and feet mutating into the shape of paws, my shoulders painfully rolling to allow my spine and ribs to change their direction and force. I hadn't felt this slow direct pain since before I had learned to accurately control the speed of transformation.

227

"Alright, roll her onto her side, so she can finish." The Doctor ordered his lackeys, who obeyed like trained rats. Rolling me over onto the left side of my altering build, so I could complete the entire process. Once he had finished, I exhaustingly panted feeling the sedative complete its course. Trying to fight slumber I blatantly perceived him say. "Once she is out, I want her fitted and finished with the administration. When she awakes, come get me." Just as I slipped into another drug-induced slumber.

Chapter 42
Cinder

When I came too, I saw at the start of my muzzle there was some sort of nylon material wrapped around my mouth. It's form-fitted preventing my jaws from opening. Moving my front feet around, I tried to move around the cold table, attempting to readjust how I was lying down. As painful as it was to force my muscles to work, I eventually managed to get myself into an upright lying position. Lying now on the underneath of my stomach, I skimmed around my enclosed concrete environment for any changes to the bland room. The chains had disappeared from the still present floor clasps that were nailed to templates in the concrete floor. Looking elsewhere, I saw that in that matching corner some of those brutes, as well as some other 'human' workers, were working on building up what I assumed was a tall chain-link fence.

"So, you've noticed the fence, they are working on." I overheard the irritating Doctor/Scientist speak. "We do this with every Shifter we get. The fence varies depending on the species and their abilities." He willingly told me. "For you, we had the fence bathed in cleansing salt while it molded together."

"Cleansing salt?" I thought, still unable to talk. "You keep saying that, and yet I don't even know what it is?" Turning over to look at the man, I growled in the 'Canid' Language, desiring more answers which I knew this blabbering man would tell me.

Receiving nothing but a cold glare, the employer eventually told me, "Cleansing salt is what we have researched to be your suspected weakness. Which as you know every Breed and Species of Unnaturals have their own weaknesses, unfortunately. Due to you being a breed of Hellhound only to have been found documented in the earliest forms of literature, it was hard to come across any information, however noting that Hellhoundism is in a subcategory of Unnaturals belonging to the Demon Family my fellow researchers and I developed 'Cleansed Sodium', also known as Blessed Salt. The same salt that Priests and Mediums use to keep away Demons. Melting it down to the Atomic Level, we eventually figured out ways to use it in not only your bloodstream but also in your surroundings." The man answered, going into his scientific vocabulary that I had grown so used to hearing from my years of living in another Laboratory, although I did note that the mood here felt much more relaxed than the last place. "Based on how your body is currently reacting to the small dose of Salts we had given you, we can easily maintain control even without the help of the fence, but our Directors don't want you to receive a differential treatment than the other Unnaturals we have here."

"Do you ever shut up?" I grumbled, upset, and irritated.

"Back to what the rest of your 'first day' holds." The Doctor spoke, temporarily strolling away from the table. "Until they get that finished up, you, 0497 will remain on the table allowing me to get some fresh blood analysis, and some DNA testing done."

"Whatever." I sighed, again rolling my blue-eyes. Dropping my heavy head down on my front legs, I surveyed the men work at constructing that cage. Noticing out of the corner of my left eye this nameless doctor I had also been 'assigned' to step back up to the side of the metal table holding what looked like a metal comb of sorts. Feeling the teeth of the comb brush through my soft-medium length black fur and savagely pull away from the recently grown Winter coat hairs with the few strokes he made, I cringed in slight agony. Afterward, the allegedly high-ranked employee walked around the table. Stopping in front of my tired vision, he blocked my view of the builders and began to draw the required blood samples. Seeing the dark-red blood samples flee out the draining needle into the collecting vial, my thoughts aimlessly ventured around in my head. "Did Jakob and Mhykal get Yalu back home? Was she okay? Did the place they send her to cause any physical damage? Or any emotional damage? Did the Shadow keep his promise to me? Did he keep Yalu safe from harm? Did he keep Jakob and Mhykal safe from harm when they went to save her?" The faith in my friends potentially ever getting me out of this place remained headstrong in my heart, although simultaneous it began to wane with the rise of challenging doubts. I didn't know where here was. I didn't know how to get a single word out to them. All I knew was that I would have to keep my faith in them for as long as I could both mentally and physically endure. I had to stay stable and willing for as long as I could until my allies arrived.

"Alright, we are all done, for now, that is." The human who still wore his work attire voiced up. The sound of his voice snapping me out of my traveling thoughts, although I was uncertain to whom the conversation was directed. Exhaustingly observing him wrap my foreleg with some gauze to stop the busted vein from bleeding out, I wondered why my advanced healing powers were not stitching the damaged vein like it usually did. "The salts we previously injected into your bloodstream have slowed the Species's healing capabilities by over eighty-five percent. We already ran that test when you were unconscious and put it into consideration, when you busted your chin from your little fight with the multi-purpose guardsmen. Instead of your blood clotting at nearly five times the rate of human blood, it now clots at about fifteen percent faster than the average human blood cell. It's still impressive, although it is quite manageable." The Doctor continued as he finished bandaging up my front leg.

"Again, do you EVER SHUT-UP!?" I snapped, snarling under what I had heard was a uniquely designed muzzle. Apparently, it was mimic of the usual canine headcollar, or a horse's halter whose nylon material wrapped around my jaws and behind my ears. Wrapping around the muzzle was a thick buckle meant to tighten the restraint around my jowls, further constricting the use of my deadly fangs as a weapon. Eyeing the man walk out of my line of sight, I lied my head down again on top of my front paws, and returned to surveying the men work on putting up what looked like two more panels of seven-foot-tall chain-link fencing, to complete the assemble.

"Looks like they are almost done, 0497." The man continued to endlessly ramble on. My nose burning from his pungent cologne, I easily located where the talkative human had wandered off to. Standing off to the left side of this uncomfortable table, I uncontrollably eavesdropped on the conversation, "Once they are done, the transporters will move you from this table and into that kennel, where you will stay until we need you again."

"Great-" I groaned, rolling my eyes at him.

Finally finishing the 'kennel.' the Transporters came to retrieve me. One set of hands grabbing at a piece of my upper scruff right behind my clipped ears dragged my head painfully up, while the other guy snaked his hands underneath my neck and stomach. Once I had been lifted, the man let go of my scruff, allowing my exhausted head to fall back down and droop over his co-worker's bulky arm. Counting each notch of the concrete panels sliding by until I had been carried into this makeshift cage, I was roughly lain onto what felt like a well-used thin blanket. Barely able to move, I felt less and less like a human Unnatural with an ability of transformation and more like a mongrel stuck behind bars. I now felt more like those poor animals at the shelter waiting for someone to adopt them, for anyone to save them. Hearing the chain-link rattle when the gate's handle was clamped down, followed by what sounded like the links of a chain get wrapped and pulled through the chain-links poles, I quickly figured out that they were taking precautionary measures.

I delayed any purposeful actions pending the exit of the last man. After he had left, I initially attempted to situate a better position to which I could lie. Throwing my body backward, I harshly flung the tired frame onto the hard concrete. The blanket offered absolutely no comfort whatsoever. Unable to adapt as easily as I assumed, I weakly began maneuvering around for another comfortable position to lie myself in. Dragging my front legs to help my body sit back up and allow me to curl up into the canine fetal position. Resembling the typical fur ball shape, I locked my tail around my face, trying to use my long dewclaws to hopefully pull the head collar off from my jaws from underneath the shadows of my short black tail. However, my equilibrium felt bizarrely off, thwarting that plan. I knew that it had to do with the amount of this 'Salt' seeping through my veins, as well as the amount used in the molding process of this fence. Breathing a tiring sigh, I dragged my drugged body into a tighter circle, proceeding to rest my head now over my tail. Stalking the empty darkness, I counted the long passing minutes before eventually by natural laws of exhaustion I fell asleep.

Chapter 43
Cinder

Surprised by the jolting blinding lights turning on, I slowly opened my blue eyes to see who was it that had entered the large-sized concrete room. Counting two Transporters and another man that was dressed the same as that other irritating man yet smelled slightly different. Wearing the same white Doctor coat over his scrubs, I examined this Doctor strolling ahead of the transporters before stepping off into that side room. Curious, I lifted my head, slowly readjusting my slightly strengthening body to observe the actions this new Scientist/Doctor was doing.

A few short minutes went by before the guy strolled into the adjoining room. Walking up to the metal table that was about twelve steps outside of that side room, I overheard his low-lying masculine voice order the low-income brutes. "Get 0497 out." As he laid what appeared to be a towel over the soft white metal and again ran into the off-set room.

Straining my eyes over to the two lackeys who were coming closer to the makeshift 'kennel', each of them holding these strange poles in their hands, I forced myself up onto my tired feet. Prepared to argue my refusal once more, however as soon as my front legs vertically locked, my equilibrium broke. Collapsing onto the floor just as my sensitive hearing caught the sound of chain-links jangle, alerting me to the chain being fed out of the gate's post. Once more,

I attempted to stand as the flight instinct overrode the primary thoughts of my challenging debates. The minute the gate's latch was flipped horizontal, my heart rapidly raced, fueling my exhausted body with the adrenaline to get up. Again, I collapsed, falling back down onto the blanket-covered hard concrete floor with such force that I almost rolled completely over onto my back. It was here that I decided to temporarily submit. The scarce strength I had to argue with my equilibrium and simultaneously fight those guys had completely exhausted. Petrified, I glanced up at the two men who now stood over the top of me. Flattening my cropped ears as one of them pulled a small metallic wired loop over the top of my thick neck, I hastily found the energy to combat the tool's hold. Tossing my weakened physique around like a fish out of water, I stressed every manageable attempt to get free from them. While flinging my head around, unable to use my jaws thanks to their unusual contraption that restrained around my muzzle, I surveyed the patient men who awaited my submission. Which eventually I exasperated, tiring myself out. Unable to pant because of that same collar I swiftly became dizzy, seeing dots in my visionary path as my brain advised me to feed it oxygen. Collapsing onto the cold dark floor, its freezing temperatures cooling my warming physique the longer I lied there with the pole jamming deep into the side of my neck. Tracking the men's whereabouts still gravely panicked, I watched one of them stroll up to me. Observing him take out a nylon leash he then wrapped it around my back legs, pulling the clasp through the loop to tightly bind my legs together. Feeling the leash wrapped around a few more times until I felt the metal clasp get hauled tightly under the self-made restraint in between a small gap that my legs naturally molded around my canine-mutated ankles. Once my movement had been limited the utensil's tightened wire was removed from around my neck. Placing his latex-gloved hands underneath my body he then picked me up. Lifted off the ground, I tiredly drooped my head yet again viewing the concrete panels that passed by.

Released onto the towel-covered metal table, I noticed that there was a makeshift table adjacent to the one I had been put on, with a bunch of syringes and other tools lying on a blue cloth. Feeling the leash's clasp that was wrapped around my back legs get attached to some other clasp, further halting the use of my restrained legs. Inspecting the second brute human grab at the hard clasp ringlet underneath my muzzle, I saw a short leather lead come out of the edge of the metal table and get tied to the head collar. Restraining my head from also being of any use while I lied on my side, my stomach completely exposed to this newer doctor.

"0497 is all ready to go." I heard one of these multi-tasked guards smirk.

"Okay, then go sit in the other room, I will call you once I am done." The Doctor demanded, slipping on the identical white latex gloves his co-workers were wearing. Waiting until the two men had closed the door attached to the small side room before he continued. "Alright 0497, I have no right to tell you who I am, but I am not that kind of guy. My name is Dr. Melundanz." The Doctor politely introduced, making me feel unusually confused. Glancing at him from above my lower eyelid, I saw this very skinny slender man with Hispanic skin-tone, pitch-black hair, and bright green-hazel eyes stare down at the number of liquid-filled syringes. "I will be taking over for Dr. Thompson while he is out on family leave. You sure did give him hell yesterday." Doctor Melundanz chuckled, picking up one of the syringes. "First, I will be giving you another small dose of a muscle relaxant sedative." Injecting the needle into my front leg, it's liquid being pushed by the syringe as it drained throughout my entire system. "That should take less than ten seconds before it starts to work."

"I know how it works." I groaned to the young Doctor. "Do you all talk so much? Does it make you feel better about how you are treating the Unnaturals whom you keep imprisoned here if you explain it all or something like that?"

Feeling my restrained back legs relax under the effects of the medications, I continued to hear the Doctorate Scientist speak. "Now that that is in effect, I am going to give you a Pheromone Upper." Picking up the second syringe filled with more clear liquid obviously labeled something different, the man again injected the needle into approximately the same location as the last drug. Hastily overcome by the rush of pheromones seeping throughout my bloodstream, I began to feel the effects of the second drug. I could sense my blood start to clot, forming on the outskirts of my canine front legs. With no control over the spawning blades as they formed out of my wrists, I unconsciously molded the Blood Cells together. "Alright, that was fast." Doctor Melundanz surprisingly spoke, following up with another injection. The drug this time seizing the pheromone creation in my bloodstream. "Now with the blocker in you 0497, I can collect some samples from those sharp blades."

"Is that even possible?" I confusingly snarled. Thanks to the Pheromone Blockers now combating the Uppers in my bloodstream, I could not retract the Blood Scythes. And because of the irritating sedative, I could not effectively use my body's muscles either.

Fearfully observing the scrawny doctor pick up what looked like a small scalpel from the table, I could feel my heartbeat start racing even faster than normal. I could also oddly feel the small surgical tool begin to cut strongly through the blood made scythe. "Even under the Sedative, and Blessed Salts in your system this blood is very dense. Its ability to clot is astonishing." The man complimented, pushing more force into slicing away at a small section of the first blade. Even under the relaxant, I could still feel the blade cutaway into the clotted blood. Producing the sensation of ripping into my flesh, a feeling I had been through many times prior. Yelping in pain, I threw my restrained body around, doing whatever I could to slip away even though I knew it was pointless. Once one piece was finally retrieved out of the blood made weapons, the Doctor then dropped the still clotted mass into a small petri dish for later examination. "All right, now that all that's done." Feeling his hand rub along the side of my stomach, running through the black fur. "Only one more

237

needle prick and then we can send you back to the kennel for now." I could hear the man smirk, his hand clutching the only syringe left. This one was full of a semi-murky clear liquid. Injecting it into my front leg, he explained, "This is the Blessed Salts. Once inside your system, it will allow those blood scythes to de-clot." The heavy liquid sodium rushed through my overworked bloodstream and instantly I felt sick while the scythes began to separate from my wrists. Not having enough control over the blood, I watched as just like in my training, the blood drop onto the towel. The bath towel easily soaking up the thick blood red cells. From there, I felt the man's short fingers prod around each one of my front legs to make sure there were no open wounds left from my abilities. Overhearing him relieve a heavy exhale, I observed the Doctor remove his latex gloves. "We are all done for now. I have to run these samples up to the lab, so I will be seeing you later 0497."

Chapter 44

Cinder

"0497." I heard a muffled voice call. The lights flickering back on, blinding me for a few seconds. "Time to eat-" one of the incoming humans said, while a total of three men entered the bland room. I could smell a strong stench of blood and meat coming from the inside of a large, metal dog bowl one of the men was carrying. The closer they got to the kennel, the stronger the scent became. Stopping at the kennel's gate, I hesitated my next set of actions. I was unsure if I should trust them or if I should fight them. Remaining on top of the blanket, still lying on my stomach, I avidly watched them, recalling that I had not a single ounce of strength thanks to those 'Salts'. The element turned drug was throwing off everything from my equilibrium, to my heightened senses, and even my increased ability to heal and recover.

One by one, the three guys strolled into the makeshift kennel, and once they were all inside, I heard one of the other employees speak, "This is how it works, we will release the muzzle from the head collar, from there, you will have ten minutes to eat your meal. Whether or not you choose to not eat is up to you, but you will only get fed twice a day. However, if you turn down an entire week of food, we will resort to force-feeding you. If you try to attack anyone of the employees that come and go from here on out, while your muzzle is off you lose both of your meals for the entire day. Depending on the damage you do, you can lose an entire week of

239

meals, or you will be force-fed until the Doctors believe your behavior has changed." Digesting these 'rules' that were being explained, I pulled my ears flat against my skull. Observing one of the men step closely up towards my side, kneeling beside me, I pushed myself away unsure of what to do. I did not want to submit, but I accepted his hands, grasping at my jaws to start unbuckling the muzzle. Feeling my jaws move again, I stalked the man who was carrying what I could only assume was one of my two daily meals.

The sweet fragrance overpowering my blurred sense of smell, I perceived my stomach bark at me, ordering me to take advantage of the free meal. Preying the man who slowly put the dish down in front of my long legs, I gradually crawled towards the food dish, my body acting purely on instinct. I hadn't eaten raw meat at all since I had obtained these abilities, nor had I ever eaten Venison in my entire life. Guided by the aroma, I ignored the rational hesitation and the appearance, obeying my stomach's commands. Chomping down onto the fresh meat, my fangs eagerly ripping into the flesh, splashing a few droplets of blood onto my palate, my stomach raved for more. As I ate the meal, I proceeded with protecting my food from these goonies, weakly standing on my four feet, I continued to devour the two pounds of raw meat, my tongue getting a waft of cooked rice every so often, although the flavor began to taste stranger the more I ate. Ignoring the feeling, I quickly completed my meal, before falling back down onto the concrete and licking the blood away from my lips. 'Allowing' the same guy to start wrapping the muzzle back around my jaws again. Locking my jaws together, yet keeping them loose enough to not give me lockjaw.

Surveying the guys leave the cage taking the bowl away as well, I observed them pull the chain through the gate to lock me inside the kennel once more before they departed from the concrete room with the naturally dimming fluorescent lights. Dropping my head into my paws, I stared into the low light darkness, wondering if the friends I had made at the Syndicate were still fighting to liberate me.

After what felt like several hours alone in the dark, the blinding lights came back on. Dancing back the shadows, I again had to adjust to the insane brightness those industrial lights gave off. Once I wasn't seeing spots, I watched another three men come in. Two of them were the same brute transporters, while the third guy I could only assume was Doctor Meludanz. As the Doctor slipped into the side room to begin to fish for his tools and equipment, getting them set up for whatever was planned next, the guards approached the 'kennel' this time without the catch poles in hand. The men did not waste any time, swiftly entering the cage and tightly grabbing at my scruff to carry me back over to that metal table. And this time around I was just too tired, too fatigued to fight. Placed on the metal table, I watched as one of the Transporters again tied down my head, clasping the head collar to the lead attached over the edge of the table.

"Is she ready?" I heard Doctor Meludanz shout from inside the side room.

"Just about. Do you want her tied completely to the table?" One of the humans shouted back.

"If she fights me for this, then I will ask for your guys' help." The hazel-eyed Doctor said stepping out of the side room a few minutes later. "Alright, everything is set up in here."

"In there?" I thought unable to crane my head and observe everything.

"Alright." The guards said, both agreeing. Overhearing a clicking noise, I felt the table jerk as if a brake had been released. Shifted around only worsened the nausea, as the table was drug out from my assigned room into this adjacent room. From where I lied restrained, I made out tall cabinets full of thousands of drugs and vials, several syringes, medical kits, and other unknown equipment. Along that same wall, I noted a kitchen sink with both paper towels and cloth towels sitting on the same counter space. Wheeled around, I saw that along the opposite wall was more cabinets, however full of more restraints such as collars, head collars, wrist and ankle shackles, chains, blindfolds, gags, as well as I.V. bags full of what smelled like various kinds of medications and hydrants. When the vehicle came to a stop, I again felt the brake get locked. My physique being jerked simultaneously with the table.

"0497, we have found a particularly important component in the construction of your Blood Scythes. That composition allows a certain degree of change to happen in the makeup of your blood cells." Doctor Meludanz said as he stood over me again, wearing the same white latex gloves. Grabbing the I.V. needle, he began to prepare my canine leg for the massive needle to get jammed into one of my larger leg/arm veins. "Dammit, I'll need to shave your fur away so I can get a good vein." Putting the needle down onto the table he then walked over to the counters full of tools and picked up an electric razor. Coming back to the table he started up the battery-run razor and began to lightly press the shears against my short black and tan fur, shaving away the hairs in a short yet wide strip. Exposing one of the larger artery veins in the legs. Dropping the razor down on the table he again picked up the needle, "Alright, here we go." Jabbing the I.V. needle into my leg, he accurately tapped the vein. "Hand me the I.V. bag." The Doctor ordered his lackeys. One of them swiftly handed the bag over to Doctor Meludanz, who then set the drip up to a hanging hook before connecting the bag to the corresponding needle. Grabbing a sedative, he swiftly emptied the drug into the same protruding vein. Injecting the medication directly above the I.V. needle's location. "We had to wait a full eight hours after her breakfast before we could even think about this." I heard the man complain as the sedative started to take over my already exhausted figure. Fighting complete exhaustion, I now overheard the conversation change directives, the tones changing. The men beginning to converse dialogue as if I were no longer conscious.

"So, why are we doing this again?" I perceived one of the men inquire his superior.

"Due to the genetic makeup that allows 0497 to create the nearly indestructible clotted blood cells into those Scythes that Doctor Thompson and I have now both seen in person, the Directors and Researchers believe that if we can further analyze the composition of her blood cells, we can hopefully figuring out how to create a Super Human without making them Unnatural, possibly further allowing us to advance our country and world with both sound Medical Science and Warfare." The Doctor returned, answering in complicated scientific vocabulary, "In the end, everyone agreed to start running some trials, and if they turn out positive, then we can get some heavy funding for this project. However, the only way to get a decent start on these 'trials' is if we harvest an extended portion of her blood."

"Harvest-?" I shockingly questioned myself. The theories running rampant in my head hastily infuriated me. The thought of being used as nothing more than an extinguishable Vessel, filled me with enough rage to again fight. Forced myself to stand up, I surprisingly managed to get my hindquarters up before I was thwarted by the restrained head collar. Pulling against the muzzle, I attempted my best to slip out from that horrible jaw-locking contraption.

"Dammit!" The Doctor snapped. "Looks like we will have to restrain her."

I could feel two sets of large manly hands grab at my scruff and grab at my flank, I howled out my act of surprise. Growling from under the muzzle, I still fought my hardest to stay up on my feet. After a long minute had passed, my legs gave out from directly underneath me. The strong weight of their heavy arms crashing down on top of me. Again, savagely screaming out in pain, just as the sound of something snapped under the crushing weight of their strong hands. I could feel my lungs heave for air the minute they lifted themselves off the top of the left side of my ribcage.

243

"Dammit!" Doctor Meludanz snarled aloud. His voice sounding full of rage. "Well, we can't restrain her chest now. You damn idiots broke some of her ribs."

"Sorry-" One of the guys apologized.

"Just get me an intubation tube now! We will have to help her breathe while we continue to harvest some of her blood, and she heals."

"My ribs are broke?" I cried, my body again wreathing in pain. "My back was still sore from the massive burning I suffered from the day I was transported here. Now I had to heal some broken ribs while these horrible human researching scientists were going to 'harvest' who knows how much of MY blood." Hardly managing to find the strength to get back up, I decided to argue my refusal.

"No, no, no." The Doctor snapped, quickly holding my body down, his lighter weight pushing down on my snapped, yet already trying to repair ribs.

Coming crashing back down onto the metallic table, I was forced to give up just as the sedative finally drew my last conscious breath. Closing my eyes, I slipped away in the yet again drug-induced slumber, thinking to myself, "How long was I going to be out? Would my friends finally get me out of here? Was this how I was going to be meet my end?"

Chapter 45

Jakob

It had been almost a month since Yalu and Cinder had been captured by Hunters. Although we had thankfully saved Yalu before anything had gotten seriously bad, we had yet to save our Hellhound friend. I remained at a loss the longer we went without knowing where the Hunters had taken her off to. I often found myself just staring at her bedroom door, expecting her to open up the door dressed and ready for the day's breakfast that Yalu had made, but I knew that there was no one on the other side of that door. I did not want to think of her being gone, however, I could not shake the feeling I had lost her. The feeling that we had lost her. Mhykal was also taking it quite hard. We would end up finding him staring out into the Garden, just endlessly staring into the horizon. When I had asked him one day what he was doing, I remember him turning to me and telling me that he reminisced the memory of watching Cinder and Yalu out sparring in the grass, hearing their laughs, and Yalu's snotty comebacks to Cinder's childish sneers. However, out of the three of us that were close to the twenty-four-year-old Hellhound, it was truly Yalu who was taking it the hardest. She had tried to put up a front for the longest time, but according to Mhykal and Valeryie they would often find the Vixen in either her room or in Cinder's room crying. They wouldn't try to comfort her for fear of her hasty judgment, yet they all felt the same. We all missed her. We desperately wanted her back with us, back under the safe sanction of the Manor.

"Hey Jakob, Braedon wants to see us," Mhykal said, coming down the corridor to retrieve me for our Syndicate Leader. "You know staring at that door won't bring her back anytime soon?" He heaved a sigh noticing that I was again staring at Cinder's dark Victorian wood-paneled bedroom door.

"I know that." I snapped back before following up with a depressing sigh of my own. "Why does Braedon want to see us?" I questioned, trying to change the subject and distract myself.

"It's about the next Raid, I guess we managed to get the Syndicates to collaborate with us on this one," Mhykal responded while we started our stroll over to the study. "Yalu and Viktor are already upstairs waiting on us."

"Okay." I exhaled. We had gone ahead with the newly constructed Government Based Institution Raid, putting the rescue of Cinder on hold or so it seemed by everyone else's eyes except for Braedon's that is. I still believed he was hiding something from us about Cinder, but no matter how much I had tried to get it out of him, I couldn't get the old Vampiric to talk. It was infuriating the longer we had gone without a single clue about her whereabouts ever surfacing, and I felt that her faith in us was dwindling the longer she also waited on us to come save her. I just had that gut-wrenching feeling.

"We will find her." Mhykal softly moaned as we ascended the staircase closest to the Study. "I promise you that, Jakob."

"I know we will find her, Mhykal," I answered, finally reaching the double doors to the Study. "It's just the case of when. I don't know what to do if we end up finding her in the SAME condition as the last time or if we find her worse off than then. I don't know how I will react if I see her that way-"

"Jakob, I know how you will act and if it is that bad, both Yalu and I will back you up one hundred percent of the way. Cinder is all of our friend, even though I think you are feeling more for her."

"You may very well be right," I said, opening the doors to the large Study where we usually met up with our Leader to converse about the upcoming Raids and Events. Putting up my customary laid-back front, I walked inside the room, hiding deep down in my heart that continued to heavily ache for our missing friend.

"Alright now that everyone is here," Braedon spoke, his tone sounding frustrated by something unusual. "We can finally get started."

"What is it?" I growled back.

"Well Jakob, plans are for tomorrow to go meet up with Calem and Saylene and start configuring a plan to quickly dismantle the Institute and free those Unnaturals."

"Is that all?" I retorted with the same irritated tone.

"Jakob?" I heard Yalu softly inquire, the tone of her question full of concern and sympathy. She knew exactly how I was feeling. Everyone here was feeling the exact same way.

"No, it is not all I have to say." Braedon snapped back at me, locking our gazes in a long staredown. Breaking first, I straightened my back up while listening to his rant about my behavior. "Look, I know life has gotten rough without Cinder being here at the Manor, and you guys are taking the brunt of it all, however, I promise you, we will find her eventually." Braedon paused. "For now, she is not-"

"No, according to you she isn't the top priority!" I snapped, clenching my fists as I proceeded to challenge him.

"Our goal is to save all the Unnaturals from these-"

"Don't give that Goal shit to me! I am all for saving the Unnaturals from the abuse that Humans have given them as well as all the tiring shit they give us. When Mhykal and I left to save Yalu, there were at least seventy new patients at the same place we had

247

gotten Cinder the first time! WHAT THE HELL DOES THAT TELL YOU?! We have not gotten anywhere with our goal!"

"We have accomplished much in the years that our Syndicates have been around!" Braedon snapped. "You should know that because you have been here the longest out of your little tight clique."

Using my supernatural speed, I swarmed the old suit-wearing Vampiric, grabbing the collar of his shirt will both of my hands, I pushed him flat against the arched floor to ceiling window, "Don't tell me about what I should know and what we have accomplished here!" I growled. Forcing the man to stare down at me, I proceeded to hold him up with one of my hands, "I have been the one down in the grind, seeing all those people suffering from their abuse in person! I have seen all their pain with my very own eyes, but I have never seen someone who has gone through as much pain as that woman has! It took her an entire year to warm up to us, too finally trust one of her own kin, and yet I get the damn feeling that you are hiding something about Cinder. Getting this feeling deep fucking down that all you care about is the number of places we shut down, the number of people we save, and the number of Raids we have on top of the other Syndicates!" Dragging our Syndicate Leader off the window, I turned around and threw him down the center of the Study. "You not once saw the pain she was in even after we had brought her home! YOU DON'T GET THAT THE LONGER WE WAIT TO TRY AND LOCATE WHERE SHE IS BEING HELD, THAT WE ARE ALSO BEING TESTED BY HER!" I snapped at him. Walking around the desk, passing by him I snarled, "YOU ARE THE LAST PERSON WHO SHOULD BE TELLING ME HOW TO ACT!" Stopping at the door of the Study, I ended the conversation with a heavy snarl, "I will help you and the other Syndicates free those Unnaturals, but until that day comes I don't want to be notified of anything else Braedon unless it is about Cinder. Until then you can kiss my ass."

Chapter 46
Jakob

Storming out of the Study, slamming the doors shut on my way out, I went back to my bedroom. Again, slamming the door shut with such force it rattled the old Victorian Windows. Taking my short-tailed black leather jacket off, I hurled it on the bed before throwing my back against the door. Crashing to the floor, I grabbed my head and screamed out my flurrying frustrations, cursing out my hatred for Braedon, my hatred for the Humans, the Hunters, the Institutes.

"I am so tired of living this game," I said aloud to myself. Leaning my dark-brown haired head against the door, I continued to quietly complain to myself, "It never used to be that way. It wasn't until those damn idiots decided to create their little Sanctuary groups that all these places started to pop up." Looking up at the dark ceiling I changed the subject on myself, "I just want to find you, Cinder, I just want to see those brilliant blue eyes of yours again. I just want to see you again."

"Jakob?" I heard Yalu ask from the other side of the door. "Are you okay?"

Opening my eyes, I once more stared up at the ceiling debating on how to answer her call. "Yeah, I am okay." I breathed.

"Are you sure?" She asked. I could overhear her shuffle around on the other side of the door before I felt her back push against the wood paneling. "You did lose your temper."

"Yeah, I guess I did. I just needed a moment to myself."

"Do you love her?" Yalu bluntly questioned me straight out of nowhere. The tone in her voice sounding softer than usual, still raspy but more mother-like.

I didn't know how to answer that. I had been in love before but only a couple of times in my entire immortal lifespan and it has never felt like this. I didn't know how to explain it this time.

After a pause, I heard Yalu softly chuckle, "Yeah you love her. But so, do I." she spoke. "It's hard not to fall in love when she became a member of our family. But-but you truly care for her just as much as Mhykal does for me."

Understanding the metaphor, I banged my head against the door before I exhaled, "Yeah I guess I did act the same way he did when we found out you two had been taken by the Hunters."

Seconds of pure silence went by before I heard Yalu shuffle around again from the other side of the door, "Jakob, let me in please." The Vixen suddenly pleaded.

Standing myself up, I put my hand on the brass doorknob, twisting it, I swung open the door to see the Caucasian black-haired, amber-eyed Vixen staring straight at me. Running into my chest she swathed her arms around my back, tightly clutching my shirt. Perceiving the change in her voice from the comforting motherly woman to the defeated and depressed Vixen, I looked down to see her head pressing deeply into my upper chest. "I miss her so much, Jakob." She cried.

Returning her hug, I firmly wrapped my arms around her, our silence the only comfort I needed. The pure silence uttered our feelings for our missing friend, for Cinder. We all greatly missed her, and yes, Yalu was right it was hard to not fall in love with her. A

Hellhound with a pure white, childish soul. Completely misunderstood. Finally finding the words, I heard my voice break under the sadness and tears. "You're right I do love her, Yalu."

Overhearing her tenderly chuckle before breaking our hug after a long-standing, I watched her wipe away the straining tears. "Then when we finally get her back to us, tell her." She told, giving me one of her typical happy smiles.

Looking down at her I rubbed my eyes, trying to rid my face of the saddened emotional characteristics. "I will tell her when we finally find and free her. I will tell Cinder how I feel."

"You better, or I will kick your ass." The old snotty Yalu returned. Putting her emotions back in check. "And I think I might remember some of those Hunters having a small conversation here and there." The Vixen then casually exclaimed. Closing the door to my bedroom, she continued to speak, "When the drugs finally wore themselves out of my system, I began to slowly recall little details about the event."

"So, you think you might know a local vicinity of where they could have taken her?" I pleaded feeling my own 'dead' heart lively skip. "What do you remember?"

"I don't recall every little detail-" Yalu said, folding her arms under her breasts.

"Please tell me what you do remember." I urged, however, trying to keep my distance from the Vixen, so I didn't overburden her. "Anything at all will help us out. Yalu please."

"I think they said something about going somewhere in Colorado." She finally answered, persuaded by my eager pleas. "I don't know where exactly, but knowing the way these places tend to be in plain sight- It's"

"I doubt they sent her to a regular Institute out of the State," I said, falling on the red comforter draped over my queen-sized bed.

"It was a Government base. I do remember those asses conversing with one another as they drugged her before took off in that plane."

"Knowing those guys, if it's like the base we are going after in Maine, it is secluded from the eyes of the public." I sighed, pausing for a glimpsing moment. "So, Colorado?"

"I heard them say that before the plane took off in a westerly direction."

Rushing Yalu, I wrapped my arms around her, hugging her very tightly while trying to not get over emotional again. "Thank you. Thank you, Yalu." Breaking away, I then grabbed my suitcase and began to fill it up with some extra clothes.

"Jakob-" Yalu interrupted. "Jakob wait!"

"There is no time." I returned, packing some of my jeans into the black suitcase. "I need to start scouting the state."

"NO! You need to wait a minute!" Watching the Vixen close the top of my suitcase and stand on it in her small petite Fox form, baring her small sharp teeth. "Wait a god damn minute! Yes, I told you that piece of information, but it was to help you calm down. We need to finish our business here first-"

"It's more like Braedon's business. He just bosses us around while he sits inside that damn room!" I snarled, my glare staring down at the black two-tailed fox.

"I see what you are saying, however, Cinder would want us to help all those people, then find her and save all those people that are also imprisoned beside her," Yalu growled back; her huge Fox ears folded flat against her small skull. "You know that is exactly what she would have told us."

Calming myself down, I bit my lower lip knowing that Yalu was exactly right. I could see that very mature Hellhound telling us exactly that same thing. Imagining her soft femininely maturing voice telling us everything word to word. "Yeah you are right, she would have said that." I eventually answered back, agreeing with her. "But I don't feel right just letting her sit and wait on us any longer-"

"And neither do I-" Yalu said, altering the forms again. Proportionally sitting on the suitcase in her human form now. "But I told her to keep her faith in you two that day. And knowing Cinder, she will hold onto that faith because that is the kind of person she is. She trusts in us, because we all made such a strong effort to not only build a relationship with her but to also create that trust." The Vixen exhaled with a heavy sigh. "Now we need to stay focused on the Raid we got first, then after that, the three of us will go together to scout out that base and try to find her."

"Yeah-okay." I agreed, acting as if I was a saddened child that didn't get his toy. "But I still don't want anything to DO with that asshole right now."

"No, you won't have to deal with them. Mhykal and I will let you in on the plans the closer we get to the day."

Chapter 47
Cinder

"Alright 0497, time to wake up-" I heard Doctor Meludanz speak, his voice ringing through my ears. His fingers trying to pry my eyes open. "Come on 0497, you need to wake up now." The Doctor continued. Growling at him, I slowly started to open my eyes back up, the feeling in my body returning. "There you are." He heaved with an elongated sigh of relief. "You stopped breathing for a few seconds there." Plopping down on the little wheeled stool, I faintly saw his silhouette move around.

"What happened?" I questioned my thoughts. I remember having my ribs broken, right before they were going to attempt to 'harvest' my blood. I recalled becoming overrun with exhaustion, but I had not a clue as to what was happening. "I know where I am; but what happened?"

"We had to intubate you to help you breathe while you were under the anesthesia." The man continued to tell me, explaining or more like rambling on about what had happened. I wanted to know, but the confusing way these people were acting made me wish they would just shut up. "You had three broken ribs and two more fractured. They healed on their own with your healing capabilities, but of course, we had to help them along the way. So, that was why we had to intubate you."

"How long was I out?" I now requested, having some of the other questions answered. Getting filled in on exactly what had happened after I had been put into yet again another drug-induced sleep.

"After you had gone unconscious, we harvested your blood for the first set of trials, which are going pretty well now I have to add. We might need more after a while, but we will wait until you've recovered some more."

"Is she ready to go back now?" I heard someone else ask. Barely able to move my head accurately around, I waited till the man came into my line of sight. Seeing it was the other higher-ranked Doctor, Thompson, I believed his name was. "Hey there 497," he smiled, pressing his usual hands-on my fur. "You were out for a while-"

"Awhile is putting it into a different category, it was only two weeks. " Doctor Meludanz snarled back to his co-worker. "She will need to be observed over the next week-"

"But she can go back to her kennel?"

"Yes, I suppose she could if you keep her I.V. steady and her stats up."

"Good, alright go ahead and take her back." My sensitive hearing perceived the brunette Doctor hastily order what I assumed were those same transporters. Watching the Hispanic Doctor Meludanz begin to unhitch an I.V. bag from its stationary post to one of those hooked mobile posts.

"She is ready to go."

"Good, move her now."

Feeling a transporter slither his hands under my fur, putting them under my stomach in front of my back legs and under my chest behind my front legs, I felt his hands cup my body, dragging my frame upwards. Angrily whining, I pathetically let them carry me back to that makeshift kennel. Surveying the tile floor pattern convert over to the concrete paneling, I counted the footsteps made in my head, in an attempt to wake myself up. The minute we had walked into the blessed salt-soaked kennel, the man carrying my limp build slowly placed me on the unfolded large full-sized blanket. The softness of the old blanket along the hard-concrete floor somehow a much more comforting feeling to me than I last remembered. Still, nothing compared to the bed I had back at the Manor, but regardless of its comforts, it was better than that hard table I had been sleeping on for two full weeks.

With the men finishing up my I.V. placement, one of them began the process of reapplying the headcollar's muzzle around my jaws. Securely buckling the straps, forcing my jaws to lock back up. Repeatedly unable to fight back, I continued to let them do their means of keeping control over me. Completing their orders, the transporters left the kennel, closing the gate, feeding the chain-lock back through the fence's two posts to lock me inside, before they left the room entirely.

Watching the two buddy-buddy unusual doctors coming out of that little side medical room, I eavesdropped in on their conversation:

"So, what are your plans for 0497 now, Meludanz?"

"Well if the results of those trials come out as good as the initial start, then by the end of next month we will again harvest another couple quarts of her blood." I overheard Doctor Meludanz answer his co-worker. "Until then, we will just keep an eye on her. Continue with the Blockers, Sedatives, and the salts. The Directors want some more tests done on her for further analysis of this Breed of Species she is, so I guess we could get a start on that as well."

"Nothing unusual." I complained, attempting to block out the thought of going through another 'harvesting'. Testing was still just as bad, but now being used for my Blood Abilities felt more abusive in my opinion.

"We could get a start on those, but for now let us give her some space to finish coming out of anesthesia and recover from her intubation. Probably start those tests in a few days." Doctor Thompson spoke up again. Viewing them both staring down the room past the chain-link fence and directly at me as I lied on my side on top of the blanket. "Besides, it will give me some time to finish catching up on some of the other Unnaturals I had been assigned to before I had to go on 'Family Leave'."

"About that," Melundanz sneered, "You owe me big time for some of those troublemakers. I know that 0497 has some history of putting up a rough fight, but she is much more adaptable than most of the other Unnaturals here." He continued still maintaining that irritating smirk as they now both left the room, leaving me to be watched under the supervision of the low light high-definition cameras variously put up in several spots. Leaving me alone in the dimly lit room, so I could have the chance to rebuild my strengths from the other side of this cursed fence. Resting my somehow still weary form, I easily drifted back off into a naturally induced slumber.

Six feedings had passed, and I had regained much of my available strength well at least as much of it that those creeps had allowed me to have. My equilibrium was still off thanks to being locked inside this makeshift kennel molded with blessed salts. I had also continuously day after day received Pheromone blockers to retain the un-allowed amount of strengths on the down-low. This was heir attempt to preserve THEIR control over me while also keeping me alive for the use of 'Harvesting'. With time passing, I found it harder to maintain my faith in my friends coming to rescue me. Although, with no available strength left in me to fight, I had nothing else to put my faith in. I had to stay faithful, just to stay sane I had to keep telling myself that my friends were working their hardest to liberate me from this horrible place.

On the fourth morning around the time I had usually received my breakfast meal, I saw the brunette-haired Doctor Thompson and his usual low ranked co-workers stroll in. Remembering that there were plans in place to run some tests for my Species Breed. While the transporters entered the kennel, repeating the same pickup and drop off, I noticed that the Doctor was still in the side room collecting whatever tools he was going to need.

When Thompson left the adjoining room, I had my headcollar restrained as well as my stomach and chest with base leather straps from what they felt like. Unable to freely move, I wearyingly listened to what he said, "0497, those samples that we had run on your first day here they did come back indeed as a type of Hellhoundism, however, your hair samples nor blood matched with any breeds we've had documented in the last hundred years our industry has been documenting your kind. So, we looked back into your file and saw that the Researchers at your old Hospital clarified you as an Infernus Cannus Umbras or a Hellhound of Shadows. Giving you the that Breed Name because of your relationship with the Blood Moon, and the proclaimed documented sightings of a Shadowed Skeleton." Doctor Thompson told, sticking my leg with the draining needle to draw a small amount of my blood from my worn veins for more samples. "And although all of that has been documented as well as your available powers, and we have found ways to keep you under control, we still don't know anything at all about your breed." The man expressed, changing out the first vial with a second. "So that's why we need to do more testing. If we can figure out your entire identity as a Hellhound of Shadows, we can hopefully figure out why all of a sudden at this point in time, a new breed such as yours has popped up out of nowhere." Switching out the second vial with an empty third, the rambling succeeded, "When you were first documented at eight years old, our Directors wanted your parents also tested to see if there was the chance a family of Unnaturals was flying under the radar. Imagine our surprise when your parents' tests came back negative, and their religious beliefs left them believing they had been cursed by Satan-"

"My religious parents had believed I had become possessed by a Demon, morphing me into a Hellhound." I thought in my head, flashing back to a memory of their argument with Doctor Masters about bringing in a priest for an exorcism.

"Then shortly after that, they ended up signing away their parental rights to their only daughter when she was the tender age of eight." Thompson endlessly voiced, finally removing the draining needle and starting to bandage up my arm once more. Trying to hold in my anger and pain when that happened, I felt my eyes start to water, drenching the black fur under my clear blue eyes. "Sorry, if I hit a nerve I can only imagine what you had gone through, but think of it this way, if we can figure out how you had gone from a human to an Unnatural in one night, through that same research we can stop this from happening to another family."

"Right-" I snarled in my head, my emotions turning to frustration. "All you humans want is to keep using me as a 'Vessel' for my blood for your Government-funded Research. Wasting both Human and Free Unnaturals' money on this pointless crap." Institutes were the same no matter what this man had previously explained. Recalling that Thompson had explained the Hospital Institute I was previously a patient at was trying to find a way to subdue my Hellhoundism, to potentially return me to society; I debated the truth in his words because not once did Masters ever say was for my benefit. No, he often told me it was for the benefit of this 'Government.' It did not matter the difference between these two 'Facilities; Unnaturals were the ones that made the sacrifices as prisoners for the same old lie. "Everything was the same again. Nothing had changed at all-" I thought my mind heading off again into the unstable mentality it always wandered off into when I began doubting the ability to see life outside the four walls. Swiftly halting myself from traveling that deep down into the endless abyss, I reminded myself, I needed to stay strong until my friends had found me. "Stay strong." I now commanded myself as I was being returned to the fangs of the kennel. "I have to keep believing that they were going to find me, that they were going to save me."

Chapter 48
Jakob

Another entire month had passed before I knew it, adding thirty days onto the thirty that had already passed. Life had only gotten harder for me to continue living after I had come clean about my feelings for her. My usual routine had only become harder to deal with, however as hard as it was, I clung to Yalu's words to Cinder of maintaining the Hellhound's trust in us. I clung to them so strongly, I knew that I couldn't give up on her, because she was expecting us to burst through the door of wherever she was being held. Cinder was expecting us to save her, and that encouraged my faith.

"Jakob focus!" Mhykal shouted at me as we ran through the long dimly lit corridor. Blindly dodging flying bullets, I observed my comrade overthrow one of the guards located at that Government Institute we were currently raiding. "Just remember we get this done without getting killed, and we can head out for Colorado." The Vampiric voiced, reminding me of the plans that we had discussed earlier.

Punching one of the other men in the face, I grabbed his gun, swung it over my leg with such force I snapped its military-grade enforcement in half. Glancing back at him, I smiled as he decked the last guard on our designated level.

"That was the last one." Mhykal panted, straightening his stance. "We need to get these doors open, and clear the rest of this level so we can start escorting these Unnaturals out."

Sighing a heavy breath, I spoke up, "The sooner we can get this done and over with, the sooner we can go save Cinder." Urging my priority, I used my gifted abilities and commenced with unlocking these 'top'-security panels that were locking away these poor souls. Quickly running through room after room, we cleaned out every room on this floor. Indeed, running into some Immortals who dated as far back as the fifteenth century, even running into an Immortal that dated further back than the eleventh century. It was surprising to know that here stateside we had Immortals who were older than the age of the country itself. As I opened the last door on the panel, I began to count the heads. "All twenty-four are accounted for," I reported back to our checkpoint through my Bluetooth Earpiece. "We are now returning to base."

"Alright, Jakob. You got clearance, please report back to S2." Yalu answered me, speaking through her earpiece.

"Alright everyone," I called to the group of Unnaturals who were either in their changeling forms, or were dressed in a straight white hospital-like surgical gown. Some were dressed in bandages. Some were still wearing collars and tags that neither one of us Rebels could break loose. Catching their attention, I softly ordered, "We will be heading out, please follow Mhykal." I announced, pointing at my comrade who gingerly smiled back to the traumatized Unnaturals. "I will round up the back of the group. We will make sure that you all make it to the outside world."

Watching the dark-haired Vampiric push his way through and start to lead the Unnaturals away, I quickly followed in behind keeping prying eyes on all slower and more-drugged patients of my kindred cousins. Ensuring my promise. Swiftly noticing one of the elder Immortals steadily creep up beside me, I inquired, "What is it what you want?" Trying to not sound harsh when I truly wanted to be left alone.

261

"I can smell your troubled mind even through whatever drugs they had given me." I overheard the bipedal black-furred Pharaoh-Hound/Jackal Cross tell. I did not want to say he was a Were-Creature, but he sure as hell looked like one. His amber-red eyes gleaming back at me with an unusually familiar toothy smirk I had not seen since Cinder was in my life. "I have smelled it before, Vampire."

"Oh, then you tell me what you think?" I inquired, staring up into his smoldering eyes from his impress seven-foot height.

"To my belief, based on years of experience, you are doubting your faith. You are doubting what to do with yourself." The hound answered, his tone trying to retain tranquility.

"Well you would be right, I guess." I sighed as we started to regroup with another group of Rebels, the ones from Saylene's Draconic Syndicate. "I am indeed full of doubt."

"And love."

That callout shocked me. How could he have caught onto my emotions that accurately? Unsure how to answer that, I remained silent.

"I've been alive for centuries, and in that existence, I have seen those same furrowed brows and darkened thoughts of doubt. You are in love with someone and this person does not yet know, nor is that same person within reach or contact." The elderly Were-Animal rambled on, stating every known detail about my current situation in such few words. "You also believe that this person is in great harm."

"Yeah, who are you?" I hastily requested the Unnatural, having enough of him telling me about what was going on in my 'life' without even knowing me.

"Forgive me, it has been years since I have truly socialized." The two-legged hound said in this astonishingly royal-manner. "I was once a Pharaoh born back in Egypt way before this advanced era. I was poisoned by my own older brother and in my death, I pleaded with Anubis to save my life so I could keep to my thoughts of vengeance. My heart was weighed as pure, so my wish was granted to return to the Mortal World, however, I was also gifted with this 'ability'. I am what is called now a Deity to the God, a soldier on this plane. I am called Peylith. I was forgotten by history, by my own son."

"So, you are in many ways like Cinder." I hypothesized, theorizing that Peylith was another version of a Hellhound except he was guided by another Religion and Gifts.

"Ah, her name is Cinder-" Peylith smiled. "Is she a Deity too?"

"I guess you could say that. Did those Researchers give you any other 'Breed Name?" I probed wanting my hypothesis proven without acknowledging his accurate prognosis.

"Not one I can remember. They called me a Canis de Anubis."

"Anubis's Dog?" I translated. "They only have given those Latin Specie Names to those with the Hellhoundism Diagnosis."

"Well I guess in the year it is now, that is what I would be identified as." Peylith sneered as we finally ascended into the shrouding darkness of the night. Into the same gloom that had allowed us to successfully complete our Raid. "Ah, refreshing Moonlight; I owe you."

"Jakob," I said, giving my name to him with my genuine smile.

"Then Jakob, I owe you my life, and please let me help repay you by helping you with finding your beloved Cinder."

"You don't have to repay me, really." I returned, trying to discourage this humble man's traits. Trying my finest to now persuade the bi-petal hellhound to not come along with the three of us to Colorado.

"No, let me do this. If what I smell is right, then you have faith in the location your unknown lover has been taken too. My job gifted to me by Anubis was to aid those in need of my help and return those to be judged that have wronged a Deity of Anubis. Your

Cinder might not serve my Anubis, but she is still a Death God's Deity and as one of the same species, I must help her. Let me repay her and you with this." Peylith said. "I will be able to return to my human form once I get these 'blockers' out of my system."

Giving up on trying to persuade this man to the traditional 'Thank You' and go on with their 'Merry life' kind of thing, I let him shadow me as I strolled over to the second station. Introducing the Hellhound to them, I proceeded with the usual follow up procedures.

"So, he will be joining us to Colorado?" Mhykal questioned Peylith with his usual jokester comical smile. Elbowing the seven-foot Unnatural at the lower chest region. Sensing Peylith's slight smile and simultaneous growl, I just chuckled away.

Chapter 49
Jakob

"Wow. Would you look at this place." Yalu happily sparked. "I can't believe you rented this place for an entire month!"

"Yeah, who would have thought that Braedon would allow us to use that much money-" Mhykal returned, staring at the three-bedroom, modern craftsman lake house I had decided to rent while we were staying in Colorado.

"It's not his money." I piped in. "It's mine. I offered my open account to the Syndicate back when I truly thought that we would make progress in creating freedom for Unnaturals and all that same old shit."

"Well, we did close that Government Base-" Mhykal returned. "And we had freed the seventy Unnaturals who had been imprisoned there."

"True, but Jakob is right babe, in the last five years we haven't made as much a dent in this as we had when for instance I first joined. It may be a slump we are in right now, but the reason we are out here is because our goal is to find Cinder. Making sure she is safely returned to our arms is our current priority. Sorry if that offends you, Peylith." Yalu reminded us before apologizing to our little follower.

The Anubis Hellhound had thankfully returned to his human form that resembled a young adult maybe around the age of twenty-one, clearing up the fact that he was an Immortal. He did resemble an Egyptian from when they reigned over way back when however with modern times, we adjusted his appearance. His long black hair was pulled back into a man bun. His red eyes returned to their human black-brown color. He was a skinny, lean yet surprisingly tall man with dark skin wearing our modern amenities of clothing. Thanks to Yalu's taste, we had gotten him to wear denim jeans and a form-fit white long sleeve which he kept rolling the sleeves up over his elbows.

"I am not offended." Peylith happily interjected, putting his hand over his chest. "She is your friend and Jakob's unknown lover, so it is only natural that she takes priority over the other Unnaturals. That is what we are called right?"

"Yes, it is what we are all called when no one wants to call us by our species or breed names." I hastily answered, attempting to hide my building frustration at this compromising man. "Now we should get inside, so we can get settled and start scanning the perimeter. We need to hurry up and locate the facility where they are holding Cinder." Stepping up the five darkly stained oak solid steps to the front deck, I opened the door and sauntered inside to make sure it was everything that had been advertised.

Inside the foyer was filed river stones on the floor, stretching all the way back down to the main open floor plan. Off to my right were the modern wooded stairs with iron railings leading upstairs to the two bedrooms. Off to my left was the living room, a large forty-seven-inch-wide flat screen hanging over the same river stoned fireplace mantle, accompanied by an 'L' shaped sectional and a glass coffee table. With everything so far lining up with the pictures from the rental website, I walked back outside to collect our supplies from the black Escalade we had painfully driven here from New York.

"So how is the inside?" Yalu asked me while she clung to her man's arms.

"Everything I paid for." I sighed, grabbing some of our technical equipment. "Go see for yourself."

"I will." She sneered back, kissing Mhykal on the lips she broke free and ventured inside. Hearing her awes in amazement of the architecture, I grinned as I tailed in behind the Vixen carrying the heavy suitcases.

"Your guys' rooms are upstairs, I want to leave the downstairs room for Cinder when we get her," I said to Yalu as she ran through the floor plans.

"Makes sense." She replied. "This house is so small in comparison to the Manor, Jakob; but I like its small capacity. Feels homey and warm."

"You are a very peculiar Vixen." I teased as I carried the suitcases to the office hidden behind the kitchen.

"Oh, and like you aren't a peculiar Vampire yourself?" She barked back at me while playing with the stove's burners.

Putting them down in the open-spaced study, I looked out at the lake view from the floor to ceiling windows. Closing the blinds, I blocked out the light entirely. We had to keep the area private from any prying eyes. Strolling back through the kitchen, I saw that everyone was now pitching in to carry the luggage inside the house. In minutes we had successfully designated our rooms and started unpacking the equipment we had borrowed from the Syndicate.

"Alright now that we have everything set up, Yalu, I want you to start putting up the Electric Magnetic Field, and the Transmitter Blockers," I said, taking command.

"On it." Yalu sparked, sitting in the computer's office chair, quickly twiddling her fingers away at the keyboard. Activating all our precautionary measures, just in case we had been tracked back, or the base had microchipped Cinder as they had with Peylith. Although, Peylith had removed his with his teeth after we had told him about the chip. It wasn't anything unusual, I guess for him except for the advancement in science and technology. In minutes, the Vixen returned, "All setup."

"Okay, good. Now we need to find the number of existing Hospital Institutes in the state. Peylith, I know you want to help us, but I need you to stay here and guard the house while Mhykal and I go search the forest and next town over. Probably be about three or four hours by Vehicle."

"Understood," Peylith said, leaving the Study before I heard his tall frame fall onto what I could only assume was the sofa. "I will wait here." The Hellhound then barked.

Grabbing the keys to the Escalade, Mhykal kissed his girlfriend again and journeyed out into the snow ridden world to warm up the car although us Vampires didn't need heat, it was a 'human' gesture; something that would make the four of us seem 'natural.' "Yalu if you could research any bouncing signals from any military bases, I am sure we might be able to locate the extended perimeter of where they are holding her. Find a signal like the one we had just raided if possible. If you find anything, I have my earpiece on me." I ordered, pointing up to my ear to hint to the Bluetooth while descending out of the lake house's porch steps.

After I had slipped into the vehicle's front passenger side, Mhykal steadily pulled it back, driving the vehicle along the faded driveway back towards the actual asphalt road that was a mile out. Driving along the asphalt road we began our journey towards town to not only look for any information regarding any Institutional Facilities, but also to retrieve some much-needed food for our growing party. When we arrived in the quaint town it couldn't be helped that our Escalade stood out. During the winter, this place usually didn't get the tourist kind of vibe, however, it was almost the busiest holiday of the year, so we were also getting the rich family down for the Holiday look too. As irritating as it was, we had to continue to maintain this 'Human' Lifestyle. Which meant we were better off not wearing our 'traditional' attire so we could hopefully blend into the public eye. While I wore my usual black short-tailed jacket, with a form-fitted dark grey long-sleeve high-V-neck shirt, topped with dark blue jeans, and some dark carpenter boots: my old friend wore a dark brown zip-up hoodie with the zipper up to his higher abdomen, a faded red long-sleeve and some worn light grey faded blue jeans with similar boots. By our genetic makeup and attire, we could potentially pass for brothers-in-law. Pulling the vehicle up to a commercial parking lot, we both took a long breath before we embarked on our entailed mission.

Chapter 50
Jakob

"Did you get anything?" I requested, walking alongside the other Vampire as we regrouped. Seeing him shake his head no followed by a depressing sigh, I continued, "So nothing?"

"No, the nearest Hospital if that is in the next town over, and when I looked it up on my cell-phone I saw not a single familiar characteristic that would even resemble the type of place we are looking for," Mhykal answered translating the vocabulary as we merged back within human citizens' prying eyes. The smell of their blood burning right under my Vampiric nose, enticing me to feast. Maintaining control of my thirst, thanks to my recent feeding and years of experience, I listened to Mhykal's statement. "Has Yalu found anything on her end?" He probed consecutively completing his report.

"She hasn't called me yet," I said, converting the earpiece hidden deep into my ear, its nude color passing for a possible hearing aid. "It sucks that we haven't found anything. I was thinking that in a town as small yet as busy as this one, we would've at least found something revolving Cinder."

"I know, but just as we have all 'told' you over and over for the last two months, 'We will find her'," Mhykal spoke, stepping in front of my path to halt my feet. Putting his hands on my shoulders and staring me straight in the eyes, he encouraged. "We WILL find Cinder, Jakob."

"I know that we will find her, but I'm afraid of what those assholes could have done to her in that time." I said, breaking the 'human character.' "I don't want us to see her and have to break her yet again of that-"

"We will figure it out when the time comes, of course after we get her back." My good friend repeated, his glare tightly fixating on my worry-hearted expression.

"I know-" I snarled, breaking away from the sincere moment.

"Jakob-"

"Hold on, Yalu is calling me-" I eagerly barked back to Mhykal. Swiftly taking my phone out of my pocket and putting it up to my ear that had the earpiece in it to mock the action of receiving a phone call, I discreetly listened to Yalu's hopefully positive findings. "Yeah what did you find?" I enthusiastically questioned. Keeping fingers crossed that it was as good as I was believing it was. Looking at my old friend, I saw that he had the same high hopes facial expression on his face.

"I found some trace signals that I believe are replicating the identically matching systematical functions as the Institute in Maine." Yalu excitedly reported.

"Were you able to track where they were coming from?" I asked, walking along the sidewalk back to the Escalade to get out of the small yet bustling afternoon crowd.

"I am currently running a tracer on the signal right now, but I would prefer if you guys were back here." The Vixen voiced, her tone somewhat frustrated yet also concerned. "This looks like it will take several hours to scan over, and you two left the house almost eight hours ago." There was a pause before an unsettling sigh pushed through the phone's speaker. "And I believe that Peylith may have broken the T.V."

"He did?" I attempted to question in as calm a demeanor as I could manage. "He probably doesn't know how it works. Well, Mhykal and I haven't gotten to the store yet, we are going that way now, then we will be on our way back to the house. Just keep Peylith busy with something, he understands English quite well so give him a book to read or-" I said while stepping into the Escalade.

"I gave him my iPod for now-" the Vixen growled back.

"Yalu, are you sure that's a good idea? I mean, he just broke our T.V." I teased, getting a dark glare from Mhykal.

"Well, it's working for now. JUST HURRY UP AND GET THE HELL HERE!" The petite woman shouted into the earpiece, her raspy voice blaring down into my eardrum, leaving a blaring ring in my poor ear.

"We are working on it-" I said, pretending to end the call and put my cell phone away in my jeans pocket.

"JUST HURRY UP." Yalu loudly ordered again before her voice broke away from the speaker.

Taking the earpiece out, I dropped the Bluetooth piece into the cup holder so I could try to rub out the ringing in my ears. "Peylith is driving your girlfriend crazy." I jested.

Putting the keys into the vehicle's ignition, I heard Mhykal chuckle back at me. "He isn't used to this era yet."

"He may never be." I happily sighed. "Alright, we need to head off to the store to get some supplies before we go back to the house."

"Did she find something?" The Vampiric seriously queried as he drove out of the parking lot, maneuvering around the older modeled vehicles.

"Yeah, she found a signal and is trying to currently trace its location which could take a while. It took her this long to find it, so who knows how long it will be before we can even get a decent proximity of its location."

"But it's a start."

"Yeah, it is a very good start," I repeated while we drove through town again to find the nearest grocery store with fresh produce, although I don't think that either one of us can remember how to tell apart the good fruits from the rotted ones.

"God, that was so exhausting," Mhykal complained as we left the grocery store. Filling up the back of the vehicle with two hundred dollars' worth of groceries; meats, fruits, vegetables, bread, junk food, waters, candies, grease. "It was so hard not to feed."

"I know. When we get back to the house, I packed a supply of blood in a freezer unit. We can feed then." I reminded my friend while I pushed my back into the soft leather cushions of the passenger front seat. "Although we will likely get an earful from Yalu about taking so long."

"It's not our fault that we don't do the shopping, or even go out as much as she does." He choked back. "I mean back at the Manor, Yalu, Valeryie, Nancy, and Alexsandria do all the public crap or just order the food online now with whatever that website is called."

"Yeah it has made us quite lazy, but one day the roles were going to reverse on us." I sneered.

"Yeah, yeah." Mhykal teased with his typical smile. Driving the Escalade around the other parked cars, he exited out of the Grocery Store Parking lot and began to drive the vehicle the few hours it took to return home, in the next town over.

Taking advantage of the long journey the two of us began to converse without the eavesdropping Vixen enforcing regulations on the dialogue. Of course, Mhykal could not help but talk about his current sex life with Yalu, making it seem like she was here still. Although it wasn't all too difficult to change the subject when the very private Vixen was with us. Thankfully, the Vampiric sensing my irritation abruptly changed the subject. This time talking about

273

similar weather patterns. The similarity between Colorado and New York. It was all oddly similar, very freaky, but I knew deep down it was not supposed to be that way. Taking charge of the conversation, I altered its subject making us commune what our plans were going to be once we had found this undisclosed location. Deciding that we were going to follow our usual raid protocol, the two of us began to discuss how much of the hard labor we were going to do once we had entered the Institute.

"We will need Yalu though for the Illusions and Trickery, so we can get passed those guards without hassling or alluding to our presence. In our last Raid, it was quite difficult to fight against them and free the Unnaturals. They were extremely well prepared to eliminate us and keep those High Risks confined. My instincts tell me that the same thing will happen once we break into the facility." Mhykal told me, his tone becoming unusually serious as we had finally reached the forest-wrapped road on our way back to the rental.

"Yeah, I know my gut is telling me the same thing, however, I have already made precautions. Contacting a couple of other guys who're willing to give us a helping hand." I seriously spoke, gleaming back at my friend with my own cocky smile. "Even if they are prepared for possible raids from the Syndicates or are prepared for escape attempts made by the Unnaturals they keep imprisoned there; we too are prepared with a few tricks up our sleeves."

Chapter 51
Jakob/Cinder

Arriving back at the house, Mhykal and I quickly walked for the Study. Making our way into the Kitchen, we found Yalu sitting on the kitchen Isle countertop messing around with her phone. Seeing us out of the corner of her amber eyes, she said with a low growl, "Finally."

"Did you get anything yet?" I anxiously questioned the Vixen.

"Not yet. I estimate possibly another ten hours before it can even find the proximity of the signal's location. They must have taken precautions after our Raid on that base in Maine." Yalu said, retaining her fixed tone. Lightly dropping her phone on the countertop, she then slid off and continued, "So did you pick up some groceries so I can at least make something decent for dinner?"

"Yeah, we'll go bring them in," I returned, turning around to exit out of the kitchen. Saddened about the estimated time we had to wait for any longitude and latitude points to spit across the computer screen, proving while technology was a great asset it to had flaws. Stepping back outside into the snow-covered ground, I began to carry the grocery bags inside, passing Mhykal and Peylith as they also walked out to aid me.

Putting down the plastic bags I had carried in on the first run, I told myself, "Don't worry Cinder, we are hurrying as fast as we can to find out where those damn humans are holding you captive. You just have to wait a little bit longer."

"0497, you need to eat-" I heard Doctor Thompson sigh at me from the other side of the chain-link fence. "If you keep on refusing to eat your meals, then we will have to resort to force-feeding you, and I don't think that you will enjoy that very much."

"Bite me-" I snarled, my voice only producing the canid growl. No 'human' words came out because of that irritating head collar. Observing the man move around the room as he continued to aimlessly ramble, I eventually gave up on following him with my sights and began to curl myself back up into a circle sleeping position.

Before slipping into another deafening dark slumber, I overheard the man further speak, a few words of the statement catching my numbing sensitive hearing, "You still have another blood draw that is coming up shortly." Pretending to ignore him, I tucked my head closer to my frame, tightening up the circle. "I know that it isn't something you like but remember-" the researching Doctor paused before continuing with the rest of the sentence, his voice now deepening, "you do not have a choice in this matter. So, ignore me all you want, but I thought I would be generous enough to let you in on that."

"Whatever-" I growled, once more only to have a low growl rumble out of my sore throat. A side effect from the intubation and what little water I was able to lap up in this form.

"There's some acknowledgment finally." The brunette man sadistically chuckled. "Alright, come tomorrow morning we will start force-feeding you, 497. Since it has been three whole days you have refused to eat." Ending on that note, the man turned around and left this bland room, this time completely dimming the lights before locking up the room.

"Alone again-" I thought to myself, sensing the obscuring thoughts return. Closing my eyes to slip into the bleak darkness that hid behind my eyelids, I saw a memory arise. A quick flash of me standing over a bloody man in mid-transformation. My fangs, I could feel were tightly wrapped around his neck-shoulder area. Holding onto the flesh so firmly. I felt my heart skip as I let go of his skin, the blood dripping down my long white canines. My jowls spreading open, I recall feeling my lips curl. Rising so high that my lips revealed the tops of my gums. Simultaneously feeling my ears pull forward, my tail curl up along my spine, and my colic rise, I hastily sprung my sleepy eyes open. Forcing my drained physique up out of the tight sleeping circle position. My legs barely could hold me up, causing me to collapse back onto the concrete ground. Falling short of the worn blanket, I petrifyingly panicked, "That wasn't me! I don't recollect that ever happening?! There is no way that was me!" Having another flash of memories come slapping back into my memory of the other people I had slain:

One was an older male human who had killed over twenty female Unnatural and Humans alike. I had allowed my human form's sex appeal to attract the man, baiting him to come after me. Almost stripped down completely nude before the man attempted to pull a simple handgun on me. Staring down the gun's barrel, I felt the same sadistic smile press along my face, my skin pulling back. Activating my long blood scythe blade out of my left wrist, I flung it against his throat, quickly slicing the flesh with no hesitation. While that man flopped around trying to hold his neck together with both of his hands, attempting to stop the spewing blood, he dropped the gun. Before the weapon could hit the ground completely, I transformed myself into my Hellhound Canine form. Covered by the darkness of the tight alley passageway, I jumped onto the five-foot-eleven man and wrapped my fangs around his throat the same way I had done with Logan. The same feeling of pure excitement, of pure 'thrill' washing over me. Holding his throat, I began to combust the man into the orange flames. Just as his soul had passed over, the life had been sapped from this man, I let go changing back to my human form and redressing. Disappearing into the darkness just as an incoming storm rained down on the moderate city.

"That can't be me!" I cried, again attempting to stand myself up onto my weak and unsteady feet. "I don't remember any of that!" I howled from under the tightly wrapped muzzle just as the next memory of another person I had killed came flooding back into my memory I again collapsed onto the concrete floor:

This time it was an Unnatural I had hunted down and excitedly murdered. Recalling being assigned to it because this specific Unnatural had lived for over five hundred years and had mercilessly disobeyed the laws of 'Death' for that period by stealing souls of young children. Again his targets were both Unnaturals and Humans, all so that he could become a 'False Immortal' as the Shadow described it. Chasing after him in my canine form, I pathetically got myself trapped into a chain-link gated cage behind a warehouse. Hearing the man laugh at me further enraged me, however, it to enrich my dark instinct to hunt. Sensing my Blood Scythes spawn uncontrollably out of my front leg's ankles and the bone spikes out of my back, I howled out in pure frustration. Waiting for the man to come back down, I ducked into the dark shadows quickly morphing back out from its darkness behind this Life Stealing Wendigo. Hastily jumping onto his back, I attached my fangs to the back of his neck, quickly ripping through the flesh. As he maddeningly swung around, I placed my paws over his shoulders, changed the positions of the scythes, and dug them into the collarbone. Clipping a major artery, I observed him spontaneously combust while he was attempting to thwart my attack. The Unnatural lost his stolen life essence from where he stood. His old body decaying into nothing more than fine dust particles. While the dust continued to burn away, I licked the blood from my lips. The metallic taste for some reason tasted so sweet, so rewarding. The smile I could again feel against my long jaws encouraged the deep panic.

"It wasn't me!" I sobbed completely overrun with fear. For the third time, I tried to again get myself up off the concrete floor. My shaky legs unable to hold my hungry and drugged body up once more gave out on me. Collapsing right down on top of them, I yelped in tragic pain. Feeling my breathing start to restrain itself, my lungs contracted. I could hear my heartbeat rampantly thudding down into my eardrums. "That wasn't me!" I again told myself. "I remember having assignments going out onto the town to yes get rid of pesky souls by the orders of that Shadow, but-" Observing through the piercing darkness as more flashes of my hunting memories came back to the surface. "I don't remember any of those details, I don't remember-I DO NOT REMEMBER ENJOYING IT!" I shouted, my still petrified body trying to stand back up. Just as the door to the room slid open allowing several Doctors and Guards to come rushing in, I continued to remind myself that I did not recall any of these events rushing back to my memory.

Hearing the gate to the kennel get pushed open, I saw through my flooding tears, the four white coat wearing men swarming around where I lied. Their hands prodding around my chest and neck, I cried out in more pain. Snapping my head upwards in agony, I now felt everything snap back to reality.

"Dammit, no one told us about this behavior-" I heard one of the unusual Doctors shout to his employees angrily. "Thompson, nor Meludanz is here right now."

"Sir, she is bleeding out of her nose and mouth." Another employee shout as he held my swinging head up. I tried my best to fight against the strength of his hands as he exposed my bleeding orphisms to his co-workers, but I was too weak to show any promise. Honestly I didn't felt any built-up pressure in my nose or my mouth telling me that I had started to bleed during my mental breakdown. "It's a lot of blood."

"About a few cups, nothing too serious. It just looks like a lot due to her also bashing her head into the floor. Plus, she is under the Cured Salts." The main man spoke up, alerting me to his leading personality. "Get her up and onto the table inside the room, I will be able to properly examine what had happened to her inside there."

"Okay-" One of the Guards acknowledged, pushing his way through the small crowd of Doctors to complete his orders.

Doing what I could to fight against him, I heard a third man dressed in a white lab coat speak up, "We can give her a muscle relaxant and laced salts to calm her down."

"While that will likely make it easier on everyone, I don't want her sedated just yet. Not until I have completed my examination, okay."

Chapter 52
Cinder/Jakob

"Alright here we go-" my heightened sense overheard the lead Doctor calmly express as he placed his hand on my neck, stroking it down my medium length-black fur coat before poking the syringe full of the salt/relaxant concoction into one of my still viable veins running throughout that region. "That should help calm you down."

Still unable to comprehend the memories that had flashed before my eyes. Those images of pure thrill and excitement while I hunted down and killed those men. "Why did I enjoy it so much?" I murmured anxiously to myself, "I knew I had to kill them, but what made it so entertaining? How INSANE had I become during those hunts?" With the Relaxant attempting to calm my racing heart and restrained breathing, I also began to feel my weak legs tingle and my throbbing headache ease.

"Okay then-" the same man spoke, still standing over the top of me. My scarcely conscious body lying coldly on the metal wheelable table. "Took a little longer to take effect, but now she is starting to calm down."

With the mixed concoction finally overtaking my nervous system, I started to feel those haunting flashbacks delay. Those horrendous moments of me losing my sanity starting to sink back down to the depthless abyss of my mind.

Feeling hands press into my black fur, I heard his voice proceed to echo throughout the small room and into my pounding eardrums; "The bleeding is beginning to stop. Probably a pressure bleed." The white coat wearing man paused as he prodded around my face, investigating the bloodstains tarnishing my brown muzzle. "I will have to remove the muzzle, so I can investigate if she bit her tongue or her inner cheek." His long fingers snaked around the leather, slipping underneath the buckle. Removing the leather strap from the metal contraption, I felt the corresponding muzzle of the headcollar start to fall off the bridge of my nose.

Just as he finished removing the muzzle, I now perceived the other lab coat wearing men determine. "Doctor Maluthe, I don't think she could have bit her tongue, lips, or cheek with that wrapped around her mouth. She would have to use her jaws just to get her tongue slipped past those fangs, and with how tight that muzzle was, it makes the probability even smaller."

"Right." the Doctor depressingly sighed, understanding the obvious. Tightly holding my jaws together, the man began to slide fabric back over my nose, pushing it up along the bridge before he rewrapped the strap around my muzzle, "That leaves the only source of the bleed to be from her nose which most likely drained into her mouth." The man rambled on about, trying to make his stupid move still seem reasonable.

"You never reviewed her file, like I had asked you to?" A familiar voice questioned.

"Doctor Thompson-" Doctor Maluthe sighed. "I wasn't expecting you to start your shift this early?"

"Well, I got a text message telling me about 0497's possible panic attack. The camera monitors are supposed to alert my cell phone when it senses any thermal or heart changes in her stats." My 'assigned' crazy Doctor verified. "I am here to not only do my job, but to also tell you that you should have reviewed the file we had faxed. There was information in it about her odd behaviors when there's a Blood Moon. Although there is nothing directly surfaced around her Canine Form, I suspect the arousal of this unusual heart rate, and the unusual, unsourced bleeds are based upon the Blood Moon that is out right now." Hearing him step up closer to where I lied on the table, "You guys can leave now, I will clean her up." Doctor Thompson breathed, his hand lightly gliding down the side of my recently healed ribcage.

"Great-" I groaned, feeling tiring exhaustion rip into my ankles again. Trying to retain myself from falling asleep because I was still terrified to repeat those memories of anguished insanity.

"It's alright, 497-" He assured me, stepping into my fading sights.

"Anything yet?" I asked Yalu, stepping into the study.

"Nothing yet, unfortunately." The Caucasian Vixen sighed, twiddling away at the computer's keyboard. "The Signal is being traced through five different towers so it will take some time to shrink the perimeter into a manageable size."

"Right-" I exhaled, rubbing the back of my neck.

"You're worried about her and tonight's moon phase, aren't you?" Yalu interrogated, standing up from the expensive computer desk.

"The Blood Moon does have me worried over Cinder's condition, especially after that last time-" I continued, leaning in the archway of the study standing still in front of the Vixen. "However, it's the sharp possibility that they are holding her at a place like the one we raided a few days ago that has me truly worried."

"We are all concerned about her especially tonight, but until we can find local proximity where they are holding her and who knows who else; we just have to keep our hopes up that she is hanging on to her faith in us and still fighting to keep living." The Vixen said, her eyes gleaming under the darkly lit room, "Just as she needs to keep her faith in us, we need to believe in her, remember that."

"Yeah I know-" I heaved another heavy breath before getting interrupted when Peylith and Mhykal stormed all buddy-buddy inside the Study, pushing me into the desk a few feet away. "What the hell you two?!" I snapped at them.

"Sorry Jakob, but Mhykal just received a message from Braedon," Peylith apologized, giving his all olden sincerest to me as I recollected myself.

"What did it say?" I inquired, trying to collect myself.

"We are needed back at the Manor, ASAP." Mhykal anxiously returned.

"Why? What is so important that it is taking us away from this-" Yalu snapped at her boyfriend, her feelings about Cinder coming to the surface.

As the Vampiric scrolled back through his cell phone's text messaging app to re-read the text he had received. "Apparently, it is because the Manor is in danger, we are needed back there to help Braedon and Viktor with follow up protocol."

"Valeryie-?" Yalu asked her focus now altered to her sister's safety. As much as she loved Cinder, her sister came above all else, even coming above her partner, Mhykal.

"So far everyone is okay, but I guess Braedon had received an email about the Manor having a Search Warrant issued by the Government." Mhykal continued to express, scrolling further down the list of received messages.

"Jakob, I know we are so close to finding out where she is being held, but we really need to-" Yalu said. The tone in her raspy soft voice alerting me to how worried she was over her younger sister.

"As much as I give a rat's ass about Braedon right now-" I angrily growled, clenching my fist as pure rage and frustration filled throughout my entire body. Releasing the tension, I quickly thought over the fact that I couldn't go alone to save Cinder, although the plan was very tempting, I knew it would be a futile attempt. Forcing my hands to relax, I exhaled my anguished frustration and finally spoke up, "Alright, we will pack up and return home to help ensure the safety-"

Interrupted by an irritating buzz that shot out from the computer's speakers. A few seconds of soundless noise settled before I noticed Yalu's facial expression change again. Morphing from worry to fixed concentration. Running up to the computer, I saw her eyes dance, the golden amber reflecting the blue-white light of the computer screen at us.

Eventually speaking up, she enthusiastically chipped, "The Signal has been traced down to a five-mile radius around this deep section in the forest that outskirts that next town over." Turning the computer's flat-screen monitor around to show us exactly where it had been circled with a red mouse marker.

Suddenly overwhelmed by this absurd feeling of determination and anxious excitement, I grabbed the computer screen to look closer at the five-mile perimeter our tracers had created. Overhearing Mhykal and Peylith take a deep sigh of great relief for the moment. Returning to our two objectives at hand, I concluded on our plan of action. "Alright, start packing up the equipment. Yalu take a picture of that so we can mimic its location on the GPS in the Escalade. Tonight, we will find out where those assholes are holding Cinder. Immediately after we rescue her, we will begin our drive back to the Manor."

Chapter 53
Jakob

Arriving at the perimeter of the area that the computer had configured for us, our group began to embark on the next step in the preliminary stages of our traditional Raid protocol, the scouting process. Leaving Yalu and Peylith with the Escalade, Mhykal, and I began to rummage around the boundary, skimming through the ins and outs of the perimeter for any clues about the building we were desperately searching for.

Breaking away from my friend, I busted through the trails, eventually finding a paved road that led deeper into the disclosed area. Keeping myself concealed in the shadows of the trees and the cloudy nightscape, I ran beside the road, keeping high hopes of what was at its end. Maintaining an endured sprint, I ran for close to three miles before my hopes were gratefully rewarded. Following the path right up to a concrete brick-based building, I overlooked the unique infrastructure. The building had an irregular structure that resembled a faded red box underneath the surprising clear sky and red-orange Blood Moon. Staying in the shrouds of the forest, I saw several vehicles parked in the open parking lot, however thanks to my enhanced sight, I also saw there were over ten cameras around the front and left-hand side of this building. Observing what I could only assume was the building's front entrance, I absorbed all of the characteristics, still following traditional protocol. The front resembled a traditionally modern public hospital, a large two-story abstract paneled glass held up at a ninety-degree angle with the front and left side of the building. Allowing the casting moon rays to seep inside of the two-story foyer. Surveying the rest of the building, I configured by the modern size of the single-floor building there was going to be a lot of square footage we were going to have to comb through.

Seeing enough, I tapped into my Bluetooth earpiece that ran on a protected server, "Yalu, it's Jakob. I found the building, track my location."

"Alright, don't think about going inside yet, Jakob." the Vixen swiftly ordered. After a few minutes of silence, she returned. "We are all on our way. Be there in about fifteen minutes."

"Okay, hurry up-" I answered, cutting the conversation while counting the number of cameras and human-figured silhouettes my vision was preying upon.

Twenty minutes had passed by, and we had all regrouped. "So-?" Mhykal questioned. "How do we get in?"

"We will most likely have to go in through the front. I did a perimeter run around the entire building while waiting on you guys. The several back doors I noted were all guarded by small groups of men per door." I answered. "The front is our best option, however, its also guarded by at least two stationary guards and five patrolling guards. Then there are also three separate cameras projected at the front doors." I reported pointing to the cameras and their distinguished angles.

"Are you sure this is the place?" Yalu asked, confused by the way it looked in comparison to the Factory-Styled Institute we had recently raided. "I mean it looks too 'friendly'."

"The way the guards are walking around, and the way that the second building looks over there-" I pointed towards a second

287

concrete building with five large garage doors hidden off to the side. "I do believe that this is the place, however according to how low some of those windows are, there has to be at least one or two floors underground." I paused for a moment to catch my breath. "And we have to recall that Humans are doing whatever they can to hide away the ugly truth of how they are treating Unnaturals, trying to disguise it as nothing more than treatments of 'Cursed' Humans."

"Right-" Peylith growled, his deep voice speaking up over the hushed noise of the light breeze. Having morphed in his now four-legged four-foot-tall Pharaoh Hound canine form. The hound seemed extremely tall for the form, but I still had faith that it was something we could use to our advantage. "Now, how do we get inside?"

"About that-" I paused again before pointing towards the inside of the open-foyer. "They should already be inside. Yalu, can you see them?" I asked the Vixen, hoping her highly advanced sight could clearly state what was going on in the Foyer of the building from our distance.

"The guards are all on the ground-" Yalu reported. "There are two tall men with what looks like wings, standing over a collection of them-wait, Jakob you did not call the twins did you?"

"The Draconic Twins?" Mhykal asked. "The ones we rescued from the Salem Hospital Institute?"

"Yeah, the older one Mikael had given me his cell phone number when I ran into him back in town yesterday. He said if we ever needed his and his brother's help while we were in Colorado, they would be available." I explained, stepping out of the shadows. "I will run inside-"

"We could just Shadow Morph inside-" Peylith spoke up, altering his form again. Once more, reverting to his bipedal human form.

"Huh?" Mhykal and I asked, deeply confused.

"Shadow Morph?" Yalu questioned.

"It's a trick I had learned after a few years having this gift of mine. It allows me to step into the shadows and come back out from another shadow anywhere within my sights or knowledge." Peylith responded. "I can also morph several sources of masses, including people."

"Okay, we can try that-" Yalu happily declared.

"Once we are inside the building Peylith I want you to stay with Yalu and try to locate the Camera room. From there, Yalu I want you to shut down the Cameras. Peylith you should be able to memorize where I'm located and 'Shadow Morph back to us."

"Understood." The Deity of Anubis answered. Closing his eyes, we began to watch the shadows of the purest black material wrap around the four of us, and before I knew it, we stepped out of a shadow behind the Draconic Twins.

Collecting myself, I shook hands with the twins, their human forms about a foot shorter than their Dragon-like mutations. Looking like identical twins, they both had light auburn hair and bright emerald green eyes. Strong jawbones, broad shoulders, and well firm handshakes. "It's our pleasure to be here, Jakob. Although this barely pays you guys back for our freedom both Matheu and I believe that it helps." Mikael announced before his twin.

"It does help us out by a lot." Mhykal joked, now shaking hands with the twins. "You guys look like you are doing well."

Ignoring their chatter, I hinted off to Yalu and Peylith to go find the Camera room while the rest of us would start to descend into the lower levels that were clearly stated on a hanging map. "Alright, we are going down to the lower levels. Remember, we need to find Cinder, but if we can also free the other Unnaturals that are being held in here who're willing to step outside in the free world, then we will also be doing that." I ordered the group as we took the stairs to the lower basement levels.

"Got it," Mikael answered. "And if we run into any Guards or Doctors?"

"Well try to not kill them," I answered back, leading the pack down the staircase. "I know they are armed with both weapons and drugs that are sedative laced, however killing humans is not our priority, nor is it our policy, understand?"

"Yes." The three answered back in unison, making me chuckle.

As we finally reached the initial first lower level, my earpiece activated. Overhearing Yalu's voice relay, "Jakob, the Cameras are down. And from I can see, Cinder is inside a small room off to the side of what most likely is her base room-"

"Thanks, Yalu, now hurry up and regroup," I answered back into the earpiece.

"Got it-" she said. Seconds later Peylith used his Shadow Morph ability, allowing the two of them to catch up to our current location on the first underground level. "I believe that she is being held at the end of this level. The second level beneath us is full of well..." She paused.

"Full of the Deceased," Peylith interjected. "It's a grave of dead bodies being tested on."

"Okay-" I murmured, feeling creeped out and disgusted at the same time. "Well ignore that and start working on getting out the willing and able Unnaturals. We will reach Cinder eventually."

"What happens if we get to her before we free the others-" Matheu asked.

"As much as I don't want to say to leave them behind, we may have to. If they are unable to move on their own accord or are too delirious, we will have to do the unthinkable." I upsettingly responded. I did not want to be the bad guy here, but in my opinion, we were here for one reason and one reason only; to get Cinder back home.

Chapter 54
Jakob/Cinder

Steadily searching room by room, we skimmed over the patient charts, reading for specific numbers, and whatever possible medications the poor creatures were on before officially deciding to break through any of the electronic keypads. If there any who weren't too drugged to be liberated, we freed them, however, I could not help but feel myself growing more and more worried the longer it took us to scroll through these rooms. I desperately wanted to get Cinder out of here, but I was so concerned about the condition and mental status they had possibly put her in, especially after reading through an endless array of charts belonging to other Unnaturals.

"Jakob?" Mhykal called. Swirling around, so my eyes could lock sights on my associate. Looking up at him after blanking for so long, I saw the worry on his face. "We have almost scavenged through this entire floor."

"I know." I sighed, standing up after breaking another keypad, using my abilities to crack the PIN's code by tracking past signatures left behind by the Humans in charge here. "I know we are almost done." I audibly voiced, reminding myself that we had five rooms left to check. Recalling that based on Yalu and Peylith's findings the second basement level was a Morgue, only further extended my concern. Although Yalu also told me she had seen a figure that resembled Cinder's canine form in a side room off to the far angle of the camera, it enforced the fact that our Hellhound was still somewhere on this base.

"I am surprised that the Alarms have yet to be triggered," Mikael spoke, his low snake-like voice extending the sounds of his consonants, slurring some of his words.

"It's because of Yalu. She not only turned off the Cameras and Monitors, but she also shut down the Alarm System." I answered back to the Draconic. "Hopefully you didn't jinx us. Mhykal said the same thing at our last Raid and shortly after the Alarms were triggered."

"Right-" my friend grinned, slouching over trying to play it off as a 'meant to happen' moment.

"Just keep any patrolling guards at bay-" I moved on, handing out more orders while I proceeded to introduce myself to the eighteenth Unnatural who was capable of walking of their own free will.

"Roger-" the twins, Vampire, and Hellhound responded while Yalu and I strolled inside the next room down the hall.

"It's unusually quiet outside-" I heard Doctor Thompson ramble on, standing up from the stool that sat beside the table, I was latched onto by that dreadful headcollar. "But I guess that happens at three-" The man paused, glancing at his expensive silver shiny watch. "No, four o'clock in the morning."

"Four-" I thought to myself, sighing out my exhaustion alongside the Doctors. "The Blood Moon should have started to set by now. The sun doesn't rise till eight anyways during the Winter- if it is still winter out." Not even knowing how long I had been locked up. I knew it wasn't quite yet a year, but the longer I remained in this alter form the more my time-sense distanced. It felt so long since the sun's rays had beaten onto my black and tan fur, or even my pale-white skin.

As the Doctor stepped out of my line of sight, I consecutively listened to him talk to himself. "So far everything is matching the recorded reports filed with your connection to this Blood Moon. Though I do not trust it as the source, I am positive we will discover ways to treat this, and that back pain you were complaining of."

"You knew about that-" I interrogated in my head, too tired to physically acknowledge him with a growl or whine.

"Anyways, for now, you'll remain hitched to that table 497, while I get some sleep. After that, we can start the second Harvesting."

"Great-" I again exhaled. I had no way to argue against it, nevertheless, I still refuted my dislike of having my blood drawn against my will and in such massive quantities.

"Of course, though we will again sedate you for that. Having you sit still for almost eight hours of a continuous slow draw is hazardous for not only your health but also for the employees."

"Whatever."

Hearing the man's footsteps silently clap against the concrete, alerted me to the man changing his shoes between his previous absence. The image dissipating out of my blurred hearing range, I stared blankly ahead at the empty clean counters. Desperately trying to keep my eyes open for as long as I could manage, telling myself that I needed to stay conscious for as long as possible. I was too afraid to return to the deafening depths that hid behind my eyelids, too scared to revisit the terrifying memories of my creeping insanity.

"That is all of them." Matheu heavily breathed, returning to his secondary humanoid form.

"We still have the second floor beneath us-" I reminded.

293

"But that floor was a morgue-" Yalu hastily interrupted.

"I don't think the entire floor is a morgue. I am more willing to believe that they have Cinder and a few more Unnaturals down below. Hiding the risks from still-prying humans." I resumed. "You have to remember that Cinder is an 'Undiscovered' Breed according to these guys. And even her Species Abilities have never been previously documented."

"That is a probable theory." Mikael returned, speaking ahead of his younger twin. "Back when we were all held at that Hospital Institute in New York, they also did a lot of 'tests' on her."

"Her screams of pain on those Red Moons would always echo through the halls-" Matheu spoke up, his eyes telling me the rest of that painful memory.

"It has been decided then, we will head downstairs. Mikael, Matheu is it possible that you can lead these guys back up. One of Saylene's Syndicate's Safe Houses is-" I said changing orders.

"Yeah we know-" the elder twin interrupted. Taking charge of the group of recently freed Unnaturals, I watched as the twins started to head back out. "Save your friend and if you ever need us again, just call."

"Don't worry about Cinder, and if the time comes, we will not hesitate," Mhykal spoke, flashing his traditional gleaming smile as he firmly shook hands with the younger twin.

Once everyone was gathered, I still leading the 'Raid' commanded Peylith to Shadow Morph the Draconics and Patients and ensure the recently escaped Unnaturals made it safely back to the outside world. We waited nearly seven minutes before the eldest Hellhound returned, notifying me that everyone had made it close enough to the Draconic's Sanctioned Safehouse. I didn't feel comfortable wasting more time on this rescue mission, however deep in my gut I felt that this was something the selfless woman would have wanted. I felt so horrid that the only voice mumbling in my head to have rescued those people was Cinder's soft femininely mature voice. My will was primarily fixated on liberating the Beauceron Hellhound that not only I but so many others at the Manor had become attached to.

"Everyone made it to the tree line on the other side of the forest. They have a little bit more to go before they meet up with Saylene's Rebels who have agreed to give them sanction." Peylith said as he returned ascending out of Yalu's own shadow.

"You had that all setup, didn't you?" Yalu interrogated.

Smiling back at her was the only answer I had available. Indeed, I had set up this entire mission on short notice. When we had finished our last raid, I had requested a private meeting with Saylene to ask for her help in the sanction of any Unnaturals I had freed when we left to save Cinder. Of course, the female Draconic Leader accepted more Unnaturals, because like I said to Braedon earlier, when it comes to the Syndicates, it was all about those damn numbers, nothing else.

Changing the subject, I urged, "Now let's go retrieve Cinder and get the hell out of here." With everyone's agreeance and understanding, we began to quietly press on. Just as our feet descended the last concrete step, we were surprisingly greeted by one of the Doctors and few guards stepping out of one of the close rooms. Making eye contact for a quick second, I gave the command to take out the guards while I would take the man wearing the white lab coat.

Mhykal and Peylith eagerly took off for the four guards, each taking two. I knew that my old Vampiric friend could handle two easily on his own when they were holding heavy firepower, so I wasn't worried about a couple of unarmed Humans with him. Nor was I too worried about Peylith with unarmed Humans, however, I was curious about his fighting style. The bi-pedal black-furred Pharaoh Hound quickly ran and grabbed one of the men with his large skull-sized hand. As the Hellhound kept his back to me, I saw the lining of his own scar-like tattoos. A large golden Ankh with a red gem sat in the middle of his back, stretched from his shoulders down to his lower back. The Ankh was surrounded with sharp Hieroglyphic Angled golden tattoos, their sharp lines amplifying the simple curved cross Egyptian Cross. There were also straight-line tattoos wrapped around his wrists, but they failed to stand out as much as that centerpiece in his back. Quickly throwing the first man at the second, before charging both, slamming his large fist into the second's gut, Peylith surprisingly took out his share of men in about the same amount of time as my old friend. With all four knocked unconscious and maybe with a concussion or two, I charged the Doctor. Using my heightened speed, I grabbed the Doctor by the collar of his lab coat.

Throwing him against the wall, I then ordered him with my hypnotic eyes activating, "Where is 497 being held?!" Assuming two-to-one these fools had gone back to calling her by her Patient I.D. Number like every other Institute had ever done. "Answer me, where are you holding 0497?!"

Chapter 55
Jakob

The lab coat-wearing man mindlessly answered me with a simple point of the finger to the same room he had just came out of. Putting the man down, I then frustratingly demanded, "Open the damn door." Thanks to my advancement in my Hypnosis, simple orders mixed with some cruel vocabulary, it didn't buffer their mindless control. It was like puppeteering, and after seven hundred years at it, the process became second nature to me. No different than typing a list of commands into a computer's programming module. All I had to do was type in the codes, and it would do exactly what I had ordered. Following the employee over to the keypad, I anxiously counted the seconds away in my head as he entered the passcode. Even though I eagerly wanted to get Cinder safely out of this 'Government-funded' base, I also get back on the road before things went anymore downhill. Pushing the unlocked door, I grabbed the Doctor by the skull as he turned around to face me, awaiting further instructions. My hand clutching the entirety of his face, pulled the hypnotized deadweight towards me, pushing it away at top speeds I rammed the back of his brunette-haired head into the keypad. Fracturing his skull and breaking the electronic locking mechanism with little effort; Not killing the man though the thought had crossed my mind. Wiping my hands clean on the unconscious man's white coat, I darted inside the bare concrete room shadowed by my fellow raiders.

Wandering around, we all saw the wet concrete paneled floor, the dark coloring spreading around the makeshift chain-link kennel towards what appeared to be droplets of water and blood still staining the hard floor. The four of us tracked the stains into an entryway off to the left side of the room. Yalu leading the way, her petite figure moving ten times faster than the rest of us. Before I could even get near her, I heard the Vixen's raspy voice shout at me, "Jakob! She's in here-!"

On instinct, I felt my heart drop down into my stomach and begin to rapidly churn all my questioning doubts. Running humanely over into the side room, I saw the longing sight of the Hellhound of Shadows I craved to see. Although it wasn't the exact image I had in mind, it was still a lot better than the first time I had seen her. Walking up to the metal table covered with towels that were carrying Cinder, I noticed that she was surprisingly still conscious. "Thank-god." I prayed aloud. Stepping around the setup of empty syringes, and scrunched up bloody cloths and rags, I finally walked into her line of sight. "They muzzled you-" I sighed as I gently cupped my hand around her squarish face, dragging it down along her long muzzle, feeling the soft fur press against my skin.

Getting a short cry out of the canine's throat, I watched her ears flatten against her skull, and out of the corner of my eyes, I observed her tail move. Going from drooping off the edge of the table and into a slightly happy wag. No words were needed for this conversation. Shortly proceeding our sentimental moment, I watched the woman stuck in her canine form attempt to move around. Her lean build flinched, banging and flopping sternly against the metal table.

Noticing the amount of difficulty the young Hellhound was having standing, I swiftly scanned over the emptied syringes on the adjacent table. Attentively reading the labels on the small syringes, it became abundantly clear that Cinder had been drugged with some sort of sedative and muscle relaxer. Gently grabbing her head to keep it steady, I noted that the muzzle was attached to more black fabric wrapped around her head and was attached to a lead tied under the metal table. Following the chain-lead, I unclasped it from its post before I went into overdrive. Time was of the essence here. Slipping my masculine hands swiftly underneath her limp body, I pulled the now less than hundred-pound canine towards me and gently lifted the dead weight off the table. "We will get that contraption off you once we safely get out of here-" I panted. Rushing back out into the corridor, I impatiently ordered. "Alright Peylith, could you use one more Shadow Morph for us?"

"Yeah, I can do another." The bipedal hellhound obliged, having returned to his lengthy human form. Grouping all around the intimidating former Noble, we watched as again the Shadows formed around us. Stepping out of the casting shadows of the tree line bearing down on the Escalade, I exhaled a deep breath of relief. The parked vehicle was gratefully still parked in the exact location we had left it, a couple of miles distanced from the five-mile perimeter edge. Counting the heads, I relieved another heavy breath after assuring we all had safely escaped the Base.

Feeling Cinder's heartbeat bang against her chest wall, thumping with a heavyweight against my hand, I saw her starting to try to fight against even me. Her ears were pulled flat against her skull, her eyes were bulging out of her head in complete fear. With everyone glaring down at the canine, standing over her, I surveyed Yalu starkly clutch up the contraption wrapped around Cinder's head. Sternly telling the spooked Unnatural, "Cinder, it is alright. We are not going to hurt you. No one is going to hurt you-"

Shortly after the canine had relaxed, we began to gently load ourselves into the backseat. Changing up the seating order, I ordered Yalu to take the front seat with Mhykal, while Peylith and I would take the back seat with Cinder lying in between us. Filling all into the black SUV Escalade, I slid Cinder inside the back-passenger side, her body still trying everything it could to fight us. We saw the Hellhound acknowledge us, even noted her beautiful blue eyes recognize the people she called her friends, so for her to challenge

299

us was strange behavior. Slowly crawling into the seat, I began to move her large, heavy head around before slowly skating my leg under it. Once we were all situated in our assigned seats, we finally embarked on our journey back to the Manor. Having already packed up the equipment, and some of the non-perishables in the back of the vehicle, we started our drive towards New York knowing in the back of the three of our heads that we had to hurry back as fast as possible.

Driving through the rest of the night and through that next morning, we finally entered our last hour stretch of the road trip. Cinder had slept all the way there, her rib cage slowly rising and falling. The soft black fur reflecting the passing streetlights. Every now and then I would see her muzzle twitch, forming a small snarl. A low growl would also escape from time to time, coming from deep within her throat. Only a handful of times along the entire trip did she toss her head up at me. If we had decided to take off the muzzle, I would've most likely had either my arm or my leg ripped open by those long fangs she had in this form.

With time counting down the miles we had left on our journey, I leaned my head against the head-cushion of the seat and took a thankful longing sigh. Content that we had gotten Cinder back to us before she faced a trauma as horrible as the one she had in her past. I couldn't imagine her having to go through all that again, nor could I imagine us having to see her go through it again.

"She is much different than I," Peyltih said, ending the calming silence. "What breed did they identify her as?"

"A Hellhound of Shadows-" I returned, rubbing my hand along her upper rib cage, noticing that although she had lost some weight, the length of her body has grown a few more inches.

"She was identified as that breed because although her blood tests had come back as a Hellhound, it was her continuous recollections of an interactive Shadow that gave her that name." Yalu now spoke up. "Cinder told me the last time those Researchers had any reports of one of her breeds it was dated as folklore back in their earliest recorded literature. The scriptures were dated supposedly even farther back than even some early Hebrew tablets."

"Taking it further back than-." Peylith politely interrupted. "A breed even older than the Deity of Anubis."

"I guess." I acknowledged, still petting Cinder. "I am just glad that we got her out..."

"Jakob, I'm sure you can take that muzzle off by now," Mhykal's voice interjected, his eyes flashing at me through the rear-facing mirror.

"Not yet." I hastily refused, "For everyone's safety, it would be best for us to leave it on until she is fully conscious again."

"She's reacting in her sleep?" Yalu probed, swiftly turning around to face me from around the front passenger seat.

"I guess you could call it that-" I said, again rubbing my hand along her soft fur. "I don't think she is fully aware of her surroundings."

"Did she regain those memories?" Mhykal now asked ahead of his girlfriend.

"Who knows."

Chapter 56

Jakob

Making our way up the driveway to the place we had all called home for so long, our small group of five were greeted by the sanctioned Unnaturals working on taking their leave, including the numerous numbers of Rebels we had working at this Syndicate. My best estimate we were currently running at a little over thirty percent full capacity, however even with that number and the number of rooms the Manor had, it was all still too much per the Human Laws. As we further approached the Garage, I noticed the families we had sanctioned here were packing up all their simplest belongings, piling them into the rented cars provided by my money, as stated per protocol for emergencies like this. While those who had managed to create unique relationships during their stay were steadily leaving in makeshift parties. As we completed our rendezvous under the direct sunlight of the midday sun, the black Escalade caught the attention of our appointed Syndicate Leader.

Putting the vehicle into park, Mhykal took the keys out of the ignition and turned off the SUV. Turning over to Peylith, I gestured, "Stay here with her, please. The three of us need to go discuss what our plans are."

"Okay." The conscious Hellhound returned. Still in his human form, surprisingly he began to roll up his sleeves again. The cold shockingly not unsettling him.

Looking down at Cinder, I rolled my hand under her large canine head and gently snuck out. Not wanting to wake her up, although I knew that with how hard she was 'dreaming' it would take a lot to abruptly arouse the sleeping beast. Finally putting my feet down on the paved driveway, I followed the Vixen and her boyfriend up to the long classic Victorian-styled front porch to go communicate with Braedon. That sneaky suspicion our Leader had something he was keeping secret from us still feeding my churned gut.

"So is everyone almost out?" Yalu cautiously inquired.

"So far. Those are the last few." Our astounding Leader answered, pointing to the four remaining vehicles who had yet to leave the Manor. "I rented out small houses for everyone. Grouping them up in groups of four to six Unnaturals per house, keeping families together of course." Braedon answered, his tone full of caution and sincere concern.

"So, all thirty-six Unnaturals have somewhere else to hide out, while this is going on?" I calmly inquired, my concern fixating once more on the safety of those that we had freed.

"Yes. I paid up for an entire month with most of the houses." Braedon responded, still wearing that black suit of his, continuing to attempt to pull off that look of authority and empowerment.

"Jeez, Jakob, I knew you were rich and the Syndicate was able to use your funds for reasons concerning the Unnaturals we had freed, but still-" Mhykal teased finally grasping onto how wealthy I truly was.

"Seven centuries of Immortality allowed me to build up tons of interest on my money." I sneered, trying to ease the mood. "Anyways as long as they are all safe and they can make those places look lived in as much as possible just in case these damn bastards want to go report in on them for interviews." I sighed, returning to the subject at hand.

303

"You got her back, didn't you?" Braedon now probed, suddenly changing the subject. Most likely using it to lighten the amount of uncertainty he had in himself and the thick tension between the two of us.

"We did, and it was a lot easier than that collaboration you had us do with the Draconics and Lycans. In and out, no problems. Cinder is in the car."

"Okay-." The slightly older Vampiric paused. "How is she?"

"Unconscious and thin, but still ten times better than how she was fifteen months ago."

"That's good. Well then, back to the subject at hand. I already set up our second location for the six of you. Assuming that the other Hellhound was going with you-"

"You set up the Mansion over the state-line in Connecticut?" I harshly interrogated. "As in the one that's off the damn coast in New Haven?"

"Yeah. It's a good place for you guys to getaway. You are one of those old rich people anyways." Braedon smirked. "I already had all of your belongings, including Cinder's newly bought clothes sent up there. It should all be set and ready for you guys to live at for the time being-"

"It is in the middle of the fucking winter, Braedon!" I angrily snapped.

"I know it is in the middle of winter right now, but we have little choice in how to deal with this damn search warrant. Okay?" He growled back at me.

"Did you do all of the other precautions? The blood? The Cameras? Were they documented with people coming in and out to make it look more like a Historical House as it should be? All of the other Unnatural signs are out as well?"

"Yes, I have already put all of the other precautions in order. All the cameras have been put in with false tapes. The Blood has already been safely stored away at the Beach House. Everything has been taken care of. We had made plans like this for reasons like what is happening. I wasn't expecting it to happen like this, but here we are." The Vampire explained.

"And Valeryie?" Yalu asked, now changing the subject yet again.

"She is finishing up packing away her things, though she is quite upset about having to relocate like this," Braedon answered, but before he could finish the Vixen had already stormed inside the front doors.

"I bet she is-" Mhykal sneered, following his girlfriend inside the Manor. Stopping at the threshold, my friend threw me the car keys and called back, "Jakob, you go ahead and take them two up to the Mansion. The three of us will meet you guys up there."

"Alright," I said catching the keys. Not thrilled about driving on the icy roads over to Connecticut, I began to descend the front porch steps. "I wish you good luck Braedon."

"Same to you-" the Leader cockily sneered.

"Where are Yalu and Mhykal?" Peylith questioned me from the back seat the minute I climbed into the driver's seat.

"They are taking another vehicle and will meet us up at the next place," I answered, trying to simplify the situation for the Immortal Hellhound.

"Okay. So, we will meet them up there?"

"Yeah." I slowly exhaled while putting the car keys into the ignition and revving up the vehicle. Though I hated driving, in comparison to my friend I was much better at it than him. Pulling the vehicle out, I drove around the rest of the circular drive and returned to the end of the property. Once we were back on the road we embarked on the journey to New Haven. "Peylith keep an eye on Cinder for me." I softly ordered, glancing up into the rear-view mirror.

"I can do that." the Anubis Deity answered back, his voice sounding excited yet somehow just as stressed as I.

"If she wakes up or starts to have another fit, please let me know," I said, locking my gaze with Peylith's yellow wolf eyes through the mirror. Seeing his acknowledgment, I took another deep breath before returning my focus on the road with a long continuous journey laid out before us. Thinking along the way, "How was I going to handle two Hellhounds by myself?"

Chapter 57
Jakob/Cinder

After we had finally entered New Haven, Connecticut, I again looked in the mirror to see that Cinder was still unconscious, and Peylith himself looked like he was ready to drift off. Driving the Escalade through the rich town, I sped directly through downtown as my smartphone started to blare its usual ringtone. Approaching a stop sign, I glanced down at the phone's screen, my eyes noticing that the screen had flashed the image of Yalu and Mhykal hugging one another and happily starring back at me. The very image I was using as the Vixen's contact picture.

Before I propelled forward, I picked up the phone, swiping the phone button over to accept the call, I heard Yalu's raspy voice speak. "We are about a half-hour away from the Manor."

As I went from zero miles per hour and climbed back up to a steady twenty miles per hour, I responded, "I am just about there, got another five minutes or so."

"Ok. How is she?" Yalu asked, abruptly changing the subject on me.

"Still asleep."

"Really?"

"Yeah, Peylith looks like he is about to fall asleep himself." I joked.

"No, I'm not-" the man tiredly argued.

Hearing Yalu chuckle on the other end of the phone told me that she had heard his tired voice shout over the speaker. "Anyways, we will be there shortly. Okay, Jakob?"

"Okay, I am just now entering the property," I said, turning onto the brick-paved cobblestone road that marked where our property stood. The house was completely secluded in over ten acres of woods on both the left and right of the property, while down beneath the Manor was our private stretch of beach. "We will see you guys shortly."

"Okay, see you then," Yalu agreed, ending the phone call.

Tossing my phone onto the passenger side's seat, I drove the vehicle up the rest of the driveway towards the seventeen thousand five hundred square foot house with five bedrooms, five and a half bathrooms, and a three-car garage. It's beige brick, European styled roofing, and structure blending it accordingly with the surrounding woods. Driving up the driveway, I drove around the frozen snow-covered circular fountain and parked the car at the front of the house.

"Are we here?" Peylith asked, readjusting his tired frame around in the uncomfortable leather seats.

"Yeah, we are here," I answered, taking the keys out of the ignition. Opening the door to the Escalade, I strolled to the passenger door of the parked vehicle towards where Cinder was lying, still unconscious of course. Looking over to the former Pharaoh who was slowly exiting out of the seat after having numerous problems with his seatbelt, I gave out fresh orders. "Now Peylith, there should be a key hidden under the rock off to the left side of the stairs-"

"Huh?" The Hellhound asked. "A key?"

"Of course-" I sighed aloud, feeling stupid. Cursing to myself for a minute, I overheard the much older than I Hellhound sincerely apologize. "No, it's not your fault," I assured, calming back down. "Well just watch her for me, while I'll get the key."

"Okay." Peylith returned, stepping out of the Escalade to stand on that same side of the vehicle and obediently observe his fellow kin.

Running up towards the front arched porch, I stopped beside the stairs to look under the small rock. Picking up the rock, I quickly found the key. Hastily clutching the little metal tool, I placed the rock back down in the same spot along the empty snow pocket before darting up the stairs and beginning to unlock the thick-arched oak wood double doors. Turning the key, I effortlessly picked the lock to yet another house I owned under my illustrious name. Then running back down the stairs to the vehicle, "Alright go ahead and go inside, explore the place. I will be inside shortly."

"Okay, but Jakob..." Peylith paused, not yet ready to leave his post. "She's awake..."

"Where am I?" I thought, trying to get my sight to adjust to the bright rays of warm sunlight battering down at me. The brightness only stronger as the blinding rays clashed against the bright white snow.

"Hey," I heard a remarkably familiar voice ring, "You're awake-"

Once my powerfully gifted sight had finally accustomed its vision to the harsh glare, I saw that familiar European face with short dark brown hair and feint amber eyes mixing with a fading hazel-like green. Wearing his usual dark clothes and that same smile as always, I recognized the Unnatural. That Vampiric friend of mine, one of the three, I had desperately urged to rescue me. Trying to again speak, I was stopped by the same head collar still wrapped around my skull.

"Here let me take that off," Jakob said, stepping further into my line of sight, blocking all the warm and brightly reflecting rays of sunlight. Feeling his hands grab around the leather strap behind my ears and start to unbuckle it, I anxiously froze. With that contraption falling off my skull, I proceeded to observe Jakob also unbuckle the muzzle's strap attached to the head collar. Sliding the entire contraption off from my face, he finally freed my jaws were free from that tightly bound contraption. Feeling his hand gently coax the flattened fur, I heard him softly remark, "There, feel better?"

Moving my jaws around as I regained more and more feeling in my mouth, I took a minute to reclaim the entire function. Eventually speaking I quietly returned, "Much better. Thank you." Taking a swift breath through my mouth, I inhaled the freezing cold salty fresh air. Tasting my freedom once more. "Where are we?" I questioned, finally recognizing that this was not the Manor I had spent the last year freely roaming around. "And who are you?" Also, recognizing the unusual man who stood beside Jakob. It was obvious he wasn't Mhykal, Viktor or Braedon, so who was he?

"That is Peylith." Jakob calmly answered me, sensing him trying to level my insecurity. "He is a good friend of ours, he helped us get you out of that Institute."

"Hello." The dark Caucasian skinned man happily greeted.

Acknowledging him, I nodded my canine head, however, I did not feel comfortable enough to communicate with him just yet. Even if he was a fellow Unnatural.

"Peylith will be staying with all of us here for a little while," Jakob explained, trying to still calm my heightened sense of insecurity.

"Us?" I interrogated, trying my best to now move my legs and get back up onto my feet. I had a million questions in my head, but before I could ask another Jakob filled in all the answers.

"We will be staying here at this Mansion in New Haven, Connecticut, until we get the all-clear from Braedon, who is staying back at the Manor with Viktor. Mhykal, Yalu, and Valeryie will all be staying here with us as well."

Exhaling another sigh, I decided it was better judgment to give up on standing for now. I could tell that the drugs were still in my system. Frustratingly cursing at myself, I dropped my head down back down into my lap.

"You still can't walk or transform, can you?"

"Nope." I quickly returned.

"It's alright," Jakob said as he began to help me out of the vehicle. "It was easier getting you in the car than it is to get you out at this angle." He now teased.

Chapter 58
Cinder

Strolling through the massive front doors of this new property, Jakob proceeded to gently carry me inside. Moving me into a semi-traditional modern living room, the seven-hundred-year-old Vampiric eased my worthless frame on top of the backless ottoman attached to the neutral grey 'L' sectional. Lying on my side for a few minutes before adjusting myself around to laying on my stomach in an upright lying position, I avidly resumed watching the Unnatural who I was still unsure I was truly seeing or not, maneuver around this massive house so effortlessly. Glancing around, I also observed Peylith wander around. His movements the complete opposite of the Vampire, telling me that he was either new to the Syndicate or that Jakob had been to this place before. Dropping my head onto the soft throw blanket, I again painfully drifted off into slumber. I wanted my conscious doubts answered, but my exhaustion bit my ankles too hard.

When I woke back up, I saw young Valeryie intently staring at me with her bright yellow eyes and long black eyelashes. "Hey there Cinder." The young Vixen loudly shouted, leaving a deep ringing in my ears again. "Yalu, she's awake."

"Yeah I am awake-" I groaned to myself using my regaining leg strength to scratch at my cropped ears with my front legs. Trying to rub out the ringing.

"Well leave her alone, you probably woke her up, to begin with." The elder sister scolded her little sibling from behind the neutral oak with rock-like cobblestone patterned marble top counters. Telling me that two to one the elder sister was cooking something. Using my nose, I easily whiffed up the strong smell of cooked food. Tasty food. Food that was not raw.

"You smell it huh, Cinder?" Valeryie asked me, still hunched down at my eye level. Looking back at her, I slightly smirked, continuing to eavesdrop on her dialogue, "Yalu is making some sort of meal with chicken."

"I can tell that it's chicken." I eventually spoke back. Shaking my head, I heard another familiar sound. The sound of that Number I.D.ed metal tag bouncing around the keyring attached to the old leather collar still wrapped around my thick canine muscular neck. As I shook away the dizziness, I decided to again attempt to get up, to move. Hoping that after spending nearly my entire day sleeping, the remnants of the drugs still running rampant throughout my system had been worn down. Forcing myself up into a sitting position on top of the cushion, I felt my front legs twitch but attempt to remain steady. Holding steady for around forty seconds, I then tried to stand the rest of my physique up. Managing to get all four legs standing on top of the ottoman, I again tried to stay steady. Locking my legs in place, I waited till the spasms in my legs calmed down before eventually moving around to the edge of the cushion, and stepping down off onto the abstract naturally faded red rug beneath the sectional. Finally, being free to move around I decided it was time I explored some of this insanely huge property that the six of us would be temporarily staying.

Slowly moving around the sectional, taking one step at a time, I overheard Jakob's voice ring out. Seeing what I believed were his legs standing before me, I released a long exhale and sat back down.

313

Looking up at him, I produced a low snarl as he spoke, his voice too leaving a nasty ringing in my poor ears, "Peylith and Mhykal are still outside sparring."

"Still?" Yalu shouted through the kitchen over the sizzling of frying chicken. "Valeryie could you tell them to knock it off and get their asses inside this house before I go beat them upside the head with this same damn cast iron skillet I am cooking with."

Flattening my ears while I listened to the usual Yalu attitude spark, I finally conceded that the images rolling through my head was indeed a reality and not some altered side-effect of all those drugs that had been forced onto me. Observing the little young Vixen take off for the back doors around the other side of the large sectional capable of sitting of at least eight people comfortably, I continued to eavesdrop on the conversation. Valeryie ordering the two men exactly what her sister had told her to, made me lightheartedly chuckle.

"You haven't regained your human form yet?" Jakob probed.

Sighing out with a frustrating breath, I answered the Vampiric, "No not yet. Probably by tomorrow. I hope by then that the Pheromone Blockers have worn their wear."

"Pheromone blockers?" He questioned, wandering around me to sit on the sectional. "I thought those drugs stopped you from changing into your Hellhound form?"

"It stops the creation of Pheromones needed to change in-between forms as well as stopping any abilities from consciously activating." I frustratingly clarified.

"Do you recall how you got locked in that form, then?"

"Pheromone Uppers and Blessed Salts." I again returned, climbing back up onto the ottoman.

"Uppers? Blessed Salts?"

"The Uppers were able to trick my body into creating the exact number of Pheromones needed for a transformation, while the

Blessed Salts were injected into my body to keep me numb and unable to function," I said laying my head back down on the blanket. Reading his confused facial expression as he strained to digest everything I was telling him. "I guess you could say that the Salts reacted to my body the same way Silver does to other Canine Species of Unnaturals. Something to do with Hellhoundism belonging to the Demonic Branch of Unnaturals."

"Going back to early literature to figure out how to control you." Jakob eventually answered after digesting everything I had told him.

"Something like that." I exhaled.

"Well, you will be back to your full potential once those are weaned from your system." He said, getting up to walk into the Kitchen and help Yalu finish everything for what I had assumed was dinner. The sweet smell of that fried and seasoned chicken pulling my fear of returning to the insane haunting memories of my 'assigned hunts'.

"Here you go-" Yalu said, strolling out of the kitchen to hand me a large platter of sliced chicken pieces. "You still need to eat. It may just be chicken for now-"

Interrupting her, I offered my sincerest thanks and eagerly began to devour the plate full of a couple of chicken pieces. The taste of garlic, rosemary, and thyme filling my palette. It was not as enriched to me in this form as the meat I was fed back at the Institute, but mentally it was fulfilling. The longer I ate away at the food, the more I felt energy flowing back into my body. My stomach ordering me for more and more, to eat faster and faster because of my small deliberate starvation I faced back at that other place. Hearing the clanging of knives and forks, the many communication tones, the moving of jaws and teeth crunching down on their own food, urged my need to eat more comfortably. Finishing my meal, I instinctively began to lick the plate clean, picking up the salty garlic seasonings on my tongue. Trying to maintain self-control, I pulled away from the plate and climbed back off the ottoman to again touch the floor.

Sneaking away from the view of the collected Unnaturals sitting at the dining table by one of the back doors, I once more attempted to embark on an exploration of the place. Using my regained energy, I forced my legs to work. Trotting around the halls in this form that I was still surprisingly more comfortable in, I used my nose and snuffed the scents of the Unnaturals to figure out who had picked what room. Yalu and Mhykal's scents were grouped together, telling me that the two were, of course, sharing a room and by my best estimate it was on the second floor. I also noticed that the one who was called Peylith, too had a room on the second story. So did the younger Vixen. Both were separate, but their scents were close, telling me that most likely their rooms were across from one another. The only scent collected downstairs was Jakob's soft cologne. Following that, I swiftly found where his room was located. The door was unfortunately shut, keeping me locked outside. Pushing on, I went to discover where my room was located. Knowing that as big as this place was, I at least had to have my own room somewhere on this property.

As I worked to find my sleeping quarters, I suddenly felt a cold hand glide by my left ear. The sensation abruptly pulling my long-cropped ear away a second later. I did not need a second glance to know where this uncomfortably inhospitable feeling came from. And it belonged to a person I honestly didn't want to see right now. Halting my gait, I turned my four-legged body slightly around before harshly growling at this being, "What do you want, Shadow?"

Chapter 59
Cinder

Turning my large dog frame around in the narrow hallway, my eyes alerted to the cursed Shadow. Keeping my head lowered, I bared my fangs as I prepared myself for what this being had planned. Once more I interrogated him, deepening my growl, "What do you want?"

"Watch your tone." The Skeletal Shadow hissed back. "You were the one that asked me to watch over your friends while you were kept inside that place."

Flattening my ears and my hackles I looked away from his red eyes, remembering that I indeed pleaded with this Shadow for the protection of my friends. "My apologies-" I contritely mumbled.

"I followed through with what you asked, now it is your time to follow through with what you promised, Little Reaper-"

"NOT NOW!" I growled baring my teeth, raising my lips higher. Staring back into his fiery red eyes, I locked gazes before again hastily looking away. Softening my tone before speaking up. "Not now, please not now. Give me time to work out how to break it to them. Considering I have to leave them, correct?"

"My smart Little Reaper." The being's voice praised. "You are correct that in order to live up to your title and occupation, you must leave behind this life." The Shadow now coldly returned, his voice also ringing deep into my eardrums. "I understand that takes time, so you will have six months."

"Six months?" I questioned, thankful for my voice being disguised under the loud conversation between Jakob, Peylith, and Mhykal over hunting or something along that line. I desperately wanted to argue with him, I wanted to rebuttal my point or at least negotiate it, however, because of that plead I made not too long ago still hanging over my conscious, I submitted. Dropping down onto my hindquarters, I lowered my head and looked away from his gaze. "I understand." I painfully obliged.

"If you take any longer than the time which has been granted to you, I will make you watch as I do them in." The Shadow now threatened me. His fingers firmly clutching my mouth, forcing my muzzle shut and my eyes to focus on that unusual warm glaze of his. "Do you understand me, Little Reaper?"

"Yes, I understand." I choked, feeling my heart rise into my throat as I excruciatingly spoke those words. My stomach churned, and my head felt dizzy with all the digestion.

"That's my smart Little Reaper." The Skeleton repeated, his fingers moving around to the top of my head, rubbing through the short black fur on top of my head. Petting me before he again disappeared into the darkness.

Taking a few minutes to calm my thoughts, I began to wonder, "How the hell was I going to tell them that I had to leave? How could I do it without telling them the entire truth?" This was just too difficult for my still-developing mind to warp around. Dropping onto the carpeted floor, I lied my head in between my paws and continued to quietly ponder to myself as I lied right in front of what I believed was my designated room: "How could I tell the only people that to have ever shown me any kindness in the last seventeen years that I had to go without hurting them? Without possibly losing my sanity along the way and perchance even unwilling being forced to kill them?"

318

I decided in time I would tell them, in due time. I had six months before I had to break away, that was plenty of time to break the news to them, right? I just had to wait for what felt like a decent time to explain it. Standing myself up to return to the Living Room where I believed everyone was still collected at, I continued to wander through all the potential ways I could tell them this, and the possibilities of their denial.

Stepping out of the hallway, I stepped down the small step that connected the two rooms, noticing that all the Unnaturals had calmed down in front of what I assumed was a television. It was so long since I had seen one of those electronics. As I eyed over what everyone was doing, I noticed that they were all indulged in their 'electronics'. The men were playing on what I now believed was a Video Game console. Having what looked like old PlayStation controllers that had been modified with sleek shiny black covers, I swayed my sights over to see that they were playing some sort of war game through the T.V. and were overpowering Peylith in whatever its goals were. Confused, I further observed the men continue to play the first-person shooter from a distance. Growing bored, I glanced my vision over to the women in our little group, curious about what they were doing. I noticed that Valeryie was texting away on her large smartphone using both of her hands to hold the phone up while twiddling away with both of her thumbs on the phone's miniaturized keyboard. Glancing over to Valeryie's older sister, Yalu, I saw that she too, was completely indulged into her own newly replaced smartphone. It looked like she was also texting away on her modern electronic, however not at the same speed as her younger Vixen sister. Sighing out, I quietly strolled around the back of the sectional and began to explore the rest of the house. The large property I had overheard we would be staying at for a little while, noting that the furniture throughout the place was much more adeptly modern and blanketed with very modern architecture than the previous location. Everywhere I looked, it was dark floors with bright but neutral décor, a complete opposite of the Manor.

319

Passing around the dining table fit for ten people, I saw that the dark-stained pine wood had a glass table stationed over it, allowing me to see up through it. Seeing the under of the glass rose vase, the red rose petals that had fallen over the table's glass cover block out the modern chandelier, which was passing warm rays down through the glass tabletop. Weaving around the chairs, I strolled out around the other side to explore the modern open-spaced kitchen. Finding nothing unusual about the clean surfaces, I went down the other adjoining hallway. Finding a small half bathroom, and an open sliding glass door that walked out to a floor to ceiling fifteen-foot by thirty-foot seasonal room.

The room all around was filling with bright green ivy potted plants, modern wicker sectional patio furniture, outdoor pillows, and many other objects discovered in a patio room. Although it was dark inside, the bright light shining off the fading full moon was enough to help me see around the area. Walking around the sunroom, I jumped onto the sectional and found some comfort on the edge closest to the window where I lied myself down and stared out past the snow-covered beach. Contently watching the crashing waves breaking onto the shore from the Atlantic Ocean, I stared up into the bright little blinking stars that shone right back down on the land they guarded. Feeling the sincerity and calmness of their bright white light, I mumbled aloud to myself. Howling out my anxiety on my very first day here in this new Manor. Collapsing my head down onto the vinyl fabric, I bundled myself up into a tightly formed circle before using my tail to cover over my eyes and slip into another worn-out slumber.

Immediately after I shut my eyes, I began to feel my body revert to its human form. My paws growing out the long fingers, my fur retreating away back to its smooth pale skin. Painfully grimacing as my snout retreated to its human female nose and soft lipped mouth. In seconds the pain too retreated, telling me that my modification had finished. Finally, I had returned to my twenty-five-year-old human form. Not caring that I was completely nude from the last time I had been in this form, I curled myself into a tighter ball. Using my own species' flame abilities to stay warm as I lied beside the window separating the house's warmth from the outside world's wintery blast. The warmth illuminating from my pale skin only deepened the blanket of condensation that clung to the inner glass of the window. Exhaling a long-contracted breath, I finally drifted off into a peaceful, non-drug-induced slumber.

Chapter 60

Jakob

    With everyone on track to finally head off to bed, I shut off the PlayStation Four console and commenced with turning off the lights around the large common area. Recalling that a couple of hours ago, I had seen the female Beauceron Shifter skimming around the floor, obviously exploring more of the house. She didn't stick around us, which I felt was an unusual pattern for someone like Cinder, who normally stayed within inches of one of us ever since she had regained her mobility. It seemed the Hellhound was always shadowing one of us, so it was indeed odd for her, yet I brushed off the gut instinct that there was something wrong. Replacing the instinct with it being nothing more than Cinder's maturing independence. Strolling around the kitchen to dim the hanging lights, I tried to remember where all the light switches were so I could complete my esteemed task, while I too attempted to solve where the Great Dane sized canine had scampered off to. I knew she could not run out of the house in her paralyzed transformation, yet I still did not know where in the house the dog was hiding. Walking down the wide hallway that was directly parallel to the back of the sectional sofa, my mind strived to configure all the spots and access points that Cinder could slip into. As I stepped past the half bath and towards the garage, I swiftly closed off the second floor and nearly all the closed-off rooms. Strolling past the open sunroom, I caught a familiar silhouette out of the corner of my eye.

Unsure about the present Aura I was getting off this person, I slowly entered the darkly moon-lit closed off patio to further investigate. Slithering around the glass, light tan wicker coffee table towards the ottoman angled along the tall nine-foot-tall window, I further investigated this sleeping person's physique. The moonlight echoing so softly off the pale-skin that I didn't need my heightened sense of sight to map out the specific details along this mystifying person who I deeply hoped was the Unnatural I had been searching for. Praying it was her and not some unwanted being who had snuck into the thoroughly secured house, I scanned the woman for key characteristics. Studying the form unfolding before my eyes, I quickly noted that this distinguished person was completely naked. Not a single item of clothing was covering the porcelain white skin. Standing a bit back in shock at the nudity, I backed into the adjacent fern pot. Attempting to hastily catch the potted plant before it crashed onto the patio cobblestone, I lowly cursed, "Shit!" Barely catching it with my left foot before the pot came slamming into the ground, I gently placed the flat surface back on the ground. Turning my gaze on the sleeping person who was readjusting it's sleeping position on the vinyl cushion, I took a heavy sigh of relief.

Stepping closer to the nude person, I continued to and investigate its key traits. Under the white moonlight, I saw long black hair draped around small shoulders and over the side of another small oddly shaped rib cage. The way the ribs looked was as if they had been broken recently. The bone also appeared to have healed improperly. Noticing how petite this humanoid was, I began to wonder to myself where I had seen this frame before. Leaning forward as I quietly questioned the darkness, "Cinder? Is that you?" I knew that if I could find a dignifying mark on the assuming-to-be woman, I would be able to clarify my gut suspicion. Was this indeed the person I had yet to say how I truly felt? Looking around the soft bare skin, I saw along her upper rib cage the start of that dignified trait I was hastily surveying the frame for. The sharp scarring that resembled a large cross. Soundlessly creeping around the table and ottoman, I began to foresee more of the long scar along her bareback and tailbone. The same long crossed scar with its scalded pale pink skin hiding in the darkness. Viewing the damaged skin, I noticed an insignificant increase in the etching along her spine, as if it had further embedded itself into her skin in her absence. Taking note of that, I thankfully sighed another relieved breath.

Gently placing my hand on her warm beating skin, I tenderly rubbed my hand down the shoulder before delicately moving the long black bangs away from Cinder's soft-skinned face. Cuffing the hair behind her little-almost elf-like ear, I proceeded to serenely stare at the Hellhound's peaceful sleeping bi-pedal human form for a few minutes. Eventually, I walked back around the coffee table and back into the living room to grab the soft white fleece blanket from the sectional. Draping the small blanket over her curled-up body, I covered the exposed skin and softly whispered goodnight in her exposed ear. Gazing one last time at Cinder, I smiled feeling ecstatic to have her back in our lives again. Content to have the female Hellhound free from the Institute's grimy hands.

"Tomorrow will be another day, Cinder." I yet again whispered before exiting out the Sunroom. Strolling back into the adjoining hallway, I casually dragged my exhausted feet towards my assigned room on the first floor across from Cinder's. Using the bright moonlight cascading through the long traditional colonial windows that were built along the backside of the house to let in the beautiful ocean scenery, I safely guided myself around the sharp corner. Entering my room, I continued to tiredly drag my feet towards the modern darkly stained four-post bed with this Elk scenery engraved into the headboard. Beginning to take off my day clothes, I threw my black hoodie onto the little dark-stained chest sitting along the edge of the footboard. As I proceeded with removing my grey shirt, and my dark jeans, I wondered about her mental stability as I threw both items into the dark hamper. Skimming through the matching material dresser, I quickly searched for a comfortable pair of sweatpants. Once I found a pair, I slipped the pair over my dull grey boxer briefs and embarked on those final steps. The minute I flopped on top of the comforter I became comatose, crashing into a desperate plea of slumber.

Waking up the next morning hearing shuffling feet, smelling the menagerie of breakfast foot items being cooked in the nearby kitchen, I rose from the dead and began to stretch my also waking muscles. Raising my arms up above my head, I extended the limbs as far as they could reach. Twisting my back around until I heard the infamous pop of my seven-century old skeletal structure. Completing the daily ritual, I began to wander over to the dresser and pick out today's clothes to which I would be wearing. Deciding that today was just going to be a day with no noteworthy events planned, I swiftly grabbed a casual off-white shirt. Not caring to straighten up my already messy bedhead, I opened the bedroom door noticing that its corresponding door across the hall was still closed. Prompting me to believe Cinder was probably still sleeping in the Sunroom. Following the sweet-aroma of cooking food, I exited out of the small corridor overhearing surprised shouts and loud voices ring out through the open-spaced, multi-functional room. Curious, my eyes scavenged around the room the corner to see that standing beside Yalu in the kitchen was Cinder eating a piece of bacon. Her appetite overrunning the urgency of privacy as she stood completely nude in front of the older Unnaturals.

"What is going on?" I asked, stepping up to the island and sitting in one of the backless bar stools. "Cinder we did bring you some clothes, you know?"

"Yeah, I kind of figured you would. I just wanted to eat first." The woman tiredly replied while she continued to devour the bacon both delicately and aggressively. It was quite a sight to see!

"Cinder you should get dressed before Valeryie wakes up." Mhykal pleaded, his ecstatic concern making me want to laugh at my old friend. But holding that urge, I agreed with him.

325

"Just grab another piece and go put something on okay? The food is not going anywhere anytime soon." Yalu ordered, in this motherly tone, she seemed to always use when she was handing out orders to the sweet Hellhound.

"Fine-" the young nude woman groaned. Watching her stuff the piece she was eating in her mouth to hold on to it, I shockingly observed her lean her hand directly over the two-burner sized fryer, right over the grease and grab a piece of bacon straight off of the skillet. Her skin not even blistering or reacting to the heat of the grease. She didn't even react when the grease popped on her wrist! Shocking all of us as she slowly strolled her nude human form back to where her room was located. Another surprise.

"She knows where her room is?" Peylith asked, his voice a little unsure about the event that had just occurred.

"Sure, seems like it. Doesn't surprise me, Cinder has a nose far better than even mine." Yalu answered while she stood over the stove proceeding to flip a small buttermilk pancake over. "Mhykal, could you go wake up Valeryie, and make sure she gets semi-decent as well."

"Uh, sure." The dark black-haired, amber-eyed, three-hundred-year-old Vampiric reluctantly agreed.

As he ascended the double-wide staircase, I abruptly asked the question hanging over my head. "Did Cinder really just grab a piece of bacon right from the skillet?"

"Yeah, she has done it a couple of other times before," Yalu answered. "She says that she doesn't feel the burning of grease, nor an open flame."

"Doesn't surprise me," Peylith said as he finally sat down on the seat next to mine also in his sleepwear. Wearing grey long sweatpants and a form-fitting black tank top to show off his muscular stature. The colors coordinating well with his dark tanned-skin and brilliantly yellow eyes. "Our species don't feel the pain of any form of heat. In all my life, the only time I have ever felt that kind of burning pain was when I had received this Gold Ankh on my back and the tattoos on my arms. Yet, I do not believe that my pain was as bad as that 'Deity's was. That scar on her back is very deeply engraved and has smaller blistering scars along her spine. I can only imagine how painful that was when she received it from her God." Anubis's Hellhound continued to clarify.

"You seem more surprised by her scar than her nudity." I heard Yalu tease while her back was still facing the active stove removing the sizzling pork.

"No, I was shocked that she had not covered more of her skin, however, when I was still living in my own time, I had seen countless nude women that had been given to me-" he now quietly sneered.

"Your time was much different than everyone else's." I teased back. "You had it very lucky when you became an Unnatural."

"I believe I did." Peylith chuckled as the other Hellhound finally came back out of her room this time dressed.

"Thank you, Cinder." The dressed Vixen graciously spoke while Cinder again grabbed for more of that greased Applewood Smoked Bacon fresh from the skillet.

"Yeah, yeah." The woman returned, as she eagerly ate the bacon. Wearing a black sports bra, some black tight leggings, and her long hair put up in a high ponytail. The black hair somehow ten shades darker passing for the darkest brunette I had ever seen.

"Going for a run or something?" I probed my sights locking on her athletic get up.

"Yeah, I want to get back some of the muscle I had lost." She answered after swallowing a mouthful of meat.

"Mind if I join you?" I overheard Peylith casually ask. "I need to start preparing myself for when I get back to hunting and returning lost souls."

"So that's your job?" Cinder asked her attention completely averted from her food.

327

I was unsure about where this was all heading off to, but I also understood where her question was coming from. They were both the same species, maybe not the same breed, but being Hellhounds alone seemed to have brought out this atypical relationship the two were steadily forming. Pushing aside any forms of doubt, I noticed Mhykal and Valeryie were finally descending the stairs to come eat. Poor Valeryie was still exhausted from staying up all night and texting her friends back in New York. With Yalu finishing up, I watched Cinder and the younger Vixen start to move the collected platters over to the dining table so we could have a nice calm breakfast before the female Hellhound could finish off all the bacon.

Chapter 61
Jakob

After breakfast, the two Hellhounds took off into the backyard to run along the long secluded beach and forest trails blanketing our property. The cold snow and salty ocean air not at all bothering them as they both altered their physical appearances. Mutating into the canine forms. Avidly surveying from the other side of the colonial window in the dining room as I drank a glass of blood to catch up on my feedings, I noticed the vast difference between the two breeds while they ran down the snow-covered sandy beach, and it wasn't just only their height.

Peylith was in his large Pharaoh Hound form, his fur was more of a soot-black, and was shorter than Cinder's. Strained over the back of his spine was that same gold Ankh and his other oddly marked tattoos, the bright gold deeply contrasting against his black fur. Watching the Hellhound use his larger height and weight against Cinder he, I believed playfully tackled her down into the snow. His firm ears standing straight up like huge satellites on top of his slender muscular skull. Peylith's whip-like long tail wagging as he stood a few feet away from the Beauceron Hellhound that stood covered in freshly fallen snow.

Glancing over to Cinder, I noticed that the attack had not phased her while she rolled herself back up onto her four feet. Her smaller height was still considerably larger than her standard breed.

If I had to say she stood about as tall as one of the Giant Breeds. Puffing out her two-toned chest, Cinder heavily inhaled the cold-air followed by a puff of white breath exhaling, her long cropped ears too pulled forward standing at attention and the pitch blue-black thick tail remaining low yet still wagging. Her head holding high, she bared her teeth back at her larger opponent and charged back in.

"They are playing," Yalu said as she picked up more dishes to take to the dishwasher. "It might look rough-"

"I thought they were going for a run?" I asked still viewing the two canines tussle in the snow. Cinder rearing up onto her hind legs to extend her reach for Peylith's face.

"They will be, but for Canid Species, play is just as important as stretching is for everyone else. It helps them build up and flex the muscles for all the same reasons it does humans." The Vixen continued to explain to me, piling the dirty dishes into the washer.

Observing Peylith again push his weight around, tossing the smaller framed Hellhound into the snow, I witnessed Cinder roll a few times in the snow before regaining her equilibrium and taking off at a deadbeat run towards the other canine. Using her larger muscle mass and surprisingly faster speed, she rammed the left side of her chest into his right shoulder. Throwing her head upwards, Cinder sprang her jaws wide and grabbed at Peylith's scruff just as he started to fall over. Noticing her push all of her dead weight into his side, I watched them both fall into the snowbank. Cinder losing her 'playful' light grip was swung off the larger Hellhound in the tussle. Rolling again in the frozen water molecules, she skidded back a few inches. Getting back up onto her feet, the younger Hellhound once more charged for the Pharaoh Hound, using her large paws she placed one of them right behind his jawline and the other front paw onto the side of his exposed chest. From there it looked as if a few words were said before she eventually let him up. Proving I guess that although the Beauceron was smaller, she was still a lot stronger than she looked.

From there I proceeded to survey the two take off into the surrounding snow-covered woods, their black fur being the only contrast against the bright white background. Waiting until the two Hellhounds faded into the distance of the large five-acre property, I decided to go back to my room and get myself changed into some actual clothes.

"Going to get dressed-" I heard my old friend smirk, looking back at him I rolled my eyes, chuckled, and continued towards my room. "Don't worry we got all of the Decorating this year."

Halting, I spun back around the corner of the hallway to stare back into Mhykal's eyes. "Decorating?" I interrogated. "What decorating?"

"Oh, you know Christmas is right around the corner." the Vampiric casually joked. "We still have to go out and get some decorations, but we got three weeks until the holiday is here."

"Are you sure that everyone is up to supporting the Holiday?" I asked, now leaning against the corner. "I mean, when was the last time that Cinder even had a Christmas? Did Peylith ever celebrate the Holiday, to begin with?"

"Well, Peylith already knows about it and is up to dealing with the Holiday. And Cinder well we would hopefully like to surprise her with it." Yalu said as she leaned in behind her boyfriend against the back of the sectional. "To Cinder, we are the closest she has to family, and what a better Holiday to bring our relationship closer than Christmas."

"Okay, okay. But you guys can do the shopping and all." I said, turning back around to again head into my bedroom.

"We will need Peylith then to help us with the tree," Mhykal said. "Considering you won't be coming with us."

"Okay." I shrugged. "I will stay here with Cinder and Valeryie while you guys are out doing your Christmas shopping or whatever you want to call it."

331

Finally, inside my bedroom, I began to take off my sweatpants so I could get dressed. Grabbing a fresh pair of jeans, I began to slip those on. Sliding one leg in at a time before pulling them up over my boxer briefs, I began to vacate the shirt I had slept in. Throwing both items into the hamper, I sauntered over to the dresser and made a hasty scroll through the drawers for a good shirt. Skimming through several folded shirts until I found a piece of clothing I could happily wear today, I eventually picked out a dark grey-black shirt with a white line straight line art going vertically down the left side of the shirt. Unfolding it, I pulled it over my head and fitted my arms through the short sleeves. Once I was finished dressing, I prepared to walk back out of the bedroom door, stopping when I heard my smartphone start ringing from off the bed's nightstand.

Huffing a longing sigh, I strolled back over to the bedside table. Standing over the darkly stained furniture, I glanced over the flashing phone screen to see who was calling me at ten-thirty in the morning. Hastily noticing that there was no contact picture attached to the caller, I read that the caller's number. Recognizing the number that I kept forgetting to save into my contacts as Viktor, I questioned. "What are you calling for?" Wondering why he would be calling me instead of Braedon. Fingers crossed that nothing had happened to the Manor when deep down I still did not care for the Vampiric Syndicate Leader, nor the Syndicate currently for that matter. I was still quite sour after how he had treated Cinder's kidnapping much different than Yalu's and wouldn't even let us bring her home until we had succeeded in 'prior obligations.'

Picking up the phone, I slid the answer button to accept the call and heard the familiar low soft masculine voice that belonged to Viktor, reply. "Hello, Jakob-"

"What's going on Viktor?" I immediately interrogated, attempting to head back towards the door for the fourth time today.

"If you are not alone, I ask you to excuse yourself." The Vampiric coldly demanded.

"Okay, I am in my room right now. What do you want to tell me?" I again questioned this time using a lower tone. Unsure about what was going on with the highly intelligent Unnatural.

"Braedon is not only dealing with Law Enforcement who are refusing to leave, but he is also having to work with Unnatural Scientists who are looking for all possible forms of Unnaturals that were being kept here." Viktor hurriedly answered.

"Well, you could have told me that while I was out in the Living Room. What do you have that it needs to be in private?"

"From what the Searchers had told us, they received the Warrant loosely based on a possibility of a tagged Unnatural Patient being held here. Apparently, the Unnatural's tag last chipped here at the Manor."

"And what of it? We have hundreds even thousands of Unnaturals that we save each year that could all possibly be chipped, what makes this one Unnatural so special?" I suspiciously inquired.

"Braedon believes that the one they are searching for is Cinder, herself. Before you go all crazy on me, Jakob, you have to think this through." Viktor continued. "How did those Hunters find Yalu and Cinder so quickly after only one trip to the Mall? And why was Cinder automatically flown out to Colorado without ever being placed elsewhere-"

"I get it." I swiftly interrupted, my mind spinning around and around as it digested the growing possibility of Cinder being tagged. There was a chance that he was right, especially when you put in the fact that they had on her so many medications, to begin with, from back when we had first encountered her. Recalling those very words that Doctor Masters had told us the same night, I started to feel chills run through my veins and down my back:

"Her abilities have been helping the Government in more ways you cursed Rebels couldn't even bother to understand."

Chapter 62
Jakob

"Was that all?" I impatiently questioned Viktor while I paced my room's floor, trying to digest the theory that Braedon had proposed.

"For now, yes," Viktor replied. Hearing the heavy sigh from his end of the phone. "For now, there is nothing else. Braedon just wanted me to warn you ahead of time just in case more Hunters come after her while you guys arc hiding out in New Haven."

"Alright, I will try to keep her on the property under the EMF Barrier." I sighed back through the speaker of the phone.

"It has also been requested that you are to keep it on the down-low. If Yalu finds out she might try to rip off our heads, or if Cinder finds out she might take off, and we will not know where she runs off to."

"I know. Alright, I will keep it on the down-low." I agreed. "I, however, will let Mhykal know so he can aid me in watching out for Hunters. How long it will stay a secret while those two are still shacking up I cannot say." I sighed, recalling how much those two told each other. Changing subject before the Vampiric would usually rudely hang up on me, I asked, "Does Braedon know when we can head back?"

"Probably not until after the first of the year," Viktor returned. "He thinks that at least it will take that long. Those guys have to do all their tracking tests and analysis which unfortunately can take a long time as we know."

Chuckling, I agreed, "Well, at least now it's faster than what it was fifty years ago, or even thirty years ago. A month or two is not that bad. Nothing like an entire year or anything like that."

"Right." The usually calm Vampiric chuckled back before hanging up without saying goodbye like usual.

"Great" I sighed, tossing the phone onto the grey and blue plaid comforter. Still pacing back and forth along the bedroom floor, I swiped my hands through my dark brown hair, dragging them down my long European Face, I released another heavy sigh. "It has been one thing after another it seems-" Stopping myself from completing the end of that sentence I then thought to myself, "The possibility of a tracking chip being implanted into Cinder's body is a large possibility especially with how she was indeed transported to the Government Institution. However, if she is truly tagged, how long would it take for those guys to track down her current location? It took them over a year to let alone track the microchip's signal back to the Manor, but still..."

Hearing my door's brass knob twist around in its clockwise position, I hesitated, stopping in the middle of my midway back pace. Waiting for the door to slowly swing open, I preyed on the identity of the unknown familiar who had yet to show itself. My Vampiric eyes swiftly noticing that it was my old friend Mhykal, I relaxed.

"Man, Jakob, how long does it take you to change?" Mhykal teased, stepping further into the average modern-sized American Bedroom.

"I had a phone call." I upsettingly returned. Glaring back at him, I walked over to the bed and picked my phone back up.

"So?"

"It wasn't Braedon that called me. And it wasn't really about the Search Warrant."

"Okay? Knowing your phone's contact list, it was still someone in the Syndicate. Most likely Viktor-" Mhykal immediately stopped, his eyes intensely dancing around to configure why Viktor had called me. "So, what did he have to tell you?"

"Well, we are most likely stuck here for sure until after the first of the year." I broke down. "Nothing unusual there. However, that wasn't the only message."

"What was the reason?" My friend pressured, his curiosity pushing the envelope on my tolerance. "Viktor hardly ever calls you up privately unless he was either told to or-" He paused. "Or unless he was told to."

Tired of the interrogating questions, I hinted for Mhykal to shut the bedroom door. Thankfully understanding the Vampiric shut the thick wooden door and patiently listened for me to begin. "Braedon had Viktor call my cell so he could explain the Search Warrant. He believes that one of the Unnaturals we had brought into the Manor was tagged-"

"More like, our Leader believes that Cinder was chipped." Mhykal interrupted.

Heaving another heavy sigh, I went back towards the center of my room and further clarified, "Viktor said that it is a large possibility especially after what that crazy disgusting human Doctor at the Salem Drive Institute told us, and how quickly the Hunters had pinned down the girls when they recaptured Cinder." Sitting on the chest at the end of the bed, I continued to intently stare at my friend.

"You actually believe that?"

"I do." I sighed. "Unfortunately, there is way too much evidence that is coming to the surface-"

"What are we going to do?" Mhykal asked. "She is not all that capable of going out on her own."

"I know that. I wasn't going to even think about pushing her out!" I snapped back, interrupting the Vampire from saying anything else. "That thought never even surfaced itself! However," I paused leaning back on the chest and looking up at the tall white ceiling, "If Cinder finds out she might try to leave on her own, thinking of us first. I know that in the least will be how she acts, especially after the whole Valeryie/Logan incident."

"Yeah. That's true. She would most likely flee for our protection."

"But we cannot let that happen Mhykal." Glancing back at him, I repeated. "We can't let that happen. She is not capable of being out on her own, especially when she is being haunted by that Shadow that tells her to do who knows what." Seeing his nod of approval, I voiced another side of the subject, "We also cannot tell anyone else about this. Yalu might try to take the chip out for the sake of everyone, including Cinder. That you should know for sure about your crazy Fox girlfriend." I chuckled. For now, Viktor and Braedon just want us to keep an eye out for any more Hunters and stay on the down-low. Only you and I can know what is going on."

"Understood." Mhykal playfully saluted me like some idiot. Smiling that same childish grin of his, he expressed, "Well, Yalu and I, are about to go out and start the Christmas Shopping once Cinder and Peylith get back from their 'Run'. I know it's still early, but Yalu wants a good selection this year."

"Okay. Tell her to keep it on the low end, like under fifteen hundred dollars." I returned. Hearing Mhykal bust up laughing, I waited for his agreement before finally dismissing the younger Vampiric. After he had left, I sat for a few more minutes on the chest, wondering to myself, how long would he be able to keep it a secret from the Vixen? If she indeed discovers our secret, then how long would she be able to keep it from the possibly tagged Hellhound who was just now starting to blossom.

337

Ten minutes later, I finally walked out of the bedroom and back into the Living room to spend some time relaxing before things got chaotic again. Descending the single step into the open concept room, I saw the two Hellhounds finally return from their run. Bursting through the back-sliding glass door after being gone for almost thirty minutes.

Both were back in their human forms, and both were drenched in sweat despite the time-lapse. While they tried to catch their breaths, I inquired. "How was your run?"

"Good." Cinder smiled back at me. A genuine smile sitting on her face. Her eyes were giving off an unusual glow that I had only seen once since she had become a free Unnatural. "It has been so long since I played out in the snow like that." The twenty-five-year-old woman reported.

"I bet," Yalu said, coming down the steps from behind the small hallway. "Hey Peylith, go shower up so we can get some shopping done. I could use both yours and Mhykal's help."

"Okay." The Deity of Anubis happily barked as he walked back up the stairs towards the bathroom to go get into a shower.

"Hopefully, he remembers how to work the dials." I joked aloud.

"Mhykal, honey go help him please." Yalu sighed into her boyfriend's ear.

"Fine-" the Vampiric painfully huffed like a teenager did when he did not want to do his chores. Stomping up the stairs, he shadowed the Hellhound's path up to the second floor.

Chapter 63
Cinder/Jakob

"Alright, I'm also going to go wash up," I said after Peylith had disappeared upstairs.

"Okay." Jakob smiled back at me.

Weaving through the collection of Unnaturals, I stepped into the hallway towards where I knew my room was. Twisting open the doorknob, I strolled into my meticulously organized room with three large nice colonial windows facing the ocean. Staring out into the vast sea, I inhaled another breath before strolling over to the dresser. Pulling open the drawers that had been appropriately filled with my clothes, I scammed through for an outfit. Still furious that one of my favorite outfits had been cut open before being disposed of during my recent captivity. Finding some fresh undergarments and a nice tight V-neck beige long sleeve with the thumbs cut out of the cuffs, I sauntered over to my closet so I could search for some nice jeans. However, as I eyed through the six pairs, I changed my mind. Feeling too lazy to wear jeans or leggings, I went back to my dresser for some comfy sweatpants. Once I had collected a decent 'I don't care' outfit, I stepped into the large adjoining bathroom. Personally, I liked this bathroom much better than the much, much smaller one I had at the Manor; the heated tiled flooring, the nice sandstone painted drywalls, the nice window with a stoned modern tub put into the bay, all of it was a pleasant change in pace that sustained my growing tastes. Glancing over at my reflection in the four-foot-long wall-length mirror, I proceeded with placing my clothes on the long double sink vanity and sauntered over to the glass shower capable of fitting four people in it. Opening the glass door, I began to set the water temperature.

With the water pressure and temperature starting to match the settings I had chosen, I began to undress. Taking off the clothes, I once more looked back into the mirror to see the same annoying Shadow standing behind me.

"Now what?" I growled while I finished undressing.

"Still very feisty aren't we, little Reaper." The voice mocked as he spun around to face me eye to eye, blocking the sight of my reflection in the mirror. Feeling his fingers grab at my chin and pull it up to look up into his red calming eyes, I felt my body start to burn while simultaneously go limp. My brain couldn't comprehend what was going on fast enough. "I know I told you six months, but I did not say that for your sake, my ignorant Reaper."

Blankly looking up into his eyes unable to look away, unable to fight him, unable to still grasp what he was doing nor saying I remained silent. Painfully listening to his strange dialogue while my scar began to savagely burn. Standing there in the bathroom in my underwear before this being, I said nothing.

Feeling his grip on my chin and lower jaw grow tight, I heard the Shadow explain, "The longer my Reaper waits to break away, the more I will take away her Sanity. Do you understand?" I wanted to verbally acknowledge, however my jaw wouldn't move. "You can speak." The Shadow ordered me before he repeated, "Do you understand me Little Reaper?" In a much deeper tone.

"I-I un-under-understand." I pronounced trying to hold back my tears of anguish.

"Good-" he ended, letting go of my chin, allowing my body to fall to the ground. Barely able to catch myself, I fell onto my knees, the palms of my hands encountering the heated floor. Regaining control, I looked up around the room, no longer seeing the sulking black-hooded Skeletal Shadow.

Cursing aloud to myself, I beat at the tiled floor in complete frustration. "I never asked for this shit!" I cursed. Using all the vocabulary I had heard throughout my life as I again beat on the tiled floor. "I did not ask to become an Unnatural! I did not ask to be used as a Guinea Pig, to be used as a Harvestable Vessel! I did not ask for any of this and-" I paused, feeling the tears run down my cheeks, "I didn't ask to be your damn Reaper!"

It was almost forty-five minutes before Cinder came out of her room. She was wearing some pretty lazy casual clothes while her hair was back up in a ponytail. Surveying her facial features, I easily noticed that something was dragging on her mind. Debating on whether to ask if she was okay, I kept my mouth shut. Viewing the woman dig around in the fridge, I clenched my jaw tighter, still debating my decision to remain quiet. All of a sudden, she slammed the door shut and stormed back around towards the patio doors to step outside.

After she slammed the patio door shut behind her, I decided against my first initial decision to stay out of her way. Changing my choices, I followed in behind her. I knew something had to have happened to Cinder when she went to get a shower. Whether it was something she remembered, or it was something that her haunting Shadow had told her, I was unsure, but I knew I had to find a way to calm her down somehow.

Stepping out into the freezing winter breeze and snow-covered patio, I sat down next to her on the stone steps. Feeling the warmth just echo from her petite physique, I took a deep breath before asking her, "I know that there is something on your mind, so what's wrong?"

"I never asked for this to happen to me Jakob," she mumbled, looking down at the snow. Her chin resting on top of her knees, with her arms bracing around her upper chins.

"None of us asked to be who or what we are," I responded. Though I knew exactly what she was feeling and going through. I went through the same thing after I had my hundredth birthday. It was the same topic I had helped explain to many other previous Unnaturals. "I know that feeling all too well."

"You were Human once-"

"Once." I simply returned. "I was turned into a Vampiric when I was twenty-eight years old. Of course, seven hundred years ago, I was treated differently than more recently turned Unnaturals are today, however, once I had my first centennial, I wondered why had I been chosen by my Sire, why I had survived her attack. Why me when there were thousands of others to choose from in that town?" I quickly skimming my past.

"But you got an answer didn't you, from your Sire?" the Hellhound probed, attention now fixated on my story instead of me trying to sympathize with her.

"I did, but not until I asked her why much later in my life." I sighed. "All that witch told me was she liked how I looked and how I treated her."

"Well, at least you still got an answer and not dragged around like a pathetic puppet." I heard her frigidly snarl, completely understanding the building frustrations she had.

"Well yeah I got an answer, but I had also been treated like her underling for those hundred years," I told. "Although I want to know what your true frustrations lie, I know you want to understand why you were chosen by whoever made you into an Unnatural, however, I sense that you're upset about not having a choice in a new problem, instead of what has happened to you in the past."

Seeing her brilliant blue eyes finally stare up at me, I again asked her what was wrong. Finally receiving something back from her. "Jakob, I can't tell you what he had told me because if I did, I would be threatening not only my life but everyone else's life."

Figuring that was going to be the answer, I put my hand on her back softly implying, "Cinder, I know you can't tell me, but I can't help you if you don't give me something to work with. I want to help you as much as I possibly can-"

Watching her break away and descend the steps into the snow with her bare feet touching the cold frozen water particles. "You can't help me, Jakob!" She wept, the tears run down her face. "No one can help me, but my damn self and I can't even do that when someone else has all the control over my mind and my body! The-the only time I-I am ever in control is when he isn't around-" the woman cried, melting the snow in a fifteen-foot radius around where she stood telling me how irritating this new problem was.

Standing up from the steps, I closed the gap between us and stood myself in front of her. Stepping closer into her circle, I wrapped my arms around her petite body, forcing Cinder to encounter me. At a loss for words, I simply remained silent. Feeling the young woman's hands wrap around my back and her head press against my chest, we continued to just stand there. It may have not been the exact response that Cinder may have wanted, but it was the only thing I could think of that would comfort her. After another thirty seconds, I heard her release a heavy breath; sensing all the frustration push out from deep down inside her small frame with that same exhale.

Eventually finding the words I wanted to say, I told her, "It is alright to feel as bad as you do right now, it is completely understandable Cinder. But, if you ever need to tell someone about your sorrows then don't be afraid to ask anyone of us to lend you an ear, or a shoulder. Okay?" Rubbing my hand down her back while we stood together, her timid childish nature afraid to pull away, I proceeded to comfort. "Everything will be alright."

343

Chapter 64
Cinder

"The longer my Reaper waits to break away, the more I will take away her Sanity-" The Shadow's voice recited in my head.

In a panic, I shot open my eyes and pushed myself to sit up. I've heard the same sentence invade my dreams every night for the last week. Each time I heard his voice, I could feel my mind go deeper into the darkened depths, feel my heart drop down into my churning stomach, feel my blood freeze. With his call ringing in my ears and sending chills down my spine, I swiped my naturally long hair away from my face trying clearing my erratic mind. Exhaling another long breath out of my lungs, I wrapped my arms around my knees still hiding under the bedsheets.

The conversation I had with Jakob had helped calm me down the first few times I had relived that moment, but the more it haunted me, the less and less power I felt behind 'Everything will be alright'. The phrase had lost its place in my head, just like all the immeasurable memories from my childhood. Even when Yalu, Peylith, or Mhykal all told me that they were here for me and that it was going to be alright, the phrase just went in one ear and out the other. I didn't want to hurt their feelings by telling them that it wasn't going to be alright, so I continued to nod my head, making them believe what they said was worthwhile.

Finally calming myself down, I got out of the bed and walked into the bathroom to empty my bladder and clean up my terrible night sweats. While I stood under the hot water inside the shower, I tried to figure out how I could get myself to break away from the only people who were ever nice to me. I needed to find a way as soon as possible, for not only the insurance that they would still live but for the insurance of my waning sanity.

"I can't just leave." I thought to myself. "If I did that, they would just try to find me again. Most likely believing that I was taken or something along that line." As I washed out the soap from my hair, I proceeded, "I can't just leave them a note, I don't even think I can remember how to hold a pen long enough for that. Besides, I'm doubtful my handwriting would be illegible anyways. And even if I did leave a note I doubt they would leave it at that." Standing directly under the shower's head, I laid my back flat against the slated wall of the glass shower and collapsed onto the floor. Staring through the steam covered glass wall and into the ocean beyond the bathroom window, I cried. "Why can't I just figure this out? Why can't they just let me go just like my parents did?"

Following an extended stay in the shower, I clothed myself, choosing this time to wear some light blue skinny jeans and a short sleeve beige shirt with the same V-neck collar. Brushing the tangles out of my hair, I left my hair down, allowing the flair of the swayed angled bangs to tell their story. Content with my appearance, I finally left my dreary lightly pastel-painted bedroom to go join up with the others who're more than likely preparing for breakfast.

"Hey, you're up?" I heard Peylith bark at me from the sectional, "You going to go for another run after breakfast?"

"I haven't decided," I answered, plopping myself down on the dark fabric sectional sofa. "I know I need to, but I am just not feeling up to it today, maybe some sparring instead."

345

"Okay, that sounds like fun." I heard Mhykal chip in just as he threw his arms down on the back of the furniture.

"Don't overwork yourselves," Valeryie interjected, mocking her sister's motherly tone.

Twisting myself around to stare at the young Vixen who was helping her older sister prepare the dining table for our 'Family' feast, I teased, "Why don't you join us, Valeryie? It will be good practice for your Species Abilities."

"You do need those." Yalu chuckled to the younger Vixen over the loud sizzle of cooking food. "It's more fun than you think, and it is something you as an Unnatural needs in order to survive."

"No, it isn't needed! The world is changing! Not all humans think that we are a disgrace! You guys just have happened to see the worst of them!" Yalu's younger sister aggressively challenged.

Having a point, I stayed out of the debate between the two siblings just like Mhykal and Peylith. It was not something we needed to get involved with, although it was something I believed was not happening as fast as Valeryie alleged. I didn't want to pressure her into learning how to fight and accurately use her powers, but it could still come in handy regardless of the word's political situation. I understood all too well that the young woman may have not had a choice when she was born or dropped off by her parents, but she did however still have a choice in what she was going to do with the rest of her life. It was like Jakob had said to me a few days ago, many Unnaturals who've been liberated and were actively molding the Human Image, such as living a 'Civilian' Life, having human neighbors, employees, or employers. And with the younger Vixen's social character, I knew she had a higher chance than someone like I would ever be.

With the argument unfolding between the two sisters I looked up to Mhykal, asking him, "Is Jakob up yet?"

"He got a phone call from Braedon this morning." The younger Vampiric answered over the shouting of the Vixens. "That was about an hour ago, so I don't know what they could be talking about. I'll go check on him." Mhykal ended as he stood up from leaning against the sectional, stopping before he walked down the hallway, "Don't break that T.V. Peylith or I swear to god, I will kick your ass all around this property."

"You broke a T.V.?" I confusingly questioned the Hellhound that called himself a 'God's Deity'.

"I guess I did." Peylith chuckled aloud as he flipped through the channels on the long remote. "Back at the other place, I couldn't figure out how it worked when I was done watching what was on the image at the time, and yes, I do believe I broke the moving pictures."

"Understandable." I laughed. "I don't understand the purpose of its addiction anyways. Never have."

"Yet you were born in this era."

"My parents weren't keen on allowing me to watch television when I was a child, I didn't even have one when the Institution was granted full custody over me. I was kept locked away in a bland room with nothing else to do but talk to the Shadow." I said while I sat on the sofa, my body turned parallel with the furniture's spine, and my legs folded up underneath me.

"I know what's that like. The bland room that is; the Shadow part I do not. Anubis rarely spoke to me, and during my 'institutionalization' he didn't even show up." The Hellhound replied. "All I did was sleep whenever I could."

"I did the same, well, when I wasn't drugged or talking with that being." I sighed, sensing a familiarity in our 'treatments'.

"Alright, breakfast is done." I heard Yalu shout to us in the open space. "Cinder could you go get Mhykal and Jakob."

"Sure." I sighed, standing myself up from the sofa. Walking down the hallway to get the two Vampires, I started to feel that sharp pain in my back once again. Stretching across my Cross-shaped scar, the burning sensation took all the air out of my lungs. Hearing the same dark skeletal voice ring in my head telling me the consequences of extending my stay. Trying to calm myself down, I took a couple of deep long breaths before feeling the pain finally diminish. The feelings of dread and hatred disappearing. As I recollected myself, I finished the rest of the journey down the corridor leading towards Jakob's bedroom that was across the hall from mine and knocked politely on the door.

"Jakob, Mhykal breakfast is ready," I said, trying to hide my weakened breath.

"Alright we will be right there, thank you, Cinder." I heard Jakob respond through the thick bedroom door.

"Don't take too long. I don't want to get yelled at by Yalu who's already had one argument today."

Chapter 65
Cinder

Once breakfast was complete, I went out with Mhykal and Peylith through the back glass sliding doors and into the snowy bank while Yalu, Jakob, and Valeryie cleaned up the dirty dishes. Dressed in my sweatpants and short-sleeved shirt I quickly asked, "Alright, who wants to go first?"

"Why don't you two practice with each other while I go back to warm up-" Mhykal answered.

"Alright-" I joked. Teasing the Vampiric I questioned, "I thought you Vampires did not feel cold upon being sort of already dead?"

"Yeah, yeah. Well, this Vampire does feel cold and does not like it still after three hundred years of living in it." The Vampiric ended, waving his hand at us as he walked back into the Mansion to apparently dress more appropriately with the surrounding weather.

"Well then I guess it's just the two of us-" I shrugged, facing the taller Hellhound who was already standing in a combat-ready position. Maybe karate or Tai Kwan Doe, whatever the stance was it still made him appear ready. "You know you really should learn to be combat-ready without a pose. It leaves your opponent off guard, giving you the time to strike." I mentored standing firm in a normal feminine position.

"I will take that into consideration the next time I fight." Peylith cooly snickered back.

Hinting at him to take the first attempt, I observed every single muscle contraction the skinny brute with darkly tan skin made as he ran directly for me. Keeping my sights locked on his feet, I counted the few seconds that were in between us. Rapidly computing that in three seconds at his current speed he would be able to close the fifteen-foot gap between us, I calmly counted down the time and patiently waited until he was about eight-tenths of a second away from hitting me before I made my first move. Dodging the strike, I leaned sideways about six inches. Using my left arm, I grabbed his right shoulder and pulled my entire body up. Flipping over the man, I rolled myself into a ball just as my hands kicked off his shoulder. Putting forth all the muscle in my arm, I sprung several feet away. Switching forms in midair, I used the four legs of my canine mutation to land on the snowy ground. My paws tapping the snow with such a heavy force that I released a small heatwave. The elevated temperatures melting the frozen particles within a twenty-foot radius around the center of my Beauceron Frame. Turning my body around, I smiled showing all my front teeth and darted for my fellow Kin. The Hellhound also twisting around to confront my counterstrike, sealed his amber gaze on me. Feeling those eyes pry deep down into my soul, I transformed back into my bi-pedal sleek human form. Leaning off to my left as I continued to close in our gap, I eyed the Hellhounds movements follow. Swiftly realigning myself, I now leaned off in the opposing direction. Approaching him, I struck my 'combat' pose and socked him directly in the upper stomach. His hard-refrained physique dropping over in shock, leaving his head open for my succeeding left undercut. Swinging my arm up, I closed my first, my body following every knitch in my mental plan. Making direct contact with the center of his face, I successively managed to knock the Hellhound back. Holding back my normal killing instinct, I flipped my thin petite body backward into a temporary handstand. As my long legs came up for that straight-line pose, I proceeded with wrapping them around his neck.

Using my superior leg strength, I uprooted the hundred and seventy-pound, six-foot man and dragged him towards me. Deciding at the last minute to alter the pose into a backflip. Swinging my body backward, I flipped him over the top of me just the rotation went a full circle. Contorting my body into a side twist, I kept my small hands firmly planted in the snow before releasing my legs' hold of the man's thick neck. Tossing the man weightlessly away into the cold hard ground, I brought myself back into an upright position. Watching the Hellhound remain on the ground his chest heaving in and out, collecting all of the cold air around the beachfront, I slowly crept up towards him remaining on guard with each passing step.

Questioning Peylith, I wondered if he had conceded defeat, "Did I overdo it?"

"A little-" he panted. "I was not expecting you to move that fast."

"Well, I have regained more of my muscle mobility since we have been hiding out here." I laughed at the Hellhound, standing over him. "You should have seen me when Yalu and I spar, we move at even faster speeds than this."

"She's right." I overheard someone's voice call from behind me. Catching the downriver scents of the familiar Vampirics I relaxed my tension. "Yalu and Cinder would move much faster than this, and their rounds would usually last for fifteen, maybe twenty minutes at most," Jakob said, helping Peylith up off the snowy ground.

"You really had to get a coat?" I questioned Mhykal, noticing his dark black short modern coat. It wasn't a puffy jacket just a nice thin-looking felt jacket. The way that it looked it told me that for sure it was of Yalu's taste and that she had most likely bought it for him.

"Shut-up, Cinder." Mhykal snapped back playfully. "Not my fault I can't maintain body heat like the two of you can."

"You could have just asked us, and we could have kept you warm," I interjected, gently placing my hand against the Vampire's cheek. Holding it there for a few seconds before I removed my soft-skinned woman's hand. "Better?"

Seeing the man's body relax from the apparent bitterness of the Winter Climate I heard him respond back this time without his teeth chattering. "How did you do that?"

"I can ventilate my Flames in such a soft and light motion that it keeps you from combusting, or from your organs melting. Keeping you just warm enough to neither get hyperthermia nor heat exhaustion. Unfortunately, it does take a lot of patience and concentration to maintain."

"Peylith can you do that-?" Jakob asked his face full of wonder.

"Nope. Never had that much control over the Flames part of our Species Abilities." Peylith quickly answered. Illuminating his right palm with an open orangey-glowing flame, I observed the other Hellhound maneuver his hand around. Making the flame dance the same way that the Shadow's eyes danced. It was captivating to survey yet frightening all the same. Standing as a reminder that I needed to hurry up and find a way to break away from these guys before things made a turn for the worst.

I was so captivated that I had zoned out of the rest of the conversation. Recalling everything that the Shadow had told me, that there was a continuous loss of my sanity the longer I hesitated to do this undesired task; I had less than six months to do this or else I would lose all of my sanity and only hurt my friends worse than if I just left them.

"Hey Cinder?" I eventually heard Jakob call. "Cinder are you okay?"

"Yeah." I breathed, pushing the truth further down, holding those undaunting thoughts deep down inside of me. Taking a breath of that cold salty ocean air, I continued, "I'm okay. So, who's up next?"

"Well, I would like to spar with you this time, Cinder?" Mhykal joked, now cockily swinging his arm around while holding his shoulder. Stretching out his 'old' immortal muscles.

"Alright." I played. "What kind of spar do you want to do?"

"I would like to work around your Blood Scythes if possible. I need some more practice with close combat weaponry."

"Sure, you do." Mhykal's old-time friend sneered while both he and Peylith backed off to the sidelines. "You just don't like it when she last sparred with bare-hands and she kicked your ass."

"No!" Mhykal snarled still in his usual playful manner.

"Right."

"Can we get on with this?" I irritatingly barked. "If I wait any longer, I may already have calculated all of your possible movements and might just kick your ass before it even gets started." I antagonized using more of my 'maturing' vocabulary.

Chapter 66

Cinder

Mhykal recklessly charged towards me, allowing my fast hunting gaze to study every one of his muscle twitches. Slipping small blood cells out from my skin's wall, I proceeded to mold the clotted blood into its iconic Scythe's blade. Keeping my arms down at my side, I remained still while the Vampiric continued to run directly towards me, his speed moving slower than normal almost mocking me. Irritated, I continued to hold steady, equipping my physique for the incoming first swing, already knowing Mhykal was predominantly right-handed I expected a left hook to come flying at me. His movements were so predictable that it felt like the challenge was almost nonexistent. Focusing on the right arm, my hunting eyes caught out of the corners that it was his left arm beginning to raise up. Seeing the tightly clenched fist coming straight at me, I ducked off to the side, parrying the first blow. Now waiting for the right hook, a part of the one-two combo he does, I was thrown off by Mhykal's flying knee coming up towards my stomach. Jumping backward, I backflipped a few feet away before transforming into my Beauceron Canine form. Hesitating a millisecond, I tried to evaluate all my missed hypothesis. His movements were not as predictable as I had originally thought. Nonetheless, I was still able to dodge every attack in time, however, the question was how long I could keep it up. Regaining the focus I needed, I took the offensive. Running towards the dark black haired

Vampiric, I used my full speed and prepared to jump up for the man's neck. Seeing his expectation of my attack, I transformed back into my human form. Throwing my still weaponized right arm up, I shielded myself from his left hook. Hastily noticing the follow-up sequence, I saw a right hook coming straight at me. Bending my body backward to avoid getting hit, I backflipped, thrusting my long legs up in a small counterstrike. While he barely dodged my kick, I proceeded to complete the flip. My nimble figure successively backflipped a few more times, pushing some distance between the two of us. Panting a happy sigh, I drove my mind into overdrive to swiftly come up with an effective strategy.

"Surprised, aren't you?" I heard Mhykal cockily question me during our small intermission.

Chuckling I retorted, "You changed up your routine that's for sure, but-" Looking up from his feet to lock our gazes, I smirked, "I think I caught onto it now."

"Oh-?"

"Observant as always." My sharp ears overheard a feminine voice speak up through the quiet crashing waves along the frozen shoreline. Seeing Yalu come up from off the small deck adjoining to the back of the house, her Vixen eyes glistening off the mid-morning sun and blinding snow.

Glancing back into Mhykal's eyes while the pupils slide off to the right corner so he could see his long-time girlfriend, I took advantage and charged forward. Reaching his body in a quick millisecond before the yellow eyes could return their attention to his opponent. Drawing my left blade flat against his neck, the back end of its blade close enough to the skin that it could nick the fine-lined hairs poking out of the small facial feature follicles, however not close enough to slice through the flesh.

"I concede-" the Vampiric quickly surrendered with the same old goofy smile.

355

Releasing the Blood Scythes, I ordered the blood to retreat into my skin and return to their arterial veins. "If you didn't take your eyes off me, we could have kept the round going." I sneered, walking around the Vampiric to greet the Vixen.

"You sure have gotten good with your Special Abilities and protecting yourself. Still prefer using them for defensive instead of offensive though." Yalu quickly observed. Eyeing her attire, I surveyed that she was wearing the new winter coat she had bought at the mall a while back, its black fabric flattering her slender body quite well.

"It doesn't feel right to recklessly charge in." I returned, shrugging my shoulders. Of course, lying through gritted teeth about the number of times I had taken the offensive and had brought the first strike down on my victims. Although that too was only half of the story, I did stay defensive most of the time. Once my victims caught sight of me, it was enough evidence for them to attempt to kill me.

"While it is true, recklessly charging in risks your trump card tricks, and exposes your fighting style, it also can allow you to defeat your enemy with one blow before they fight back Cinder." Yalu lectured. However, I felt like it was more of a scolding than a lecturing with how her tone spoke. "Anyways, when one of you guys are done, can one of you bring me to the Market, so I could get some more food? Feeding six people three times a day adds up."

"Sure, I can do it." I heard Jakob volunteer.

"Would anyone else want to come with us?" I heard the Vixen casually offer after callously ordering someone to drive her to get more groceries.

"No, I don't feel comfortable enough to head back onto the town," I declined, flashing back to when I was hunted down by the Hunters and brought back to an Institution.

"It's okay, Cinder." I blankly heard Jakob's warm voice comfort.

"I'll go considering I lost to her in less than five minutes." Mhykal sighed, his voice happy, but comedically sad about his defeat, lightening the mood again in his usual mannerism.

"Peylith?" Yalu asked the other Hellhound of our group.

"No. I'm good here." He too refused.

Strolling into the mansion-sized Coastal House, our group split in two different directions. Those of us that were staying plopped down on the sectional sofa, while those that were going to go off to the Store for Grocery Items went off to their individual rooms and got dressed. Coming back down the stairs and out of the hallways all dressed for Civil Living among Humanity, Jakob zipping up his lightweight winter jacket announced, "Alright then. We will be back."

"Okay then. See you guys later." Valeryie surprisingly declared, her eyes glued to the tiny screen of her smartphone.

Hearing the front door slam shut and the engine of what sounded like the Escalade start to drive down the driveway, I stood up and walked into my bedroom. Feeling the urge to break away from the remaining Unnaturals who were staying here at the Manor. Once I had closed the door to the room, I wandered over to the bed and plopped myself down onto the thick comforter. Granting my mind, the ability to wander as it usually did, I again wondered aloud to myself how was I supposed to break away from the people that surrounded me with such kind hearts and good wills. The same people that had saved me from that dark grasping paralysis and cold-hearted scientists at the Institution.

"How was I going to do that without hurting them? I can't just disappear?" I aimlessly thought aloud. Staring up at the wooded ceiling of my room, I then reflected, "But, if I don't manage to get away soon, I will only end up hurting them more. I can barely even manage possibly breaking away from them mentally without it completely breaking me. Although, I guess it's my only option considering physically harming them is way beyond my grasp."

357

Continuously debating on how to break away from everyone on the orders of the Shadow, I easily lost track of the time. Looking out the window, I saw that the sun's rays were now starting to set into the distance. Figuring by now that everyone had returned, I rolled off the bed and walked towards the door.

Just as I reached the doorknob, I saw the door's brass knob start to twist and turn. The motion informing me that there was someone on the other side of my assigned bedroom's door. Someone who was trying to get in. Stopping myself from grabbing the door, I moved back and permitted the door to swing open.

As the door opened, I witnessed that the person on the other side of it was none other than Jakob. Questioning him, I wondered why he wouldn't have knocked first like he normally did, considering his courteous nature.

"Sorry, I didn't knock Cinder, Peylith told me that you had gone into your room. I presumed that you were sleeping or something." The European Vampire apologized to me with utmost sincerity and a small bashful laugh.

"It's okay." I sighed with great relief. "So, you guys are back now?"

"Been back for a little while now actually, but I was told to come collect you for dinner. You know how Yalu is about these 'Family-like Obligations."

"Yeah, I know." Seizing another sigh followed by my sly smile. "She can be very strict about these things." Shadowing Jakob out into the hallway, I closed the door to my room behind me, catching a glimpse of the dark fiery orange-red eyes from the skeletal shadow. The cold gaze reminding me of my time-limit and the continuous loss of my sanity the longer I remained. Pushing that image into the back of my head, I tried to maintain the familiar character I had built up and settled in among the people I felt like I could start to call my 'Second-Family'.

Chapter 67
Cinder/Jakob

The Shadow had begun to haunt me regularly as more time passed, urging me to hurry up with separating myself from the Syndicate and its Rebels. I did what I could to ignore him as best as I could, but with his haunting message still rampaging through my head, it became ever so difficult. I could feel my mind desire to keep intact with its sanity, filing away all the plans and predictions for how to break away from them. With no luck, my poor deranged mind could only tell me to slowly ease off from being around my friends. Ordering me to spend more and more time inside my bedroom, even commanding me to lock the door to maintain a wall of separation. Demanding me to call it 'Privacy' so I could hide the truth to the Unnaturals who knew so much more was going on.

"How much longer do I have Shadow?" I questioned, my voice the only one echoing throughout the empty room. I knew that cruel being was still hiding somewhere inside my bedroom's shadows.

"With as much as my Little Reaper is worrying over her friends' relations and concerns, it would be about half of what I mentioned earlier." He coldly answered a few minutes later.

"Three months, that makes it all that much harder-" I complained lying flat on my back on top of the made-bed.

"Are you done fighting this?" The skeleton asked me as he stood over the foot of the bed, his human skulled head coming into view of my blue eyes.

"It's hard to deny it when someone is keeping a tight short leash over your sanity-" I growled back in my head.

"Still as defiant as always, stupid Reaper."

"Shut-up," I growled this time aloud at the cloak wearing man. "I just told you what choice did I have in this matter!"

The Shadow rushed over the foot of the bed, reappearing on top of me through the darkness of the moonlit room. One of his cold bone hands strapped around my neck, and the other over my mouth. Full of shock and fear, I felt my body freeze. Paralyzed. The usually cold and calm being had gone dark and violent, stuffing me with an overwhelming amount of fear. I had been trained on how to fight this, yet I couldn't move.

"My Reaper needs to watch her tone." The Shadow threatened, his icy voice freezing the skin on my left ear. Staring into his burning ember eyes, I felt my eyes mirror the same color as he resumed, "Or else she will lose more of her sanity and will only have one month to break away from her friends." Changing the vocabulary on me, he then sternly asked, "Do you understand me, Reaper?"

Feeling his hands release from my mouth and neck, I blindly responded, "Yes I understand." The words escaping my mouth before I could even recognize what I said. Getting the feeling like I was nothing but an obedient soldier serving a cold general.

"Good. Now hurry up and get this over with my little Reaper." The Shadow ordered me, his voice the only reminder of his existence.

Rolling off the side of the bed, I leaned my back against the mattress and stared out the window at the large white moon who stared back through the glass panes. Wrapping my arms around my legs I curled up into a fetal position, softly whispering, "I don't want to do this..."

Stopping midsentence when I heard a knock on the locked door. Three hard taps along with the thick-heavy wood. Through scent alone, I could tell it was Peylith, making this an unusual occurrence, causing me to hesitate to answer.

"Cinder are you awake?"

I didn't answer right away. Again, I hesitated how to respond. Eventually, I returned with a soft-toned yes.

"Could you unlock the door?"

"Yeah hold on." I returned, forcing my numb body to stand back up and walk over to the door. Pressing my thumb and finger on the quick lock of the doorknob, I unlocked the door before twisting the knob and unrolling the entrance.

"Are you okay? Your scent smells emotional?" The Egyptian Era Hellhound asked, standing there in the doorway in his dark-skinned Human form.

"Just thinking." I returned calmly. "Reminiscing. What do you want Peylith?"

"Okay, well Jakob and Yalu wanted me to come get you. They got something they want to show you."

Again, hesitant to answer, I simply nodded, following my fellow kin out into the small corridor towards the living room. Venturing out into the open-concept floor plan, I saw a warm-light echo off the neutral-toned wallpaper. Coming down the single step, I discovered a huge seven-foot-tall Douglas Fir Tree. The smell of pine needles eagerly filling my heightened sense of smell like the fragrance of a strong perfume or cologne. It was full and fresh, and...gorgeous.

"Ah, there you are Cinder. Finally came crawling out of your darkroom, huh?" I heard Yalu tease me as she came around the other side of the tree that rested between the entertainment center

361

and the banister of the main staircase. "So, what do you think? Isn't it gorgeous?"

Memorized, I nodded staring at the little lights, gold and red balled Garland, and the many complimenting gold and red ornaments adorning the tree's small prickly branches. I was so taken back by the warm feeling echoing off the decorated tree that I didn't know how to respond.

"Was it too much?" I asked, spinning around to face Cinder after putting on one of the last ornaments. Hoping to see this genuinely happy smile along her face for once, however, I witnessed a much different face sprawled across the young woman's face. "See Yalu I told you it may be too much-" I growled to the Vixen who had ever so eagerly persuaded the rest of us into getting a Christmas tree while we were staying at this bland Mansion.

"No-" Cinder interrupted, her voice speaking so quietly that it was hard to understand. Looking at her face to examine her features, I saw through her messy deep brown hair, and her pale skin, noticing her soft blue eyes here reverting to the smoldering embers as they echoed the light source of the Christmas tree lights. The brilliant blue glazed over with pure emotion as it released small tears from the ducts in the corners. Glancing around the rest of the young woman's fine features, I recognized that genuine smile spread across her face. The same smile I had not seen in so long had shown itself once more. "It's perfect." The Hellhound softly spoke, carefully stepping closer towards the tree. Her attention completely captured by the essence of the Douglas Fir. Exactly like a child when this time of the year came around.

"It's okay." I smiled, putting my hand on her shoulder as I faced her.

The woman rushed me, wrapping her arms tightly around my back. Surprised by her outcome, I gently folded my arms around her back returning the hug.

"Thank you. All of you." I heard her whisper softly.

Resting my head on top of hers, I answered back to her, "You are welcome Cinder." Glancing over to Yalu, Mhykal, Peylith, and Valeryie, I could see written all over their faces the level of appeasement they too were feeling. "Tomorrow we will celebrate Cinder's and Peylith's first Christmas with the Vampiric Syndicate." I enthusiastically proclaimed.

Chapter 68
Jakob

With the Eve of Christmas ticking past the stroke of Midnight signaling to us the passing seconds into the arriving day, I hinted over to Mhykal and Yalu that now was the best time to start passing out the collected gifts we had hidden under the tree. It wasn't tradition to open them so soon after the stroke of Midnight, but it was the best time for all of us. Especially when everyone was already wired.

"Okay, then why don't you start handing them out?" Yalu questioned me with the look of 'Go right ahead and start'.

"Start handing out what?" Peylith confusingly asked as he leaned back in his seat on the sectional.

"You are going to start handing them out now?" Cinder asked perplexed while still standing in front of the tree admiring the decorum. "Isn't it a bit early for that?"

"No!" The younger Vixen chipped in excitedly. "It's past Midnight! And by tradition, we can open the presents on Christmas Day."

"We are all awake and it is Christmas now, so why not open them up anyways?" Yalu said, sitting down on the sofa beside her younger sister while calling the slightly younger Hellhound. "Come sit down, Cinder, so those two can start passing out the gifts."

The Hellhound obediently followed the stern Vixen's passive order. Walking away in her soft grey sweatpants and loose white V-neck shirt, Cinder sat beside Yalu, between her and Peylith along the corner of the sectional, a seat that she had seemed to prefer here in this house.

Once everyone was settled into their seats, I looked over to Mhykal flashing him a slight nod and sly smile before commencing to dish out the few presents we were able to collect in such a brief time. Reading the tags on the 'Holiday' gift-wrapped boxes aloud, the two of us speedily handed them out to everyone. Even making piles alongside the ottoman of the sectional where my long-time friend and I were planning to sit.

"This is the last one-" the younger Vampiric said, grabbing a medium-sized box wrapped in red plaid wrapping paper and topped off with two different sized green bows above the tag. Reading the small oval tag on the present Mhykal continued, "It says to Cinder, From Jakob, Yalu, Mhykal, and Peylith."

"You could have said from everyone, honey." Yalu teased her boyfriend.

"Well, I'll do that next year." He jeered back, sitting down on the ottoman beside me. "Alright everyone go crazy."

In no time at all, the eager teenager Valeryie and eager Immortal Peylith began to savagely tear into the wrapping in record-breaking times. Noticing both rip open the boxes with much ease, I wondered if they even noticed the gifts that we had gotten them:

I knew that Peylith had gotten some more clothes besides that same outfit he was stuck in since we had broken him out of that Government Institution. Several new outfits that Yalu, of course, could not help but pair up to each own box. Not only had we gotten him those, but we had also bought him a custom made four-inch-wide burnt leather dog collar that had the outer shell of the leather cased in gold and layered with blackened Anubis Hieroglyphics. I had to pay quite a lot to get that ordered and made especially in such a short period, but I guess having good relations with businesses going back as far as I have been alive, helped.

While Yalu's little sister, Valeryie had gotten a brand-new cellphone, something I still could not understand why she needed. The young Vixen also received some of her favorite band shirts, which the elder sibling had yet again paired up with matching pairs of skinny jeans. That teenager had more clothes than anyone else in the Syndicate, including some of the older members and the Founders, such as myself had. She even outranked her sister with the size of the wardrobe, unfortunately, she only wore about fifteen percent of the entire ensemble.

As I opened my presents, I noticed Yalu was adoring her few gifts that Mhykal and I had bought a couple of weeks ago. A few new dark boots that her boyfriend had surprisingly remembered her asking him for a few years back. One ankle bootie pair with short block heels, a pair of over the knee stilettos, and a black summer wedge with a mid-length heel. As well as one long little black box, with a special gift hidden away inside. Keeping an eye on her behavior, I watched her show the opened box to Cinder and her younger sister.

"Mhykal-" I hinted, elbowing my friend in the gut, "She opened it."

"Yalu?" I heard him call, his focus diverting to her before he opened his girlfriend's gift to him. "What do you think?"

"Mhykal, honey, you know how much I hate jewelry," Yalu growled to the Vampiric before she cut herself off. "But I do love it." As she pulled out the faded white laced choker necklace with a large Emerald pendant that resembled every same shade and color in her eyes, it was evident how taken she was.

"I'm glad you love it-" Mhykal answered back with that same cheesy smile he usually gave his mate once he had achieved granting her genuine happiness. "Umm Yalu-"

"Yeah?"

Glancing back over to my friend, I wondered as to what had made the man stutter. It wasn't something he normally did. Looking into another similar black box, I saw sitting in the middle of the velveteen lining was a pale pink and white stick with a small monitor on it. Off to the broader end of the stick, close to the monitor was an assumed positive, judging by my friend's reaction. Mhykal's hand vigorously started shaking as he held the box. Swinging my sights over to see Yalu's intent glare staring back at her Vampiric boyfriend, I confusingly waited to see what the gift was just like everyone else.

"No?!" He eventually shouted out to the world, sounding shocked. "You aren't-"

Interrupting him, the Vixen blurted out, "Yup. You're going to be a Father, Mhykal!"

The news completely shocked all of us. The room went quiet, fast. The first one to break the astounding silence, surprisingly was the steadily maturing woman, Cinder. Hugging her oldest friend, she choked out, "Congratulations."

"Thank you, Cinder." Yalu smiled, returning the hug. The tender-hearted moment lasted a few seconds before Cinder went back to pleasurably opening her gifts. Keeping tabs on the Vixen, who now proceeded to step closer to her lover, I watched Mhykal drop the black box and the positive pregnancy test, before happily hugging his girlfriend. Further tenderizing the sweet moment.

With everyone calming down and finishing up with opening their presents, I reviewed my gifts. Some new Raid Gear, and a new set of Whiskey Glasses specially engraved with my initials in the bottom of the glass. It was only a few things for me, but that was okay, I liked simple anyways. It was the thought that matters, right? While Mhykal had gotten some more pajamas, and the pregnancy test. Lastly reviewing what Cinder's gifts were, I noticed that she had opened all but that last gift-wrapped present. The one gift that was from all of us. Although the stuff she had previously unwrapped were items her close friend Yalu had bought, lots of neutral based clothes, and a couple of pairs of ankle-booted wedges.

As we all waited for her to hurry up and open literally the last present, Cinder slowly grabbed the small rectangular box. Unwrapping the box in its unusual wrapping paper, the Hellhound started to slowly lift the top. Laying the box on her lap, she then began to push aside the foil paper, I anxiously waited for her response to the gift we had all presented her with. Seeing the change in her facial features, the happy yet surprised look on her face soon enveloped into a saddened look. Her eyes quickly tearing up, telling Yalu, Mhykal, and I that she had immediately recognized the dark blue nylon slip-collar with a chain choker in the front.

"Where did you guys get this?" She asked us, wiping the tears away from her face ever so gently.

"It was still in the car when Mhykal and Jakob went to save us," Yalu answered, speaking in that famous motherly tone of hers as she rested her hand on Cinder's knee. "Matter of fact, all of the items we had bought that day were still locked in the car."

"I hope you like it-" Peylith chipped in. His deep masculine voice trying to be soft and sincere, knowing the story of how the Vixen had talked the female Hellhound into getting a fresh collar.

"I love it." Cinder hastily interrupted.

"Then why are you crying?" Valeryie questioned in her ignorant teenager way.

"Because of the meaning behind it," I answered back to the young Vixen. "There is a sentimental value with that gift that brings back positive memories for once."

Chapter 69
Jakob

After everyone had finally gone through their gifts and things had started to calm down, we began to clean up the empty boxes and torn holiday wrapping paper. Everyone pitching in to toss the garbage into a large plastic bag for collection.

Once we had cleaned up our self-made messes and had put everything back in order, Valeryie and Peylith had gone off upstairs into their rooms to get some sleep in before the sun rose. While Yalu and Mhykal had started to work on remembering the possible date when their baby was conceived in the kitchen. As for Cinder, she continued to admire the new collar she received.

"You really like it, huh?" I asked, sitting down next to the Hellhound.

"Of course, I like it." She mumbled. "I was originally unsure about the idea of a new collar-"

"Especially when your collar had a significant meaning behind it, but also when to humanity, it resembles how the man keeps control over the beast." I returned, staring down into the box at the collar she had yet to touch.

Glancing over at her face, I saw her long bangs fall off the top of her ear, slightly covering up her fiery orange left eye. Her soft tone speaking louder, "Yalu told you, didn't she?"

"Yeah. She did. Yalu told both Mhykal and I about it when we saved her from the Institute." I answered still staring at her.

"When you guys found out about us being captured by the Hunters?"

"Yeah. All of your guys' belongings were still in the car, and the car was still in the same parking spot from where the signal took." I replied. "When we had saved Yalu, she found the collar and told us about why she bought it. How she had managed to persuade you into getting one, by wanting all of our scents on the nylon, like how that leather one you bear wrapped around your neck carries the scent of your parents on it."

"I guess it was their way of still trying to say they cared about me, but I knew it was Masters' plan all so he could maintain some control over me." The Hellhound softly growled. "They thought I was so naive, so childish all those years, all those horrid years I spent locked away in a small room as a lab rat."

"Her demeanor changed?" I quietly thought to myself, noticing that she was leaning forward on the edge of the sofa, her arms lying on her knees and her hands grasping each other so tight that her knuckles were starting to turn white. I could feel the darkness resting deep down in her heart swiftly climbing its way to the top, and this time it was not sadness or grief. Swallowing before I decided to speak up, "Well it wasn't our intention to bring up those memories, Cinder-"

"I know that Jakob." She hastily snapped, her hands still shaking. Releasing the grip on her hands, she turned to face me, both of her eyes a dark amber red. "I know that it wasn't your intention."

"We just wanted to give you a fresh start." I told her, "A new outlook about your newly gained freedom and a way to hopefully move on from your past but not forget it." My voice softening so I could tranquilize her anger.

Observing the red retreat to that extraordinary bright blue, I unwound my bundled nerves. Hoping for a reply, I kept silent for a bit, allowing her amazingly fast-working mind to digest what I had just told her. Cinder spun back over to face the dark navy-blue collar again, hesitating for a split second before she finally reached for the collar. Her shaky hand picking up the nylon chain choker styled collar that Yalu had picked out. Holding her collar as if it was the first time she had ever held one, I watched her turn over to me, speaking ever so softly, "Well then it should be that same person who broke me out of that cell, and gave me that freedom that should put it on."

"Umm, okay-" I stuttered. Honored and confused at the same time. There was more than one person that had saved her that day from Salem's Off-Grids, I was also not the only person who broke her out of the cell. Shoving away the confusion, I gently grabbed the collar from her clenched hand. "Alright, now you just need to change forms." I softly directed.

Observing Cinder hastily change from her two-legged human form into the four-legged canine form, her soft pale skin swiftly being consumed by the short to medium-length black and brown fur so fast that even with my increased eyesight sense I barely noticed the change. In such a short vast time, the Hellhound had changed from her disguised human form into her Breed's Identification canine form. Telling me that she had mastered the transformation part with much ease.

Seeing the Beauceron staring back at me with those blue eyes as she sat on the couch still in the same location, I got the idea that I needed to hurry up and get it over with before she changed her mind on me. Placing the nylon collar down on the coffee table, I slowly reached my hands out for the thick leather collar still coiled around her neck. Cinder held her head still, however her body froze up. Going stiff with uncertainty, an understandable yet terrifying behavior at the same time. Coaxing her, I gently clutched the metal buckle behind her head on the upper part of her neck and steadily began to feed the strap back through. As the collar went loose from around her neck, my ears caught the sound of the scratched-up dog-tag ring while I quickly removed the leather from her fur.

Looking down at the rounded rectangular tag which read Cinder's Institute Patient Identification Number of 0497, I hesitated to ask the question I had on my mind. Finally growing the courage to speak, I blurted out, "Do you want me to keep the tag?"

Cinder sat there in her canine form, her eyes still watching me very intently. The modified cropped ears standing straight up at attention, quickly went flat against her head. Lying her body down on the sofa, she crawled up towards my lap, her large muscularly sleek canine body stretching out to attempt to smell the underside of the collar that had for so many years laid along her neck. Surveying the location on her body where the thick collar had just been discarded, I noticed how flat the hairs on her neck were. The closer I observed, the more I saw the details of her abuse. There were noticeably small scars from what I would assume were either needle pricks or from the collar itself. Watching Cinder now shake her head, feeling the freedom of no longer bearing this heavily weighted collar on her neck, I wondered if putting another restraint on her was a good idea. It was as if I was delivering her from one hand of ownership to the other.

"Keep the tag, please. However, don't put the tag on that collar after all this is supposed to be a new freedom." I heard her speak in her canine form. "I won't need it to remember all that had happened to me."

"Alright, then I will go ahead and put this one on you, Cinder," I explained, dropping the old collar with the still attached dog tag on to the coffee table and reaching for the new one while I still had the hundred-pound dog lying in my lap. Feeling her head move around to most likely watch what I was doing, I slowly advanced closer towards the collar.

Grasping the new collar off the table, I gradually brought the nylon towards my abdomen, so I wouldn't spook the cautious Hellhound who was still stiff, but surprisingly calm. Gently moving my fingers around, I began to play around with the setting of the size on the slip-on collar. Estimating how big it would have to be in order to properly fit around the canine's massive neck without causing harm to the already damaged skin. Eventually finding a reasonable size, I used my fingers to lift the dog's muzzle, informing her of my desire to slip this object over the top of her giant head. Patiently waiting till she allowed me to pull it over, I drove it passed her square head, her long flattened cropped ears and onto her neck. Once it was safely around her neck, I once more began to mess around with the size setting on the collar while the Hellhound did her best to also adjust to the new object that firmly sat wrapped around her neck. It was obviously uncomfortable.

Finding a nice size that was still breathable yet snug enough, so it wouldn't always fall off the high rise of her neck, I continued to engage with the Hellhound, "There you go. How does that feel?"

"The metal is cold." Cinder first replied to me. Chuckling alongside her, I heard her calmly resume as she brought herself back up to a sitting position on the gray-sectional. "But it is much lighter than that one." She announced, her blue eyes glaring back over at the thick three-inch collar. Silence filled the room once more before the Hellhound softly spoke up. "Thank you, Jakob."

"You're welcome Cinder. You deserve that new freedom." I acknowledged.

"Oh, that looks beautiful on you in that form," Yalu said, coming out from behind us, grabbing a hold of Cinder's body and hugging the canine transformed woman. Bringing the dog up off her front feet as she was pulled against the back of the sectional. I could see Cinder show her long fangs, yet I didn't feel like it was at all aggressive. It felt more like content and happiness, the darkness that I had felt just minutes earlier, I could no longer sense coming out of her heart. However, just because I could no longer sense it didn't mean it was no longer there either, and that had me only more concerned for the sake of the woman that I loved.

Chapter 70

Cinder

Shortly after we had finished our small gathering, the rest of the party decided to slip off for some sleep before the chaotic day we knew was going to unfold. I didn't know what to expect from this holiday, but based on all the blabbering Yalu frustratingly complained about, I wondered.

Sneaking off into my room to mentally prepare myself to be further haunted by the cursed Shadow being, I once more closed and locked the door. But this time he didn't approach me from the darkness, nor did his cold voice echo in my mind. The room was completely quiet for once. Thankful for the peace, I strode over to the bed I was temporarily calling my own and flopped down on top of its poorly made mattress. Lying with my head towards the footboard, I stared up at the ceiling wondering to myself, "Why did they have to celebrate 'family' so close to when I was supposed to break away? I know it was not their fault, but it just wasn't the best time for it..." Hesitating, I wondered, "How much longer could I hold out without being interrupted by him?"

Remaining quiet for several minutes, I waited for that expected interruption from the Shadow who had been hanging over my head for the last three weeks. When fifteen minutes slipped by and I had yet to sense or interact with him, I finally decided to try to get some sleep. Hoping as I closed my eyes that this cursed being would also stay clear of my conscious.

Waking up to hearing a knock on the door and the jiggle of the brass knob, I shot myself up out of the bed. Waiting for a calling, I stayed in front of the door, unwilling to reach for the knob until I knew who it was on the other side. Attempting to smell for any scents on the other side of the wood, I caught a stream of Jakob's scent. It was faint, but I could positively identify the elder Vampiric's scent. Lowering my guard, I decided to go ahead and unlock the door.

Just as my fingers switched the knob's locking mechanism, the door slammed it's way open. Barely able to dodge the door running me over, I prepared to snap the Vampiric's head off for trying to hit me. "What the hell-?" Was all I could manage to get out before I noticed a different figure standing in the doorway. Taking in the familiar characteristics of this man, I felt every single nerve in my body freeze. I could feel my heart begin to erratically beat out of control, beating so hard that it felt like it could burst right through my chest wall. My poor legs grew numb, becoming stiff and unable to move. I was frozen over with fear.

There standing in the doorway was the slicked-back, silvery blonde hair man whose face was heavily scarred. Wearing his same old white lab coat and carrying himself that same way he did back at the Institute. Feeling the fear rise up from my stomach into my throat as my heart started to pound even heavier I attempted to ask the cruel man who had been put in charge of my wellbeing back when the Salem Institution was granted custody over me. As I tried to utter the words, my vocals quivered. Fighting the urge to run, I continued to attempt to speak though nothing came out.

"Awe, what's wrong 0497?" I heard the Unnatural Specialist ask me, his voice ringing clear as day in my ears.

375

Finding my voice, I fiercely interrogated, "What are you doing here?!"

"You can't figure something that simple out?" The man laughed aloud as he stepped further in. Backing myself up in more fear, I awaited his reply, my mind too tired to try to create an appropriate response to his question. "I am here to collect what belongs to me." He informed me subsequently a few seconds later.

Fighting back my raging fear, I formed my Blood Scythes out of the back of my wrists and waited for him to close the gap between us. Something that wouldn't be all that challenging as I recalled how this man took pleasure in standing over the top of his 'patients'.

"Do you think those stupid blades of yours can kill me?" The cruelly toned Doctor Masters mocked, his words sending chills down my body. Completely freezing me over despite my body's willingness to kill this jerk. "What's the matter you damn brat? You don't seem to have that same hatred for me like you used to?" He probed, now standing directly over the top of me. Still unable to move, I stared up into his cold blue-green eyes, preparing myself for the same old torturous treatments the man use to force upon me back when I was both mentally and physically impaired. With my petite build unable to move whatsoever, I fell to this man's mercy, feeling my Blood Scythes start to de-clot. "Looks like your weapons have failed you, just like your pathetic body, 0497."

"Shut-up!" I thought in my head, still unable to speak a single word, let alone utter a sound.

"Looks like you and your annoying pals will all go down together-"

Finally interrupting him, I angrily screamed, "Shut-up!" Quickly transforming into my Hellhound form, I lunged for his face with my jaws swung open, I prepared for round two. Just as my paws were supposed to reach his shoulders, my ears could hear movement coming from Jakob's room across the hall. Trying to terrifyingly decide on how to react to this situation, my body came crashing down on top of Doctor Masters. His slicked-back hair coming undone with the sheer force I had brought upon him. Standing on top of the Doctor, I went against the urge to kill this man and instead ran towards Jakob's room. Worry over my friends' safety taking urgency.

In my canine form, I rushed right out into the hallway, my four legs moving me almost four times faster than my two legs ever could. Swiftly reaching the Vampiric's room, I barged past the doorway and again altered forms. Steadying my gait, I cautiously entered unsure of what was awaiting me on the inside. My overactive imagination of course already expecting the worst possible outcome, but before I could attempt to survey the new environment someone called, "Cinder-?"

Feeling a masculine hand grab at the back of my left shoulder, I quickly reformed my Blood Scythe out of instinct. Pushing the edge of the blade against the skin of the neck, right where one of the most important arteries in the human body ran. Driving the right wrist blade into the skin, I felt another masculine hand grab at that arm in an attempt to stop me from severely injuring or possibly maiming this unknown identity. With the front edge of the blade slicing the fine hairs on the neck, my arm eventually came to a complete halt.

Once more that same voice rang in my ears, calling out my name, this time full of more fear and urgency. "Cinder! Hey, wake up!"

Confused, I started to feel my tiny frame forcefully shake. Trying to fight against this suspected man's arm which was still tightly gripping my forearm to stop the blade from imminently ripping into flesh, I yet again overheard the voice call out to me.

With the next call, I noticed that all around me the surroundings were beginning to blur and rapidly spin before fading into a penetrating darkness. Shutting my eyes to keep from becoming dizzy, I eventually felt the spinning world seize. Shooting my eyes wide open, I hastily saw that I was still in my bed, still in the same position I had fallen asleep in. As I steadily regained my senses, I noticed that I had my right arm was raised over my head, the Blood Scythe still exposed and lying with the blade's edge against someone's neck. Trying to adjust my eyesight, I began to finally make out the features of Jakob who was leaning over the edge of the left side of the bed, doing his best to hold back my Special Power from slicing into his flesh. With reality hitting me, I hastily retracted the blades, forcing the blood to return to the strong veins lying beneath my skin.

"Finally-" Jakob graciously sighed, thankful I had come to when I had.

Looking over to stare up into his haunting Vampire yellow gaze, I tried to wrap my head around what had just happened. Trying my hardest to understand if all that I had gone through really was just a bad dream, a nightmare. As I fought to find the right words, I apologized "I'm sorry Jakob-"

"It's alright Cinder." He thankfully replied with another heavy exhale, "I'm just glad that I was able to catch your arm before you sliced my head off."

Forcing myself up into a sitting position on my bed and allowing Jakob to sit alongside me on top of the dark blue comforter, I proceeded to apologize. "I really am sorry about that." I couldn't find any other words to describe it.

"It's okay. Really." He paused for a minute. "It was my fault anyway for barging in, but I had to come get you for breakfast."

"It's already morning?" I wondered aloud, perceiving that the was trying to abruptly change the conversation's subject, so I would not feel so bad for nearly killing one of the most caring people I knew. Looking out one of the windows which faced the frozen ocean shoreline, I answered my question. "Looks like it."

"It's actually eleven o'clock. But when I knocked and you didn't answer, I thought you may have wanted some time alone like you have been wanting a lot of here recently; which is understandable, but when I heard you violently shout out to some unforeseen person I decided to..."

"Please just stop talking Jakob." I interrupted him.

"Sorry." Jakob now apologized to me. "Have you had those before? As in those kinds of nightmares?"

Standing up off the edge of the bed, I turned to face the Vampiric, "I have not had them in a long time since-" Pausing, I wondered if I should even tell him about the last nightmare I had. "We should head off to eat, any longer and Yalu WILL kill us-" I teased, now being the one who altered the subject.

At first, he seemed hesitant about my direct change in behavior however he then agreed to my statement. Returning with his comical remark the two of us both made our way out of the bedroom, through the hallway and back into the common area where our close friends were happily waiting for us to come eat.

Chapter 71
Cinder

Two weeks after Christmas, everyone seemed to move on ahead with normalcy, our routine had stuck through both Christmas and New Year's. Every morning it was wake up, get ready for breakfast, eat, then I was off to either spar or run along the wooded trails generally with a partner, followed by lunch, and after that, I would normally hide out in my room until dinner. It was the same thing for me every day, and for them it was the same questions every day. Questioning why I kept secluding myself, why I kept locking my door, why this and why that. It was making me truly begin to wonder if they were starting to catch on. I had less than two months now until I had to leave, and it was heartbreaking the more I kept thinking about that dreadful day. The more I worried over it, the more I could hear my ferocious, psychotic ideas take over. Even though I was fighting every second of it, I could feel myself beginning to lose the energy to.

"Alright, that's good news." I overheard Jakob speak as he walked down the small hallways that connected our rooms to the common area.

"What is?" Mhykal asked from his seat on the sofa, while I was attempting to catch my breath after my normal routine of sparring with Peylith, followed by a rigorous run.

"Oh, well-" he returned, putting his cellphone into his pants' pocket.

"You just heard from Braedon, right?"

"No Viktor, but it's still good news, nonetheless. After lunch, we will start packing our things up and returning to the Manor."

"Wait, we are going back home?" Valeryie questioned with the happiest expression on her face I had yet to see since we had come to this Connecticut Coastline Mansion, "About time."

"We will start packing after Lunch, okay," Jakob repeated to her while he walked into the kitchen to help a now pregnant Yalu set the table.

Sitting down at the same seat I had sat in for the time we had been stuck here for a reason that had yet to be disclosed, I surveyed the platter full of pre-made sandwiches and snacks get arranged in the center of the glass dining table. While everyone else also situated themselves around the table to get ready for the second meal of the day, I felt the same cold hands touch both of my shoulders. My natural instinct was to slice the cruel being's arteries, however, I knew that this person didn't have any veins considering he was just a skeleton made of nothing more than a perilous black mass.

Grabbing for some of the food, I consciously interrogated the Shadow, "What do you want?"

"Just checking in on my naive Reaper."

"Right-" I subconsciously groaned while grabbing a couple of ham sandwiches and a handful of leftover chips. "Can't you just wait till I go back to my room like you do every other day?"

"Don't get ahead of yourself, little Reaper." The Shadow whispered in my ear before fading out. The sensation of his hands tightly clutching my shoulders diminishing.

"Whatever-" I sighed in my manic mind.

"Cinder are you okay?" Peylith asked me, alerting me to the probability of my fellow Kin catching onto my small dialogue. Taking a small breath, I prayed he did not see the being as I could.

"Yeah." I exhaled, grinning back at the other Hellhound, hiding the truth. Lying like I normally did now, another part of the same old routine.

"You sure?" He continued to prod.

Staring into his amber-yellow hound gaze, I stuttered an answer that was half true and half false, "Yes, I'm okay. Just excited to finally go home, although at the same time I am worried about what awaits us when we get back home."

"It's alright Cinder." Yalu interrupted, eavesdropping on our conversation. "For you, it's whatever you want, for me it's going on Maternity leave soon, and for everyone else, it's eventually returning to the regular schedule of the Syndicate. This is not the first time we have done this, and it probably won't be the last time either."

"Yup, for as long as there are those Institutions and inhumane laws treating Unnaturals so cruelly we will continue with the Syndicate's work," Mhykal spoke up. "However, while you were gone you missed out on Jakob's hissy fit."

"You had a-" I spontaneously questioned Jakob.

"Braedon had his priorities all screwed up." The Vampiric returned. "Needless to say, I threatened him and told him to go shove the Syndicate and everything else up his ass."

"Oh."

"If we can't protect and fight for our members then how can we protect and fight for them as well."

"He was worried over you." The elder Vixen interrupted. "Jakob was thoroughly concerned over your wellbeing and your faith in us the longer we waited to try to find you. So yes, he fought Braedon about the priorities, and nearly well, let's just say he could have seriously injured the Syndicate's Leader."

Once more, I exhaled a heavy shocked sigh. I had no idea that had even happened in my absence. I knew that they cared about me and fought to get me back to the Manor, but I did not know that Braedon had tried to push it off. Making me wonder what had made that Vampiric dislike me. Looking down at my plate of food, I felt my heart pause. The more I heard about this story, the more my heart ached about having to leave someone who was so willing to fight for me. I never had anyone fight that hard for me for in years.

"But it's all good. You're here with us now, and you will be back home shortly." Jakob spoke up, staring at me from across the dining table.

Expressing the same grin I had gotten so good at expressing in my granted freedom, I decided to hurry up and finish eating so I could return to shrouding myself in my room with my tormenting thoughts. While I finished eating, I noticed that everything had grown quiet again well besides the sounds of everyone's teeth crunching on chips or tearing away at their sandwiches.

Shortly after Lunch had finished, we all pitched in with the clean-up process, before returning to our rooms and begin packing up our clothes. Although I only had a handful of outfits that were returned to me from the Manor, the few clothing items I had bought with Yalu that day at the mall, and the few outfits I had obtained over the Holiday, I still aimlessly wondered in my head, "Would all this really be okay?".

Stepping into my room I gently shut the door and locked it the same way I did every day. Turning around, I saw the bright rays of the mid-day sun poking through the modern panes of the window in my room. It's warm light beating into the room, almost as if it was telling me it was okay to move on. Taking a heavy exhale, I carried one of my gifted suitcases back over to the bed, placing it on the bench at the end of the footboard.

383

While filling the suitcase up with my items besides the outfit I would wear on my journey back, which I had yet to pick out from my neutral toned collection, I called out to the Shadow, "What were you wanting to discuss with me out there? Was it about the time I had left sane? If so, I already know."

"Well I am glad that it's finally broken through my Reaper's thick skull, but no it was not what needs to be discussed." The Shadow said, leaping out of the dark shadows to produce a semi-physical being.

"Then what?" I now asked, changing into a more comfortable outfit for the long drive back to the Syndicate's main base of operations.

Sliding into some comfortable skinny jeans, I awaited an answer. A few minutes later, I heard his low dark voice return, "It can be discussed at another time and place, for now, enjoy the time you have left with them."

"What are you rambling on about?" I questioned, slipping my form-fit long sleeve over my black sports bra and began to put back on my new nice cuffed beige wedged booties with trudges along the soles.

"For now, I will sulk in the shadows until then." The Shadow spoke, acting as if he had something hidden from me or something cruel planned like usual.

As I put on the same winter coat Yalu had bought using Jakob's money, I stared back at the Shadow, locking our two different colored gazes. The warmth and comfort of that orangey blazing amber eyes I had grown so used to now felt like a deceitful trap awaiting me. The quietness lasting for a few seconds before he broke away, returning to the dying shadows of the changing sun tones in my room. "Sometimes I wonder about your true desires." I ended zipping up the suitcase.

Chapter 72
Jakob

"Is that everything?" I asked while Peylith closed the back lift to the black Escalade, now filled with several suitcases containing everyone's attire.

"Yup that's everything," Yalu answered me with a teasing smirk. "Mhykal and I will be taking the car, while the four of you guys take the Escalade."

"Sounds good to me." The younger Vampiric cheerfully agreed, sneaking up behind his mate for a devious hug. "Gives us some more alone time."

"Is that all you talk about?" Valeryie huffed at the two looking up from her cell phone for the first time in ages.

"You will understand it one day." Her sister debated. "When you finally get a man of your own."

"Alright, well we should start heading back. I would prefer to get back home around the same time as the late-night traffic. Be easier to sneak under the cover of the nightlife."

"Well, it takes a few hours to get there without any moving traffic, so what is your plan, Jakob?" Mhykal returned, leaning his chin on Yalu's left shoulder.

"I would prefer to take the back roads, for now, then drive along the main roads the closer we get to home."

"Okay, and with the traffic that will almost double our drive time."

"In other words, we should start driving in about an hour if we want to make it in time with the rush hour but also stay a bit ahead of it." Valeryie ever so intelligently interrupted.

"Exactly." I sighed, "Until then, I would enjoy having one last glass of blood before I return home."

"I could use one myself." Mhykal sneered, breaking away from his girlfriend's hips.

"You better clean it up once you are done," Yalu growled. "I am not cleaning up your bloody whiskey glasses!"

"Yeah, yeah." I shrugged off before I returned to the warmer, snow-free house. "I was already planning on cleaning up after myself, I don't know about your lover though."

"Hey now-" Mhykal comically snarled at me as we walked side by side.

Elbowing him playfully in the traditional manner, I continued to snicker, "You know I am just joking with you two. You two will make great parents seriously."

Trying to playfully jab back at me, my longtime friend returned with a gracious thank you. Acting as if he had never heard me compliment him before. "You will be a great uncle as well, Jakob." Strolling inside the house, we grabbed our special 'Blood' Drinking glasses and advanced to the wine storage in the sunroom where we had hidden away the 'Donated' blood. Filling up my glass with the necessary plasma cells needed to survive as a Vampire Unnatural Species, I heard Mhykal once again speak up. A serious look spread across his face, "Jakob why didn't you profess your attraction to Cinder while you were helping her with that new collar? You know she wouldn't have asked for you if she didn't feel at least similar towards you."

"I know that, but I don't know how to say it," I replied, gingerly sipping away at thick cold metallic blood cells. "When she was eyeing that collar, it was like there was this dark aura just flowing around her. I could sense all of the hatred and the darkness that rested in her heart if that makes any sense."

"No not really, but I do sort of understand what you mean. She has started to act odd. Separating herself from everyone on a regular basis. She's acting suspicious for sure, and it has only grown since Braedon and Viktor made that theory about her being the one who's leaking our location." Mhykal returned. His ability to evaluate and respond to situations like this always taking me back a bit. "I think, for now, we just have to keep an eye on her. I really don't want to believe that she was told to do this, but those two situations are creating a violent cocktail."

"Yeah, I know." I sighed, flashing back to that time she and I were outside on the patio steps, where she was completely overwhelmed with becoming an Unnatural. "Mhykal?" I asked. "I don't think she is being controlled by them that's for sure." Having another flashback of when Cinder refuted how she hated the Researchers and Scientists thinking she was stupid and naive. "If it's anyone that is making her act so dark and causing her to separate herself it's that Shadow-"

"That same one the Shaman told us about when we freed the Off-Grids?"

"Yeah, I think so. I mean, you remember what he told us. A shadow that lurks over her, one that even the Spirits avoid. One that even the Dead dredges." I returned.

"Corrupting her heart with darkness yet leaving her soul still so innocent." My friend interrupted me. "Yeah, I remember that. I also remember that day you and I went into the Ward on the Blood Moon, the first time we saw her in that form. Acting as if we weren't

387

even there. Talking to something we could not see." Finishing up his first glass of blood before heading onto another.

"I vividly remember that. I also remember seeing that thing when I hid away the memory of her killing Logan. It was like he was enticing her to lose control." I said as I filled my glass up for a second round, feeling my energy return.

"The more I am thinking about this, the more I am worried about her sanity and safety," Mhykal said before taking a large swallow.

"Yeah, however, there isn't much we can help her out with when she can't even tell us what is going on-"

"Are you guys about done, it's almost time we start leaving," Yalu urged, peeking her head into the dimly lit sunroom, considering per protocol we had to close all of the curtains.

"Yeah, just have to clean up the glasses." I jested, finishing my second glass.

"Okay, then hurry up! I am so ready to get back home and start planning out my maternity leave." The Caucasian Vixen smirked, trying to rush us along. A bit surprised that she was so excited about having a child.

Walking out of the sunroom, I went to clean the whiskey glasses while Mhykal cleaned up the empty wine bottle we had hid our limited blood supply in, before dumping it in the recycling bin at the end of the property. Finishing up with washing the tiny dish load, I quickly hand-dried the two glasses and put them back in the glass cabinet hanging beside the fridge while Mhykal put his winter coat on, preparing for his rigorous journey to the bin. Grabbing my winter coat, I slipped it on before also slipping back out in the outside world.

Stepping past the front door's threshold, I saw that Valeryie was already inside the Escalade with darkly tinted windows while the two Hellhounds were both in their canine forms. The much larger

Hellhound Peylith was attempting to nip at the smaller Cinder, trying to entice her into a play tussle. Though I could tell she was not in the mood for their customary play. The hair along her neck and back were raised, her ears were laid flat back against her head and she was bearing her front fangs at him. There was no actual language said between the two that I could understand, yet the actions were obvious.

"Alright, you two that's enough." Yalu snapped at them, stopping the canines both dead in their tracks. The Hellhounds' ears dropped, snarls faded, and tails tucked as they fixated their attention on the Vixen. "Just get in the damn car now." Following in with the orders they both piled into the vehicle, Peylith stepping into the front passenger seat while Cinder stepped into the back, her nicely dressed winter outfit standing out against the black painted vehicle. "Ready Mhykal?" The Vixen now exhaled, turning to stare back at her partner.

"Yup." Mhykal acknowledged. Turning his attention back to me, he further resumed, "Okay, we will be right behind you for most of the way Jakob, considering you know most of the roads here."

"Yeah." I sighed, splitting from the group to get into the Driver's front seat of the black SUV.

Chapter 73
Jakob/Cinder

The drive back to the historic Victorian Manor was surprisingly quiet. To no surprise, Valeryie was on her phone chatting with some of her friends I assumed by the way her phone danced in the rear-view facing mirror. Meanwhile, Cinder was fast asleep in her human form, and Peylith was looking out the window still surprised by the advancement in Human Technology, thankfully he wasn't breaking anything. Even through the busy highway and rush hour traffic, it remained quiet, a feeling I treasured.

Driving around the oval driveway towards the large garage, I pulled the vehicle off to the side just as the red sportscar that Mhykal owned snuck up behind us. It's quiet purr silently driving past the Escalade and into it's designated spot inside the massive garage. Taking the key out of the ignition, its sudden stillness alerting the rest of the passengers to our arrival.

Regrouping behind the SUV, I opened the back hutch allowing everyone to grab their designated luggage. "Take it all to your rooms and get resituated. Peylith, I will show you to your room after I talk some things over with Braedon." I gently ordered, struggling to keep my tone as calm as possible during the untimely hour.

"What do you want to talk to him about?" Yalu asked, hurriedly reaching for her suitcases, however, her boyfriend was fast on feet, yanking them away from her grasp.

"Is it about the reason why we had to vacate everyone from their rooms?" Mhykal too queried, eagerly grabbing another suitcase that belonged to his soon-to-be child's mother.

"Mhykal would you quit that!" The Vixen snarled, smacking him on the back of the head. "I can still carry my own bags!"

"Ow, sorry-"

"Anyways-" I interrupted, watching Cinder and Valeryie already work on carrying their luggage inside the Manor. "Yeah, I want to talk to him about something first, before everyone starts to return over the next few weeks."

"Okay, well considering the number of suitcases here between Yalu and her sister, it will be a little while before I get caught up with you."

"Jakob can go talk to Braedon on his own." Yalu hissed at her boyfriend while carrying two of her medium-sized cases towards the house.

"Yeah, I know that-" Mhykal exhaled, looking back at me and over to his girlfriend with the same uncertainty a child had picking between his two parents.

"I will be fine; I won't try to kill him." I insured my fellow kin. Picking up my suitcases, one medium and two large ones, I shot back to the male Hellhound "Alright just follow me, Peylith."

"Are you sure you do not want my help?" The Egyptian Hellhound questioned, his teddy bear side poking through the intimidating height and brute muscle mass.

"Once we are inside, I am sure you can ask Mhykal," I answered him while the two of us trailed everyone else inside, passed the covered front porch and beyond the thick double front doors. The minute we stepped inside, I led the Hellhound towards the common area which lied beyond the newly lain foyer, of course having to stop a few times to grab his attention. "After we get everything back to some normalcy, you can spend all the time necessary to get become accustomed to this grandiose place."

"Okay." He returned still in awe at the height of the double ceilings and double staircases mapping out the foyer. Once inside the common area, I left the Hellhound alone to go upstairs into my room, intent on completing my task.

Coming back out of the room, I strolled back down the catwalk/corridor towards the Study where I knew the Syndicate's Leader was hiding. Glancing down over the railing, I saw that Peylith was indeed trying to offer his help to Mhykal. Thankfully, the Vampiric took the Hellhound off of my hands. Taking a long heavy breath, I proceeded with entering the Study.

"Oh Jakob, I thought you guys wouldn't be returning till tomorrow," Braedon said from behind his desk.

Walking up towards the mahogany desk, I smirked, "Well you got your information wrong because I told Viktor after Lunch, we would be preparing to head out."

Quickly shifting the subject on me, Braedon ensued, "What do you want to talk to me about? Now that you seem to have a much cooler head."

"I am still pissed off at you for how you acted a few months ago, though I am trying my damn hardest to remain civil." I snarled, sitting down on one of the newer Victorian chairs, indeed trying everything I could to keep my boiling blood from simmering over. Taking a minute breather to center myself, I resumed, "I am here to ask you, do you truly believe Cinder is the one that is tagged?"

"Home at last." I sighed, flopping down on top of my four-posted bed with dark navy-blue blankets. Turning over onto my back, I long fully stared up at the ceiling. "Well, for now, it is my home. I don't want to leave them-" Sitting myself up on the

392

comforter, I debated if I should even worry about putting my clothes back in the armoire. Heavily glaring at the black suitcase that laid on the floor at the foot of my bed for an extended period, I decided to put the items away. It was something to distract myself, even if I knew I wouldn't be here for much longer.

As I put away the clothes, I felt the scar on my back start to burn. The pain beginning to constrict all the air out of my lungs, placing further strain on my aching heart. Biting my lower lip, I thwarted the ability to tranquilize myself in an attempt to bear through the pain. Collapsing down onto my knees, I threw my limber figure against the wall connecting the bedroom to the attached bath, preparing myself both mentally as well as physically for the long haul this time around.

Telling myself, "Just calm down. Take slow breaths. It will pass." seemed to help for a short duration. Sitting alone in my room, I rapidly pleaded, "Please pass soon. Please." Simultaneously wondering in my head, "Why did this thing have to burn at the most minuscule of times?"

"I am just going off what they told me." I heard Braedon speak, trying to turn my interrogating questions away from his thoughts on the manner.

Going along with it, for now, I pushed my questioning, "What did they tell you?"

"After they had searched the property with their warrants, I was able to request my inquiries and thankfully get some answers. From what one of the men had told me, there was a chip implanted in a 'runaway' Unnatural who was considered extremely dangerous. While they were waiting for the chip's GPS location to seize movements for a small extended amount of time in hope of allowing recapture, the GPS location happened to stop on this property; the date they told me was around the same time that we had the Hellhound in our care."

"Then why did they wait to pull the search warrant at that specific time?" I frustratingly interrogated. "If it were Cinder who was truly tagged by the Institute then when she was at the other one in Colorado, wouldn't they have told Salem that they had her? Why didn't they follow the GPS tracker to the state during her two months in that facility?"

"I don't know!" Braedon quickly shot back, his eyes looking away from my harsh glare, "It was hard enough just getting them to answer those questions."

"So, you just naturally assumed it was her?! You know we have other Unnaturals we've saved from that Institute, and the ones who decided to stay here, could have easily been chipped. It could have been any one of them!" I snapped at the other Vampiric, who was as old as I, "So, why put all the blame onto her?!" Surveying Braedon further advert his attention away from my burning glare, I knew deep down he was now trying to advert his true answer. "Answer my question!" Still no response, I stepped up towards the desk and again ordered him finally losing my patience, "Answer the fucking question Braedon!!"

Chapter 74

Jakob

"You want my answer, huh Jakob?!" The same as always suit-wearing Unnatural man shouted back at me. Darting out of his chair, Braedon slammed his hands on the mahogany desk.

Yelling with just as much volume, I returned, "Yes, I want your answer! Stop beating around the damn bush!" Locking gazes with the man, we remained in a dark staring contest.

Braedon, of course, being the first one to give in like normal, slunk back down into his chair and began twiddling on his computer. Moving the wireless mouse around on its fabricated pad, I began to wonder what explanation this man had come up with. What excuse would it be this time? Eventually, his deep voice spoke up after a few intense minutes had slithered by. "In the few weeks transcending between her killing Logan and the day that the Hunters had kidnapped both Cinder and Yalu, the cameras posted on the front door caught her sneaking in and out of the Manor in the early hours of the morning."

"What has that got to do with anything?! Valeryie has also been caught sneaking out of the Manor on several occasions, as well as many other Unnaturals." I questioned, trying to calm my rising hatred for our Syndicate's Leader and his feelings towards Cinder. "I ask you once more, what has that got to do with you continuously blaming Cinder?"

"Jakob, just watch the Security Camera's footage." Braedon snarled, hinting at me to come watch the footage I only naturally assumed he had pulled up on the computer screen. With a deep exhale, I stood myself up and wandered around the mahogany desk to view the footage. "Look, I know that there are all kinds of Unnaturals who sneak in and out of the Manor at all times of the day, that's why I had the cameras put up, however something about the way she acted when I brought up the subject just keeps eating away at me."

Watching the footage that had been saved on the computer, I indeed saw Cinder walking out of the front door at two, three, and four o'clock in the morning on several days. I could understand where some of his confusion was coming especially when at that current point in time she was just beginning to adjust to the outside. "How did she act when you asked her about this?" I wondered aloud, beginning to slightly understand the need to investigate this a bit more.

"I don't know how to explain it. It felt like someone was whispering into her ear, telling her what to say. She was good at it for sure, but-"

"Our years of experience with lies and liars-" I interrupted. As I continued examining the footage for the time when the Hellhound returned, along with the actions she represented upon that same return, I felt my stomach start to churn. I didn't want to doubt anything about Cinder, especially with how much I cared for her, yet the evidence was beginning to sway my faith. "However-" I attempted to continue as I finished reviewing the camera's footage, noticing that there was a light double shadow effect pulling from Cinder's shadow. "I don't think that she was doing it of her own free will," I told Braedon.

"Huh?" The Vampiric confusingly asked, his gaze completely fixated on what I was going to say next.

"Only Yalu, Mhykal, Peylith, and I know about this. I don't want to go against Cinder's wishes here, but I guess even someone like you who oversees this place deserves to know this in the least." Stepping away from the computer screen, I strolled over to one of the chairs. Shadowed by Braedon, I resumed my explanation once he sat across from me. "I know it is going to sound weird, but just go with me on this. There is a Shadow being that follows Cinder and from what I have physically observed, the being does have a profound sense of control over her."

"Okay, when and how did you see it? And none of that still doesn't help the fact that-"

"I don't know if she was the one that was chipped or not, that resulted in the Syndicate being searched by the Government, but you can't go putting all the blame on her when she has that creature enforcing her to lie and act out." I heavily breathed, trying to maintain as much tranquility as I could when Braedon was yet again pissing me off. "Although it has never taken a physical form to my eyes, I saw it when I hid way that memory of her killing Logan."

"When she killed Logan to protect Valeryie-" Braedon swiftly interrupted, attempting to comprehend the information I was reporting.

"While that part of the story is true. Cinder only killed Logan by the forewarning she received from this Shadow. She also told me about the unfairness of being a Hellhound." I hesitated, recalling Cinder's frequent pauses in the middle of our conversations. Excusing herself with unusual reasons such as 'She wasn't supposed to tell us' or 'She couldn't tell us.' "I am telling you this, because you can't go blaming everything on her when Cinder is hardly in complete control over her own damn body."

Standing up from the Victorian chair, I prepared to stride out of the Study only to overhear Braedon's voice call, "I will try not to blame her for it, however, her odd behavior should nonetheless be evaluated."

Just as I reached the end of the rug, I stopped myself to react towards our Syndicate's Leader statement. Questioning the several century-old Vampire with my voice hitting a low tone, one I hadn't used in a long while, "What do you mean by evaluated, Braedon? She will not be used by you, like you have used the rest of us!"

"She will be a significant help to our cause, and a better benefactor to the Syndicate. I have seen most of her combat skills during her sparring."

Rushing back to him, I picked him up by the collar of his tuxedo and held him up in the air. "I don't give a fuck what you think! I will not let you use her like that, nor will I let Calem or Saylene use her! I will not let anyone of you guys tarnish how she thinks of us!" Feeling the twist in my stomach get worse, I tightened the grip on his collar, "If anyone of you foolish leaders tries tarnishing that faith she has in our Cause, it will make you no better than those Government assholes who're trying to do the same thing to not only her, but to all of the other Unnaturals we have saved over these past ten years."

"Jakob-" My ears now perceived someone else's voice quietly utter inside the Study.

Looking over my shoulder I saw Yalu and Mhykal standing in the doorway. Slowly putting Braedon back down on the floor, I again attempted to take my leave, but hearing my long-time friend call out to me made me stop dead in my tracks. "Hey man-"

Pushing his hand away, I growled at him in the same low tone, "Leave me alone." as I pushed through them. This was not how I wanted to spend my first day home, although at the same time this had been a great weight bearing down on my shoulders that needed to be lifted.

Walking in the direction of my room hoping to escape the dark confines and calm myself, I noticed Peylith was still waiting on me to show him his room. Quietly cursing to myself, I spun around and descended the stairs making my way towards the common area where the other Hellhound was patiently waiting. "Sorry about that Peylith." I sighed, taking a deep breath.

"No, whatever it was that had pushed you over must have been on your mind for a long time." The dark tan-skinned toned man with amber yellow eyes consoled. "It does not bother me."

"If you don't mind me asking-" I questioned while leading him towards the designated room I knew had yet to be assigned to anyone. A room about four doors down from the other Hellhound we had living under our roof. "When you lived in the Egyptian Era, how did you handle problems that weighed so heavily on your heart?"

"Well, we would usually pray to our designated god or goddess for hopefully some guidance on the situation. If we could not get a hold of our Deities, we would, in turn, offer a plead to their messengers." He explained to me. Speaking in such a manner where I could truly see the amount of experience this man had with life, despite what little knowledge the former Pharaoh had of the modern world.

Stepping towards Cinder's room, I couldn't help but lock my eyes on the door, noticing that there was that same dark aura piercing out of her bedroom and this time, the sensation was much stronger. Going against my gut feeling to go check on her, I proceeded to lead the other Hellhound in the direction of his room. "Well, I guess it wasn't that long ago that even we too had done the same thing, but it was to the apparent monotheistic religions."

"Yeah?" Peylith pondered before wisely exclaiming, "Although there was no point in asking me the question when it seems you already know the answer."

"Yeah, I just wanted to get my mind off that argument between Braedon and I." I sighed, rubbing the back of my head with a cheesy grin.

"Was it about Cinder?" He pursued.

"Yeah, it was." I returned, looking down at the dark wooded floors as we were just getting beyond the third room past Cinder's.

"I won't ask why-"

"Hey Peylith, when you were busy serving Anubis, did you often have things you could not say to others, or have things you had to do which you had no control over?" I questioned him after a few succumbing seconds of silence, now desiring an answer to the other question I had rampantly running through my mind. The one which remained unresolved in my heart.

Looking over at him I observed him glance down on me, flashing a quick smile before taking a deep breath, "Yes, there were things I could not tell anyone, even now after many years of silence there are things I still cannot tell anyone, even you guys. As for control, I have always had control over what I wanted to do." That last sentence made my heart drop, and my gut twist and turn. Continuing to listen to his answer, "There were tasks I had to do, and unfortunately, I had no control over when they arrived, but I still had to do them. Why? Do you think her 'God' is abusing her?"

"I don't know, but the way she acts around many subjects is like she is completely terrified to even mention them-" I said, coming to a stop in front of his assigned room.

Watching Peylith lay his hand gently on my shoulder, I stared up into his taller frame, "Jakob, she is still young. I am sure there are many things she is terrified to tell you, especially when she has been forced to grow up in a Hospital room that is no different than a Prison Cell. So, try not to worry over it too much."

"It's hard not to." I thought in my head while my heart and stomach still felt so hurt. Snapping back to reality, I spoke up as I opened up the door to his room, "This is your room, here. It is the fourth one down from Cinder's room, which is right across the hall from Yalu's room." Avidly watching him enter the moderately-sized room, I quickly told him that I would be in the common area or my room on the second floor if he needed anything before closing his room's door and returning the way I came.

Chapter 75
Cinder

With the screeching pain in my back increasing, I internally debated who to call for help. I had heard loud shouts coming from outside of my room not too long ago, and while I knew not who it was, I figured that it was better to not get involved. However, I also did not want to call upon that being who was lurking in the shadows and was only going to aide me once I had decided to disembark down the opposite path of my close friends, my second family. Sure, it was inevitable, but I was not yet ready to leave them.

Feeling my heart constrict, again forcing all the air out of my lungs, I punched my left hand against the bedroom-bathroom adjoining wall. "Damn it-" I coughed, barely able to speak without losing consciousness. "It's not fair-" I continued to complain in my head while it still tragically weighed my available options. Punching the wall repeatedly as my right hand nevertheless clung to the skin above my breast and over my heart. "It is not fair-" Bending over into a fetal position, I tightly grasped for my heart that was in agonizing pain and heaved for air.

Before I felt the last grip of my conscious slip away from me, a familiar voice spoke. The male voice deeply ringing in my left ear. "What's wrong you damn brat?! Are you in pain again?" Lifting my head while fighting against the urge to slip away, I barely made out the figure standing beside me. His knees bent, so he could still stand over me yet remain at eye level. "Shall I make it go away?" Making out the figure as the same man who was just in my horrid nightmare, I quickly reacted. Throwing myself back against the wall before trying to stand myself up, I tried to prepare for what I knew instinctively was a needle full of unwanted painkillers. But my poor body collapsed once more. Falling back on top of my knees, I attempted to bellow out in pain, however before I could get a single note out of my throat to fearfully call for help, I felt his hand's grip around my mouth. Mumbling my voice, while now straddling over the top of my dressed body, forcing it to fall flat along the hard floor. "Shhhh, we don't want them to hear us." He stated before taking a quick pause. "Now sit still, 0497! This will only hurt for a little bit." I overheard the cursed Doctor shout at me in the same low tone he usually did when I had made him mad. Staring at his scarred face, into those lifeless sadistic blue-green eyes of his, I felt the prick of the needle strike at one of my unprotected veins. Quickly losing the will to struggle against him, I pitifully allowed the undesired drugs to enter my veins, allowing it flow through my bloodstream on the way to my nerves and shut off the pain signals that were running towards my brain. "That's it, just relax and sleep. It will all be over with shortly, stupid child."

"You aren't here-" I argued my subconscious. "You are not here!" I again urged, "There is no way that they would let you get passed those front doors. Not without giving you a fight-" Stopping when I remember the last vivid nightmare I had, remembering the footsteps, the sounds, and scents of others in that Mansion, I worriedly cried, "No! There was no way!" Trying to calm myself down, I indeed began to feel the pain in my back fade and knew that despite my drugged body, I had to find a way to fight them. As my mind argued passing out into the drug-induced slumber, I regained control over my breathing and commenced the next step: trying to overcome the cruel and abusive Doctor Masters.

Patiently pretending that the drugs were working their way through my blood system, I waited for the weight of his heavy frame to stand up off my body. Feeling his hand push off my mouth then move under my chin so he could 'professionally' evaluate the percentage of my consciousness that was still awake, I proceeded to count the seconds it took him to remove the hand from around my neck area. I knew in the past it took him about ten seconds to evaluate the condition I was in, so I just counted them inside my fear-ridden head.

When the tenth second finally succumbed, I decided now was the time to fight back. Feeling the grip release, I shot my eyes open. Through with the pretending, I commanded my legs to work. Using the wall as my guide while my weakened legs now tried to persuade my demanding mind to not push the limbs.

"Still have fight in you, huh 0497?" Doctor Masters cockily barked to me. "I wonder how well you will be able to fight me when you can hardly stand at all..."

Grinning back at him, I noticed that something seemed off about his presence. Beginning to see through his lab-coat wearing body, I finally spoke up in between my returning breath, "You are not here. You're just another figment of my wearing mind. A sign of my steadily losing sanity." While the memories of that cruel cursing man faded away, I continued to reinforce my thoughts, "You are not here! You, nor your hired Hunters, and Guards are here at this place!" Straightening up my back as the numbing sensation in my legs dissipated. "You will never reach this place, nor will I ever let you hurt them like you did me." Taking a long deep breath and slowly closing my eyes for a quick second, I repeated the sentence in my head. Telling myself it was okay to trust the declaration, to believe in the statement, even if I knew deep down in my heart that it was not one hundred percent proof, it was all I had.

With the final resemblance of Masters finally vanishing into the shadows of the setting sun, I turned myself around to face the large arched floor-to-ceiling Victorian window. Feeling its last warm rays punching its way into my skin, I took another settling deep breath. Standing there in the middle of my room for a few minutes soothing my rapidly beating heart as my pale-like skin was still absorbing the basking light, I serenely observed the Sun exchange its watch with its rivaled brother, the calmly lit Moon. The colors in the sky were as breath-taking as the nightmare I had just endured. Watching the orange rays turn to a soft white, I proceeded to contemplate my next move, recalling that just like the Moon whose job was to observe the world it watched over, I too had a job. One I was dreading to partake in.

Debating what my two choices were, I verbally wondered, "I could either embark down this road now, or I could wait two months before heading down it. Nonetheless, I was still going to have to go down it, and no matter what choice I made, I was still going to hurt them. Something I had just told that nightmarish image of Masters I was never going to allow him to do. Although-" I paused when I recollected the words the Shadow had crudely told me, "If I waited till my time was up, I would end having to watch with no control over my body as he hurt those same people." Staring up into the moon, I wondered what one was the better option. I had repetitiously been reviewing the options I had, endlessly debating them over and over and over again in my head. "With less than sixty days at most, forty-nine in the least, I must hurry up with a decision."

Hesitating for another ten minutes while two sides of my conscious deliberated between one and another, I finally decided on what I needed to do:

"In order to protect them-" I announced to the empty room.

Right before my eyes, I saw the dark mist form out of the Shadow. The red beating eyes that belonged to a cloak-wearing, walking, talking skeletal being exposed themselves out of the faded yellowish-white skull. Trying to retain a calm state, I exhaled one more breath while the last of the entire Shadow reformed himself.

Arguing my now doubting mind, I repeated, "This is in order to protect them, to protect my second family, to protect the people I love and cherish."

"You have finally come to your senses, my Little Reaper."

Chapter 76
Cinder/Jakob

"It is not my senses I have come too, Shadow." I snarled back, pulling my long side-swept bangs over my left ear. "You can read my thoughts, so I know you know the reason behind my decision."

"So, my Reaper, how do you plan to leave your friends?" The Shadow's cold voice asked me, standing blocking my view of the dimly lit moonlight rays.

"Well there's no way to go on without them trying to stop me-" I answered, hesitating with each passing word. "And I have no idea how full proof this plan is, but I need to get away somehow."

"I will leave you to your plans, Little Reaper." The Shadow spoke to me before attempting to fade into the abyss. "But do know this, the clock will not stop if my Reaper fails to get away from them."

"About that-" I asked, wanting the fading being to remain for a bit longer so I could further procrastinate. Getting no response from him before he disappeared into the nothingness of the resting shadows, I recklessly complained, "Great, make me leave just so I can get my questions answered." Taking a quick breath to prepare myself for this unplanned breakaway, I proceeded, "I truly dislike you."

Attempting to calm my uneasy stomach as it digested everything I had been told by both Braedon and Peylith, I heard the click of a door's knob being twisted. Glancing up from my view of the rug-covered floor, I saw a shadow starting to move down the corridor. Curious to see who was going to be approaching, I avidly followed the approaching shadow. I knew that there were more than just the three rooms down the long corridor, but I hoped it was her who was finally coming out into the light. Making note that the shadow's figure belonged to a man, I relaxed my anxious nerves, my fluttering heart slowing its sporadic rate.

When the shadow finally lurked out into the common area, I saw that it was Peylith who had left his room. Taken back by the amount of time it took the Hellhound to make his way back out of his room, I casually inquired, "So, how do you like your room?" Trying to keep the true feelings I was harboring down deep.

"Oh, yes. Quite well. I can't get over the 'design' the-"

"The architecture, you mean?"

"Yes, that. The woods, the bed. It is not like the Cabin or the house by the ocean." Peylith answered me, plopping himself down on the couch opposite me. "Everything here is older than the world outside, but so well preserved."

"It's Victorian." I chuckled. "It's supposed to give you that old yet regal and wise feeling. Although the Era died long ago, it is still remembered greatly. Besides, when Unnatural's come here, they too are all taken away by the stature, architecture, furniture, style, and wooded privacy from the nearby city. Matter of fact when Cinder first was able to move around the place on her own-" I paused, chuckling to myself when I remembered Yalu giving her room and the tour of the premises. "She wasn't as surprised as you are, but she observed every little detail that she could."

407

Peylith busted up laughing. "I'm sorry Jakob, but seeing you talk of my fellow kin like you do is making me understand the way Yalu and Mhykal have-"

"How they have tried to push me to confess my..." I stopped speaking when my sensitive ears alerted to the sound of another person approaching the room. Looking away from the Egyptian Hellhound, I laid eyes on the other Hellhound we had living here, the very woman to whom we were discussing.

"Oh, hey Cinder."

The woman stopped at the beginning of the rug, choosing to not sit on either couch. Looking at her long magically dyed black hair that was pulled up in a high ponytail, I noticed she was wearing the same clothes from back when we had left the Mansion. With it now being almost three o'clock in the morning, I was curious as to why she was still dressed like that. This wasn't part of her usual routine. Quickly noting that the Hellhound was wearing her light beige winter jacket with a long soft faux-fur leather collar that hung low around the breast area and matching cuffs, my gut warned me that she was going out into the world to attempt to blend into society. "What is going on?" I silently inquired, "Was I about to see her prepare to do the same thing I had seen her do from the footage?"

"What's with the get-up?" Peylith asked, beating me to the punch.

"Are you going out somewhere?" I followed up.

Watching Cinder put her hands in her back pocket of her dark skinny jeans and start the usual lean that women pulled off, I waited to hear her answer to our questions. With my full attention shifting onto her model-like fit frame, I listened to her response. "I was just going to go running on the trails out back-" the Hellhound swiftly answered. "It's a little colder than I expected it to be, so I thought I would bring my coat with me."

408

"Yeah, our internal temperatures can only handle so much out in the cold." The elder Hellhound remarked as he casually leaned further back into the sofa.

"Would you mind if I tag along?" I questioned her. My gut still advising me that something was deeply wrong with her current behavior. Something was off about the way she was talking.

"OOOOOOooooooo-" Peylith cooed, winking his amber eyes at me in the same irritating way Mhykal did when the Vampiric too teased. A nasty habit.

"Shut-up," I growled back at him in a hushed but low tone. Glaring back at the Egyptian with my own low amber gaze, I continued to wait for another answer.

"Did he catch on?" I asked myself, trying to maintain a calm composure despite the butterflies who were ferociously fluttering against the lining of my stomach. "No, I don't think so, there has to be something else on his mind-" I continued to think, hastily wandering around in my head. Noticing that Jakob's usual scent was off, his usually calm and collected scent reeked full of fear and worry. Focusing back on the subject at hand, I inhaled a quick breath before answering the man's offer. "No, I was just hoping for some time alone to think," I told him, trying to give my utmost sincerity. "There has just been a ton of things going on-" I sighed, flashing one of my 'learned smiles.'

"Alright. Be careful the moon isn't all that bright out tonight." The Vampiric warned, the tone in his voice sounding so sad. As if I had just broken his large heart.

"Maybe next time, Jakob." I smiled, finally dismissing myself from them. It wasn't the goodbye I wanted to give them, but it was all I could offer for now. As I walked towards the door connecting the back patio and open garden space to the house, I felt my heart

409

skip a beat before heavily pounding against my rib cage like it was preparing to pierce through the bone. Turning the handle to the glass door, I swung open the door and slipped out into the complete blackness of the night. Hurriedly strolling towards the trails where I knew once I was far enough from the prying eyes of my friends and those cameras; I could easily escape from the Syndicate, until then I was keeping my head down and staying in this uncomfortable human form.

Getting up from the sofa, I strolled over to the glass door so I could watch where the suspiciously acting Hellhound was going. In the pitch-black night, I could see that she was now maybe about a good twenty or thirty feet out from the house, still making her way towards the trails. However, I knew that up there in those trails there weren't any cameras or eyes to watch her, and that made my concern surrounding her behavior only worse.

"You really love her, don't you?" Peylith probed, his voice breaking the astonishing silence that had overcome the Manor.

"I guess you could say that, but for now my confession can wait," I growled back, still observing her petite body decaying into the night. The silhouette steadily blending into the outline of the woods surrounding the property. A few minutes after she had faded away into the pitch blue blackness of the night, I hastily rushed up the adjacent stairs.

"Hey, where are you going?"

"Going to grab my coat. I'm heading out there." I called down to the Hellhound who still sat on the sofa ever so casually relaxed. Completely oblivious to everything that was going on around him.

"She told you not to though."

Chapter 77
Jakob/Cinder

Running back down the stairs to the lower level of the Manor, I rushed right for the door. As I traveled through the door and down the patio towards the trails my mind had yet to decide if following Cinder was a good idea. It was stuck between catching up to her and debate my offer or pursuing her until I had a better understanding of what she was doing. Either one I chose, I knew there was a risk of me blabbing out all the reasons behind my suspicious actions, so eventually, my mind decided to do both. Hoping along the way that Cinder's scent tracking was not as accurate as Yalu and Peylith had reported.

Tracking in behind her footsteps which were still heading towards the woods, I quickly noticed a change in the pattern of her footsteps. There was a small stop followed by the small boot pattern turning back towards the house before it seemed Cinder returned pressed on. I felt my stomach drop as I let my mind wander off with the various reasons she would have stopped like this in the middle of the field.

"I thought I told you, that I was wanting to be left alone."

Staring straight at the Vampiric who had boldly followed me out into the frozen winter wasteland, I put my hands in the back pockets of my jeans and waited for the half-ass excuse I knew he was going to give me. The time I had spent here had alluded me to everyone's traits, and I had figured that Jakob was an obedient man who acted on impulses whenever he felt something was off, so his pursuit told me that I had arrived at a situation I greatly wished to avoid.

"Oh Cinder, I thought you were already on the trail..." the Vampiric lightheartedly chuckled with me trying to pretend he wasn't examining my misguided footsteps.

"I was just about to step foot on the trail when I caught onto an incoming scent," I upsettingly replied. "So why are you following me?" I inquired trying to keep my boiling blood under control.

"Well, I know you wanted to be alone, but you have been separating yourself from all of us for so long that it has gotten very worrisome Cinder. Everyone is concerned for you." Jakob responded. The tone in his voice exploiting how much he honestly cared.

My heart hurt. Felt as if it was breaking in two, while slowly constricting all of the blood supply from appropriately flowing. My stomach churned and my skin crawled while I digested Jakob's statement. Taking my hands out my pockets, I soundlessly mumbled, "This is so unfair."

"Unfair?" I quietly questioned. "What is unfair?" With my thoughts returning to silence, I wondered, "What else is that THING making you do now?"

"Jakob-" I heard Cinder call out. Looking up into those beautiful vibrant blue eyes of hers, I saw the creeping darkness in addition to the varied emotions residing inside. This was something she definitely didn't want to do, but what was it.

"What is it?" I questioned, closing in the gap between the two of us. The freshly fallen snow crunching under my black shoes.

"I don't want to do this, Jakob. I really don't want to." The Hellhound cried back.

"Do what?" I again called out, nonchalantly stepping closer and closer.

"I have to leave."

"Leave? Nobody said you have to leave-" Watching Cinder back away from me, I finally began to piece things together. It was that cruel dark Shadow I had seen when I had peered into her memory, it was he who was forcing her to do this.

"I'm sorry, Jakob." She apologized, again taking a few more steps backward. Her petite body turning around to return to the secrecy of the woods.

Quickly thinking on my feet, I used my Unnatural Vampiric increased speed and ran right in front of her. Completely blocking her path. Hurriedly wrapping my arms around her small frame, I brought it in towards my chest, "Don't be sorry, it is not your fault." I told her. I could see in her eyes that she was desperately trying to wrap her fearful but still-childlike mentality around what was going on. Although Cinder had matured in most parts since her release from the Salem Institution, she was still lacking control over the fear department. The more fearful she was, the more child-like she became, and I could tell in those soul-catching eyes of hers that the Hellhound was truly terrified.

Seconds after I had wrapped her in my arms, the Hellhound quickly broke free from me. Her body illuminating this massive amount of heat that melted right through my winter jack, scalding my forearms. Glancing down at my arms, I saw through the holes in my jacket that my skin was beaming shades of reds and pinks from the burns. The heat was just steaming off my skin in the below-freezing temperatures. Completely in shock that Cinder had just harmed me, I continued to question what the hell was going on.

413

Moving my sights up from my arms, I listened to her again apologize, this time with double the amount of sincerity and fear in her voice.

"It is not your fault Cinder," I called out to her through the searing pain in my arms while my supernatural healing powers tried to return the skin back to what it once was prior to the injuries. "I know that it's not your fault!"

"I can't stay here any longer!" Cinder swiftly shouted, her voice interrupting me. Alerting me that in her depthless mind, this was what the Hellhound HAD to do. This was what she was told to do. Told to leave the Manor, and highly likely the safety of the Syndicate as well.

"WHY?!" I shouted back at her, craving an explanation for this occurrence. "Why can't you stay here?"

"I can't tell you-" she cried out, the tone in her voice telling me she desperately ached to explain everything, but she was too afraid to. Just like all the other times. "Just let me leave! Forget about me, like everyone else has-"

Observing the woman again try to burst past me, this time moving at a much faster speed than before, I was barely able to catch her with my damaged arms. Tightly clinging to her left wrist, I remained persistent. I needed answers.

"Let me go." She urged, her fearful blue eyes once more locked on to my gaze as she proceeded to try and break free without hurting me this time around.

"I can't," I shouted at her, simultaneously pulling her towards me, again attempting to comfort the spooked woman I loved. Not frightened by the possibility of getting burned.

Continuing to fight against me, she refused my willing comfort. "Just let me go! Please!" She again yelled back at me, her eyes now watered over. I knew this was painful for her. I could see it in that emotional gaze of hers. I could hear her heart just bursting away at her rib cage, trying to beat out of her chest.

"I can't do that!" I repeated.

"Why?!" Cinder blurted, her hands touching what remained of my jacket. "Why-why can't you just let me go like everyone else has?" Quietly murmuring the question so only the two of us could hear.

"Why?" I restated, looking down at the beautiful woman. "Because-" I paused, swallowing my words before attempting to speak up. "Because I love you, Cinder-."

Chapter 78
Jakob/Cinder

"I can't just let you go, because I love you," I repeated as the words began to sound clearer. My mind frantically working in overdrive so it could comprehend the results that were likely to happen in correspondence to this statement. Knowing how her mind also worked when she was scared, I figured that this was either going to turn ugly, or it was going to turn out how I had hoped it would.

Standing there in silence with the confession finally out on the table, I awaited a response while we remained closely tied together. I waited and waited under the shifting moonlit sky, it's rays our only source of light. Comforting her for what felt like forever, I eventually heard her murmur, "Why?" Another eternity went by before my sensitive Vampiric hearing caught onto her voice again inquire. "Why did you say that?"

The words felt like needles being impaled into me. This wasn't quite the answer I was expecting from her. Swallowing once, I decided to answer her question. "Why did I say that?" I restated. Hesitating for a brief moment while I tried to think of a reasonable excuse, "Because it's true. Because I do love you. And it's also because I don't want to see you in so much pain...it makes my heart ache every time I see you this way."

"Jakob." Cinder said, putting her hands up against my chest to push away, putting space between our chests. "I don't want to leave." The Hellhound cried, "I really don't want to go, but-" She paused. Looking down at her, I surveyed the color in her eyes begin to change. The blue crossing in her right eye to the glowing fiery orange. "But I don't have a choice, I must go. I must."

"Cinder, you do have a choice-" I comforted.

"NO, I DON'T!" She argued, her arms fully extended to put as much room as possible between us.

"Yes, you do Cinder!" I shouted back, putting my hands around her forearms. Watching the color in her left eye start to also split the colors after the orange had consumed the right pupil. "You may not know this, but there are always choices. You must know that you don't have to leave me, that you don't have to leave us. "

"NO, I DON'T HAVE A CHOICE ANYMORE!"

"Anymore?" I confusedly repeated. Thinking quietly to myself, I used my supernatural strength to hold onto the Unnatural who was desperately struggling to fight free. "What does she mean by anymore? What has that thing done to you that you feel like you don't have any choices left? That you don't feel you have control over your actions? Why did you just scan right over my confession-?" Between trying to find the right question to ask and trying my hardest to hold onto the struggling twenty-five-year-old, one-hundred-pound petite woman I began to feel extremely overwhelmed.

"LET ME GO!" I shouted through the howling wind which had just started to blow across the empty field.

"NO! I WON'T LET YOU GO, BECAUSE-because I don't want to lose you, Cinder." Jakob rebutted, now relying on his superior strength to hold me within arm's length. "I don't want to see you back in an Institution! I don't want to see you in that same paralyzed state you were in when you first came here! I don't want to see you, the woman I have been in love with for so long, in pain like that again!"

The words came flying at me so hard that it made my heart feel as if it had just dropped into my stomach before rapidly rising back up into my throat. All the hairs on my arms and neck were standing on edge while they remained hidden beneath my jacket. I sincerely didn't want to leave him or the others, but what choice did I have? My time here was over, so why couldn't they just let me go? "Why did he keep saying that word? That hopeless word? That word that I knew the definition of but could not remember the feeling behind?" I thought to myself as he kept uttering the 'Love' word over and over again.

"Cinder please-"

"No. Stop talking," I ordered, seizing my struggling for the moment. "Just stop talking," I repeated. "Just stop." Walking closer towards him, so close that I could feel his warm breath leave his immortal body and drift the top of my head. With the howling wind making it harder to hear, and the blowing snow harder to see, I again ran over the ways I could break away. I didn't want to hurt him any further than I already had, nor did I want to harm any of the others that I had gotten so close to, but feeling the prowling eyes of the Shadow lurking in the woods awaiting my breakaway, made me fear for the worst the longer I waited. I had to hurry up.

Looking up at the taller sleek build of the European descendant, I stared up into his amber eyes. Staring directly into the lining underneath of the greenish-hazel human gaze I knew was beneath, I took a small exhale after finally deciding on how to break away. Pushing my emotions aside and calming my racing heart so I could clearly decipher all my soon to be actions, I leaned up onto the toes of my wedge boots, lifting the heels just a couple of inches up so I could equally match my height with his. Bringing my head closer towards his, I took a secondary pause trying to recall all the times I had observed my desired action. Keeping my eyes locked on his for another second, I gave a soft exhale and proceeded to bring my face in closer. Pulling my cheeks back into a small grin, I softly closed my eyes and pressed my lips against his. Allowing my heightened sense of touch to feel everything around me. Jakob's lips were chapped from the harsh winter, but they were uniquely soft. I could feel my supernatural body temperature significantly begin to rise the longer we held our mouths together. The intimacy while pleasant was short-lived. Breaking my lips away from the short-lived kiss, I opened my eyes to see that the Vampiric's head was now trying to lean forward, craving another I naturally assumed. His eyes were still closed and his lips were partially open. Dropping the soles of my boots back on solid ground, I proceeded to feel his head press against mine. Our foreheads touching, the skill still in contact while my rising core temperature continued to keep the two of us warm in the moonlit snowstorm.

Everything was quiet again while the two of us just stood there. No words were being said. I had stopped fighting him. It was just pure silence. After a little while, my grin faded, and I exhaled a heavy sigh. "Jakob." I softly mumbled as our heads still nuzzled one another, the frigid air condensing the warm carbon dioxide that was being released from our heavy breathing. "I'm sorry."

"Sorry?" I thought. Trying to ask the question, I felt a lodge in my throat rise, making it hard to breathe. A quick shear stabbing pain hit my stomach. Looking down at the woman who I could visibly hear crying, I watched her step back from my already scalded body to expose the source of my newfound pain. In the dimly lit night, I saw the dull red blade piercing out of the left side of my gut. The similar blade style of a scythe or sickle. I had been stabbed by one of Cinder's Blood Scythes! As my brain swiftly received the pain signals that were running up the nerves, I coughed. Bringing up some blood with the spurt, I barely succeeded in saying her name before I began to feel faint. My knees instantly grew weak and made my legs give out from underneath me.

Prior to collapsing onto the hard-frozen snow-covered ground, I felt the same soft feminine hands grab at my arm. Her unnatural strength coming to the light as she held my two-hundred-pound deadweight muscular figure, and simultaneously pulled out the right wristed blade from my gut. Helping me lie on the ground before I could regain my surroundings, I watched in and out of consciousness as she leaned her head in again. Her lips once more pressing against mine, granting me one simple long kiss. Breaking away only milliseconds later so I could stare into those burning bright orange eyes with dark blood red tints, I barely perceived her voice mutter a crying statement.

"Jakob, I love you too." She said as more tears fell down her cheeks. "And that's why I must leave."

"Cin-" I coughed, spewing out some more blood from my bleeding wound, "Cinder-"

"I'm sorry-" she said, mutating into the long-legged sleek furred large Beauceron canine form. Watching the change of her human eyes into the canine ovals, I observed the blurred shadow of her black fur approach. Shortly after, I felt sharp edges wrap around my neck. My breathing strained as my mind finally focused on the next weapon the Hellhound was using. Feeling more warm blood seep out of my open wounds and mouth, I felt the many sharp daggers which I could only assume were her fangs release their impenetrable hold. Her square canine face coming back into view with my blood dripping down her dark lips and brown marked jaws. "I'm sorry Jakob." Cinder called just before she took off into the deep woods surrounding the open Garden space. Disappearing into the secluded trails.

"Ci-cinder." I attempted to call out while trying to stay conscious. Focusing on the cold temperature, I knew I had to find a way to keep her from leaving this property, to keep her out of the hands of that controlling Shadow. Using my leftover strength to move my right arm, I stretched my hand into my sweatpants' pocket for my cellphone. I knew with the amount of blood loss I was facing that I didn't have the strength to make a phone call, however, I did know the sequence to trigger my GPS location. My fingers began to twiddle around in my pocket for the home button of my smartphone. With a spasm running through my hand, I fought through the muscle aches to reach for the designated switch. Pressing three times on the home button with the reprogrammed sequence, I activated the GPS Tracker Services. "Alright," I thought in my barely conscious mind, "Ple-please hurry-"

Chapter 79
Jakob/Cinder

"Shit! Jakob what happened?!" I heard someone shout out in the blackness. Fighting myself to stay awake, I forced my eyes open again.

"There is blood everywhere-" Another person loudly voiced while my sensitive sight attempted to now clarify the blurred beings who I could only assume were the higher-ranked Syndicate Rebels I called my closest friends.

As my sight finally clarified who was all there, I began to murmur my passing thoughts, "Mhykal-"

"Jakob- don't talk-" I heard Yalu speak, slipping my head in her lap, "Babe go back and get Viktor-" she now ordered the father of the yet to be born child, "Peylith and I will stay here with him-"

"Yalu-" I whispered, trying to use my free left arm to point out behind me. "She-"

Although my voice was barely audible for them to hear, I proceeded to listen to the elder Hellhound growl, "I can smell Jakob's blood scent moving-"

"PEYLITH WAIT!" The Caucasian Vixen called out into the pitch blackness of the snow ridden world beyond where I lied helplessly bleeding from what I could only assume were two vital spots.

"PEYLITH WAIT!" My sensitive hearing could accurately decipher a familiar voice shout out into the blowing wind.

"They found him-" I paused, looking back down the trail I had just ran up. Taking a sigh of relief, I turned back towards the wooded trail before rubbing my muzzle through the snow to wipe off some of the blood I had sprayed onto my fur. The frozen water quickly melting from my muzzle thanks to my still increased core body temperature. "That's good," I told myself as I started to increase my gait and run deeper into the depthless woods. "I tried my best to avoid his major arteries." My thoughts raced, "Knicking them just barely enough to disable him from following me, but not enough to kill him."

Minutes later, my panicked mindset worked in overdrive, forcing me to work my exhausted muscles harder. My long cropped ears picking up on the sounds of crunching snow and breaking twigs. My hound-like nose instructing me there was a familiar scent swiftly approaching. The pounding of my heart increased twice fold as I began extending my gait to build up my speed. I knew that I had to run faster to hopefully outrun the speed demon I now had pursuing after me.

"Cinder!" The savage Hellhound angrily called out.

Out of the corner of my eyes, I saw the blurred figure of the male Hellhound chasing after me in his four-legged Pharaoh Hound form. Ignoring his savage calls I continued to work on running through the snow towards the edge of the property. My breathing becoming painfully restricted the more I pushed myself. "Come on, run faster!" I pleaded.

"Cinder!" Peylith again barked, his voice much louder this time. "Why do you have Jakob's blood in your scent?!"

"Great-" I huffed between breaths, my tongue rolling out of my panting mouth.

"ANSWER ME CINDER!" The canine shouted, the tone in his voice growing more aggressive. My nose following the upriver wind drafts alerted me to how dark his scent was becoming. Fear, anger, all of the pessimistic emotions came flowing out of the exposed skin pores and mixed with the scent of dramatically raging heat soaring from his Species Abilities. "WHY DO YOU HAVE JAKOB'S BLOOD ON YOU?!"

"DAMN!" I cried. "JUST LEAVE ME ALONE!"

"NO!"

Barely avoiding running into a tree, I side-stepped, shaving almost a four to the six-foot gap I could have extended in my chase. Trying to swarm around the massive collection of pine trees, I finally remembered that there was a fallen log up ahead and a small six-foot sharp drop behind it. If I could just jump over that cliff-edge, I might be able to avert the larger Hellhound in possibly a max distance of thirty-feet according to my panicked mind's mathematical calculations. "I just had to try it-" I thought as I finally reached the small clearing that hid along the trail's pathway.

Running straight for the log I knew was hidden beneath about ten inches of undisturbed snow, I began the second nature preparations for jumping. My back legs muscle's locking up like a springboard on top of the fallen aspen trees as my front legs lifted off the snow pulling towards my chest. Releasing the tightened muscles, I felt my toes kick off the snow-covered slippery bark while my front legs broke out ahead of me and allowed me to stretch out into the open air. Thanks to my plenty of experience running through the trails, jumping over rocks, fallen trees, and even using standing trees as unnatural trampolines, I wagged my tail around for some balance while beginning the accelerated decline in the direction of the frozen lavender field that lied beneath the sheer cliff.

Upon my brutal faulted landing, I released a massive heatwave that had uncontrollably escaped through my sweating paw pads. Seeing the snowmelt in a complete three hundred and sixty degrees radius around my body, I observed the sleeping wildflowers become exposed to the harsh climate. Unfortunately, I had just given away any possible cover I could have received. "I don't want to have to fight him." I quietly cursed. Desperately glancing back up at the small cliff, I locked my gaze onto the grey black-furred canine with unusually dark amber eyes. Seeing him hesitate on hunting me down, I turned my back and returned to making my getaway. Hoping that he wasn't going to follow me, and just was going to allow me to leave this place in its entirety behind.

My sore feet had just started the beginning steps of the extended galloping gait when my eyes saw the same creature come charging out of the dark shadows of the collected forest trees planted before me. His tongue rolling in and out of his mouth because while his breed of Hellhoundism was built for speed, it was not built for endurance like mine.

Baring my long canines at him, I refused to falter. Mirroring my snarl, my elder Kin, lifted his curling lips to bare his fangs. "Cinder, I don't want to have to fight you, just answer my questions-" Peylith ordered through his intimidating snarl, trying to breathe in the frigid air.

"Neither do I-" I snapped back, folding my ears flat against my square head.

"I know it hurts, but hold on for just a little bit longer." I could barely hear Viktor comfort as he used his unique powers to heal the open wounds Cinder had ripped into my flesh. "Just a bit longer-"

"God, they are really going at it-" Yalu murmured, still holding my head in her lap, trying to, I guess comfort my half-dead immortal self.

425

"Wh-what?" I attempted to question. Desperately seeking to understand what could possibly be happening out of my sight.

"I'm going to go check on them-" Mhykal spoke up from his position beside Yalu, standing between us and the darkening shadows.

"It-it was...wasn't her fault-" I tried to clarify, coughing up more blood as I heavily breathed in and out.

"Oh Jakob," Yalu cried. Lifting my head, she helped my limp body exhale the blood and saliva which was rapidly collecting in my mouth. "Viktor, why isn't your powers working?"

"It is, but-" the scientific medical Vampiric said, trying to keep his hands on my gut so the golden-light emitting from his hands could attempt to revert the damage that was done to my intestines.

"But what?! Viktor, we need to get him up to the Manor, so we can get him some painkillers and transfusions!"

"Yeah, I know that! I was just wanting to at least stabilize him before we attempted to move him, however, these wounds seem beyond even my level of expertise." The Vampiric audibly diagnosed. Hesitant for a moment, the two of us waited for the next part of the conversation. Sitting in the silence, under the dying moon-light and slowly falling snow, I finally overheard the sounds of sharps snarls, barks, cries, whines, and shrieks filling the white noise. The chilling echoes, alerting me to the grave possibility that the much older Hellhound was fighting against his much younger Kin. "Alright, fine. Once we get him some painkillers, I think I might be able to work on reverting the wounds."

As they lifted me up onto my feet, wrapping my arms around them to help stabilize myself, I felt my two friends start to drag me towards the house. Managing to use my own two feet, I limply walked with their aide in the desired direction. I knew I needed to get myself healed up first, but I couldn't help worrying over the health and well-being of Cinder, especially when she had so easily confessed her love to me just before ripping into my neck.

Reaching the Medical Ward, the Vixen finally asked, "Where is Cinder anyways?"

Chapter 80
Cinder

"I told you I don't want to fight you!" Peylith shouted at me as he continued to dodge my snapping jowls. Watching the canine swipe out into the shadows, I lost control over my floated emotions, releasing another implosive heatwave that this time busted into an array of bright orange flames. Creating a circle of wall-height flames which attacked the rim of trees surrounding the field of lavender wildflowers, thankfully forcing Peylith to reappear out of the sulking shadows. Standing wide-open in shock, the Hellhound locked his gaze onto where I stood.

Only seconds passed by before he charged for me, reenacting the same scenario from our many practiced sparring matches. Coming in with the first swing, his long muzzle's jowls spreading wide open. Ducking my head to dodge his attack, I made a wide swing from under his neck. My body shifting perpendicular against his chest before I leaned off my left side and rammed my corresponding shoulder into his chest. Acutely turning on my right side so I could bring my jaws towards his neck, my fangs swiftly ripping through the short black hair and into the skin and flesh lying beneath. With Peylith's extra height, I was forced to lift my front legs a couple of inches up off the ground, risking exposure to my chest and upper stomach. Effortlessly being swung around while the Pharaoh Hound tried to shake me loose from the back of his neck, I tightly hung on. Hearing the angry cries of pain and frustration further triggered my hunting instinct that was steadily consuming every inch of consciousness.

Eventually, Peylith managed to swing me off from my perch, my fangs slicing the skin on their way out. Blood spitting out from the wound as we separated ourselves. Landing on my feet, I scanned for another opening, so I could attempt to paralyze him from chasing after me. "I need to hurry this up," I told myself as my eyes hastily observed every little bit of movement the other Hellhound did while trying to regain his bearings.

"Cinder!" I overheard somebody else shout from behind me.

My ears fell flat against my skull when my mind registered the voice, acknowledging it as Mhykal's. From the tone, I deciphered the aroma of frustration, confusion, and fear the Vampiric had about our current predicament. I knew that with a speed-built Hellhound, and an experienced three-hundred-year-old Vampiric who could definitely outrun me, I had no choice but to attempt to paralyze them both without killing them. "This plan of mine was not turning out how I was hoping it too at all, but you knew this didn't you-" I snarled with a smile. "You had all this planned out didn't you, Shadow?"

"What-" was all I heard come out of the Vampiric's mouth before I got tackled by the much larger framed Hellhound. The air getting beat out of my chest, swarmed out into the below-freezing air. Before I could regain my bearings, I was thrown into the recently unfrozen wildflowers. My hundred-pound canine weight crushing the lavender's pedals as I came toppling down over the top of them. Trying to get myself back up, I again was thrown back into the flowers. Peylith's front left paw pressing heavily down into my neck, forcing me to remain where I fell. Dreadfully scanning around the field of flowers and their long stems, I continued to hear Mhykal shout. "Peylith! What are you doing?! What is going on?!"

"Cinder just answer my question!" He growled to me, his long neck hanging low while his lips were centimeters away from the scarred left ear.

429

"Just let me go!" I shouted back, trying to fight like a trout out of water so I could get back onto my feet.

"Why is Jakob's blood on you?!" Peylith hissed, asking the same question.

Hastily swallowing, I snapped my jaws at him, "Get off of me!" Swinging my head up, I gave my silent answer. Peylith pulled his head back, barely avoiding my blood-stained fangs from scraping his long muzzle. Kicking outward with my back legs, I hoped that one of the swings would be enough to thwart the canine morphed man to get off of my smaller frame. Hearing my heart rapidly race and feeling it beat against my small chest, I was alerted to my current level of panic and fear. "You don't understand!" I shouted. The fear beginning to take control of the consuming instinct to hunt down my two friends. While Peylith maintained his one-paw hold on my neck, I finally managed to sock him with my left back leg. My paw kicking the Hellhound directly under his chest's sternum. The canine quickly bounced off of my frame from the shock of my heavy-powered back legs. Taking advantage of Peylith insistingly shaking his head to regain his balance, I hastily twisted around and bounced back up onto all fours. Having enough of this running for the meantime I decided to revert to my human form.

"What are you saying?" Mhykal questioned. He too forced to shout over the roar and flicker of the wall of flames. "Cinder, what are you saying?!"

Turning to face the Vampiric with a slightly larger muscle mass than his long-time friend Jakob, I locked my gaze with his. Taking a deep breath to attempt to calm myself before unwillingly moved on with answering his questions. "I didn't want to do it, but he wouldn't let me go." I softly spoke, activating my Blood Scythes in preparation to fight the two of them. Recalling the strong bond between the two Vampirics, and how this one acted when one of his close friends were injured, I told myself to stay on guard for incoming reactions.

"Cinder-" Mhykal murmured, putting his hands up in an 'okay settle down' motion.

"I really don't want to hurt anyone else, Mhykal." I pleaded, holding my arms down at my side, keeping my weaponized blood sheathed.

Before he could respond to my plea, I watched through his body motions that my previous obligation was coming back at me. Whether it was still his current form or if it was one of his other two forms, I barely had enough time to respond. Twisting around, I ducked below his incoming left hook from his alter canine form. While still hanging close to the ground, I swiftly vaulted backward going into a walking crab position. Straightening my arms, bending my back, I quickly went into a short backflip. Lifting my legs in the process I then wrapped them around his extended arm. Crossing my ankles and tightening my knees, I locked his arm in a strong armbar. Instinctively the now bipedal formed Hellhound attempted to raise his arm so he could shake me off, but my agility out gravitated his muscle mass, allowing me to complete the flip's rotation. Swinging him over the top of me, I threw him down into the wildflowers. A little bit of karma. Flipping over to standing on my hands and feet, I reformed back into my canine form.

Raising another snarl, I locked my gaze once more on the Vampiric, who was attempting to help stand Peylith back up on his feet. Over the racing thuds of my heart, I continued to debate how to handle this situation, as well as the new arising situation of my natural hunting instinct: that creeping rush of possibly enjoying this, of enjoying seeing the people I deeply cared for get hurt.

With my ears paying close attention to what they were saying, I stayed put in my location as my mind fought over three different mindsets: sanity, fear, or rationality.

"What is going on?" Mhykal questioned the newcomer to the Syndicate. "Why did she attack you?"

"I don't know myself," Peylith growled, returning to his human form that was still wearing what I would have guessed were his sleepwear. "All I know is that mixed in with her scent is the odor of Jakob's blood."

431

"She's the one that attacked him?!"

"I would assume by her answers however they are not direct-"

"What's going on?" I heard Mhykal question as he looked back into my direction, his demeanor being illegible to my deranged mentality.

"I need to leave." I murmured. Shaking my head, I heard the keyring of the chains attached to my nylon choker collar clang against one another.

"And go where?!" Mhykal interrogated me. Clarifying that he had heard my murmurs. "Cinder, what the hell are you talking about?!"

"I need to leave! I can no longer stay here!" I shouted back, snapping my jaws together. My lips curled so high that it exposed the brim of my pink gums and the top of my fangs. "I have to go-" I paused when I felt something disrupt the flow of my erratic thinking process. Something broke inside my head. Something shattered like glass.

Chapter 81

Watching through an opening of pine, aspen, and oak trees and a strong wall of flame, I could see our target start to wreath in pain. From my position on this slightly elevated cliff, I observed the target bend its neck over, the muzzle pointing down into the dark purple field of flowers. Activating clear characteristics of the next stage...

"Well, it looks like your 'Reaper' has awakened it," I said with a deep sigh. Resting my square model head into the palm of my hand whose elbow rested on my raised knee, I continued to express, "However you already knew that all this was going to happen, didn't you?" With no answer from my fellow associate, I softly chuckled. "Typical you."

Further surveying the target snarl, I squinted my eyes, hoping to get a better outlook on the distanced little quarrel I had been surveying. Observing what I believed were five white spikes steadily grow out of what I would assume was the creature's spine, I awaited the last part of this 'awakening' to consume the Unnatural as it usually did with our past clients.

The two comrades who the 'Reaper' had turned against both stood on their feet, completely in shock over their transforming companion. Unable to clearly hear the conversation, I again assumed that they were either questioning what was going on, or what was happening to their comrade. Curious, I looked over to my associate who was hiding in the darkness of the overpassing clouds. Only a glimpse of his scarred boney skull, could be seen from the shrouds of his shadowy-blended cloak. Staring into his spooky red-orange glowing eyes, I shifted my lengthy frame around so I could stand up on the solid ground inches from a thirty-foot sheer cliff edge and announced, "I'm going to move closer."

"No. Any closer and my 'Reaper' will sniff you out." The skulled man quickly rejected.

"And then what? Your 'Reaper' will slice my fucking head off?" I questioned, mocking that name he had given the Hellhound.

"Yes."

"Cold as ever," I smirked, plopping back down on the frozen snow-covered rocks. Sitting in the same pose from prior, I continued to avidly watch from the designated distance our target was supposed to reach in its attempt to escape from this Rebelling Syndicate. "But then what about those Hunters who are moving in on their location?" I asked, noticing a few hundred feet out in another clearing was a group of unwanted humans who were tracking what I assumed was one of those three Unnaturals down below. A normal tradition those bastards did.

"They will not be able to get past the firewall."

"I guess you're right there. That is unless they came with some stupid plan to deal with a Hellhound's flames," I smirked while returning my full attention to the fun that was unsettling inside that wall of brightly burning orange flames. Taking note that the longer this fight was going on, the flames' heat was greatly increasing as well as changing color from the fiery orange into a much hotter pale blue. It was another attribute of the 'awakened' form.

Observing the color-changing flames, I also noticed our target charge straight for the other Hellhound I had been warned of. That dark-skinned male swiftly altered into his canine form that was at least double the size of ours, alerting me that this one was much more experienced. But, then again when you are going through a countless number of applicants for this Species, you really don't get enough time to build one up.

Taking a deep sigh, I prepared for the worst outcome to happen. The larger one although fast wasn't as fast as the smaller one's new form that surprisingly managed to attach its jaws to the side of the opponent's neck. Surprised, I then watched the smaller canine while still holding onto its much older Kindred, kick off the ground and drag one of its right front legs up over the back of the neck. The canine's far front leg passing over the far shoulder before it seemed to lock in place. The action, however, was too distant for even my eyes to see from where I sat.

"You saw it, didn't you?" My shadowed associate quizzed me.

"No!" I growled, watching the larger Hellhound try to spin around so it could grab at the smaller one's back, however each time it tried the canine with the Gold Ankh on its back kept running into the bone spikes that had grown out of our target's vertebrae. Over the eerie shrouds of snarls, cries, and whelps, I continued to grumble, "What was I supposed to see? I mean, I saw your 'Reaper' swing it's leg up over the shoulder of the other Hellhound, but- there isn't anything so damn special about that maneuver."

"That little trick that happened is why I picked that child to become my 'Little' Reaper."

"What trick?" I questioned, my patience's fuse slowly lighting away. Squinting harder, I tried to at least get a glimpse of what he was talking about. While watching the spectacle still go on, I observed the third member of the little group attempt to get involved. Grabbing at the 'Reaper's' neck with his bare hands to attempt to rip off the Hellhound like a parasite to its host. Somehow managing to succeed, this Unnatural got our target to detach itself from the elder Hellhound who seemed to be in more pain at that then prior. Straining my squinting eyes to look at the unusual marking residing along the Hellhound's Gold Ankh tattoo, I noticed a huge laceration bracing from one end of the shoulder to the other. "What did I miss?"

435

"Our 'Reaper' has a trait called 'Iron Blood'." The Skeletal Shadow clarified, casually standing beside me hidden underneath the leaning pine tree from behind us. "You will better understand it once she is returned to my custody."

"Done talking in that annoying narrative, are you? And did you just say it is a female?" I questioned with a sly smirk while still actively watching our target take on two opponents. "Anyways I won't prod, though it seems 'she' is starting to become exhausted."

"As expected. Nonetheless, it's still satisfactory results."

"Typical cynical you" I smiled back.

Continuing to silently survey in the distance, the two of us noticed the female Hellhound collapse onto the field of lavender flowers. The spikes shrinking back inside the spine seconds later. As the other Hellhound and Unnatural carefully crept up towards our unconscious target, I carefully evaluated how to go about the next situation while the two Unnaturals our target opposed began conversing with one another.

"Everything is still going according to your plan, right?" I questioned, standing myself back up when the non-Hellhound Unnatural began to pick up the unconscious female, and the elder Hellhound began to attempt to remove his kin's wall of blue fire which was surprisingly still standing.

"So far."

"Alright, so what do we do now, Zachariah?"

www.ingramcontent.com/pod-product-compliance
Lightning Source LLC
Chambersburg PA
CBHW020231110726
47898CB00004B/1229